THE LAST
IMPRINT

BEST-SELLING AUTHOR
ACE COLLINS

ELK LAKE PUBLISHING INC.

PUBLISHING THE POSITIVE
Plymouth, Massachusetts

A Christian Company
ElkLakePublishingInc.com

Copyright Notice

Cover and Interior Design: Kelly Artieri, Derinda Babcock, Deb Haggerty

Editor(s): Deb Haggerty, Cristel Phelps

Author Represented By: WordServe Literary Group Ltd.

PUBLISHED BY: Elk Lake Publishing, Inc., 35 Dogwood Drive, Plymouth, MA 02360, 2023

Library Cataloging Data
Names: Collins, Ace (Ace Collins)
The Last Imprint / Ace Collins
450 p. 23cm × 15cm (9in × 6 in.)
ISBN-13: 9798891341043 (paperback) | 9798891341050 (hardcover) | 9798891341067 (trade paperback) | 9798891341074 (e-book)
Key Words: DNA memories; Speculative fiction; Action/Adventure; Ancestors; Cultural memory; CIA operatives; Mystery
Library of Congress Control Number: 2023950847 Fiction

Table of Contents

Prologue 05

One 13

Two 23

Three 33

Four 41

Five 51

Six 57

Seven 63

Eight 73

Nine 83

Ten 89

Eleven 103

Twelve 111

Thirteen 119

Fourteen 127

Fifteen 133

Sixteen 141

Seventeen 147

Eighteen 153

Nineteen 161

Twenty 167

Twenty-One 173

Twenty-Two 177

Twenty-Three 187

Twenty-Four 191

Twenty-Five 197

Twenty-Six 203

Twenty Seven 213

Twenty-Eight 219

Twenty-Nine 227

Thirty 231

Thirty-One 235

Thirty-Two 241

Thirty-Three 247

Thirty-Four 253

Thirty-Five 259

Thirty-Six 263

Thirty-Seven 269

Thirty-Eight 275

Thirty-Nine 281

Forty 287

Forty-One 293

Forty-Two 299

Forty-Three 305

Forty-Four 311

Forty-Five 315

Forty-Six 319

Forty-Seven 325

Forty-Eight 329

Forty-Nine 335

Fifty 339

Fifty-One 345

Fifty-Two 351

Fifty-Three 355

Fifty-Four 361

Fifty-Five 367

Fifty-Six 373

Fifty-Seven 377

Fifty-Eight 381

Fifty-Nine 389

Sixty 395

Sixty-One 399

Sixty-Two 405

Sixty-Three 409

Sixty-Four 413

Sixty-Five 417

Sixty-Six 421

Sixty-Seven 427

Sixty-Eight 433

Sixty-Nine 439

Seventy 443

The Beginning of the Next
Adventure 447

Prologue

11:22 p.m.
Tuesday, August 14, thirty years ago
Paris, France

One bullet. That's all it would take this time. That's all it ever took.

One bullet. Only man could create something so small, that when combined with a touch of gunpowder, could so quickly stop a heart from beating or a brain from thinking. Only man would want to possess something like this.

One bullet and everything becomes nothing—no more words, no more thoughts, no more regrets, and no more dreams. One moment there is life—blood pumping through veins and breath entering lungs—and then, thanks to that one bullet, blood is spilling onto the floor from a limp body that no longer has any use for air.

One bullet. That's all it would take this time. That's all it ever took. And just like a postman delivered the mail, William Dixon was to deliver that bullet. And nothing, not snow, nor sleet, nor dark of night, could or would keep him from his appointed rounds.

One bullet.

———◆———

Tall and lanky, William Dixon, known as the Grim Reaper or Doctor Death to his acquaintances—he had no friends—was a humorless man with deep set brown eyes and a square jaw. Women found his haunting, unrelenting gaze hypnotizing, while that same look completely unnerved men. He wasn't the "love them and leave them type" because he had no capacity for love. Yet, he also didn't hate. Dixon was not a cruel person, he was not amoral, he simply didn't allow himself to be governed by the same set of rules as those that provided both comfort and order in the real world—a place he avoided whenever possible. For Dixon, emotions were all neutral, and that's what made him such an effective killer. And on this dark night, just like all the other times he'd used a tiny piece of lead to stop a life, he felt nothing.

Dixon had accepted this assignment without reservation. Did the target deserve to die? No. But he also couldn't be allowed to live, the stakes were too high. After all, what was one man's life when compared to the effects of having to rewrite history? A new history where the good becomes the bad, the bad becomes the good, and the foundations of time are uprooted and tossed asunder. A history that robs the world of its security and creates far more questions than answers. So, unlike so many others that had come before, this hit would have a clear purpose, it would guarantee order, it would remove a problem while erasing a need for answers. It was almost noble. He would squeeze the trigger and send a man into the next life simply because it was the best thing to do for humanity.

Dixon had arrived at the small Paris flat thirty minutes before. During that time, he'd carefully searched for weapons, but paid little attention to anything else. Now, as he counted down the minutes until his target would walk through the door, he made a second pass through the rooms to get a feel for the man who lived and would soon die here. Using the glow from an antique Tiffany lamp, he inventoried the shabby one-bedroom apartment's combined living room and kitchen. The whole dingy space was no more than twenty by fifteen. The furniture appeared either second or even third hand. In the few photos, no one looked happy. Hanging on the walls were faded travel posters held in place by thumbtacks. The carpet hadn't been vacuumed in weeks or maybe even months.

As he strolled into the kitchen, he noted dishes piled in the sink while partially opened cabinets revealed a couple of cans of soup and a box of oats. Dixon moved to the small refrigerator. There was just a single jar of mustard and two eggs. With no warning, a large, brown roach dashed out from under a sagging metal chair and raced across the kitchen tile to a hiding place behind the overflowing trash can. Unless someone made a trip to the market, the insect would soon starve to death.

Shifting his gaze back to the door, Dixon studied a small desk, empty except for a stack of personal journals. Walking across the room his eyes fell onto the only one that was open. The two pages he scanned contained scribblings about the 1761 coronation of the English King George III. The writings detailed events witnessed by someone who had obviously been there. Ironically, this was not an old book, the pages were crisp and white, and the author had not used a quill, but rather a modern ball point pen to record his observations. That would have puzzled any other visitor, but not Dixon.

On a shelf beside the desk was a copy of the works of Milton. While Dixon could care less about the author or his books, a business card, now doubling as a bookmark, drew his interest.

Jean Bissett
Dealer in Rare Books
20 Lu Plaza
Paris

Dixon slipped the card into his inside suit coat pocket, before strolling across to the flat's small bedroom. Somehow achieving the impossible, it was even more depressing than the living area. There was only an electric alarm clock on a water-marked black nightstand. Nothing hung on the walls. On the dusty lime-green linoleum floor, beside the unmade twin bed whose sheets looked closer to gray than white, was an empty bottle of rye. Two more sat on the dresser. A glance into the small bath revealed a trio of fifths, all but drained, resting on the edge of the tub. This man wasn't living, he was just marking time.

The sound of footsteps on the tile floors of the outside hall, easily heard through the building's paper-thin walls, prompted Dixon to move back into the living room. He had no more than eased onto the arm of the couch, and, using his gloved right hand, pulled his CIA service weapon from his shoulder holster, when the door opened. The agent was no longer alone.

Jean Bissett was a small, clean-shaven man with dark eyes. The look on his face echoed the hopelessness on full display in the man's flat. His features were like that of a small dog. His nose was long, jaw weak, and skin pale, and his hair was the color of straw and hadn't been combed in some time. There was a nervous twitch causing his left eye lid to flutter, and his left shoulder hung like a retired baseball player who'd pitched far too many games. He was casually dressed in jeans and a wrinkled, short-sleeved, light blue dress shirt. When the surprised Bissett finally gathered his wits and spoke, his voice was high and uneven.

"Who are you?" The question was not a demand. In fact, there was absolutely no expression evident in those three words. In a high, steady pitch, he uttered them in the same way a cabby would have asked, "Do you need a ride?"

Dixon's response was brutally blunt and honest and delivered in a rich baritone that suggested, if he'd chosen a different career path, he could have been an FM radio announcer. "I'm the one who has been assigned to end your suffering."

"You don't sound like a doctor or look like a priest," Bissett cracked, "so are you my executioner?" His morbid opinion was followed by a nervous laugh and an even darker observation. "The priest walks with you to the gallows, the executioner pulls the cord or throws the switch, and then the doctor ironically rules you no longer need his services. What a trio!" He paused and licked his lips. "So, which are you?"

"Close the door," Dixon suggested.

This was not a request—it was an order which Bissett immediately followed. Once the task was completed, the uninvited guest pointed with his gun's barrel toward a wooden chair beside the desk.

"You didn't answer my question," Bissett countered while standing in front of the entry. His tone was now even, his voice steady. It appeared the small man was finding a bit of grit.

"I have a job to do." Dixon explained.

"I take it, from your accent, you're American."

Dixon nodded.

"CIA or FBI?"

"CIA."

Seemingly satisfied with the explanation, Bissett eased into the chair, and, after resting his right arm on the desktop, crossed his ankles revealing scuffed brown dress shoes and socks that had long ago lost their ability to hug the man's legs. Once comfortable, Bissett sized up the visitor and asked, "Your job? Is it to extract information, kill me, or both?"

"I'm not interested in information," Dixon admitted. "Lots of folks know history, but only a few have the power to change it. So, you see, it's not what you know that's important, rather it's what you might remember. And the world can't afford to be privy to those memories."

"And you actually believe I'm one of those few who has the power to change history?"

Dixon shrugged. "We think so."

Bissett chuckled. "Look around you? What kind of power does an abject failure have? I'm scorned, ridiculed, and mocked. Five stays in mental institutions have not been able to remove the chaos from my jumbled mind. I live in a slum, and I can't even afford my rent. On top of that, I dig for my supper out of people's trash. How could I cause the foundation of the world to shake?"

After bitterly summing up a life that revealed little but failure, Bissett casually spun in his chair, turned toward his desk and pulled the top right drawer open. A second later he reached in, produced a MAC 50 9mm pistol, aimed it at his guest and cracked, "It seems we have what you Americans call a Mexican standoff."

"This isn't my first dance," Dixon casually quipped. "The clip's empty."

Click!

Bissett then pulled the trigger a half dozen more times before frowning and tossing the gun onto the desktop. Evidently sensing there was no way out of the trap, he posed a question. "Why are my memories so frightening to you?"

"Your memories aren't. It's your grandfather's memories that can't be revealed."

"I never met him," Bissett reasoned. "He died in the war. He never shared anything important with anyone including my grandmother. What could I know about my grandfather that would mean anything to you?"

"We know what you are, and …" Dixon cocked his left eyebrow. "… more importantly, we know what you can do."

"Might be able to do," Bissett corrected the interrogator. "Don't you get it? I can't call up the past upon request. It doesn't work that way. Besides, what do you think I might remember? The truth is what scares you and your government might never come to me. It could just remain behind a locked door forever."

Bissett was brutally frank, and it was time to exploit that admirable quality as the weakness it really was. Dixon pushed off the couch and strolled over to the window. While pretending to study the quiet street, he posed a question. "Are you happy?'

"No!"

Dixon turned back toward his unwilling host. "Will you ever be happy?"

Bissett brought his hands in front of his face, fingertips touching fingertips, and shook his head. "I doubt it, but why does that concern you?"

"I like to read sad stories. I live for tragedy. I especially enjoy digging into tortured lives. Let's call it a hobby."

"Sounds depressing."

"A man is only as strong as his ability to control his mind. Consider the creativity of Edgar Allan Poe. He was brilliant but spent most of his forty years in a fog of loneliness and pain."

"What does that have to do with me?"

"Poe was one of you. He had the same gift you have. And it ate at him the same way yours eats at you. Oh, he tried to control the memories that were battling for real estate in his brain. Numerous examples of his efforts can be found in his stories. You see, he wrote of things he had not personally witnessed but had been seen by his ancestors. And in time, the memories became too many and too much for him to handle. Then came the booze and drugs.

"Look at you, Bissett. Your IQ is over one-hundred and eighty. You finished at the top of your class at university. You were once considered one of the greatest artists of your generation. But here you are at forty, and you're completely washed up. You haven't picked up a paint brush in years. Your talent is wasted because you can't hold onto an original thought for more than a few seconds at a time. And with each day, your head is filled with more and more memories. The tap is open and can't be turned off. The stories rattle around your brain like a dozen trains all going in different directions. They're invaders who don't belong in your mind, but they won't leave, and you can't drive them out. Even in drunken sleep, they demand your full attention. And it's just going to get worse. Your gift is not a blessing, it's a curse. There's only one exit, and you know what it is."

Bissett nodded. "Don't think I haven't been tempted?" He paused—his eyes now damp with tears. He was no longer talking, he was pleading. "There has to be a reason I have this. There has to be something I should be doing with the gift."

"Anything that drives us to insanity is hardly a gift," Dixon's tone was now as grim as his observation. "I've been watching you for the last ten days. Last week, you almost killed a woman. You grabbed her throat and, in a rage you couldn't control, tossed her against a window. And why did you do that?"

"It wasn't my fault. My head was filled with images. I thought she was …"

The man who'd been close to the edge since he walked into the flat was now coming completely unhinged. His ability to determine what was real and what was fantasy was hanging on a thread so thin a house fly likely couldn't balance on it.

"She was what?" Dixon demanded. "That woman you almost killed; what did you think she was?"

"A Nazi prison guard," he screamed. "I saw her as Schmidt. But the minute I shoved her, I realized the truth. And I grabbed her before she fell through the window."

"Four stories straight down. She would've died. You would've killed her. Let's face it, you can't control what's in your head any more than you can dictate when the sun sets or comes up. Perhaps the next time you have one of those flashes, it'll be a small child who's in front of you. What if you grab that kid when your memory becomes so vivid it seems real? What happens when you choke that child to death?"

Dixon allowed his words to hang in the air for at least a minute before adding, "This has now become a lot more than knowing what someone did in World War II. This is about a man who is so out of control he'll soon murder someone. I've witnessed that potential with my own eyes. For history's sake and the sake of those alive today, maybe even an innocent child, you must be stopped!"

Suddenly, Bissett's eyes went blank, and he began to tremble. It was as if he had entered another universe or was lost in a time and place void of earthly parameters. Finally, after at least a minute of silence, his vision cleared, the shaking stopped, and Bissett was no more a meek man. "I see it. I know what you can't afford for me to share. I remember what my grandfather witnessed and why it scares you so …"

Dixon's gun was equipped with a silencer, so there was little more than a pop. The bullet caught Bissett in the forehead and drove him back into the chair. Before the smoke cleared or the blood dripped from his face to his chest, the CIA agent crossed the room and checked for a pulse. With death confirmed, the assassin picked up the phone and dialed a familiar number.

"Clegg," announced the voice on the other end of the line.

"Inform the team the job is done."

"Good. See you in a week."

Dixon placed the phone back into the cradle, gathered up Bissett's journals, turned off the lamp, and exited the flat. Within an hour, he was on a plane headed toward the United States, his assignment finished. It was time to relax.

———◆————

One bullet. That's all it took this time. That's all it ever took.

Chapter 1

11:09 p.m.
Sunday, September 11, the present
Bill's Diner, Indianapolis, Indiana

Holding the fate of others in your hands is something no one should take lightly. Yet, after making one decision that stops a heart and ends a life, making the next one is a bit easier. And, after a while, it becomes almost routine. But at night, when you're all alone, the events always come back to haunt you. So, it's not the deeds that doom you to a living hell, it's the memories.

———◆———

Tim Clegg eased into the back booth at the almost deserted diner, loosened his tie, and checked his phone. He was solid, built like a bulldog with a chin to match, and moved like an offensive lineman. His brooding eyes were brown, his close-cropped hair more gray than black, and his lips thin. He'd spent more than forty years of his life on the road. The strain of constantly traveling all over the globe was evident in his heavily lined skin. Now, having a few minutes to cool his heels was something he treasured. And while the place chosen for the meeting was nothing more than a greasy spoon, at least it was quiet, calm, and almost empty, and he'd take his peace on earth wherever he could find it.

A short, chubby waitress ambled up to the table, and when her large brown eyes met his, she smiled, "What can I get you?"

Food, like they served at Bill's, an out of the way diner about five blocks from downtown Indy, was probably as tired as the faded racing posters tacked to the walls, but he had to eat something, and maybe just maybe, this would be the one dive that actually had a cook with a hint of talent. Did he risk a full meal? After glancing into the woman's pale, round face, logic overruled risk and he queried, "How are your pies?"

"The cherry's not bad."

"Give me that and a cup of black coffee." He considered the order for a second as she scribbled the information onto a pad, "Do you have apple?"

"Yeah, do you want to change your order?"

"No, I'll stick with the cherry, but I've got a friend who'll be here in few minutes. He'll want apple and coffee with cream."

"Coming right up."

Through tired eyes, Clegg studied a photo taken at one of the first Indianapolis 500s. The winner was leaning against his roadster drinking milk from a quart glass jug. Except for one clean area where goggles had covered his eyes, the driver's face was smudged by smoke and dust. Clegg could identify with the black and white image. During his time with the agency, he too had traveled a long way only to often end up where he started, but unlike the driver, he wouldn't ever be able to wash off the dirt. Regrets? He had a lot more than a few, and if given the chance to live life over again, he'd have done something much different than play in the spy game. He'd have settled down, married, raised a family, and embraced a world that might have been boring and commonplace but was also safe and clean. But instead of being a normal Joe, he'd opted for chaos and years spent rolling in muddy waters.

Where had he been yesterday? For a second, he couldn't quite remember. Was it London or Paris? Did it really matter? Then he'd flown across the Atlantic only to get a message upon landing at DC to get to Indy and meet Stone Smith. The word out of the Vatican was a loose-tongued drinker in Indiana knew where another imprint was located. If the rumor was true, a life and death decision would have to be made, and made very quickly before things got out of hand.

The waitress dropped off the order when Smith, Rocky to his friends, walked in. His closely cropped dark hair was graying at the temples, his eyes were light brown with a hint of hazel, and he carried himself like the athlete he'd once been. Tonight, as on most days, he wore a blue suit with a dark tie and white shirt. With only a nod, he eased into the booth just as the waitress walked away.

"I hope you don't mind that I ordered for you," Clegg sounded like an off-duty drill sergeant. Even when he was not agitated, his voice was intimidating. After digging into his cherry pie and swallowing the first bite, he smiled. "Not bad. The crust is actually kind of flaky."

Smith nodded. "I haven't had much to eat in two days. You know, there're parts of this job that just turn my stomach."

Unlike his boss, Smith had a smooth, disarming way of speaking. He didn't deliver remarks in machine gun bursts as Clegg did, but rather spilled them like they were coming from a barely opened facet.

"Sometimes, Rocky, we have to dig in sewers to uncover information. If we don't, then the cost might be in the millions."

"Lives or dollars?"

"Both. Now how long has it been since we worked something together? A year?"

"Ten months. We were both in Istanbul trying to turn a terrorist into a friend. It didn't go well."

That was an understatement. Two agents had been killed along with five locals, and it'd cost more than five million to keep that news out of the press.

"You ever get tired of it?" Clegg asked as he gulped a mouthful of coffee and frowned. It was as bad as the pie was good.

Smith shrugged. "I'm an only kid, a military brat who never really had many friends, but even loners get lonely. Sure, I'm tired of it."

"You still have time to get out. What are you … forty?"

"Forty-one."

"What was your college degree?"

"Business. And believe me, I've considered walking away. But when the place where I get my mail is no more familiar than the motel I stayed in last night, could I ever really settle down? Wouldn't I get antsy? Being in a different place each day gets in your blood."

"Yeah, but where does all that traveling get you? I'm over sixty and I never feel at home anywhere. I'm like a lost piece of luggage that keeps being moved from plane to plane, and no one ever claims me." He took a sip of coffee before adding, "And I just keep flying."

There was nothing else to say, the sad ode was complete, so both men ate a few bites of pie in silence, and Clegg used those moments to immerse himself into thoughts of a life that now seemed wasted.

Over the decades, he'd lost far more battles than he'd won and had been stuck in the mud much more than motoring to someplace he wanted to be. Most of the time, he had almost no control. Someone higher up was always pushing the buttons. But, there were a few times when he'd taken charge. There were moments when he had gone outside the lines. And though he rationalized he'd done it for the right reasons, in truth, it had been all for him and the team. Still, those acts now haunted him and caused him to constantly look over his shoulder. He was suggesting to Stone that escaping the CIA was a good idea, but in reality, Clegg was the one who needed to take that advice. He sighed, looked across the table and made a stark admission.

"You know, Rocky, I've spent thirty-five years on wild goose chases and the other five wondering what to do with the bird I caught." He frowned before turning his mind back to the case at hand. "Is this a wasted trip or were you able to dig something out of … what was his name?"

"Rhett Marks?"

"Tell me about him."

Stone's eyes reflected his distaste for his assignment and the man he'd met. "Marks is such a negative force that when he enters a room, it feels like two people have left. I don't think he loves anything, including his wife, and he complains about everything. Five minutes with this guy is like five years with anyone else."

"How hard was it to mine the info?"

"It wasn't like in Rome. I didn't have to employ any rough stuff. I went into his office and asked him about some life insurance. He suggested we talk at a local tavern—a dingy place where losers go to forget their pain. Suited him to a T. I bought him some beer and let him ramble. After assuring him I'd purchase a policy, I steered the conversation to his family. It took an hour and four drinks before I finally got him to talk about his sister. He enjoyed bragging about her and her accomplishments. When he found out I was single, he even wanted to set me up with her. After a couple more beers, he confirmed what our sources at the Vatican shared. She's an imprint."

"I was hoping she wasn't. I really didn't want to have to go through this again." Clegg sighed before filling in some blanks, "As soon as our sources told us Factor might be an imprint, I had the folks in DC get to work on her background."

"What did you dig up?" Smith asked.

"The research department created a family tree. At first glance, there didn't seem much of a problem. A couple of her ancestors interacted with some movers and shakers, but it was minor contact. Then I looked at her more recent past. Her father and mother, Carven and Kathleen Marks, separated before Maxine was born. Six months after they got back together, the child was born. That bit of timing put me to wondering if her father was actually her father. A week ago, I had someone covertly enter her home to obtain a DNA sample. I've been waiting on a call to confirm those results."

"Was her dad—if he is her dad—anyone special?" Smith asked.

"No, Factor's memories likely hold nothing that'll hurt us. Her mother's experiences are inconsequential as well. But we'll keep digging." He took a deep breath and frowned. "What did the brother tell you about how far advanced Factor's imprinting is?"

"Based on what I heard, I'd peg her as gifted as the man in Ukraine the Russians snuffed out."

"That's not good," Clegg suggested.

"Why?"

"Because she's well educated, incredibly intelligent, and very stable. That means she might be able to handle the flood of memories longer than most. And the more she remembers, the more likely she might see something that could change history."

Stone shrugged. "When I was briefed, it was explained that imprinting always kills the imprint."

"Based on what we've learned, it always does. It's a fatal disease. Like ALS, once it infects you, it just keeps growing. The memories overwhelm a person, and madness slowly seeps in. The two who weren't killed or didn't commit suicide became babbling idiots. They ultimately died from lack of sleep. Their minds wouldn't turn off. It's kind of the opposite of Alzheimer's. That takes away all your memories while imprinting gives you far more than you can handle."

"Imagine being murdered by your ancestors' experiences."

"The theory goes that each of your ancestors' memories is imprinted on the DNA. When those memories are awakened, they flood a mind that has limited storage capacity. And just because we've identified only a handful in this generation, doesn't mean imprinting is new. Our research indicates that several people in the past had the ability to relive their ancestors' lives. One was the author Edgar Allen Poe."

"Generations of memories waiting to be unlocked. Imagine my knowing my father's life as well as I know my own."

"Rocky, you'd only know a small part of your dad's life. Thanks to information we stole from the Russians, we know the memories that come back only include the experiences before the imprint was conceived. The genetic sequencing ends there; from that point on the experiences placed in the DNA chain belong to the new generation. So, as her mother was twenty-four when Factor was conceived, Factor would only be able to see the first twenty-four years of her mother's life. That would be true of every generation until the beginning of time. Based on what we know, only one imprint has gone back more than five hundred years. That was the doctor the Russians murdered."

Clegg's ringing cell stopped the discussion. He tapped the phone. "What do you have?"

"And hello to you, Tim," the tech announced.

"We'll catch up later," Clegg barked, "tell me what you found out."

"Okay, Mr. Impatient. Sometimes DNA is much easier to match than at other times. Especially when that DNA belongs to someone who used to be one of us."

"So, are you saying the person Factor thought was her father wasn't?"

"You pegged it. Dr. Maxine Factor is not related to Carven Marks. Her biological father is actually a former operative here at the CIA. Small world, huh?"

"You're kidding."

"Wish I were. You will be too when I tell you the agent's name—William Dixon."

"Are you sure?"

"Absolutely. And no one knows where Dixon is now. He disappeared a decade ago. Here's some irony for you, rumor has it the Russians used him to take out the imprinted doctor in the Ukraine back in 2011. If that's true, he's a gun for hire."

"Anything else?"

"Nope."

"Great." Clegg snapped off the call. After setting his cell on the table, he raised his cup and nursed his coffee, letting it swirl in his mouth. As a confused Stone looked on, Clegg finally broke the silence.

"What do you know about a man named William Dixon?"

"I saw him once. I heard that he dealt with explosive international situations and was sent in to help stop potential government coups."

"Yeah. The ramifications of the jobs he did for this country still resonate across the globe."

Clegg didn't go into detail. He couldn't allow Stone to know the real work Dixon had done. To take out one cleric in Iran, Dixon blew up a commercial passenger jet—two-hundred and forty-seven innocent lives perished that day. And in London in '75 and '81 he killed two members of parliament. The Brits still believe those men died in accidents. If powerful forces in Europe and the Middle East found out what really had happened to certain government and religious leaders there would be hell to pay.

"How does this change things?" Smith asked. "I mean Dixon being the father."

"When was Maxine Factor born?"

"August 10, 1983."

Clegg shook his head in disgust. "Give me everything you know about her as fast as you can."

Smith nodded. "Though young by academic standards, after just six years at Washington-Lincoln College, Dr. Maxine Factor is viewed as the faculty's rock. She's a leader and a force. Unlike many of her colleagues, she's not eclectic or eccentric. Though a woman of solid moral character, Factor's also a bit of a gambler. She's lean, athletic, and honey blonde with Carolina blue eyes, and so naturally attractive, she is intimidating. The students call her hot. Her choice of style, dark suits, sweaters, slacks, and flats, projects a woman comfortable in her own skin and not influenced by fads. She is so practical her colleagues rib her for buying makeup at discount stores rather than embracing the legendary brand whose name she shares. Likely due to her passion for reading, she is wise beyond her years, as well as a spiritual person who constantly challenges those around her to seek knowledge and find their calling. When giving advice, she sometimes pushes the envelope too much, becoming frustrated when her friends and students lack the energy or passion to chase their dreams, and at times she voices her irritation a bit too loudly. That has led to several trips to the president's office for stern lectures. But he doesn't challenge her much—he can't afford to lose her. Even Ivy League schools would gladly hire her. She's that good. She's a woman who seems to have her pulse on what matters. I think I'd like her."

Why couldn't she have been a maid? Clegg took another gulp of coffee. He had to let Stone know about some of the dirt to ensure the agent understood the seriousness of this matter, but he couldn't spill too much.

"Rocky, you can't share it with anyone, but there are at least five assassinations Factor could remember. We can't afford for our enemies or allies to find out we've conducted diplomacy through murder."

"I didn't know about that," an obviously stunned Smith whispered.

"You aren't alone, not even the presidents who were in office when those events happened knew about them. We were a small team that, in times when the world was about to explode, made those calls on our own. We judged our missions on who could best bring stability and who offered the United States the most bang for the buck. So, it went beyond just politics and religion, it also focused on the financial aspect of the equation. And we didn't make those decisions lightly. We took our time and examined all the options. We weighed the lives of thousands against the life of an individual or a few individuals. But if we decided that murder was the only option, the man who always did our jobs was Dixon. If Maxine Factor remembers any of those missions, we're in huge trouble. And, as I've shared the information with you, this is something that could hurt you as well."

"What if she already has remembered them?" Smith asked.

"If that's the case, and she goes public with the information, we could be looking at a complete disruption of multiple alliances across the globe."

"So, we have to nab her."

"No, you can't keep someone like this under wraps. She has to be eliminated."

Smith paused in mid bite, his face frozen in shock, before whispering, "But the chief won't allow that. That's not how this CIA operates. At least not now."

"Yeah, I know, but he's not going to find out. This will be the same kind of operation we ran when we used Dixon." He sadly shook his head before suggesting, "Let's hurry back to DC. I need to inform the other three members of the old team. And because you know about this, you'll be going rogue as well. There's no backing out now, kid. Do you trust me?"

"Absolutely!"

Blood would once more be on Clegg's hands, but there was no other way. A woman had to die. It had to be quick and clean.

Chapter 2

6:22 p.m.
Monday, September 12
Patriot's Trail, Washington-Lincoln College,
Mount Vernon, Illinois

Some memories warm you, some are as cold as ice, but they're all yours and yours alone. You own them. But when your mind is invaded by those you have never met, and their memories begin to both direct and haunt you, things change. The invaders challenge your ability to know a time, a place, or even yourself. That's when the gift becomes a curse.

———◆———

A bullet zipped by Maxie Factor's ear at 2,500 feet a second before digging deeply into a century old oak. Without John Miller yanking her to the ground and then dragging her behind a rock wall, the university history professor would have been taken down a moment later by a second shot. That steel projectile rocketed just over Factor's head before finding the same tree as did the first messenger of death. This was a moment that cell phones were made for, the very time when instant communication was needed, but as this meeting had been "unplugged," she didn't have hers. There was no time to moan about that now, but Factor did make a mental note to never let that happen again. That is, if there was a time beyond this one.

"What in the world?" Miller's words had barely cleared his lips when two more shots rang out, these bullets bouncing off the top of the native stone fence before ricocheting into the underbrush. As the short, stout math instructor hunkered lower toward the ground, his agile colleague pushed her back into the fence and grimly nodded. The pattern she'd all but ignored was continuing, and this time there could be no arguing … someone was trying to kill her!

As she hid behind the barrier, momentarily safe from the sniper, Factor thought back over the past seventy-two hours. Three days ago, she'd been driving down a rural road, and her car's brakes failed. The only reason the vehicle didn't plunge off a cliff and into a ravine was her frantically setting the emergency brake. Miraculously, that measure stopped the Mustang with a mere ten feet to spare. When the vehicle was towed into a garage and examined on a lift, the mechanic suggested two brake lines might have been intentionally cut. Factor laughed it off, had the car fixed, and headed home.

The following day, noxious fumes would have killed her except a faculty meeting had run long and delayed her departure from campus by two hours. Before she returned home, a neighbor had smelled the leaking natural gas and reported it to the city utility company. The crew surveying the small house discovered a pilot light had failed, and a safety value had not cut off as designed. The team had no explanation as to why that had happened. It was at that moment, the mechanic's warning about the brake lines gained a bit of traction. Still, as she went to sleep that night, Factor rationalized both events as nothing more than bizarre accidents.

But now this ambush, much more direct and unforgiving, confirmed someone was out to get her. But why? What had she done to sign her own death warrant? As she had no enemies, logic prescribed this had to be the actions of an angry student? Yet that seemed too extreme to accept. After all, history classes, unlike theology or political science, rarely stoked much passion even for those majoring in the discipline.

"Max," Miller whispered. A tenor in the local choir, his voice was even higher now. "What in heaven's name is this all about?"

Factor's eye's sparkled, her full lips were drawn tight and her shoulder length hair hung limp. "Not sure!" she finally cautioned. "But I'm betting it's me they're after, and not you. And I've no idea why."

"Then can you give me a way to get out of this mess? I need an exit, and I need it pretty quick too!"

Factor frowned as she recalled a similar night many years before. When pinned down by enemy fire, four men tossed rocks into brush to draw fire and then raced down a hill in the opposite direction. It'd worked on a hillside in France in 1918, but what about now?

"Are we safe here?" Miller begged, unknowingly breaking into a scene from another place and time. "Can we just wait it out?"

Factor rolled over onto her knees and studied the surroundings. She knew this park well. It covered more than a thousand acres and was owned by the university. Both faculty and students used the area for jogging, biking, and hiking. The trail the pair had been following led along a ridge and looped back to the school's main grounds near the football stadium. During the day the path provided excellent views of Stots Creek, but as dusk settled in, the stream was completely lost in shadows. That worked in their favor.

"What do we do?" Miller demanded, obviously scared to death. At this moment, the mathematician had every right to be.

Factor leaned close to Miller and whispered, "We're going to have to make a move. Give me a second, and I'll figure a way to better our odds."

"A history teacher talking odds doesn't give me much confidence. That's my turf."

Factor dismissed the dig. Much like it had happened on that night in World War I, she figured the sniper was probably working his way down the hill and into a position where he could get a better angle for a clear shot. She turned her eyes toward the sky, the sun had set, twilight had arrived, and within a few minutes the darkness created by the woods would perhaps provide enough cover for an escape. But century-old experiences dictated that waiting on those minutes was anything but wise. A man named George Wilson, a wisecracking Iowan with a wife and two kids, had hesitated and paid for it with his life, while the four soldiers who ran lived to talk about that day.

"John, if we stay near the ground and work our way down the hill using that row of cedar trees for cover, we can put some distance between us and whoever's trying to ventilate our coats."

"Isn't just staying put better?" Miller argued.

"No, I'm sure the guy's working toward a lower angle right now and when he gets to a point just down this path, the fence won't help us. We'll be sitting ducks. Consider this, birds that are flying are much harder to hit."

"Okay, I guess I'll trust your judgment," Miller's tone indicated he lacked confidence. "After all, you're the one who has studied military tactics. But let it be known I'm following you under protest."

Crawling over to the edge of the dirt path, Factor found two fist-sized rocks. Rejoining Miller, she handed one of the stones to her cousin.

"I don't think we can duplicate David's feat," the math teacher wryly cracked. "Besides, he could see Goliath."

"We're not tossing them at the shooter," Factor explained. "We're going to throw both of them into the brush about fifty feet to the north. That should direct the fire in that direction and give us time to head the other way."

"Should?"

"History professors don't make any guarantees—we just weigh the past against the future to decide the best course for the present." She forced a smile before continuing, "After we throw the rocks as far possible, I'll lead the way. Just keep your head down and run as fast as you can."

"Have you looked at this body? I'm not built for running. My long, wide torso and thick, short legs make me clumsy and slow. My dad always said, 'Johnny would finish ninth in an eight-man race.'"

"You'll make it. And like I said, they really want me, not you."

Factor pushed off the ground and threw the stone. Miller followed a second later. Just as it had in 1918, the bluff worked, at least temporarily. As the rocks rattled the brush, a series of shots rang out. Mumbling a quick prayer, Factor sprinted to the cedars and hid in the shadows until Miller arrived a few seconds later. Not waiting for him to catch his breath, Factor pushed out of the shade and toward the base of the incline. The sniper hadn't been distracted for too long. As Factor emerged into the open ground, two more shots rang out, one hitting the dirt beside her feet and the other striking and then rebounding off a rock. Though the firing stopped when she raced under the shade of a dozen pine trees, Factor continued to rush down the hill at breakneck speed. She didn't ease out of her sprint until she got to the creek. At that point she glanced back and watched her cousin, arms flailing, tie and jacket bouncing with each stride, awkwardly loping down the hillside. If they hadn't been racing for their lives, Miller's attempt at summoning grace and speed from a body intended for heavy lifting would have been funny. Somehow, he made it to the shade without tumbling to the ground or drawing fire. When he was finally by her side, Factor glanced back at the heavens. The sun was now completely behind the horizon—only a few deep red streaks flared across the sky. It was almost dark, and the odds were now getting much better.

"Okay, John, let's work our way along the creek bed. The college owns an old barn a few hundred yards to the south. I've actually used it a few times as a classroom to explain and showcase construction techniques from the 1800s. Once we get there, we'll lock ourselves in and take a break."

"Can't we wait a few minutes to grab our breath? I'm gassed. That's the furthest I've run in twenty years."

"No," she commanded, "That guy's surely working his way toward us. At least, that's the way it played out a century ago."

"What do you mean by that?"

"No time to explain. Let's get moving."

After five minutes of pushing through bushes, wading in ankle deep water, and climbing over rocks, Factor spotted the barn. Using her right hand to signal for Miller to follow, she ran in nearly pitch darkness across a small open meadow, found the key hidden between a rain gutter and the eave, unlocked the door, and pushed the building's side entry open. A few seconds later, when a huffing and weak-kneed Miller was also inside, Factor shut and latched the entry.

"Are we safe?" Miller asked between shallow breaths, his dark eyes trying to make out what was in the thirty-by fifty-foot barn, "or are we going to have to run another marathon?"

"Should be safe," Factor assured him. "The school keeps the double doors barred, and I locked this one, so no one's getting in." She frowned before noting, "Now I've got a bone to pick with you. Why did you demand I leave my cell back at the office? This is the moment 911 is made for."

A still panting Miller frowned. "I-I-I wanted to talk to you about the offer I'd gotten from a college in Colorado. I needed your full focus and didn't want any interruptions." He shook his head. "None of that seems important now, and I'd give anything to have my phone too."

"Yeah, we've had a few distractions anyway. But I'm warning you, never again dismiss the merits of embracing the latest technology."

Factor, her eyes growing more accustomed to the darkness, took inventory. They were sharing the accommodations with an ancient grain wagon, some hand tools, twenty or so bales of hay, and a 1940s Ford tractor. Now a bit more secure, she walked a dozen feet over to an ancient wooden bench and sat down. Her cousin soon joined her and again asked a question he'd posed fifteen minutes before.

"What's this all about?"

"I don't know, it's pretty obvious someone's been trying to kill me, but I can't think of a single reason why."

"Are you saying this isn't the first time?"

"Yeah, this is the third attempt in four days."

"You aren't dating a married man, are you?" Miller's tone indicated he was serious.

"No, and before you ask, I don't owe any money, and I don't know of a single student who's mad at me."

"If you'd been kind enough to mention there was someone trying to kill you," Miller quipped, "I'd have asked someone else about the offer. And then I wouldn't have had to go out and walk in the woods. Dr. Simpson would've just bought me a cup of coffee in the student center."

"Next time you want advice, I vote for Simpson as well."

The math professor, his breathing almost normal, glanced around the room. "Max, are you sure we're safe in here?"

"Safer than we were out there. I don't think there's any way he could get into this old building. But keep your ears open. If you hear someone walking around outside, let me know. I can use a shovel as a weapon."

"Yeah, that'll match up against an automatic." He glanced around. "You're claiming we're safe, but I feel trapped."

Standing, Factor walked over and picked up the spade and a pitchfork, returned, leaned the tools against the bench, and sat down.

Now it was time to wait and maybe pray. For the next five minutes, the only sounds were the breeze through the trees and the creaking of the old barn's walls. Perhaps the sniper had given up. Maybe he'd lost them and, figuring they'd called the cops, had left. That logic seemed sound until Factor caught the odor of gasoline. A few seconds later, when smoke seeped under the barn's large swinging front door, her heart sank. If the shooter couldn't get inside, he was going to burn them out.

"Do you smell that?" a suddenly paranoid Miller questioned.

"Yeah," she answered, determined to keep her wits and sound calm. "He's torching the place. There's a hundred-gallon tank of fuel behind the barn. He must've broken the lock and helped himself."

"Lord, I can't think of anything worse than burning to death." Miller's normally calm voice was cracking like a teenage boy's, and his next words proved he was not cut out for playing a hero. "This can't be real—it has to be a bad dream. I can't die. I have two kids, and Molly needs me. I've got to get out! I don't want to roast like a pig. Max, what in God's name have you gotten me into?" There were tears streaming down his face, and his body was shaking like Jell-O.

Miller was right, this was a nightmare, one that fit right into a Hitchcock movie or TV's *The Blacklist*. As she considered their next move, the barn faded from view and an almost forgotten memory came into sharp focus.

There was a race up the stairs to save two children and then, with flames rushing across the floor, a frantic leap from a second story window to the ground. But downstairs, a woman, struck by both fear and panic of not just the fire, but the band of Sioux surrounding the house, had prayed and waited for help rather than breaking a window and rushing outside. Her screams would haunt her family for years.

As the memory faded, Factor found herself once more in the present. "John, we have a slim chance out there—in here, we have no chance at all."

"Don't talk to a wide man about slim chances, the two don't work together."

"If we stay where we are, we'll either be overcome with smoke or burn to death. Think about this logically. This place is a tinder box; it'll go up in minutes. Take my word for it. You don't want to die in a fire. I've witnessed that. The pain's beyond comprehension."

"Yeah, I'm sure that's true, but I also don't want to catch the kind of lead poisoning that guy's giving out." He paused, his eyes catching hers, and then demanded, "Wait! When did you witness someone burning in a fire?"

"Just follow my lead!" she announced, ignoring his question.

"Oh sure, I followed you this far, and what has it gotten me? I'm going to die one way or the other, and I've got you to thank for it! Dad always said, 'Stay away from Max, she's trouble!' I should have listened to him."

Smoke was now filling the upper reaches of the building and flames were visible along the edge of the roof. No longer able to hold the fort, Factor hurried back to where they'd entered a few minutes before. As the fire rapidly climbed the barn's wooden siding, she unlocked the entry, nodded once, and over the sounds of the blaze, yelled directions, "Try to get to the woods and find some cover. He'll probably be aiming for me."

Miller nodded and coughed. "No offense, but I hope you're right."

As they stood at the entry, fire was now eating away at the barn's roof, and black smoke was moving closer and closer to the floor. Breathing was all but impossible. Soon the tractor would be consumed and, depending upon how much gas was in its tank, might explode sending shrapnel in all directions.

Pushing the door open, Factor coughed twice, took a breath, and stormed out into the night. She'd made a half a dozen steps when two shots rang out. From the corner of her eye, she saw the first hit a tree—the second zipped passed her head and dug into the barn's wall. The parallels to 1918 and France no longer rang true nor did the memories of a fire in 1867. As the awkward Miller tripped and fell, Factor halted her life and death race and turned toward the front of the blazing building. Outlined in the fire's glow was a thin man, medium height, holding a rifle aimed squarely in the history teacher's direction. Not wanting to be executed without a fight, Factor lowered her head and dashed toward the shooter. For the first time in over a half an hour she drew a break ... the gun jammed. The assassin was still attempting to get the weapon's chamber cleared as Factor closed the last of the twenty feet separating her from the would-be killer. Recalling a Harvard and Yale game from 1915, Factor assumed the role of a Bulldog linebacker on a full blitz, slammed her shoulder into the stranger's chest, driving him backwards toward the barn until they both stumbled to the ground just a few feet in front of the flames.

As the rifle fell to the side, Factor sprang to her feet. Kicking the weapon away, the professor turned to face the person intent on ending her life. The sniper, once again standing, looked about thirty, his hair dark, his skin swarthy, his eyes intense and focused, and his knees bent and flexed. As if possessed, the shooter charged forward, hands extended toward Factor's throat. Yet, before the menacing fingers could reach their target, the professor, using a move taught to every GI in World War II, stepped to the side and tripped the assailant causing him to stagger to his left in an attempt to regain his balance. With the barn now completely engulfed in flames, one memory was replaced with another, and Factor, relying on instincts and experience that were more than a hundred and fifty years old and learned in the days of bare knuckle boxing, delivered a right cross to the stranger's jaw. The well-placed blow sent the man staggering backward toward the burning building. With his arms flailing, the assassin tripped over a rock and fell, knocking over a half-filled can of gasoline As he tumbled into the dirt, the remaining liquid spilled out, soaking the his pants and coating his shoes. The rest snaked across the ground toward the barn. When the fuel met the inferno, it created an instant river of flame leading back to the sniper. Within moments, his clothes were on fire. As he rolled in the dirt and cursed, the barn's front wall gave way, collapsing onto the now helpless man. He didn't even have time to scream before being consumed by the inferno. Just like in 1867, as the smell of scorching flesh filled her nose, Factor once again realized how horrible it was to burn to death.

Driven back by the heat, she jogged over to Miller and helped him to his feet. After taking a final look at what was left of the barn, Factor led the way across the meadow to the edge of the woods. When they could no longer feel the fire on their backs, they turned and silently watched the flames finish consuming a building that had stood for more than a century.

Standing just inside the darkened woods, Factor wondered if there were others hungering for blood just like there had been in France during World War I. She couldn't answer that question any more than she could guess why she'd suddenly become a target.

Chapter 3

12:49 a.m.
Tuesday, September 13
Wallace Hall Room 315, Washington-Lincoln College,
Mount Vernon, Illinois

Trust is being able to share something that sounds crazy. Confidence is having the ability to know that and do it anyway.

———◆———

At this moment, Maxine Factor was drawing blanks. She'd never been a target or been responsible for a death. Now she was both.

"I just don't get it," an exhausted Miller announced while unwittingly speaking for both of them. "I've known you since you were born. No one would want to murder you. That guy must have escaped from a mental institution. He's a lunatic—that's the only thing that makes sense."

Getting up from behind her desk, Factor walked over to a third-floor window. With both hands in her slacks' pockets, she stared out on the quiet scene where decades old streetlamps illuminated well-traveled concrete walks, yet her mind didn't note what her eyes beheld. In fact, she saw nothing of the present—her focus was completely on the past. As she combed through memories to uncover a way to justify why anyone would want her dead, frustration kicked in. She needed another point of view, someone who might see something she was missing. But that would require coming clean about things even she couldn't understand, thus placing herself in an uncomfortable and vulnerable position. And she was a woman who'd spent her life disguising and hiding her weaknesses and insecurities. Could she open that window to her soul? Was it worth the risk of being considered a fool or worse?

As Factor contemplated her options, thoughts of a relative who'd served in the French and Indian War popped into her head. William Duncan had been a soldier and a philosopher, and he'd adhered to the notion you have to trust someone even if that trust led to ridicule or laughter. He'd first embraced that old adage in a lull between fierce fighting, and on that long-ago day, he'd opened up his heart to a short, stocky soldier from Maine. Her cousin was born in Maine as well. Perhaps that was a sign Factor was to tell him what she couldn't—and didn't—tell the police.

"I've got to trust someone," she thought not realizing she'd also spoken those words

"What did you say?" Miller asked.

Factor resolutely turned and studied her cousin. With his thinning hair and thick neck, he appeared two decades older than his forty-one years. His jacket torn and grass stained, his shirt's tail hanging over his ample stomach, Miller looked a great deal like Otis from the old *Andy Griffith Show*. Yet the man's brain was like a computer, and it was that kind of mathematical logic that might provide a formula for dealing with a problem so complex Factor couldn't get her head around it.

"John, do you remember that plane crash I was in two years ago?"

Sitting in the Windsor chair in front of Factor's oak desk, with one short leg crossed over his knee, Miller looked up and nodded. "Sure, the school's private plane had engine problems. The pilot did a great job landing on a country road. As I recall, you hit your head on the door frame and ended up in a different world."

"Yeah," Factor conceded, still hesitating to reveal the whole story, "but I wasn't really injured that badly."

"Tell that to folks around here, and eyes will roll. Most of us thought you were going to die. I think the docs gave you about a fifty-fifty shot of ever waking up. And, if you regained consciousness, they figured you'd have some memory or fine motor skills issues. You're a walking miracle!"

"Any brain injury scares people," Factor noted, "but all I really had was a severe concussion and some cerebral bleeding. Don't forget, within three weeks, I was back home and fine. Within six weeks, I was beating everyone on campus in racquetball, including Riley, our chauvinistic head football coach."

"Max, you're the exception to the rule. Either that or you're the luckiest woman on the planet. You beat the odds and came out fine. But I don't see what this has to do with having someone try to kill you. Everybody likes you! Heck, almost every woman on campus wants to be you! In fact, some men do too. You're as close as we get to a rock star in the academic world."

Factor shrugged. "Remember your math, one and one always equals two, so don't exaggerate."

"I'm not!"

Should Factor now move on and tell her cousin the whole story or just drop it? Did she really want Miller to hear the lunacy of a tale that even she scarcely believed?

"Once again," Miller quietly demanded, "how could that crash tie to what happened tonight? Did you find out someone sabotaged that plane or the school's mechanic failed to spot a problem?"

"No, nothing like that. That'd be easy to deal with. I'd just tell the cops and move on." After folding her arms over her chest, Factor opted to continue in the vein of her almost forgotten ancestor from the French and Indian war. Just as Duncan had, she'd lay out the facts. "John, at first the only real issues after the accident were headaches. For a couple of weeks, they were so severe they often made me sick to my stomach."

"I didn't know about that," her cousin chimed in, his tone empathetic.

"I didn't tell anyone, including the doctors, I just figured I'd learn to live with them. And in time, they went away—only to be replaced by something both fascinating and horrifying."

"Something could be worse than migraines?"

Factor nodded. When she'd shared her story with three others, they'd shaken their heads and chuckled. At first, they believed she was pulling their legs. Then, they told her if her dreams were creeping in and battling with reality she needed to get some real professional help. Yet their advice hadn't pushed her to visit a psychiatrist—instead it had driven her to researching her issues. And over the past few months, she'd developed a theory that made sense … at least in a 1950's cheap science fiction movie kind of way.

"John," Factor began, taking either a leap of faith or showing a complete lapse in judgment, "do you remember the story that got a lot of national play a few years ago about the woman in a car wreck on the West Coast? She was in a coma for weeks, and when she came out of the fog, she spoke nothing but Swedish."

"Yeah, and she'd never been to Sweden and never even known anyone who spoke that language. No one could explain how she was able to do that. I figured it was some type of elaborate hoax. Just an original way to get a video to go viral on social media."

"And a year before that," Factor moved to sit on a corner of her desk, "a high school student in Georgia was kicked in the head during a soccer game, and when he awoke from a coma, he spoke Spanish like a native. And he'd never even studied the language."

"I didn't know about that case. While this is fascinating, what does this have to do with you and what happened to us today?" He shook his head before muttering, "I still can't believe someone shot at me."

A cold shiver ran down Factor's spine. Even though every bone in her body demanded she hold her tongue, it was time to really open the can and spill the beans. "John, I've conducted my own research on those two unique cases. In my study, I discovered something others had missed. In the case of the woman, her great-great-grandparents were from Sweden. They'd died about eighty years before she was born. And the boy's great-grandmother was from the Dominican Republic, but once again, he'd never known her. So, while the medical community had no way of explaining how these two spoke new languages after their brain injuries, I locked onto a theory."

"Which is?"

"It sounds crazy."

"As if this day hasn't been one for the books. So, shoot! Ouch! Let me rephrase that employing a more carefully chosen verb. Would you please spell things out for me?"

She smiled at Miller's rather dark humor before launching into a theory that was sure to bring more laughs. "I believe that most, if not all, the experiences of our ancestors are written onto our DNA. Hence, somehow, and I can't begin to explain that part of the equation, the woman's injury unlocked her great-great-grandparents' native tongue, just as the soccer player's head trauma revived the DNA from one of his ancestor's lives. Both suddenly recalled information that was always there but had been inaccessible. For lack of a better description ... a neural pathway had been opened."

Miller shook his head in disbelief. "You're trying to tell me that my brain has all the knowledge of the language of my mother's parents? If that were true, then why did I have so much trouble with French in high school and college?"

"I'm telling you there's a lot more than French imprinted there." Factor had swung open the door to her mind, so now it was time to really allow her cousin to enter. With slow and measured words, she continued. "Since my accident, I've had vivid memories of my mother's life before I was born. And they aren't from stories she told me or inspired by photos I've seen."

"What do you mean by memories?"

"John," Factor's normally solid, alto voice almost trembled with excitement as words burst out like machine gun fire. "I've experienced sitting in my mother's grade school classrooms as well as going on fishing trips with her father. I have my mother's memories of different students she taught when she was a very young English teacher. A kid named Richard Meeks was a real card. She both loathed and loved him. I've lived World War II through my grandfather's eyes. I was also there when my grandmother read his letters from the war-front. She memorized them, and I can now recite them word for word, and you have to know this ... I've never seen them, those letters were destroyed in a fire in 1974, and, a few years before she died, she told me losing that correspondence all but broke her heart. I also know her recipes and sewing secrets. And that's just the beginning."

"You must have heard stories and forgotten them," Miller argued, "or perhaps you used what you had heard as a foundation and your imagination took over."

"No, my mother never talked about the things I now see so clearly, and I never knew my grandparents. These are not memories as much as they are real, first-person experiences. Somehow my head injury unlocked my ancestors' lives. And I feel as if I walked step by step through their experiences with them. I was, or maybe I should say, I'm there seeing through their eyes."

A suddenly intrigued Miller leaned closer. "How far back do you remember? You mentioned your grandparents, but does it go beyond them?"

Sensing she might've somehow convinced her cousin of something, Factor couldn't really believe herself—she moved her tale forward. "More experiences come each day, and they come in reverse order. It's like I'm traveling back in time. I can tell you in detail about my great-great-great-great-great-grandfather's experiences in the Revolutionary War. And this morning, as I ate my breakfast, I was thinking about things that happened in a small village in Wales in 1631, when another of my grandfathers celebrated the birth of a son. I can see these events as they played out, I can smell the smells and taste the tastes. It's as if I was there fully living each of those moments. I see everything they viewed and hear what they heard. In cases where my ancestors saw historical figures, I can point out the way paintings we now have of those men and women are inaccurate. It was both amazing and overwhelming. And I fully recognize that it sounds crazy!"

"You're serious? You're not pulling my leg?"

"No, I'm dead serious. The plan I employed today, by throwing those rocks to redirect fire to give us time to run down that hill, which was from my great-great-grandfather's experiences in World War I. I had to get out of that barn, even if the guy was going to try to shoot us because of the experiences of another ancestor. In fact, a few more of my relatives showed me what to do tonight. And if they hadn't, we'd both be dead."

"Max, if this is true, and let's say it is, what does it have to do with the reason someone would want to kill you? I mean, so you can see into the past, what kind of threat is that to anyone?"

Factor leaned back onto her desk. "That's what I can't figure out. I mean none of my relatives were famous or involved in anything that was important. My people didn't alter history; they just lived it. In my mind, the only thing this does is give me a greater understanding of the fabric of the past and how to employ that knowledge as a person and a teacher."

"Well," Miller noted, "what you said about just living and not altering history is pretty deep, but would that be worth anything? We both know you can't change history. What is written is written, and it can't be rewritten. So, in my mathematical mind, that means your gift, as you call it, is not the reason someone tried to gun you down."

"I've come to the same conclusion. All I have is a different point of view than other people. But someone is trying to kill me."

"Was, that man is dead now." Miller uncrossed his legs and rubbed his shoulder before asking, "Who else have you told about this gift?"

"Three people beyond you. My old college friend, Heather, my brother, Rhett, and the third a pastor, Dr. Wylie, who preached at my family's church when I was growing up. He's now in a big church in DC. You know all those people."

A weary Miller shook his head. "I doubt any of them would want to kill you for your gift, so there has to be something else at work here. I mean just because you have vivid memories of times gone by doesn't put a gun in someone's hand and provide a motive for murder. It simply doesn't add up. My guess is you've seen something you shouldn't have seen in the modern world, and if that recent memory is triggered, someone would be in trouble. So, I think you need to focus on events that are a lot more current than a baby's birth in Wales."

Moving back to the window, Factor glanced back at the now sleeping campus. Perhaps her cousin was right. Could it be this wasn't a conspiracy but just one deranged man who had grasped upon something in Factor's life that had provided a reason to kill? But what was it? Maybe there were others stalking her right now. That thought quickly drove her away from the window.

Chapter 4

10:47 a.m.
Thursday, September 15
Newsroom, Chicago Herald-Times, Chicago, Illinois

A true journalist really cares nothing about his or her own life. They live for the story, and each story becomes a drug that drives them to go places where death awaits and is eager to pen another obituary, maybe even their own.

———◆———

At thirty-five, Mason Hardin was arguably the youngest old-fashioned reporter in the world. In a time when most journalists flocked to online and television reporting, Hardin had ink in his veins. And as he continued to toil in the print media, the six-foot, three-inch, former quarterback for the Southern Illinois Salukis, who bore a striking resemblance to classic film actor Gary Cooper, seemed to always find the dynamic stories others missed. So, it was hardly surprising his written words had once pushed one of the city's most powerful politicians into jail, won a Pulitzer Prize for exposing corruption in the federal prison system, and provided the only firsthand report of the assassination of the man many had assumed would be the next president. On top of his riveting eyewitness reporting, his work had uncovered clues leading to the arrest of the person who pulled the trigger that had stopped Ted Weatherby's life. Yet, though it had happened last week, Hardin didn't bask in the glory, to him that was old news. The only story the scribe cared about was the next one. On this foggy morning, Hardin's dark blue eyes were searching computer files attempting to link one of the president's cabinet members to a twenty-year-old real estate scam. He was sure Dennis Richardson was involved, but so far, he'd been stymied in uncovering evidence to prove it. Still, he wasn't ready to give up, and was so absorbed in his search he almost didn't notice when another reporter called his name.

"Mason," Marsha Chambers shouted from across the busy room, "there's an envelope on my desk that has your name on it? Do you have a secret admirer or something?"

Hardin looked up from the screen and across three empty desks toward his gutsy colleague just five years out of Northwestern. The thin woman with wide shoulders and narrow hips had been raised on the south side of Chicago by a single mom. She'd grown up in the projects and somehow beaten the odds and escaped. Her long black hair, dark eyes, and caramel skin made her both mysterious and exotic, but it was her wit, intelligence, and drive that gave her a triple dose of charisma. She had all the markings of the next major media star, and he figured in the very near future she'd be working at one of the news networks.

"Did the mailman goof again?" Hardin asked.

"No, this one looks as if it were hand delivered. There's no stamp and no address. There's just your name. I guess they got the wrong desk." She smiled before asking, "Did you hear about the assassination attempt on the college professor?"

"You mean the woman at Washington-Lincoln College?"

"That's the one."

"Heard about it, but not interested. It doesn't smell like news to me, at least not the kind that rattles windows in New York and LA. Probably just some kind of weird domestic thing or a case of mistaken identity."

"So, not enough meat for you?" Chambers asked as she continued to wave the envelope.

"I like stories that have layers and are framed by people with strong personalities. How many history teachers do you know who'd make interesting copy? Most of them should be reading bedtime stories to insomniacs. They'd fall asleep in no time."

Hardin looked back at the screen. He'd been digging since six this morning and was getting nowhere. Perhaps, it was time for a break. Pushing away from his desk, he casually strolled to where Chambers sat still waving the white envelope between two of her perfectly manicured nails. Grabbing it out of the air, he tore off the end to find a single piece of paper.

"I can see it's handwritten," Chambers observed. "Invitations or showers are about the only things people hand write anymore and you don't seem like the wedding or baby type. Are you being invited to a party?"

As he glanced through the few hastily scribbled sentences, Hardin shrugged. This was either a threat or a not-so-veiled warning, but either way, it made no sense. After going over it twice, he glanced back at Chambers and asked, "What's an imprint?"

"Is this a trick question?"

"For all I know it might be," he admitted.

She shrugged. "The first thing that comes to my mind is something you heat up with an iron and press onto a shirt—like a logo or maybe a team name."

"That doesn't work. In this case, it seems like some kind of code." He then grinned. "Are you trying to prank me?"

"No," she protested with a wave. "I've been known to prank people, but I had nothing to do with this. Besides, I only prank my friends, and you ..."

"Then listen and try to make sense of it." He cut her off before she could toss out an insult. Looking back at the white letter-sized paper, he read, "Hardin, this is the biggest scoop of your life. An MVI imprint is slated to die. A scribe might be the only hope in preventing the death. The same enemies that want me dead are hunting for the imprint. If you join this chase, they'll be after you too. So, you'll have to save her to save yourself. Time to get out of class and do what you were called to do." He glanced over at his associate before adding, "It's signed with the letter U. You're the one who went to the second-best journalism school in the country. What do you make of this?"

"The best journalism school."

Hardin studied the woman still sitting at her precisely organized desk. While she seemed to be chewing on what she'd heard, it was evident she wasn't ready to spit out any of her thoughts. "Well," he impatiently probed.

Chambers frowned before exposing a glaring fact. "It'd take me all morning to list the people who want you dead. You've stepped on enough toes to keep a quartet of podiatrists in business. So, the fact someone lusts after your blood is not news. You've fully earned the title SOB. And that's about the nicest thing most folks call you."

"Yeah, at times I can be a SOB … and I get threats every week, but they aren't worded like this. They're direct, blunt, and usually filled with profanity. Besides, history proves those who actually kill reporters don't send an advance notice. This is different, it doesn't have the feel of a crackpot."

Chambers pushed her chair back, stood, and suggested, "Let's go to the break room where it's quieter and we have some privacy."

"No," he quickly countered, "let's go to the morgue. There we'll have a better chance of being alone, and you can talk freely. Besides, if we go to the break room I'll eat another donut, and I've already had three."

"Three?"

"Don't judge me."

Chambers led the way to the stairs. Three flights up and a turn to the right was the newspaper's library lit by a bank of unforgivingly harsh fluorescent lights. The entry was propped open, and the room was lined with file cabinets containing stories dating back more than a century. This twenty-by-forty-foot lair was once hallowed ground and constantly used by reporters digging for background on everything from sports to politics to fashion to obituaries, but that was in the past. Now, in the information age, where almost everything was a Google search away, this morgue was largely a museum—a relic from another era.

Once the door was closed, and the pair eased into two of the library table's ancient salon chairs, Chambers opened the conversation. "Let me see it." As Hardin watched, she took the note and studied what to him seemed to be an invitation to danger.

"Give me your read," he demanded. "Do you think I should be concerned or is someone trying to send me on a wild goose chase?"

She placed the paper on the table and shrugged. "I don't know if you're being pranked, but if it's real, I can give you a few observations."

"I'm waiting."

"The writer is likely over seventy, or if he's younger, he has some kind of disability that affects his fine motor skills. While the cursive style is carefully followed right down to the loops in the 'L's', the writing's not fluid."

"So, which is it … old or disabled?"

"I feel like you're playing me. I've been your student and your project since the day I arrived. You're always finding ways to test me. So, am I the one who's really being pranked? Did you set this up to make me look stupid?"

"No, you're not being pranked. My pranks are much cleverer, like the time I convinced you a bull got loose at the stock exchange. Watching you make those calls was priceless."

"I'll get you back," she swore. "Just waiting for the right time."

"Well until then, tell me is the writer a senior or a person with a disability?"

"The flow is there, but shaky, so I vote for a senior citizen. Probably a male."

"Why a man?"

"The size of the letters and the language is more like a man would use. I think a woman would be wordier and far more delicate. This note is straight 'who, what, where, when stuff' and exhibits no compassion or empathy. It reads like neither a warning nor a threat, but an order. In other words, while your mom might say, 'Honey, do you have time to mow the grass', your dad would bark, 'Get your lazy butt out there and mow the yard now!'"

He nodded. "I think you and I are on the same page, but I wanted to make sure and not cloud your observations by sharing mine first. Here's something you missed. I believe the man who wrote this once worked in our profession."

"What makes you so sure?"

"The word *scoop* is a term that hasn't been used much in the last two generations but was common in print media's golden era. The writer is, therefore, tempting me to get involved in a case by employing language that fits another age and time. So, I'll bet the guy has ink in his blood. I'd lay odds he spent most of his life nosing out stories."

"And our generation doesn't use cursive writing," she added. "So, the penmanship means he's not a young guy pretending to be old."

"What I need from you now is an idea of what imprint means. The writer is using it like a noun not a verb."

"And he also calls the imprint a she," Chambers added. "So, the imprint has a sex. That makes it alive."

"Is the female imprint an animal or human?"

"How about a teacher—they imprint knowledge on students."

"I don't see how that works in this case. Can you think of anything else?"

The morgue grew quiet as a tomb as both its occupants considered a new way to view a familiar word. Hardin was still coming up with nothing, but a sudden smile indicated Chambers had made a mental breakthrough.

"It could be cloning. A project cloning humans would be a huge scoop. The moral implications boggle the mind. It'd be the story of the century in political, medical, scientific, philosophical, and religious circles."

"But why would that put my life in danger? The note's writer says very clearly that if I get involved, the imprint's enemies are also my enemies."

"A living human clone would be a target for a host of different religious groups. They'd see that person as not being created by God and, therefore, having no soul."

"Would they have a soul?" Hardin asked.

She raised her eyebrow. "We could discuss that all day and get nowhere. For the moment, let's put that topic on the back burner and focus on the here and now. I can see how human cloning could fit into what the writer is hinting at. I think it's the most logical thing we've come up with."

"You came up with—I'm still shooting blanks."

She smiled. "If it's cloning, could this be an invitation to investigate a person involved in funding or maybe research? If you were to head down that road, then someone might want to kill you before you found out what was really going on."

"Marsha, there's more logic in your idea than anything I'm coming up with but think about what you just said. Both the cloners and those against cloning would be out to get me. I'd be caught in a crossfire."

Chambers shook her head in excitement. "And consider this, if you found this cloned woman, your life would be saved because you'd have the living proof to go with your story. So, you have to get there before the cloners and anti-cloning forces find you."

What she was saying made sense. It was like she'd read between the lines and picked up on the obvious message he'd missed. But who did he know or whom was he currently investigating who could be secretly studying or funding a program like this?

"You look like you're still drawing the wrong cards," she noted.

"For the moment I'm not coming up with any names. As we are at a dead end, let's look at something we haven't talked about. What do you think the MVI means?"

"It could be for some kind of institute or business. Does that match anything you're investigating?"

"No."

"MV could be Missouri or Mississippi Valley."

"Maybe, but that's still not connecting any dots for me." He drummed his fingers on the table with his left hand and rubbed his chin with his right. Then, like a bolt out of the blue, something from the long-forgotten past hit him. He remembered in his college days studying a course in the history of reporting. The instructor had pointed out that in days before press conferences were recorded digitally or with tape recorders, journalists had their own version of shorthand. Most often all caps coupled to single letters were only used for people or places. FDR was Franklin Delano Roosevelt, JFK was John Fitzgerald Kennedy, and during that same time WDC was the nation's capital, CI was Chicago, Illinois, and LAC was Los Angeles, California. Hardin reached across the table and grabbed the note. As he eagerly looked at the words, he suddenly recognized the writer's unique signature. How had he been so blind?

"You got something?" Chambers asked.

"Yeah, I'm pretty sure the MVI is a person or a city and a state. If it's the latter it has to be in Idaho, Iowa, Illinois, or Indiana. So that narrows it down a lot. And, on top of that, I know who wrote this note."

"Who?"

"Ulysses Goldsmith."

"The old syndicated columnist? But he died a few weeks ago."

"Yeah, he taught one semester when I was in college. The course was on the history of reporting. Each of us had to decipher notes he'd penned. In mine, he always wrote the letter 'U' in a very different manner than he did on the others. He double looped the right side almost like a figure eight. When I asked him about that, he explained he wanted me to think about 'the you' and to focus on what I could accomplish if I truly put my full abilities to use. He told me over and over again, 'Just think about what *you* can do.'" Hardin scratched his head and grinned, "Goldsmith was the first to believe I had that kind of potential. There's no doubt his prodding drove my passion for uncovering the stories others missed. When I won my Pulitzer, he sent me a handwritten note and the last raised part of the 'U' was written with the double loop. I should've realized it was him when I first read this note. And remember, this man covered most of the greatest stories of the last sixty years, so if he's giving me this scoop, it has to be big!"

"But how does a dead man deliver a note? He died ten days ago, and the note didn't get here until today. Someone brought it in." She smiled before vocally jabbing, "Are you thinking he's a ghost that's now haunting you and giving you assignments?"

"I don't believe in ghosts, but I believe in Goldsmith. Let me see, last I heard he lived downstate somewhere."

"The obituary said he died in Mt. Vernon."

"Yeah, that's it. And that might be the MVI in the note."

"And," Chambers noted, "Mount Vernon is where the college professor ... Maxine Factor ... was almost killed. Perhaps the case that you didn't think was big enough to cover is tied to Goldsmith."

Hardin drummed his fingers on the table as he voiced the beginning of a plan. "I'll have to start by finding someone who cared for him or handled his estate. Maybe they can provide some answers about when the note was written and who might have delivered it."

Wagging his index finger, he all but shouted at Chambers, "You want to go on a road trip?"

"You're leaving now?"

"You have any deadlines?"

"Not until I hear from a source, and that might take days or weeks. Besides, I'd like to explore the case of the hit on the professor."

"Good, then let's get moving. I'll grab my laptop and meet you at my car."

It took ten minutes for Hardin to shut down his desktop, grab his briefcase, tell Editor in Chief Barry Watson that he and Chambers were on a hot lead, and make it to his car. Chambers was already waiting beside the apple-red 1965 Corvette convertible. After he unlocked the passenger door the old-fashioned way with the key, she slid into the vehicle's cramped cockpit. A few seconds later, he joined her, put the key in the ignition and turned the switch. The engine cranked but didn't start. After pumping the accelerator a few times, he tried again. Nothing! Six more attempts led to the same results. He was thinking a myriad of words, most containing four letters, but used none of them.

"We can take mine," Chambers suggested. "It's newer and has satellite radio."

Hardin frowned. "It was running like a champ when I drove it this morning. I can fix this. I've rebuilt this engine four times. Just give me a second to look at the engine."

Hardin released the latch and got out. A seemingly bored Chambers exited as well. When he raised the hood, what they viewed was numbing. Four sticks of TNT had been lashed together and tied to the powerful V-8.

"That's a bomb," she whispered. "Why didn't it go off?"

"It appears to have been wired into the electrical system," Hardin apprehensively explained as he nervously looked around the parking garage. His heart rate plunged when he realized that except for a few hundred cars, they were seemingly alone.

"Mason, you didn't answer my question. Why didn't it go off?"

Hardin turned his focus back to the homemade explosive. "Either this guy was careless, or someone scared him off before he could fully check his work. Take a look. The lead to the coil isn't making contact.

He may have accidently pulled it away when he was strapping the dynamite down. Whatever the reason, we were just a spark away from being blown apart. We better call the cops and let the bomb squad remove this thing. I think this is out of our range of expertise." He spat and growled, "Who'd be so callus as to destroy a classic car?"

"Really? That's what's bothering you?"

"Well, that and a couple of other things."

"Do you think this has anything to do with the note?"

He shrugged. "There're a handful of people who'd love to see me playing a harp or roasting over an open flame."

"I'm betting on the latter."

Ignoring the verbal jab, Hardin leaned closer to study the bomb. While he told Chambers the truth—he did have his share of enemies—he'd fudged on one thing. None of them would likely go this far to get him out of the way. They'd be much more interested in coming up with a way to ruin his credibility. So, he was banking on this being the work of those who wanted to keep the reporter from knowing what an imprint was. Rather than pour water on his quest, they'd lit a fire.

He looked from the car to Chambers. "What if old age wasn't the cause of Goldsmith's death? Even if he was in his nineties, as I recall from his obit, his passing wasn't expected. What if the same people who did this moved the veteran reporter's expiration date up a bit?"

"That's intriguing, but only a theory right now."

"How much do you want to be a top reporter?" he asked. "How much passion do you have to expose the truth?"

"Is this a test?"

"Not one I created, but one that's nevertheless aimed at both you and me. Is your motivation strong enough that the story means more than your life?"

"I'll get my car."

As the woman purposely marched across the garage, Hardin pulled out his cell. After the bomb was diffused, it'd be time to dig into a grave for information that might prove unnerving. Proving himself to be the off-the-wall adrenalin junkie others had long ago labeled him, he beamed. There was something exhilarating about working on a story that might lead straight to a brush with death.

Chapter 5

3:30 p.m.
Thursday, September 15
County Courthouse, Mount Vernon, Illinois

Learning the name of the person paid to kill you almost always brings more questions than answers. And without the answers, what's behind you might be just as deadly as what's ahead.

———————◆———————

At precisely one-thirty, a handsome, young, administrative assistant ushered Maxine Factor through a ten-foot-tall door and into the office of the District Attorney. Rather than exit, the employee took a seat on the far side of the room. As he did, short, muscular, redheaded Ramsey Lewis, sporting a gray suit and wire-rimmed glasses, looked up from his desk, smiled, then stood and extended his hand.

"Dr. Factor, sorry to have to call you on such short notice."

She noted her host's firm grip. "If it has anything do with why someone would be trying to shoot me, I don't mind at all."

"Take a chair," Lewis suggested. After both were seated, the district attorney focused his pale green eyes on a note pad. "What can you tell me about Assad Kattan?"

Factor shook her head. "I can't tell you a thing. I've never known anyone with either of those names. Is that the man I …?"

As he ran the fingers of his right hand through his wavy hair, the obviously disappointed DA explained, "That's the man who tried to kill you."

Factor leaned forward in her chair. "What else do you know? Where did he come from? What kind of person was he?"

"Kattan was born in Syria, came to America with his family when he was six, was raised in New York City and, based on records at a local motel, showed up here about four days ago." Lewis loosened his striped tie and glanced back at his note pad. "He was in the import business, mostly antiques from Europe, and had no criminal record. He served a hitch in the Army during the Iraq War and was a decorated and model soldier. He wasn't married, had no kids, and according to those who worked with him, wasn't any type of fanatic."

"Once again," Factor explained, "I have no connection with the man, at least none that I know of. Except for a few years spent getting graduate degrees, I've lived in Southern Illinois all my life. While I've visited New York a dozen times, I never lived there and, to my knowledge, never met this man. And if you'd been to my house you'd know that I'm not into antiques. So, nothing lines up."

Lewis returned his gaze to the file.

Waiting for what she was sure would be another round of questions, Factor glanced around the room. The office was large, and with its eighteen-foot ceiling and tall windows, had an open, airy feeling. With the exception of the computers, the furnishings appeared to be about the same age as the courthouse, and according to its cornerstone, the building had been constructed in 1914. It could've been the twin of a courthouse in Friar County, Ohio, except for the curved front staircase and the lack of a central bell tower.

"I'd guess that as a student of the past," Lewis cut in, "this building's history and craftsmanship probably fuel your fertile imagination."

Factor nodded. "Reminds me a lot of a courthouse in Ohio."

"So, you've seen the one in Friarstown?"

"No," Factor admitted, "I've never been there."

"Well, you must've seen a picture of it then."

"In truth, I don't think so, but nevertheless, I can tell you the differences in the two."

"How?"

"A century ago, my great-great-grandfather on my mother's side was the country clerk in Friarstown. For more than a decade, he all but lived in this building's twin." Factor pointed to the far corner. "On June 13, 1922, he was looking out the window studying the city, thinking about the congestion created by automobiles, a mode of transportation he never fully accepted. He never even learned how to drive. At that exact moment, even though he was barely out of his twenties, he had a heart attack and fell to the floor. He lived another decade but never fully recovered. My great-grandmother was born about a year later. According to family stories, my great-great-grandfather actually returned to this office's twin to visit the DA in 1933, and after looking out that same window, he died."

"Interesting." Lewis drummed his fingers on the desk for a few seconds and glanced back at his notes. "My relatives have never been into details like yours must have been. What a rich and dynamic story your great-grandmother passed down."

Factor now wondered if spilling out that much information might've been a mistake. To move the conversation in a new direction, she made a troubling observation, "It's unsettling—that I'm responsible for that man's death. It doesn't matter that he was trying to kill me. Taking a life is never easy or clean."

"You sound as if you speak from experience."

In a bizarre way, Factor was speaking from experience. There were many bodies buried in the deep recesses of her mind or, maybe, her DNA. Either way, she knew what it was like to witness a final breath or view eyes that were open but unseeing. As there was no way to explain those experiences, it was best just to invent a cover story.

"I've read so much about murder, war, and tragedy," Factor explained, "that I feel as if I've seen it a thousand times. Because of that, I can fully relate to that old spiritual, 'Were You There'."

"The dead can haunt you," Lewis suggested.

"You have no idea."

He glanced back at his notes. "Do you have any connections to the Middle East?"

"No, I've never been there. My history courses are confined to the study of the Americas, so I've not really taught or lectured about that area either. To my knowledge, I don't even have any friends in that region of the world."

"What about your family—do any of them have any ties that might upset someone with a terrorist mentality?"

Factor eased back, closed her eyes, allowing her mind to drift though a myriad of memories, some her own, and others belonging to several generations of ancestors, before ultimately centering her thoughts on a great-grandfather who had worked for Shell Oil in the 1920s. As she immersed herself in another time and place, the memories drew into sharp focus.

Clyde Evans had been in Saudi Arabia for almost two years. Most of the man's time in the region was mundane, but two unique experiences jumped out. One was a dispute with two locals after a shady poker game, and the other, a visit to a very wealthy man's harem. But neither of those events created any lasting ill will. So, almost a century later, why would they matter? On top of that, her great-grandfather had not known anyone named Kattan. At least none that made any impression.

"Dr. Factor, did you come up with something?

She shook her head. "I can't think of any family connections with the Middle East. My brother, Rhett, is my only living relative, and he's never been there. He's married, has two kids, and sells insurance in Eastern Indiana. His wife is a third-grade teacher. They barely travel out of the state much less have international connections."

"Weren't you married once?" a hopeful Lewis inquired.

"Ah, Eli—not one of my better decisions. It was a five-year circus, and neither one of us wants to buy another ticket to that show."

"Where is he now?"

"Los Angeles, remarried, and works in advertising, and I haven't heard from him since he unfriended me on Facebook four years ago. Let's add that I'm not on his Christmas card list either."

The DA leaned forward and placed his elbows on his desk. "Does he hate you enough to want to see you dead?"

Factor chuckled. "Now you're grasping at straws. Eli wouldn't mourn much at my funeral, but he'd rather just avoid me than do anything to me. When we split, he didn't as much despise me, as he'd become bored. He told his friends I was as dusty and stale as the old books I studied. That's not something a woman wants to hear."

Lewis frowned, tugged at the collar of his starched white shirt and grumbled, "There was a reason Kattan targeted you. Until we figure that out, I have no idea if you're safe. Maybe he was hired for the job and now that he has failed, someone else will step up to fill his shoes."

"Or maybe," Factor suggested, "he just didn't like the article I wrote on the Civil War for *The Smithsonian Magazine*. Do you have any other questions?"

"No, but if you think of a connection, please let me know. I'm not going to get much sleep until I find out why you were a target."

"Neither will I," Factor assured him.

Rising from her chair, the professor walked out of the office and down the stairs. After exiting the old courthouse's main doors, she stepped into the sunshine and took a deep breath. For a moment, she was reminded of a day in Paris. The air had been crisp, and there was a smell of pastries coming from a nearby bakery. As she'd considered going into the corner shop, a handsome man dressed completely in black had approached and asked if she knew the way to the Caron de Beaumarchais Hotel. She pointed to her left and, in broken French, explained it was about five blocks. Her eyes followed as he happily sauntered down the sidewalk. Only after he'd passed a horse-drawn taxi and become lost in the afternoon crowd of pedestrians had she noted the partially built Eiffel Tower in the background. Soon a world's fair would be coming to the City of Light but unfortunately, she'd be back in the States before it opened.

Stepping off the curb and shaking a memory that wasn't actually hers from her mind, she crossed a parking lot to her 2015 Mustang GT convertible. As she did, she attempted to make sense of a mind that now shuffling lives like innumerable individual cards in a bridge game.

When this ability first appeared, it had been fun, and the images of past moments had come in slow, steady waves, but now the memories were coming so fast and were so vivid she was having problems determining which were hers and which belonged to another time and another person. And which of those times and which of those ancestors, if any, held the key to discovering why someone was gunning for her? Or were those jumbled memories keeping her from remembering something in her own past that might save her life now?

Chapter 6

10:15 a.m.
Friday, September 16
Wallace Hall Room 315, Washington-Lincoln College,
Mt. Vernon, Illinois

There is an old proverb that says what has been done in the dark will be brought to the light. That concept of lies and deeds never staying hidden had long been used in songs, sermons, books, and motion pictures. As a plot device, it serves as a way of creating suspense before presenting the consequences of one's immoral or illegal actions. Yet the wrongs of the past are not always exposed or righted. Lost in memories, buried by corruption, the guilty often aren't prosecuted and thus never have to pay for their wrongdoings. In more cases than not, the past and present never collide, the rain of destruction never happens, and what was done in the dark remains forever hidden.

———◆———

Leaning back in her chair, a stoic Factor turned her head upward to study the slowly moving fan. That's all it took to put her in another place and time. As the clicking of typewriters and the smell of cigarettes filled her senses, the wall calendar said 1881. Telegrams were spread all over a man's desk, the very man whose eyes she was seeing through, and voices were discussing the news of a president being shot.

"No!" Factor whispered. "I'm not going there."

Willing herself back to the present, she closed all the mental file drawers to the past and left open only the one reserved for her own experiences. To maintain her focus and fight off formerly lived lives frenetically demanding her attention, Factor retrieved a legal pad and began to outline the story of her time on earth. For three hours, she reviewed everything from birth to grade school to high school to college to marriage and her divorce, and then to her work at the university. Nothing stood out. Sure, she'd upset a few people along that journey, but no one had been hurt badly enough to seek revenge, not even Eli.

Looking at her notes, she added a series of trivial experiences to them ... her first kiss, a vacation to Colorado, hitting a winning shot in a basketball game, a crazy night in Vegas, and her parent's funerals. Nothing popped up. For the next half hour, she dug deeper into more mundane elements of her past, trying to uncover a thread that might unlock something she'd seen she wasn't supposed to have seen. But each of those treks just led to another blind alley. She hadn't been at the scene of a crime or observed a drug deal going down. She'd never witnessed a bribe or gotten facts about an election being stolen. In fact, her computer had never even been hacked. She'd never even had a credit card compromised. Her life was nothing if not boring. That fact led to a comforting thought—maybe Kattan had mistaken her for someone else. Yeah, that was it. That rush of security lasted only as long as it took to take a sip of sweet tea. That made sense for the first attempt on her life. Maybe he'd gotten the wrong car to tamper with, but it didn't ring true for the next two. The house with the spewing gas had been hers, and the gunfire was also aimed in her direction. She had to face it—the hard facts proved the stranger had come from New York just to kill her. But why?

Sitting up, Factor rubbed her brow and summoned logic. Who benefited from her death? Eli didn't—he'd been cut out of her will when they divorced. In the event of her passing, her modest estate that wouldn't be enough for even one additional scholarship went to the university's history department. Besides, as she was a much honored and often published historian, she meant far more to the school alive than dead.

The ringing of the desk phone offered a welcome escape from a mystery that seemingly had no answer. Talking to someone—anyone—would beat continuing a hopeless conversation with herself and those residing in her brain.

"This is Dr. Factor."

"It's Ramsey Lewis."

"Have you found anything?"

"Yes and no. After talking to NYPD, I'm sure that Kattan was not connected to you in anyway."

Factor frowned and leaned back in her chair. "Well, that makes no sense."

"On the surface, no," Lewis admitted, "but Justin Weiss, who's assigned to New York City's organized crime division, told me that Kattan was a suspect in a couple of murders. While not good enough to work for the mob, it seemed he might've occasionally been a gun for hire for other groups. When Weiss heard how this thing went down, he seemed pretty sure that Kattan must've been hired to rub you out."

"But there's no reason," Factor argued. "It'd be like taking a hit out on Mr. Rogers."

"Now that would really be a waste of good money," Lewis teased. "You do realize that Mr. Rogers is dead?"

"I was speaking metaphorically."

"Whatever. At least what happened to you does give Weiss a reason to ask for a search warrant. Perhaps he'll find some financial records that'll lead us to the person who ordered the hit."

"I can't imagine who that would be," Factor lamented, her tone revealing the frustration she was now feeling. "I've spent hours looking over every facet of my life and have come up with nothing that'd be worth a cheap lawsuit much less murder."

"Maybe, thanks to something they find out in New York, we'll be able to discover what you don't know. In the meantime, if I were you, I'd maintain a low profile. Be sure and lock all your doors and keep your eyes open. Weiss told me that hiring Kattan and having him travel likely cost in the low five figures, so there's a good chance the person who wants you dead is negotiating with another hired gun even as we speak. Maybe the next one won't be as sloppy as this guy."

"That's hardly comforting," Factor cracked.

"I hope I'm wrong," Lewis assured her. "You're scheduled to speak at my Rotary Club in a month, and I booked you. I need you alive for at least another thirty days."

"So that's the real reason you're working this case so hard."

"Seriously, watch out for yourself."

"I will."

After setting the phone back on her desk, the professor was again flooded with a dozen different memories. As she tried to sift through the mental messages from different people, times, and places, one pushed its way to the front as if demanding to be heard.

It was the evening of March 5, 1836, and all around her were ragged, exhausted men. Some were drinking coffee, others staring at the stars, and a few seemed lost in prayer, but the one thing each had in common was the hopeless look etched deeply onto their faces. The eyes viewing this scene were those of a young woman silently begging God to show her a reason these men were about to give their lives at the Alamo.

Factor, now completely consumed by the almost two-century-old memory, was only shaken from the haunting scene by the phone. With the smells of coffee cooking over a campfire still lingering in her nostrils, she picked up the receiver.

"Dr. Factor."

"It's not over," a voice whispered. "You won't live to share the truth. They won't let you."

"What are you talking about?" Her heart was racing, blood pressure rising, and she felt a sudden chill on her neck. After taking a deep breath to control her emotions, she whispered, "I know nothing."

"You might find out everything," the voice assured her, "and if and when you do, you'll be able to uproot the foundations of our civilization. They know that, and they won't let you live."

"Who are you, and why do you want to kill me?"

"I don't, but many do. Six others have been given the gift, and all six are dead."

The call abruptly ended. Hitting the phone's caller ID button proved a futile act. Someone obviously knew how to bypass technology. The screen showed there had been no calls since Ramsey Lewis. But even if she didn't have a number, at least she knew more than she had before the call. Her life was hanging in the balance, not because of anything she had done, but due to her ability to see the past through the eyes of those ancestors who'd lived it. But what was lost in history that could create the disruption the caller had spoken of? After all, the past was the past, and it couldn't be changed. A modern world was built on that principle. She taught that in her classes. Yet obviously, someone believed something buried in history must stay lost or things would be dramatically altered. Factor's future, and perhaps the past she saw in the experiences of others, now seemed to hinge on uncovering that lost truth. And she had to accomplish that search before someone made her life nothing more than a memory.

Chapter 7

The way, the truth, and the light are often obscured by those who are supposed to lead the lost. When the way becomes twisted, a lie replaces the truth and the darkness blots out the light, the found can become just as conflicted as those whom the world sees as lost.

———————♦———————

Rev. Dallas Arnold's private office was huge, at least forty by fifty, filled with leather couches and walnut tables. On the walls hung ten original oil paintings focusing on biblical history and one hundred and six framed photos of Arnold with various celebrities. Yet, it was the eight-foot-tall portrait of a benevolent, smiling Arnold, on a wall behind the man's massive cherry-wood desk, that caught the visitor's eye. There could be little doubt the artist had been instructed to make Arnold the focus. The mega-church pastor was wearing a white suit, white shirt, and gold tie. In his hand, he held a Bible that was at least two feet wide, and in the background, standing on a hilltop, was a very white, blue-eyed Jesus, painted as if he were looking down on a favorite son.

Being alone with the portrait gave the visitor a chance to really size up the person behind the religious empire. The look on the painted face, along with the way the sunbeams spotlighted the pastor's head, almost as if they were a halo, captured Arnold's view of himself. He was the focal point of his work. It was all about him. Jesus may have been the product the preacher used, but it was the endorser of that product—Dallas Arnold—who was the most important part of the equation.

As the visitor turned his gaze to the image of Jesus standing well behind the preacher, a large door located on the back wall opened, and Arnold, dressed in a blue suit, white shirt, and red tie, walked into the room. He looked to be a man expecting applause. When none came, he moved forward and shook his guest's hand.

"I've heard a great deal about you," Arnold announced as he pointed to two chairs positioned by a window overlooking the church's golf course. "By the way, you're anything but easy to find."

"Those who know me have no problem."

Arnold smiled. "Maybe this'll be the beginning of a friendship that'll put me in a place to use your services on a regular basis."

The guest, his dark eyes almost lifeless, his face void of emotion, eased down into the leather, high-backed chair, and after unbuttoning his gray suit coat, crossed his legs. A smiling Arnold dropped into the other seat and immediately took control of the conversation.

"I'm sure you know I'm one of the most powerful men in this nation. Most of the top politicians and business leaders have my number at the top of their directories. They call me before making a move. They realize, that far more than anyone else, I can deliver money, votes, and consumers who'll remain loyal through thick and thin."

The guest, his eyes firmly locked on his host, said nothing. After a long, uncomfortable silence, when Arnold shifted his gaze from the visitor to the view of the eighteenth green, the preacher continued. It was hardly surprising his focus remained on the thing he loved the most.

"It was anything but an easy road to get to this point. I started preaching when I was a teen, did a lot of tent revivals, took a break to go to college, where I made top grades in everything from economics to literature, then landed on television, and now have a ministry that brings in tens of millions of dollars annually. Did you know the last president all but bowed down to me?"

"I've read your bio," the guest finally chimed in, "and, because of some digging, I also know the real story of your life. Let me cut to the chase. Your father was a wealthy oilman, you were such a party animal only your family's money kept you enrolled in school. Your grades were so bad that you still pay the college you attended to keep your transcript secret. You do actually bring in tens of millions annually, that's the truth, though only about a tenth of that is funneled into your church work. The bottom line is what you run is not a ministry—it's a business operation that serves you and you alone."

Arnold, his face twisted like a prune, stomped his foot and barked, "I beg your pardon."

"I'm not judging you," the guest continued, "I'm just trying to cut through the bull and let you know I've done my research. Now, would you like me to list what else I know about the real Dallas Arnold? Would you like me to explain why I believe that in that portrait …" He pointed toward the wall. "… the image of Christ should be replaced with a man from a much warmer environment? Before you answer, I want you to chew on this. You have your flock fooled, and while a former president and a parade of businessmen might bow to your ability to deliver the votes or sales they need, you don't intimidate me. You see, I know who you really serve. Everything you do, in the pulpit or behind the scenes, is not for God or country, it's for Dallas Arnold. Now, do I get up and leave, or do you tell me why you put the word out on the dark web that you wanted me to do a job for you?"

After more than a minute of silence, Arnold stopped feigning disgust and smiled. "You seem pretty sure of yourself."

"I'm seventy-two years old, I've been a lot of places and done a lot of things. I'm still in excellent physical condition, my mind's sharp, and my vision remains 20-20. I work because I enjoy the challenge, not because I need the money, though I charge more now than I did when I first broke off on my own. I like Cuban cigars, tailored suits, remote and exclusive resorts, rare art, and even rarer wine. But there's one thing I don't like, and that's wasting time. Now, skip the trash about your fictional life story and tell me why I'm here."

"For starters, I sent you a hundred thousand as a good faith gesture."

"And it only buys my attendance, nothing more." The guest paused and licked his lips. "Do you know what I do?"

"Yes."

"What is it?"

Arnold took a deep breath and crossed his arms. He studied the visitor as if reconsidering his plans before finally nodding. "I have a job that's worth two million."

"You didn't answer my question."

An uncomfortable Arnold shrugged. "I know what you do."

"Then say it."

"You take care of problems."

The guest laughed. "No, the folks who work at prisons take care of problems. If that's what you're looking for, go find a retired warden."

"Okay, I know what you really do."

"Then say it, or maybe you aren't saying it because you're trying to fool yourself into believing that stopping a heart from beating is nothing more than dealing with a problem." The man stood, buttoned his suit coat, and in a calm tone continued, "This isn't like unplugging a drain or tuning up a car. This isn't grounding your child because he broke curfew. Those are problems. This is not. You brought me here to talk about something much larger than a problem."

"You know I know what you do," Arnold argued, once again refusing to really explain what he wanted. "That's why I wired you the advance. That's why you're here."

The guest was now out of patience—his hot glare could have melted ice. When he finally spoke, his voice was firm, his manner direct, and his message clear. "You're in the business of exposing sin. You stand up each Sunday morning and demand people confess what they've done wrong. Another thing, you constantly talk about folks rationalizing their way to hell. By not admitting why you had me come here today, you're trying to avoid the fact you're asking me to commit the biggest sin of all. The person who's really committing the sin of taking a life will be you. You'll order it, you'll pay for it, and you'll benefit from it."

"Let me explain," Arnold cut in, "you really need to understand my position."

"I know your position. You're the judge who's delivering the sentence. At least Pilate tried to find a way out of putting Jesus on a cross, but you're offering two million for me to drive in the nails and pierce the side."

Arnold rose, pointed his finger in the other man's face, and declared, "What I'm doing is protecting Jesus."

The visitor's answer was calm, his expression stoic, "I don't think he needs protecting. I'm out of here."

The guest had taken three steps before Arnold yelled, "What do you want?"

The visitor spun on his heels and snapped, "The truth. Your money, fame, and power don't mean a thing to me. I don't care who you are or what you can do. But I do care about working with people who'll at least admit why they want me to pull a trigger and take a life. Without hearing that, I don't work."

"Okay," Arnold resolutely shook his head, "I'll level with you, but could we at least sit down again." After both men were back in their chairs, Arnold looked out the window. "There's a woman who has the ability to see everything her ancestors saw. It's like she was there. And, as a man of God who serves the church, I'm afraid she'll remember back to the time of Christ. I'm scared that one of her relatives was there when they crucified Jesus. I'm frightened that she'll confirm my savior didn't rise from the dead. I don't want to find out I'm living a lie."

"You can't afford for others to believe that," the visitor cracked. "For you it's nothing but a product you're protecting."

"Whatever."

"By the way, the woman's an imprint."

"What?" Arnold asked.

"What you described is someone whose brain has the ability to see the memories of direct ancestors in great detail."

Arnold looked shocked. "You know about this?"

"I've been paid to knock off two imprints. Now, where did you get your information?"

"My first source was a pastor in DC. Then I called the Vatican, and my contact there confirmed it."

"That's surely the first thing you've said that has been completely honest."

"I beg your pardon."

"So, if you've talked to the Vatican, then you know imprints are capable of looking backwards in time, but surely your source told you no one has ever gone back further than five hundred years before they cracked up. You see, the mind has a limited capacity and can only handle so much information."

"This woman is stable and bright. Perhaps she's different."

The visitor shook his head. "It's doubtful, and I'm sure you realize that. Arnold, you always play the odds. You cozy up to politicians only after you know they can win. You only use businessmen who can serve your needs. And when you have affairs, and I know you've had many no matter what you've told others about being chaste, it has been with women who can't afford to ever speak out. You're a vampire who gets your blood, or actually your money and power, by paying to have people dig up dirt. So, let's be blunt, there're a lot of really good Christian people, and you aren't one of them. You're a grifter, a person who doesn't believe what he says, but you have the special ability to seem sincere. With that in mind, this has nothing to do with faith, You want this woman out of the way for another reason. And it's much more personal."

Arnold frowned and looked back toward the window. When he next spoke, he posed a question. "Do you know what it's like to build an empire?"

"No."

"It's not easy, and to know that everything is balanced on keeping an unfortunate episode of your life out of public view is numbing."

"What's done in the dark will be brought to the light. At least that's what my grandfather told me when I was a child. So, this isn't about saving the Christian church, this is all about you."

"Yes, I'm afraid it is."

"Then what is it the imprint might find out that could make all of this," the guest waved his hands to emphasize the grandeur of the room before adding, "come falling down?"

"What's your name?" Arnold demanded.

"What name did your source give you?"

"They didn't. They just told that me you'd killed scores of people."

"That's all you need to know."

"They also told me you have a perfect record. When you are …" Arnold paused as if searching for a word before continuing, "When you are employed, you always finish the job. No one has escaped you."

"You're almost right," the visitor admitted. "I found out early that everyone has a weakness, something that can distract them, something that can steal their focus, if only for a second. I found that out because there was one man who accidentally revealed mine. That caused me to make a rather unfortunate mistake."

"What happened to him, the man you missed?"

"I don't know. We found another way to ruin him, one like you often use. After that he dropped out of sight and has never been heard from again. And believe me, I've looked."

"So, you still want to kill him?"

"First, I want to thank him for teaching me a lesson. Since that day, I've never lost my focus. Then, once that was out of the way, maybe I'd finish the job."

Arnold nodded. "What did he discover that …"

"You'll never know. No one will."

The preacher's gaze caught Dixon's, and when it did, he once more demanded, "I want a name!"

"Some have called me Doctor Death—others the Grim Reaper. I'm not going to give you any more than that. Now you tell me what the imprint might remember."

Arnold spoke in tones so low the guest had to lean forward to catch his words. "When I was in college, I got a little carried away on a date."

"You raped someone."

"I don't like that word."

"I don't like rapists. Now continue."

"She never told anyone. I think she was afraid it would damage her more than it did me. But until she died a few years ago, I was always scared she'd come forward."

"Then the imprint must be her daughter."

He nodded.

"Are you the father?"

Arnold shook his head. "No, that was years before this woman was born."

"You don't have to kill her. Save your money and my time. Just deny it and say she's nothing more than a woman looking for publicity. I'll just keep the down payment and walk away."

Arnold sighed. "If only it were that simple."

"There's more? You said there was just one episode from the past. Have you been holding out on me?"

"What does the name Ezra Brittan mean to you?"

"He was a black teen accused of flirting with a white girl at a dance. If I remember correctly, it was the first dance that was fully integrated at the school."

Arnold, his face void of color nodded. "He didn't flirt with her, he danced with her. And ..."

"You were one of the men who, later than night found him, dragged him behind a car, and then lynched him."

"Yes, and no one anywhere knows who those four white men were. We were all in high school then, but now ..."

"You are the mega-star preacher," the visitor announced.

"And two of the other three are very well known. If she remembered that, we would pay dearly."

"But how could she if she's not related to you."

"That night, after I assaulted her mother, I was so full of myself and whiskey, I bragged about killing Ezra. I even shared the names of other boys. Now, do you understand why I can't afford for her to live?"

The visitor cocked an eyebrow and smiled. "In my research on you, I discovered one of your high school friends is currently a senator. As I remember, another is an odds-on favorite to be the next nominee to the Supreme Court."

"You see, it's more than me." Arnold looked back toward the golf course and sighed. The confidence he'd displayed when he'd entered the room was gone. "You said you have killed others like her. I think you called them imprints. Why?"

"Those hits involved maintaining the stability of governments not protecting the reputation of a murderer turned con artist. In those cases, the imprint might've remembered things that could have altered history."

"So much better reasons than mine," Arnold acknowledged.

The hired gun stood, shoved his hands into his pockets, and looked out the window. "Protecting the present from the past is something I've always found interesting. It opens up a myriad of topics for debate. Consider this, an imprint might actually be able to pinpoint when life began." He turned to face his host. "In other words, when a person actually becomes human. Think of what that would mean to how people view abortion. An imprint would know if life happened at conception, birth, or somewhere in-between. And, think about this, what if an imprint were privy to information that painted some of our founding fathers as being far less than who we believe them to be?"

The guest once more took a seat. "Let's say we do find a way to keep an imprint alive long enough to remember back two thousand years. The world was smaller back then, there were far fewer people, and the imprint might be connected to someone who met Jesus. That alone would prove that Christ really lived. A few minutes ago, you expressed concern about what would happen if one of those ancestors witnessed Jesus not rising from the dead. But let's turn that upside down and say the imprint actually saw—through the eyes of an ancestor—the resurrection. Consider what that would mean to all the other religions."

"It would change the dynamic of everything," Arnold agreed.

"Either way, it would alter the powerbase of not just nations, but of the whole planet. In other words, while knowing a few things, such as when the spark of life comes into a baby's being might make things clearer, there are far more powerful things that could blow this world apart."

"What are you saying?"

"I'll give you a bank account number. Send a million to that account today, and the other million will be due when I finish my job. Now who's the woman?"

"The file is on my desk. You can take it when you leave. She's a college professor in a small town in Illinois. Her name is Maxine Factor. Does that mean anything to you?"

"No." Doctor Death pushed out of the chair, crossed the room, and picked up the file. After studying it for a few minutes, he looked back at his host. "This shouldn't be a problem."

"How long will it take?"

"A week or two."

"That long?"

"I have to study her first. When I learn her movements and routine, then I'll plot my mission. When I do a job, the kill is neat, and I get away clean."

"You make it sound so cold."

"As I told you earlier, this is you killing this woman not me. I'm just the weapon, you're pulling the trigger. I'll leave much richer and my conscience will be clean, but you'll have to live with the fact you murdered someone to cover up your sins. That'll be your burden to carry not mine. I hope it's worth it."

It was a numb Dallas Arnold, a man who had been put in his place and forced to look into a mirror and see an image he didn't like, who now stared out a window seeing nothing but his own sins.

After placing the file under his arm, Doctor Death announced, "I'll start the job when I receive notification the first million is in my account." He then casually walked to the door and exited.

Chapter 8

4:15 p.m.
Friday, September 16
1301 Holly Avenue, Mt. Vernon, Illinois

Finding the truth is not a universal driving force. In fact, most would rather avoid it. But a journalist is almost rabid in the quest to uncover that truth. And that's why so many scribes die young.

———◆———

After their arrival in Mount Vernon, and once Mason Hardin had tracked down Ulysses Goldsmith's housekeeper, who'd finally agreed to meet with him, he found her waiting on the porch of Goldsmith's small, brick, one-story home. Outfitted in a pink dress and looking to be about sixty—with her cheerful greeting, she could've been the spokesperson for AARP.

As soon as Chambers switched off her 2017 Honda's engine, Hardin opened the passenger door and rushed toward the housekeeper as if the hounds of hell were on his tail. He bounded up the steps. "Miss Elliot?"

"It's actually Mrs. Are you Mr. Hardin?"

"Call me Mason. My partner is Marsha Chambers."

"You're from the Chicago paper?" Elliot asked.

"Yes," Hardin assured her, "*The Herald-Times*. And I was also one of Mr. Goldsmith's former students."

Elliot, her brown eyes shining, pushed her hand through her salt and pepper hair. "Oh yes, U said you were one of his best. He was very proud of all your accomplishments. He also was thankful you stayed in the ink … as he called it."

"I'm humbled and I can assure you my blood is ink."

Elliot nodded understandingly before posing a question. "You said you wanted to know more about how he died and perhaps what he was working on when he passed?"

"Yes, we do," Hardin assured his host. "He wrote to me hinting he was doing something big, and I was to finish the story if he couldn't. I'd have been here sooner, but his letter was delayed. My big problem is he wrote it in code, and I haven't been able to fully get a handle on what he meant."

"He often spoke in riddles," Elliot agreed, "when he spoke at all. Why don't you two step inside, and I'll give you a tour. As we walk through the rooms, I'll tell you what I know. Remember, I cooked a meal each day for him and cleaned his house a couple of times a week, but we didn't talk much. I have no clue what he was spending his time on when he died. But I can tell you this. It was consuming him. The last month or so, I don't think he slept much. Almost every time I was here, he was on his computer. When he wasn't writing, he was researching. It was like he was possessed."

Hardin smiled. "That was just like Goldsmith, once he got a lead he was like a dog with a bone."

"Just follow me," Elliot suggested as she opened the front door, "things haven't been touched since that morning …" It was as if she didn't want to finish her thoughts. Perhaps she'd been closer to Goldsmith than she admitted.

The living room was small, the furniture modest and worn, the tables stacked with books and magazines. A few framed photos, family members Hardin assumed, hung on the walls, and a half empty glass of water sat on a table next to a maroon recliner. As Elliot led them into the dining room, Hardin turned to face Chambers.

"The house reflects the man who taught me. It's simple and welcoming."

"Like an old shoe," Chambers suggested, "a well-worn old shoe."

"It was the house he was raised in," Elliot explained, "built by his grandfather in the early 1900s. U's mother and father moved in about 1924. He lived here until he graduated from high school in 1944. When Mildred, that was his mother's name, died in 1996, he began to use it as a summer place. About a decade ago, he moved back for good."

Hardin glanced from the small dining room into the kitchen. A few dishes were stacked in the sink, a newspaper was spread out on the table, and two cookies rested on a napkin. The ladderback chair he'd likely used on that last day was turned over and laying beside the table.

"There was a glass of milk there too," Elliot explained, "but I poured it down the sink. I wasn't going to let that milk sour and stink up the whole house."

"The chair was that way?" Hardin asked.

"Yes. It wasn't like him not to pick that up. In fact, it wasn't like him to not eat his cookies. He did that every night about nine. I should throw them away and straighten things up." She paused as the reporters walked over to the table.

"*The Post-Dispatch*," Chambers noted.

"And not a new one either," Hardin observed. He glanced through several stories before landing on one that might just be tied to this mess. While tapping on the feature, he looked back at Chambers and announced, "Well, the local professor you were intrigued with appears again."

"Story of a plane crash," Chambers said after she'd scanned the story, "and Dr. Factor was the only one injured. Maybe you and I are both curious about the same story after all."

"Perhaps."

"Would you like to see his office?" Elliot called out.

"Lead the way."

Elliot turned and walked down a short hall before opening a door and entering a room. She stepped aside. "This would've been his bedroom when he was a child. That he died here seems fitting."

The walls were lined with bookshelves. A library table served as a desk, and on it was a decade old iMac. By the room's only window, a Royal typewriter sat on a table. Hardin walked across the room to study the ancient "word processor."

"He told me he wrote his first story on that," Elliot declared. "Though it hasn't been used in decades, I knew he still loved it. From time to time, I'd see him pat it as if it were a pet cat."

"You say he died here?" Chambers asked.

"This is where I found him. He was sitting in that old wingback chair by the window. It was as if he were looking out into the backyard just thinking about life. The coroner figured it must have been a heart attack."

"They didn't do an autopsy?" Hardin cut in.

"He was ninety-five, and though he'd been in good health, his death didn't really surprise anyone."

Hardin walked over to a four-drawer, oak file cabinet and pulled out the top drawer. It was empty. He repeated the action on the other three, and the results were the same. Surprised, he turned back to Elliot. "What happened to the files?"

She shrugged. "I dusted that thing at least once a week. I know for a fact all the drawers were crammed full two weeks ago."

"Have any relatives been here?" Hardin asked.

"He didn't have any. He outlived his sister and he never married."

"Who gets the estate?"

"He left it to a local history professor, Dr. Maxine Factor. She had him speak to her classes each semester, and he grew to think of her as a daughter."

Chambers leaned close to Hardin and whispered, "She keeps coming up."

He nodded and looked back at Elliot. "Has Factor been here since his death?"

"No, she hasn't. She was at the funeral, but I doubt if she knows she's getting his stuff. The will hasn't been read yet. The lawyer's waiting to pay off the bills."

Hardin nodded, moved over to the computer, and hit the power button. As it was old, it took a while to boot up. Once the screen came to life, he sat down and began to go through files.

"Begin with the most recent," Chambers suggested.

"I am, and the most recent is from four years ago."

Elliot shook her head. "That can't be possible, he worked on that thing all the time." Her cell rang. She pulled it out of her dress pocket and looked at the number. "I need to take this. You all just do what you want to do. I'll move to the porch and talk to my sister."

When Elliot was out of earshot, Hardin made an observation. "Okay, all his operating programs are up to date, his browser was still being used on the day he died. He had a Microsoft Word update three weeks ago. He was using this Mac, so where are his files?"

"Look in the trash?" Chambers suggested.

Hardin clicked and opened up the garbage. There were some recent things. He dragged them to the desktop and began to open them. Nothing more than a man's personal musings.

"Okay," Hardin observed, "the note he sent hinted at something huge, and none of these things are it. I have to believe if they were on the computer, the person who stole the paper files would've taken everything and then wiped the drive."

"Are you sure?"

"Well, logic governs my thinking. Someone was here and took files out of the cabinet, so they would've fired up the Mac as well. If they grabbed the documents for the story he was working on from the computer, they could've put them on an external drive, yet, if that were the case, the originals would still be on the computer or in the trash. They aren't in either place. So, that leads me to believe that Goldsmith didn't save his important files on the Mac's hard drive."

"Then where are they?" Chambers asked.

"When I was taking his class, I quickly learned that he trusted no one. He always hid his notes and stories until he published them. In the age of typewriters, he even removed his ribbons each night and took them home."

"His paper files are gone," Chambers pointed out.

"That's a not a big deal."

"Why do you say that?"

"The file cabinet had no lock, which means whoever took them got nothing. What he was working on has to be on an external drive, and it has to be hidden in such a way that whoever grabbed the files in the cabinet wouldn't have found it."

"We would be looking for a hard drive or a thumb drive," Chambers suggested.

"Think like someone in his nineties," Hardin suggested.

"Okay, it's going to be hidden somewhere where I don't have to climb or stoop." She glanced around the room. "And I'm going to want to be able to get to it easily when I'm ready to work."

Hardin eyeballed the shelves. "We'll have to go over everything that would be in reach of a man who was five-foot eight. You take that wall, I'll take this one."

He moved to the shelves and began pulling back books to check if there was anything behind them.

"Mrs. Elliot's not a very good housekeeper," Chambers called out, "These shelves haven't been dusted in a month or more."

Hardin stepped back and studied the ones he had been searching. They were dusty as well. "Marsha, are there any places on your shelves were the dust is thinner than in other areas?"

"No."

"That means the books haven't been moved in a long time." With one hiding place eliminated, Hardin looked around the remainder of the study. He'd been visually scanning the study when he chuckled.

"You got something?"

He pointed to an artificial ivy plant sitting on an end table beside the chair where Goldsmith had taken his final breaths. Walking over, he pulled on the leaves inserted into a foam cushion. But under it was nothing. The wingback chair, a closet, and an end table also came up clean.

"We've looked everywhere," Chambers noted. "Perhaps he took it to bed with him every night, or maybe the people who grabbed his paper files found it as well."

"We'll check the bedroom in a second," Hardin agreed, "but I still think it's here and …"

Grinning, the reporter walked over to the antique typewriter and reached inside. Resting on the hammer arms was a thumb drive. He held it up. "What better place to hide your last story than in the machine you used to write your first one." He moved toward the Mac and was about to plug it in when he heard footsteps headed in their direction. He'd just dropped the drive into his pants pocket when Elliot reappeared.

"My sister is such a nut. She actually believes her dog can sing. I've spent the last ten minutes listening to a German Shepherd howl. And it was not "Old Man River" like Emma thinks." She glanced around the study before asking, "Do you want to see his bedroom?"

"Sure," Hardin replied. "Lead the way."

The bedroom was filled with awards but offered little else. Based on what was on the nightstand, it appeared Goldsmith had been reading a biography of Branch Rickey. Chambers shuffled through the pages and came up blank. Nothing else stood out. As they had the thumb drive, there was no reason to search the rest of the home. At least not right now.

When they'd made their way back to the living room, Chambers posed a question. "How long had Mr. Goldsmith been dead when you found him?"

"I'd brought him supper the day before around six. I came back in the next morning at nine. He was cold, so it had likely been a while. As he was dressed in the same clothes he'd been wearing the day before, I'm guessing he didn't even go to bed."

"Was there anything strange about the way his body looked?" Chambers asked.

Elliot paused and balled her hands. She suddenly appeared apprehensive. When she finally spoke, she sounded like a child who'd been caught with her hand in the cookie jaw.

"I know this sounds sick, and I shouldn't have done it, but I really enjoyed my years working with U so much. After I called the police ..." She toed the floor a bit with her right foot before finally whispering, "I took a picture of his body."

"Let me see it," Chambers demanded.

The housekeeper pulled a phone from her pocket, tapped in her code, pulled up the picture, and handed the phone to Chambers. The reporter carefully studied the image before giving it to Hardin.

It's been said a picture is worth a thousand words, and this one met that criteria. Though he was sitting in the chair, Goldsmith didn't look relaxed.

"You see that?" Chambers whispered with her back to Elliot.

"Yep, he was placed in that chair. If he'd been looking at the backyard, his legs would've been stretched out side by side, not with that strange bend." Hardin used his fingers to enlarge the image. "Mrs. Elliot, the blue shirt that Mr. Goldsmith is wearing looks fairly new."

"I bought that one and two others at the men's store about a week before he died. I think that was the first time he'd worn it."

"What happened to it?" Hardin asked.

"The clothes he died in were sacked up by the funeral home and returned to the house. They're in the closet."

"Could I see them?" Hardin asked.

As Elliot retrieved the clothing, Hardin airdropped the photo to his own phone. When the housekeeper returned, he gave her the cell and took the bag. After dumping the contents onto the couch, he went for the shirt. Two of the top three buttons were missing. There was also about a half inch tear on the left cuff.

"You see the stain?" Chambers asked as he turned the shirt inside out.

He nodded. There was a nickel-sized dark circle about a third of the way down on the left side. It was only visible from the back as the stain had not penetrated the pocket.

"Mrs. Elliot," Hardin announced, "as a former student, I'm going to take the clothes with me to remember my mentor. I hope you don't mind."

"Well …" She hesitated.

"I'll make this guarantee," he added, "if you let me have the clothes, I won't tell anyone about the photo."

"Okay."

Saunders smiled. "Thank you so much for your time.

The reporters didn't speak until they were in the car and headed back to the motel. It was Chambers who finally broke the silence.

"He was murdered."

"There can't be any doubt. But don't judge the locals too harshly. They didn't know Goldsmith had found something big. Naturally, they'd have seen his death as just a result of old age. When we return to Chicago, we can get the shirt analyzed and learn what was injected into his heart. Right now, it's more important to see what's on the thumb drive. Once we get into those files and discover what an imprint is, and why it's so important, we might want to find Dr. Maxine Factor. The fact the old man thought of her as a daughter and left her his estate, and then someone tried to kill her, could well be tied to why Goldsmith had to die. We couldn't save him, but we might be able to save her or at least let her know she's a target."

"And perhaps she knows what an imprint it."

"I doubt that," Hardin answered.

Chapter 9

9:45 p.m.
Friday, September 16
19 Julius Way, Rome, Italy

Is everything black and white? When does wrong become right? Is there a time when doing something that's against the law is the only way to save the law? Those questions have been asked since the beginning of time and never definitively answered.

———◆———

T he apartment was dark and smelled of years of cigarette smoke. The floor was dusty, the furniture worn, and the ashtrays full. One overhead light was turned on. Four men, all in their forties and fifties, dressed casually, sat around a badly scarred dining table drinking wine from paper cups. None looked happy to be there. One finally voiced their combined angst.

"It's a fine world that has us contemplating going against the Pope," Francesco Russo emphasized. While Russo's olive complexion and dark eyes reflected his Italian roots, his black T-shirt and blue jeans hid his occupation. Like his three comrades, he was a priest working inside the Vatican, and tonight, the librarian was playing with fire rather than cataloging books.

The apartment belonged to Russo's brother. Piero was a truck driver hauling freight in Spain. He used the flat on those rare occasions when he returned to the city of his birth. Russo knew where his sibling hid the spare key and figured this residence in the city's slum district was the perfect place to hide a gathering of men who were considering murder.

To Russo's right, Andrea Colombo, a tall man with high cheekbones and thin lips, was tapping a pencil against the table. The forty-four-year-old was displaying more worry lines than a man twice his age. A part of the church's financial division, the accountant was much more comfortable balancing books than he was plotting death.

In the chair nearest the kitchen, Alessio Moretti, a fat man dressed in blue slacks and white shirt, was munching on peanuts while staring at the slowly moving ceiling fan. The most important of the group, he was a cardinal and a personal assistant to the Pope. Of all those in attendance, the fifty-nine-year-old's opinion surely carried the most weight.

The only non-Italian was Atlanta-born Jacob Cole. Seated directly across from Russo, Cole was fair-skinned and blue eyed. The former college basketball player was just over six-six, and though fifty-two, still looked as though he could play. His job in the public affairs office saw him penning the most important stories the Vatican issued to the media. Essentially, he was the Pope's press agent.

"As I see it," Cole suggested, speaking Italian with a distinct American accent, "what the Pope wants is not as important as the foundation of the church. So, we must find a way to eliminate the woman. History proves, and each of us well knows, that sometimes an individual must be sacrificed for the good of society."

"Perhaps," Moretti noted, "but not this time. We know for a fact that none of these people—imprints if you will—ever lives long enough to remember back more than a few hundred years. It's my belief that nothing she'll learn will challenge the faith."

"It's not the church's ancient history that concerns me," Russo argued. "My faith's strong enough to know that Jesus was real, and he rose from the dead. So, even if she was able to remember back to the time of Christ, it'd change nothing. What bothers me is that she might expose some of the church's more recent, awkward political alliances. If some of that dirt comes out, think how that'll affect those who call themselves Catholics. We'll lose the next generation. They'll see us as a political force and not a force for God."

"Francesco is right," Columbo chimed in. "I'm not worried about our faith being challenged. For me it's about avoiding scandal. You don't have to go back too far to find alliances that, if exposed, would shake the foundation of the church. We've been guilty of having some rather despicable bedfellows throughout the years. Need I remind each of you that our alliances have sometimes been anything but holy."

"I think we're overreacting," Moretti suggested. "This woman only sees what her direct ancestors saw. She knows no more than that. There are no memories on DNA from single men. We serve a church where priests don't marry. Logic dictates she could never know anything about our work. So, if any organization is safe from what her relatives might have experienced, it'd seem to be the Catholic church. As none of us in this room or who work at the Vatican or have worked at the Vatican in the past five hundred years have passed on our experiences to anyone via DNA, it should close the book on our worries. We have nothing to fear."

"I wouldn't go that far," Cole confessed. "Our DNA doesn't always die with us. Though it's well hidden, I have a child. Let's not fool ourselves, there are plenty of other priests who've served in the Vatican through the centuries who undoubtedly have had children as well."

The small apartment suddenly became a tomb. For several seconds, no one dared take a breath.

"You have a child?" a shocked Moretti finally whispered.

"Are you a virgin?" Cole demanded.

Moretti said nothing. It was Columbo who finally found his voice.

"I tend to believe Jacob is right. We all know there're priests who have offspring. In a few cases, history has recorded as much. And, if we look back over the church's past, as recent as the days when Hitler rose to power, we have things that must not ever be revealed to the public. If there is even a chance this woman might have a relative who knows the unique ways we have had to deal with diplomatic situations, and if she saw those things in her memories and the press found out, then we'd be guilty of deeply wounding the faith."

"The faith or the church?" Moretti asked.

"What is one without the other?" Columbo asked.

Moretti balled his right hand into a fist and slammed the table. "The faith is pure and honest. If the church isn't, then the two are not the same. If there's someone in this woman's family line who took part in something immoral that will bring shame to the church, then so be it. Let her expose that. Perhaps that's God's way of making us more like who we need to be. I will have nothing more to do with this."

Moretti stood and stormed out of the apartment. As the door slammed the room was once again quiet. No one said a word for five long minutes.

"He's right," Cole finally acknowledged, "the moral thing to do would be to let it go."

"Where's your child," Russo asked. "Do you know?"

"She's a schoolteacher in Kansas. She has two children and her husband's an accountant."

"Does she know about you?"

"No, and if she finds out, it might ruin me. We all know that. But how many others would be ruined if my sin were revealed? So many people have had faith in me, have held me up as a role model—how I would hate to lose that. Besides, I don't want her to know who her father is. Her life is far too perfect to have her conception cast a dark shadow. But, as Alessio pointed out, what we personally want, or even fear, shouldn't cause us to fall into the trap of justifying a far greater sin."

Russo nodded. "I'm well aware that no one has to tell us right from wrong. No one has to explain to us that taking a life is breaking a commandment. But we also know the potential price if we don't act. As much as it pains me, I think we have to eliminate Dr. Factor. You see, I'd rather burn in hell than allow harm to come to the church I so love."

Columbo drained the last of his wine before suggesting a different course. "My friends, moving in haste often takes us down roads we don't need to travel. I've traced Dr. Factor's family tree back six hundred years. Nowhere in that line, if the records are correct, is there anyone who's connected to the church. As no imprint has lived to remember any further back than that, I sense we're worrying over nothing. The Pope has been told of her existence and has little fear about what she might recall. I have less apprehension because I know her history. So, for the time being we'll let her be."

"I wish I had your faith," Russo admitted. "But I'll agree that moving too quickly is not in our best interest. With that in mind, there's no reason for us to have to decide this today. We just need to keep a handle on it. I have contacts at the CIA. A man I know, but whose name I cannot share, has informed me they're looking at Miss Factor very closely and deciding what needs to be done. My friend also assures me he won't allow the church to be damaged in any way. So, I think we have far more important things to worry about. To put it in a way a child could understand, we have both the back and front doors locked."

"How much influence do you have over your friend?" Columbo asked.

"Some. Why?"

"If the woman's memories begin to go back further than the other imprints, could he arrange to have her kidnapped? Then we wouldn't have to kill her, only control her and keep her locked up behind our secure walls."

Russo nodded. "I will see."

"Fear of the truth is a strange thing," Cole suggested as he rose from the table. "We teach that the truth will set us free, and yet, we live as if it's capable of ruining everything we know and love. My fear of the world finding out the truth has now driven me to consider murder—if only briefly. Francesco, thank you for opening my eyes a bit. Yours and Andrea's solutions are far better than mine."

Russo frowned. "I'm no saint—your fears are my fears. I just believe the poor child will go crazy and die by her own hand before she remembers anything that might harm the church. And sadly, I'm not going to do anything to stop that. In fact, I'm praying for it."

Still at the table, Columbo sighed. "I don't feel good about waiting, but it's far better than killing the woman. I'll worry until we confine her and prevent her memories from ever coming to light."

"Let me handle your worry," Russo suggested. "In truth, I'm betting the Americans will kill her before she remembers much of anything."

"Is it moral for us to allow that to happen?" Columbo asked.

"I'd rather not answer that question," Russo whispered.

With little more that could be said, Columbo moved toward the door. The American followed the Italian into the hall and down the stairs.

Russo sat alone in the darkness. He had talked a good game, but that was really just for show. He needed to appear to be concerned, but also look as though he'd fallen in line with Moretti. This strategic move gave him options to move in secret if things got out of hand. For the moment, simply because of assurances from Washington, he could be patient.

Chapter 10

9:17 a.m.
Saturday, September 17
Wallace Hall Room 315, Washington-Lincoln College,
Mount Vernon, Illinois

Knowing who to trust is far more important than most realize. Put your faith in the wrong person and you often lose control of not just that moment, but all the moments that follow.

————◆————

Maxine Factor sat at her desk, grading papers. Outside her window the fall sky was dark shades of nickel, and the leaves were contemplating the rich hues in their futures. Even with the campus all but deserted, her office door was closed and locked, but that failed to provide a sense of security. As she often explained to her students, what you didn't know could not only hurt you, it could kill you. For the moment, it was what she didn't know that had her on edge.

A decade before, when Factor was still in grad school, her mother dug into the family roots. That four-year search took her across the country and even to England, and enabled Kathleen Duncan Marks to trace the limbs of the family tree back eight generations. At the time, her daughter had encouraged her mother's new hobby but was far too busy with her studies to pay much attention. Now that tree called out to her.

Pushing aside student-penned papers on the origins of the Revolutionary War, Factor turned to her desktop, clicked on a file, and a few seconds later, her mother's labor of love sprang to life. As she studied the names, dates, and places, Factor sensed that somewhere in that tree was the answer she needed. Perhaps, if she looked at each branch long enough, memories would spring into her conscious mind, revealing the reason she was a target. She studied every name with the intensity of a lion stalking its prey, but fifteen minutes later, she had nothing. It seemed that no matter how hard she concentrated, the memories of the past refused to spring to life. The fact they wouldn't come when she beckoned was maddening.

She leaned back in her chair. Why had the past experiences flooded her mind when the hired gun was shooting at her? Why had her ancestors been able to influence her actions then, but wouldn't visit her now? The answer was so obvious she almost overlooked it. Adrenaline triggered those memories. The memories came when she saw, smelled, or heard something. So, looking at her mother's labor of love was a waste of time—she could only encounter the past by engaging in the present.

A knock at the door pulled her back to the moment, which wasn't a moment she wanted to embrace. Her body tensed as she leaned forward. Was it just a student with a problem or a person with a deadly agenda? A second knock followed the first. Slowly rising from her desk chair, Factor tiptoed to the shelves holding displays of pop culture items she'd collected over the years. Ignoring the 1958 Mickey Mouse ears, postcards from World War II, and a stack of *Time Magazines* from the 1930s, she reached for a game-used Louisville Slugger baseball bat once swung by a St. Louis Cardinal third baseman named Ken Boyer. Wrapping her fingers around the thin barrel, she raised the thirty-four-ounce club over her shoulder and tiptoed to the door.

"Who's there?"

The response was immediate; the man's voice assured and calm. "Elton Carter."

She'd heard of Carter, but who hadn't? Carter was a person who would be of great interest to any historian. He had given millions to university history departments across the country. The mention of his name caused even veteran teachers' hearts to flutter.

His family's story was something half the people of the world could identify. Carter's great-grandfather had made millions in railroads, and the next generation of the family had invested that fortune in oil. By 1950, Carter's heirs oversaw an empire that included mining, textiles, publishing, electronics, and agriculture. Yet, her visitor was the family's black sheep. According to what she'd read, this Carter was less an industrialist than he was an adventurer. At forty, he was a playboy who, when he wasn't attending lush parties or squiring beautiful women to night clubs, traveled the world in a quest for relics from the past to give to museums. For several years, one of the cable channels had aired a series devoted to his exploits. His being at her door just didn't add up.

"How do I know you're really Elton Carter?" Factor demanded while considering how much force it would take to knock down her locked door. As old as it was, likely little more than a strong kick. As she contemplated moving a chair under the door's knob to offer a bit more security, a small piece of cardboard was pushed under the door. She leaned close. The information on the business card checked but did that really prove anything?

"Mr. Carter, if that's who you really are, why are you here?"

"Obviously to see you. I might add, seeing is a great deal different than just talking to you through a door."

"You'll pardon me if I have problems believing someone like you would want to visit with me."

"You do yourself a disservice," he countered, "because of what I've discovered, there's no one I'd rather talk to."

Factor walked back to her computer and did a quick Google search on the supposed visitor. Pulling up a recent photo, she studied it and then returned to the entry.

"Do you have a cell phone with you?"

"Yes."

"Take a selfie in front of my door so my name can be seen."

"You're serious?"

"Absolutely."

"Okay, I've taken it. What do I do now?"

"I'm sliding my business card under the door. Text the photo to my cell."

It took little more than a heartbeat for her iPhone to vibrate. Moving back to her desk, she compared the image on her computer with the one on her phone. They matched. Still not confident enough to drop the bat, she walked across the room, unlocked the entry, and stepped back.

Even if he hadn't been one of the wealthiest people on the planet, he was still the kind of man most women dreamed about. He was six-two, solid but lean, gray eyes, skin tanned, and hair jet black. Today, he was casually dressed in a yellow golf style shirt and jeans. He wore the look well.

"You seem apprehensive," he noted as he dropped into a chair.

"I have reason to be."

"Are you about to go work out with the baseball team?" Carter nodded at the bat.

"I've found that taking a little hitting practice from time to time keeps me sharp." Factor closed and locked the door, backed into a wooden side chair, and eased down. After resting the baseball bat across her lap, she queried, "Now tell me why you're so far off the beaten path. Last time I looked, Mount Vernon wasn't a party town, and according to the media, you're quite the party animal."

"There's a price on your head," Carter proclaimed as he folded his arms and leaned back. As she considered his ominous warning, the billionaire added something even darker. "Just because the first guy failed doesn't mean your troubles are over. But I'm assuming you're aware of that."

Her fingers once again circled the bat's neck. How would he know that unless …?

"No," he announced as if reading her mind, "I'm not here to kill you, I'm actually here to help protect you."

That made no sense at all. Carter might be good looking, but he was no superhero. What was the real story behind his unexpected visit? It was time for Factor's favorite verbal tool … sarcasm.

"Why would a world-wide celebrity take on the role of white knight for little old me?"

"That's a fair question. You probably know that I've financed a great many historic digs."

"I'm not a gardener," she shot back, keeping the wall of disdain between them, "or a gravedigger. I teach in classrooms and my specialty is American history, so I don't spend much time at ruins."

"Touché."

Factor suddenly realized her guest spoke with the same rhythm and tenor as his great-grandfather. They even looked alike. Josiah Carter had been ruthless and cunning. When he'd tried to buy a piece of property from Factor's great-great-grandfather, he wouldn't take no for an answer. Not long after his visit to the family home, their barn had burned, and now that smoke was now seeping into her lungs. She could taste it. She dismissed the present and plunged into the past. The Carter Company had eventually gotten the land at the price they wanted by destroying everything in their path including John Crawford's health. Factor reflexively reached for her chest to try to ease the pain that was very real but was a part of an ancestor's past.

"Is there something wrong?" the visitor asked.

Suddenly, both the physical pain, the putrid smell, and the ancient mental anguish were gone. Factor was back in the present wondering if this vision had been a warning sent across the generations. And with that in mind, had she invited a man into her office she couldn't trust? It was time to play Sam Spade.

"Mr. Carter."

"Call me Elton."

"Not sure I'm ready for that. You may not know this, but your great-grandfather drove one of my relatives into bankruptcy over a piece of land. No matter what you've been told, Josiah was ruthless and cold. He knew no mercy and showed no compassion. He ran over those who got in his way."

"He was a snake," Carter agreed. "On top of that, the three generations of my family that built great wealth were all that way. My brother Jeremy and my sister Suzanne have inherited those qualities—they slither ran than walk."

"And you don't?"

"I'm a rogue who loves wealth because it paves the way for me to fully explore my fantasies, but I care nothing about power. I'd rather work with people than lord over them. If someone offers me something I want, I buy it, but I make it a policy not to destroy those I work with or who work for me."

"Words are cheap."

"Mine aren't."

"Would the long list of women whose names have been spread across the tabloids agree with that?"

"There have never been any lawsuits. I've never had anyone sign a nondisclosure agreement. They never confused my honesty with my immoral urges. When I happened upon a woman who looks like you, I naturally came up with a plan of conquest. So yes, I embrace passion whenever possible, but I've never forced myself on anyone."

"They just fall into your bed willingly?"

"I seem to have a certain charm."

"And charm seems to have much more power when it is accompanied by deep pockets," Factor suggested.

"How much money would it take to charm you?" he shot back.

"Let's go back to why you're here," Factor suggested, feeling more than a bit insulted.

"I'm constantly on the quest to discover the most treasured relics of history. I'm looking for everything from the Ark of the Covenant to the Amber Room."

"And," Factor cut in, "you've already found Cleopatra's emerald ring, some of the bones of the apostle Paul, and the Old Goat's haunted silver mine. But the most valuable thing I own is one of Elvis Presley's Sun Records. So, once again, why are you here?"

It appeared their verbal dance was suddenly over. It was time to level.

"Fine. Right now, there are only a few people who know about your gift, and I happen to be one of them."

She arched her right eyebrow. "My gift?"

"Yes, the fact you've unlocked your DNA's memory core."

She was shocked. There were only three people who knew about this, four if you count the cousin she'd told a couple of days before, and none of them had contacts with Elton Carter.

"How did you find out?" she demanded.

"From a source at the Vatican."

"What?"

"The Catholic Church often asks for my help in uncovering relics that help validate Christianity. Someone told them about you. Beyond the Pope, there are four others at the Vatican who know. One of them let me in on their little secret. By the way, the guy kind of thinks it would be better if you were dead. But don't worry, he's not going to act on his thoughts. At least not now. He's waiting for others to do the job."

"But I've told no one," Factor argued, "except my brother, a pastor, a cousin, and a college friend."

"And that college friend works where?"

"In the State Department. Right now, she's in the embassy office in Rome."

"And there you have it."

Heather had sold her out. For what reason?

"Why would she tell anyone about me?" Factor demanded. "I told her to keep it our secret."

The visitor grinned. "I learned a long time ago that if you want to keep a secret, you only tell your dog. People like to impress others with unique stories and scoops. They can't help it. At some point, your friend evidently felt your gift would make her more interesting to a young man she wanted to date. That pillow talk ended up being sold to a person who took the story to the Vatican."

As anger swept over Factor, Carter continued.

"You're a threat. If my contact told me, you can bet he told others. And as there's a Vatican quartet who can sing a song about you, who knows how many are aware of your gift. And you scare all them right down to their core."

"Why? What do I know that could mean anything to anyone?"

A pained expression crossed his face as he delved into his own memory. "Betty Rydell was a housewife from London. Ten years ago, I visited with her. She was a woman of average intelligence but her recall of past generations was like listening to family history come alive. I especially loved her memories—given to her by a great-great-great-great-great-grandmother—a milkmaid. Imagine this ... she named all the cows she milked. That was in the days before the American Revolution, and we were just colonies. The stories she told me, while illuminating to one who loves history, are insignificant. Here's what's important. In time, the flood of information flowing into her mind overwhelmed her, causing a complete breakdown. When one of the medical professionals treating her told a few friends about Mrs. Rydell's unique condition, someone beat her to death."

"Why?"

"My guess is that what she might have remembered could've altered history in some way."

"But you can't change the past."

"But," he argued, "if the past is based on a lie, and that lie is revealed, then the foundation of history becomes unstable. Because of that, the present and future could be altered."

As a historian, she could understand in part what Carter was driving at. Some things in history had become almost sacred, and those events had led to the formation of governments, theologies, and traditions. Change just one element and people's view of each of those elements would be altered. New information about former heroes is why Americans were now changing the names of buildings and tearing down monuments.

"How did Rydell call up those old memories?" Factor asked.

"She didn't, they just came to her with no warning. And when they came, she couldn't turn them off. In time, they took over every moment of her life including her sleep. Did you know there had been others?"

She nodded. "I received a telephone call warning me that there were six who had my abilities, and all six were dead."

"And at one point or another, all six were targets."

"Why?"

"I don't know. Boris Stravinsky, Herman Duistman, Misato Kamimura, Jamar White, Amanda Reason, and Molly Rydell have nothing in common other than their unique ability to remember ancestors' lives in first person and vivid detail. None of them ever met or communicated with each other. In fact, none of them even knew that there were others like them. I've hired teams to dig into their family trees, and my researchers have so far found no links to major events or famous relatives."

"So why were they hunted? Why would someone want them dead? To make it even more personal, why would someone want me dead?"

"I was hoping you'd know."

That was anything but the answer she wanted and needed to hear. And so, with both of them lost in thought, the dialogue died for several minutes. When her guest finally broke the silence, it built another bridge to the past.

"I could use some coffee."

Gladys Schlieff had spoken those same words on a Civil War battlefield in 1864. The diminutive, eighteen-year-old woman had been serving as a Union nurse for a year. During that time, the blood of countless men had stained her hands. In just a few weeks, she'd watched more people die than lived in her tiny hometown of Spring, Ohio. Now, on a hot July day, in a tent filled with ten soldiers whose bodies had been literally blown apart, the price of war had become too great a burden to handle.

"We haven't had any coffee for months," Dr. Howard Day grumbled. "It seems we ran out of it about the same time I lost hope."

Gladys nodded, took off her blood-soaked apron and strolled out of the tent. The rays of the sun brought no relief. The only thing that seemed sure was that she'd never know laughter or joy again.

Desperately needing to get away from the burdens of fighting a losing battle against death, she tossed logic aside, strolled across the field and into the woods. At least in the shade, the heat was not as oppressive. Feeling a sense of relief, she leaned against a sweet gum tree and closed her eyes. Exhausted, she must've fallen asleep on her feet and then a man's pleading voice awakened her.

"Are you a medicine woman? Maybe a doctor?"

Startled, her body tensed; her eyes opened. A soldier in a tattered gray uniform was pointing a rifle at her face. He was not more than five-and-a-half feet tall. His complexion was ruddy, and a worn hat held down shaggy, dark, greasy hair. He was evidently too young to grow a beard.

"I'm a nurse," she whispered.

"That's good enough," his reply displayed his southern roots. "My friends are hurt, some are dying. We need help."

In spite of the heat and humidity, a cold fear rushed into her heart like a winter storm. She'd never felt so alone, helpless, or chilled.

"You're coming with me, lady."

Mustering what little courage she could find, she shook her head. "I can't, my place is here."

He jabbed the gun in her direction. "If you don't go with me, I'll kill you. Believe me, I will. The only thing I've got to live for is my buddies. You have to save at least one of them, or I don't think I can keep going. I've already lost everyone I love. Now turn around and start walking."

"Are you revisiting the past?" Carter asked as he directed her attention back to the present.

After shaking her head, she returned to the moment. How had he known the door to another time and place opened? She didn't have to wonder long.

"The look you had on your face was just like Molly's when she got lost in the past. What was the trigger?"

Factor got up, set the baseball bat back in its place, slowly walked over to the window and looked out on the campus. As she studied two students casually walking in front of Old Main, she felt Carter's gaze. She knew he was waiting for her, but what was there to say? In the light of what he had told her, her situation seemed as hopeless as the Rydell woman's.

"If I could see into the future," Factor announced without turning, "I could understand why my gift might have some value. I'd know what companies to invest in or horses to bet on. But all I can do is relive different lives from my past. How does my knowing the way Gladys Schleiff felt on a Civil War battlefield or what she did with her life matter to anyone today? How could her experiences be a threat?"

She turned to face her visitor. Rather than provide answers, Carter just shook his head before offering, "I don't know."

"I don't give up easily," Factor explained, "I'm a competitor. I played volleyball in college and was the best setter in our conference. I'm known for wreaking havoc on a racquetball court and going for blood when I play *Hearts*. I never quit, but today I feel as hopeless as my grandmother several generations back felt in 1864."

"She must have survived. After all, you were born."

"Elton Carter, why are you here?"

"To help you."

"Then answer this question. Who's trying to kill me?"

He shrugged. "I don't understand why anyone would want you dead. To me, you're a gold mine."

"I don't get that."

"Consider this, one of your ancestors might know of buried treasure or undiscovered works by famous artists. That's just the beginning. Beyond the historical significance of what you could do with your gift, smart businessmen, like my siblings, would see that there was money to be made from your memories. How much would depend upon what your ancestors did and witnessed. But the potential is there. As an example, at this very moment there are millions of dollars in hidden loot ready to be found, and locked in your mind might be the key to a treasure or two."

"So, I have the potential to find a pirate's booty or buried gold from the Civil War. Is that why you're interested in me? Am I just a tool to bring you more wealth and fame? Or are you like P.T. Barnum searching for the next freak to display? Come meet the woman who can tell of the great days of the past. She'll bring history to life! Get your tickets here!"

"No, I don't want to exploit you—I want to save you. You're important to me because one of your relatives may've met Cleopatra, and you might finally paint a picture of what history's most seductive woman looked like. Or maybe you can tell me more about Plato or Moses. If you can remember back far enough, the list goes on and on."

Factor sadly nodded. "All you've done, Mr. Carter, is show me that I have value. History proves that valuable things need to be possessed not destroyed. That doesn't answer the question of why someone is trying to take me out."

"Dr. Factor, I made a terrible mistake. I visited with Molly Rydell, and I tried to tap into her memories, but I didn't understand the need to protect her. I'm not going to repeat that mistake. I want to protect you. But to have a chance at doing that, you'll have to trust me."

"And what do you want in return?" Factor demanded.

"A look into the past. A chance to actually see history in a way no one else has."

"And maybe some treasure," she quipped, "or a roll in the hay?"

"Whatever we'd find, I'd give away," he assured her. "When you're as rich as I am, money doesn't mean anything, but in my case, knowledge does. And, yes, you're beautiful, but that's not why I'm here either."

She didn't have to consult with her ancestors to know that words often held no value, but in this situation, she had to trust someone—wasn't it best to extend that trust to a man who had almost limitless resources?

"Mr. Carter, you hinted that Betty Rydell went insane. Did that happen to any of the other people who shared my gift?"

"What happened to them is not important."

"I'm afraid it is. I've recently figured out that on most days the memories come and go based on my senses. It's a word, a thought, a smell, a sound, or something I hear that triggers them. But as they come more often and more quickly, I lose myself for longer stretches. Will there be a time when so many lives are living in my head that I can't contain them? Will I get to a point where I drown in memories … or my brain explodes? You see, I'm not as worried about being assassinated as I am about being consumed by the past and, therefore, losing who I am in the present."

"I can offer you the chance for protection," he suggested. "My money can help keep you out of harm's way."

"That's not the answer I need to hear."

"You have much more depth than Rydell. Your mind is far more developed. I think that means it can hold a lot more memories."

"You can only fill a bucket with so much water before it spills over," she countered.

Carter's eyes reflected deep concern. It seemed genuine. "Dr. Factor, do you know what the few medical professionals who've studied this kind of thing call what you have?"

"Crazy? Delusional?"

"No. You are an imprint, and what you have is called imprinting."

She frowned. No matter what it was called, it still seemed her future was a road leading to death or insanity or both.

"May I call you Maxine?"

"Just Max."

"Okay, Max. I know a doctor who had the chance to examine two of those like you. She knows more about imprints than anyone in the world. I think the first thing you need to do is let me take you to her. I can arrange for us to meet in a place that's safe, so you won't have to worry about dodging assassins."

"And what about my classes?"

"Based on what happened a couple of days ago, I think the president would approve a sabbatical. In fact, after I write a large check for the university endowment, I believe he'll be more than happy to find an adjunct to take your place for a few weeks or months."

She glanced around her office, a place that defined her, and where she kept the most important tangible elements of her life. If her fate was the same as the other imprints, this might be the last day she'd spend here. And here was her life, her calling, her reason for living, and she didn't want to leave it or this world. Still, maybe Carter was right. Maybe it was time to go somewhere to hide and come to grips with her new identity as an imprint. Perhaps it was time to accept an invitation and embrace a bit of trust. If she was right, she might have another day, month, or year. If she was wrong, she might be walking out the door with the man who'd killed Molly Rydell. After all, history had proven time and time again that if you have enough money, you can get away with murder.

Chapter 11

12:09 p.m.
Saturday, September 17
Holiday Inn Express, Mount Vernon, Illinois

Life is full of riddles, and most are never solved. Those who try to find all the answers usually drive themselves crazy. But when a riddle is unlocked, the answer can redirect a person to things they never dreamed of and maybe even places they shouldn't go.

———◆———

M ason Hardin spent most of the night trying to crack the thumb drive's encryption code. The sun was up, and the locals were headed to church when he threw up his hands, poured a fresh cup of coffee, his fifth since breakfast, and sat down in a chair. As he closed his eyes, he thought back to his days in Ulysses Goldsmith's class. Goldsmith demanded his students embrace research to justify every word they wrote. He required each essay employ the rules found in the Associated Press Stylebook. And he always placed the letter grade at the top of each paper followed by a slash and the numeric grade. It couldn't just be one, it was always both. And earning an A or making a score in the nineties was as challenging as running a marathon. Because it came with so much difficulty, winning Goldsmith's ultimate approval meant a great deal to him. That was surely the reason Hardin could still recall in detail all eight essays from that semester. To this day, he remembered the subject, the letter grade, the numerical mark, and even the comments.

Hardin's first assignment had been to write a history of the Cold War. He'd worked two-weeks perfecting a paper he was sure Goldsmith would hold up as an example of the proper method of taking research and transforming it to riveting commentary. All his hard work only earned a B and an 81. Because of the importance of the class, Hardin pushed even harder on his assignment on the causes of the Great Depression. That one garnered a B and an 84. It would take four more papers to get an A and score in the nineties.

"Great balls of fire!" he whispered.

Marsha Chambers had been lying on the bed napping when Hardin's exclamation woke her. After rubbing the sleep from her eyes, she sat up. "You get something or just channeling Jerry Lee Lewis?"

He sat down at the desk, opened his laptop, and quickly entered his letter and number grades in order from his semester with Goldsmith. After hitting the return button, his smile lit up the room. "I've broken the encryption."

"How many files?" Chambers asked as she popped off the bed.

"Don't you want to know how I broke the code?"

"I don't really care. I want to know how many files."

"A dozen, and they go back about six months. But you really have no interest in knowing how I broke in?"

"Once again, I don't care how you broke the encryption, only that you did."

As the first file appeared on the screen, both reporters leaned close and began to read. What was written gave them some of the answers they needed.

I've always believed that the human brain is underused. That our brains have the capacity to do so much more than we ask of them. And yet, never could I have conceived what a Vatican source shared with me today. It seems there are a handful of people in this world who have had their brains unlocked. What do I mean by that? Apparently on our DNA are the memories of our ancestors. Those who have been gifted can access those experiences. The name science has chosen for this very elite group is imprint. And these imprints, while very rare, offer us a chance to see history in a much different light than any of us could imagine.

"Do you grasp what he's suggesting?" Chambers asked.

"Yeah, if I could meet an imprint whose great-great-great-grandfather worked in the Lincoln White House, just consider what new information I could learn about the president. In fact, think of how history might be rewritten if I had access to those who had really seen it. I'd be covering stories on the Civil War, the American Revolution, the Crusades, and even back to the time of Moses as if I were conducting interviews with an eyewitnesses. I might even find out what happened to lost civilizations and discover if the story of Atlantis were true. And that's just the beginning."

Hardin scanned the remainder of the file, which was little more than a wish list of the history Goldsmith was hoping to learn. With rabid anticipation, he clicked on the next one. Sadly, it was more of the same. Goldsmith was writing about times he wanted to investigate and questions he would ask, but he was no closer to finding an imprint. The next ten were essentially more wish lists.

"This is some wild stuff," Chambers observed after scanning the eleventh file.

"If we can find an imprint," Hardin suggested, "we could write a story that'd rock the world! That's what was driving Goldsmith. He understood this could be the key to unlocking unexplained mysteries. Think of the new knowledge this might give us about Plato or being able to record more of the lessons taught by Christ."

"Open the last file," Chambers suggested. "Perhaps it'll give us a name of an imprint."

Hardin clicked on a file from two weeks ago. These notes read much differently than had the others. Goldsmith was no longer a man filled with excitement; he was a person drowning under a wave of great guilt.

I didn't know what it would mean to actually discover an imprint. I thought it was just a story. When a contact from DC, a preacher friend of mine, told me one was living right here in Mount Vernon, I was flabbergasted. And best of all, I already knew her. I was so excited that I shared my discovery with my CIA contact. And that's where I made my mistake.

Mason, if you find these files, it probably means someone has killed me. By learning what it means to be an imprint, I have put myself in danger. But, I'm an old man, I've had a full life, it's the imprint who needs protecting. Please do everything you can to keep her safe. I've discovered, thanks to my sources, she might see something in one of her relatives' pasts that will dramatically change history. If I am right, and she can prove my theory, or maybe I should say one if her ancestors were there to see the truth, and she remembers that moment in time, then we will have uncovered the biggest story ever told. I won't give you her identity. If someone else somehow breaks the code and opens my files, then it would put her life in danger. But I know you'll figure it out on your own. Everything you need is in my files. Just remember how I think and try to see the world through my eyes.

This might well be my final chance to share this story with you. As Sherlock Holmes might say, "The hounds are at my door." But I have faith you can finish my work and save the imprint's life. You're my only student who never received a failing grade, so please don't fail me now."

-U

Hardin leaned back against his chair and considered Goldsmith's final entry. The old man's faith in him was overwhelming. Essentially, he was asking Hardin to not just save a life, but to help alter history in some way. It was mind-blowing!

"If I'm right," Chambers hypothesized, "Goldsmith was feeling guilty for having put this woman's life in danger."

Coming out of a cloud raining overwhelming responsibility, Hardin nodded. "Yeah, he must have given her identity away to someone. That has to mean one of the two people he trusted is out to either kill or capture the imprint."

"He said you would be able to figure out who she is."

Hardin shrugged. "I hope he hasn't misjudged me. Right now, I don't have a clue. I'll send the files over to your laptop. Let's both read them in order again. If there's a change in the writing style, a strange phrase, anything that jumps out, let me know."

For the next hour, the two reporters silently went over every file searching for something that might hint at who the imprint was. When that failed, they read the files out loud to each other. Nothing worked!

"You think it might be in code?" a weary Chambers asked.

"No, I know his style as well as I know my own. If there had been a break in rhythm, I would have seen it."

She scanned the laptop's finder. "What's this file you didn't open?"

"Nothing!"

"How can you be sure?"

"Because Goldsmith found out the woman's identity in the weeks before he was killed, and that's a photo file that was actually created in 1998. How can it tie into this? I'm betting he accidentally dragged it over from his computer's main drive."

"Just for my sake, Mason, open the .jpeg and let's look at it. If Goldsmith kept it, it must mean something."

Hardin clicked on the file, and within a few seconds, a black and white photograph of an older man and younger woman appeared on the screen. The man was wearing round glasses, dressed in a white coat, shirt, and dark tie, and seemed to be applying makeup on a striking blonde who appeared to be in her twenties.

"That photo's ancient," Chambers noted. "Do you have any idea who it is?"

"Goldsmith loved classic films. Watching movies that were made in the thirties and forties was one of his favorite ways to unwind. Based on the quality of the photography, I'd guess this has to be a studio publicity shot. The woman's makeup, hair, and clothes indicate the time frame is somewhere in the late twenties or early thirties. But I really have no idea who either one of those people are. Lord, this is frustrating."

"Could it be a clue?" Chambers asked.

"My gut tells me it has nothing to do with the imprint."

"What if one of those people is an imprint?"

Hardin leaned closer to the screen. As he studied the image he shook his head. "If this photo was taken in the 1930s, as it most assuredly was, then both of these people are dead."

"Maybe," Sanders mused, "one of those two is a grandparent of the imprint he found. Perhaps we need to discover who they are and then trace their family tree."

"Interesting theory, but that's not the way Goldsmith's mind worked."

"So, you don't believe this is what he was talking about in his note to you?"

"How can a file, created more than two decades ago of a photo from ninety years ago, be tied to something he cracked this month? Look— there are no hidden words, nothing appears out of place. It's just a shot he kept, maybe for something he was researching back then. Let's go back through the Word documents one more time and see if there's something that pops out. Maybe the fifth time will be a charm."

As Hardin opened the next to the newest file and slowly read it out loud, Chambers began a web search. Ten minutes later, she brought her MacBook to her partner and pointed to the screen.

"The actress in that photograph is Jean Harlow. Soon after this photo was taken, she would become one of the biggest stars in Hollywood. She tragically died at the age of twenty-six in 1937. The man applying the makeup is Max Factor. His name is still one of the most revered in the world of cosmetics."

"Thanks for the history lesson, but where does that get us?"

"Who was a target for murder earlier this week, and who is going to get Goldsmith's estate?"

"The professor at the college."

"Do you remember her name?"

He snapped his fingers. "Dr. Maxine Factor."

"That's who you've got to save. Factor has to be the imprint."

Hardin nodded. He was plotting their next course of action when his phone rang.

"Hello, it's Mason."

"This is Fortes, I'm the cop assigned to find out who tried to blow up your car."

"You got something?"

"We found a print, but it doesn't seem to match anything in the database."

"So, nothing?"

"On the bomb, no, but I got your landlady to let me into your apartment and …"

"And what?"

"It looks like a tornado landed in the middle of your place. The same's true of your partner's digs. They wrecked Chamber's condo just like they did yours. Do you have any idea what they'd have been looking for?"

"No, there's nothing of value there, at least in mine. Nothing at all."

"There's something else," the cop announced. "When I closed your door, there was an explosion. It knocked me across the hall. So, your car wasn't the only thing that was wired to blow up. Someone's real serious about doing you in. We found a bomb in Chamber's condo and defused it."

Hardin looked back toward Chambers and frowned. Suddenly, this whole caper was a lot more complicated and dangerous. The people who were after him surely knew he had confided in her. Now, he to find Factor so he could also save Chambers.

"Anything else?" Hardin asked Fortes.

"Not right now. We're working on cleaning up the mess the bomb made. If we discover anything in the rubble, I'll call you. In the meantime, I think it'll be best if you and Miss Chambers find a place to spend a few days. A spot where no one can find you!"

"I'll work on that."

Hardin ended the call, slipped his phone inside his pocket, and closed his laptop. His expression was grim as he looked toward Chambers, "We have to pack up and get out of here now."

"Why?"

"Based on what I just learned, the story we're working on is much more lethal than the bomb they put in my car. They trashed both our apartments. Whoever got to Goldsmith surely knows we're in Mount Vernon."

"But we just figured this out. We didn't even have the woman's name until five minutes ago. How did they know to go after us even before we knew what we were after?"

"Goldsmith shared what he knew with someone else. When he did, he likely let it slip that he was thinking of using me to help him. Or, maybe, the person he told assumed I'd be included because of my relationship with Goldsmith. If either of those things were the case, then he must have known Goldsmith very well."

"In other words," Chambers observed, "there's a Judas in the mix. Someone the old man trusted betrayed him."

"And we have to find out who that is."

"How?"

"We break into Goldsmith's home and look for his address book. I noticed he still had a landline. We need to track down the information on all the calls he made. I figure the person who killed him took his cell, but just in case we can look for that as well. And, after we do that, we've got to find a place where we'll be safe."

"What about Factor?"

"Her life depends upon us discovering who Goldsmith told. Until we know the name of that person, we can't help her. In fact, the worst thing we could do right now is be seen with her. No use putting both targets in the same place at the same time. Now, let's get packed."

As he began to throw things in a bag, a sense of uneasiness settled in like a fog on the River Thames. Right now, someone was likely watching them, and if that were true, they had targets on their backs. He'd stupidly brought Chambers into a possibly lethal trap.

Chapter 12

6:22 p.m.
Saturday, September 17
1219 James Street, Arlington, Virginia

For those with money or power, humans are as expendable as cash, and they serve the same purpose. They are tender to buy or protect something of value. For that reason and a thousand others, to those with great influence, life is cheap.

———◆———

Rocky Smith studied the ranch-style home's living room. The house gave off a strange vibe. Perhaps it was the dated furnishings, all from the 1960s, or maybe it was the presence of people who really didn't want to be here. Either way, this wasn't a place anyone would want to visit or call home. Walk-in freezers had more warmth. Yet for reasons that he couldn't grasp, his boss called this home.

Beyond Tim Clegg, Smith had never met any of the men gathered to discuss the problem created by the imprint, but he knew each of them by their reputations. At the CIA, they had once been viewed as the cream of the crop, but that was decades ago. Now, they appeared to be nothing more than retired codgers looking for a golf game. Yet, retired or not, with just one phone call, they'd immediately dropped everything and left lives they loved to come back to a world they were trying to forget. This seemed to prove that who they once had been was still a vital part of their fiber. Or was there more? Were they here for reasons beyond Dixon and the imprint? Was there something in their pasts creating the apprehensive looks and nervous stares? Perhaps that would soon be revealed.

Sitting in an aqua wingback chair by the door was Bristol Owen. Now seventy-five, Owen wore the look of a man who had spent forty years in the spy game. His deeply wrinkled face revealed no emotion, and his relaxed posture indicated a person who couldn't be rattled. It was Owen who'd greeted Clegg and Smith when they'd arrived, and it was Owen, after the four had exchanged small talk, who finally opened the door and allowed the elephant into the room.

"So, the imprint's father is Dixon?" He brought his thick fingers together and balled them up before adding, "We should have killed him years ago."

"Yeah, like anyone could do that!" Rick Elder said. A former college track star, even at seventy he looked as though he could have still run a hundred meters in ten seconds. "If all four of us had taken Dixon on at the same time, when the cops were called to investigate, they'd have found a dead quartet on the floor. Meanwhile Dixon would still be singing a tune."

Elmer Vanover, a grizzled red-head who'd just hit his sixty-fifth birthday, was leaning against the living room wall, arms folded over his chest. "I'm tired of Dixon. He made my life miserable when we served together, and now, he drags me away from Florida to do it all over again. He's like a bad habit you can't lose."

"But," Clegg pointed out, "alive or dead, and at this point we don't know which, Dixon has the potential to expose a lot of the dirt none of us wants to have dredged up."

"Does she realize Dixon's her father yet?" Vanover asked.

"I don't think so," Clegg admitted. "I believe by now the memories are coming back in waves. That's the pattern observed with other imprints. So, obviously the risk is getting greater. If she remembers what happened in Liverpool, Paris, Madrid, or Berlin, we might be looking at an international crisis that can't be contained. Don't forget, on our orders, Dixon killed two members of parliament and one of them had royal blood. If that's traced back to the us …"

The can of worms had been opened. Clegg was behind black deeds even the agency didn't know about. His brief description of the group's past activities proved Clegg was powerful, his reach was long, and he was no Sunday school teacher. While Smith was hardly shocked by the information, it was stunning how Clegg so easily admitted it.

As Smith watched, Clegg rose from his chair and walked over to the home's picture window. In the fading light, he seemed to study the suburban street for a few moments. When he finally spoke, his voice was calm and his words carefully measured. "If what we did when we worked with William Dixon is revealed, it'll open the door to a much deeper investigation. If that happens, we'll all be dead men. Don't kid yourself, there's no escaping we went outside government boundaries and ordered murders, but that might be the least of our problems." Pushing his hands deep into the pockets of his pleated navy slacks, he continued staring out the window. "If it hasn't happened yet, at some point, Maxine Factor will remember her real father—she'll see through his eyes. Since he was in his late thirties when she was born, there are a lot of things she'll know that'll put the standing of the United States in jeopardy and make us targets of both friends and enemies." He turned to face his old comrades. "Can we allow her to reveal the truth?"

They were silent for several minutes before Elder made an admission. "I'm not the man I once was. I have a family, and my focus is on things other than national security. I rarely watch the news and haven't read a newspaper in a couple of years. I have a granddaughter who's nine—I just want to spend more time with her. That's the only real goal I have." After running his hand over his bald head, he added, "Each time I'm with Layla, I have a sense of joy I've never known."

"So," Clegg queried, "you vote to kill Factor?"

"I no longer have a stomach for violence," Elder admitted, "and, as strange as it sounds, that's the reason Factor needs to be eliminated. Our association with Dixon would be the fuse that ..." He shook his head.

"So," Owen chimed in, "you don't want to be a part of murder, but you're voting for it."

Elder nodded. "If the woman remembers what Dixon did, violence will come back into my life. Let's face it, if the truth comes out, someone will be hired to kill all of us. And I won't give up the years I want and need to spend with my granddaughter."

"That's cold," Owen observed. "You're not worried about what might happen to this country and its standing in the world. You want a young woman killed so you can play games with a little girl."

Elder was unapologetic. "Yes, I care about me. Maybe you can be noble about all this. But I was away from my family serving this country for far too many years to want to give up the time I've got left. Let me be honest, every night I go to bed wishing I'd never been a part of any of this. It haunts me! Even the payoffs repulse me. And you, Owen, you need to think about what getting those means."

"We all feel that way," Vanover chimed in. "I take drugs to sleep. I avoid looking in mirrors. I try to pretend I was never a part of the CIA or this committee. And, yet, I'm here because there's a woman who might bring some light to what we all did in the dark. I have so much I don't deserve and didn't earn, and it's all covered in blood."

"So that means you want her dead?" Clegg asked.

"Hell no," Vanover sighed. "I just can't find a way to let her live."

"Bristol, what's your vote?"

The big man pushed off the wall and walked to where he and Clegg were almost nose to nose. He held that pose for at least a minute before hissing, "I hate you." He turned back to his other former partners, "I hate all of you. But I don't hate any of you as much as I hate myself. We played God more times than I care to recall. How many deaths did we order? Does anyone remember? Was there ever a time we had a meeting when, after discussing the pros and cons, we voted not to kill someone? No, in every case we convinced ourselves the person we'd marked as a potential problem had to be eliminated. And why? For what reason? We wrapped ourselves in the flag and justified those hits as signs that we loved America. If what we did was so good for the USA, then why are we so scared of that truth now? Why do we want to make sure no one ever reveals we were behind those events?" He paused and then whispered, "I can tell you why, but do you really want to hear it?"

"Tell us," Clegg suggested.

"Who was the first hit?" Owen asked.

"Johnson, the senator," Elder replied.

"Did he kill someone?" Owen asked.

"No, he had dirt on the president and ..."

"And that dirt involved the CIA," Owen finished. "That night, the four of us spent ten hours deliberating Johnson's fate. And just before dawn, we voted to protect the country from the truth. We called Dixon, and he made it look like an accident. And how did we feel afterwards?"

"Sick," Elder suggested.

"Yeah," Owen agreed. "But here's the sad part. Each time we looked at another target, and each time we called in Dixon to execute the person we'd decided could not afford to live, we felt less sick. And on each occasion, we spent less time discussing the dynamics and ramifications of what we were doing. And, as the hits mounted, we grew numb. And now, can each of us say beyond a shadow of a doubt that what we did was the right thing?"

They went silent once more. It was as if they were remembering a life they wished they'd never lived.

Owen shook his head, "So, we just rationalize another murder now?"

"Do we have a choice?" Vanover asked.

Elder laughed, but there was no humor in it. A dark cloud hung over the room for several moments before Clegg finally spoke.

"I think Rick's right. We don't have a choice. If we'd never voted to kill anyone before tonight, we might have, but not now. That was the first step that opened the door to other things we still don't talk about. Let's face it, once you begin covering up, you just have to keep doing it." He looked back toward the window, his voice now just a whisper, "The problem is, this time we don't have Dixon. One of us has to do the job."

"You're serious?" Elder asked. "Except for you, Clegg, none of us have ever murdered anyone."

"It's the only way," Clegg explained.

Smith once more studied the old team who had gathered to deal with something that had dredged up memories they seemed unable to handle. For all appearances, these were once idealistic men who had wandered into immorality and somehow believed they could walk away from their deeds. But no one can really hide from a past that includes murder.

Owen sighed. "Can you imagine what might be written about us if this news ever got out? What would our friends and families think? Gentlemen, we'd go down in history as four of the evilest men who ever walked on this planet. Our names would be linked with those of Ted Bundy and Jack the Ripper."

"We never actually killed anyone," Elder pointed out.

"So what?" Owen screamed. "Does the fact that people like Dixon pulled the trigger or built the bomb make us any less guilty? We have blood on our hands—it might be invisible, but it's there, and now, we're about to have more."

"Yes, we are," Clegg agreed as he pulled a deck of cards from his coat pocket and dropped them onto the coffee table. As his eyes flashed around the room, he spelled out the rules. "We each pick one. The low card designates who has to take out Factor. Who wants to go first?"

Elder reached down and, with no hesitation, pulled a card from the middle of the deck. When flipped, it revealed the ten of clubs. His expression showed relief. It looked like the odds were in his favor.

Owen was next. His big right mitt hovered over the table for several seconds before choosing the top card. As everyone looked on, he tossed a king of diamonds down onto the floor. Owen was free and clear.

Vanover moved to the table. His hand was noticeably shaking as he pulled out a card from the bottom. He took a deep breath before dropping it onto the table. The six of spades landed face up. He was in trouble, and it showed in his eyes.

Then came the person who'd called the meeting. With a steady hand, he grabbed the card on the top and casually held it up. Clegg had drawn the ace of diamonds. Smith wondered if the deck had been stacked.

A dejected Vanover pawed the carpet with his right shoe. He didn't want any part of this, but as a member of the old team, he seemed ready to embrace something he knew was terribly wrong. Yet, before he could agree, Clegg made an observation.

"Rocky hasn't picked yet."

Shocked, Smith studied Clegg. The man was serious.

"He wasn't part of the team," Elder declared. "The kid doesn't need to have this dropped into his lap. After all, he made none of the decisions that got us into this mess, and he hasn't profited by them either."

Owen and Vanover both nodded in agreement. But Clegg was unmoved. "Choose a card, Rocky." This was not a request—it was an order.

A stunned Smith stood and made his way to the table. He eyes remained locked on Clegg even while he reached down and made his pick. He didn't bother looking at what he'd chosen, but rather held it up for the others to see. Only Vanover displayed any emotion. His smile told Smith all he needed to know. The job of taking out Maxine Factor would be his.

Tossing the deuce onto the carpet, Smith moved back to the couch. As he did, a relieved Elder, Vanover, and Owen hurried toward the door. There were no goodbyes. They rushed to their cars as if a storm were beating down on them. It was surely the fastest they'd moved in more than a decade. Only when the trio had driven away did Clegg speak.

"Tough break."

"Hardly."

Clegg shook his head, "Someone had to lose."

"Yeah," Smith agreed, "and that someone had to be me. I thought it was strange you wanted me to come to this reunion, but now I know why. You set this whole mess up to make sure each of them voted to do what you wanted, and then, you put them on the spot in order to let them sweat for a while. But you'd already decided who was going to do the dirty work. The whole thing was rigged."

"If they didn't have the guts to kill in the past, they sure couldn't have done it now." Clegg strolled over to the table, and as he began picking up the cards, he made a promise. "I can protect you. I've got that kind of power. You take Factor out, and I'll make sure you can walk away from the agency with enough money to last your lifetime and four or five more. You'll live like a king."

Smith shook his head. "What makes you think I'll do it?"

"Because, if you don't, you'll die. And I've always believed that when faced with the choice of being noble or living, folks picked the latter. In truth, you want to get out of this racket, I've given you a way, and you should thank me."

"I should be grateful for having to kill a woman?"

"You should be happy it's not you who's the target. Because if you don't do it, you better have your will in order. This woman dies because of what she will remember, but you'll die because of what you just heard and who you saw."

"I won't ever talk about what I just witnessed," Smith argued, "you know that. She has nothing on me. Dixon and I never met. And I was not involved in any of the things your team ordered. I don't have blood on my hands."

Clegg smiled, "But you will. And I'm sure of that because you want to live. You see, humans are predictable. We can always come up with ways to justify actions we find morally repugnant as long as we benefit from what we do. Rocky, think of this as winning the lottery—I guarantee you'll come out of this a multi-millionaire. On top of that, this is your ticket out of a life you don't like and into a world where you can have anything you want. I'm really doing you the biggest favor you could ever imagine. I'm offering you a new identity and a new life. Few people get breaks like that."

Smith was well aware that Clegg had the ability to end his life. Other agents who had resisted orders had disappeared in the past. He was trapped. There was no choice. There never had been.

"Let's say I do it," Smith said. "Where does all the money come from?"

"There's a person who also needs Factor to disappear. There's twenty million in an offshore account. Once the job is done, it'll be released. And don't worry about my friend the billionaire reneging on the deal, I know all the skeletons in his closest."

"Why don't you take it?" Smith asked.

Clegg grinned. "There's another pile of cash waiting for me."

"What about the source that gave you the information?"

"He's already dead. He was far too noble to play the game the way I needed."

"Just like that?"

"Yeah, just like that."

Clegg pulled out his weapon and casually wiped the barrel against his coat sleeve. The act was a warning. And Smith knew it. He was trapped. Though he didn't want to kill the woman he'd been investigating, he'd rather have Factor dead than have Clegg punch his ticket. He stood, moved to the door, and stepped out onto the small porch. This might be his one shot at being a millionaire, and it was time to take it.

Chapter 13

1:11 p.m.
Sunday, September 18
Hwy 142 South, Outside Mount Vernon, Illinois

When you begin to run from the past, you usually don't get to stop until you're dead. You see, no matter how fast you are, escaping the past is impossible.

———◆———

She and Carter should've left the day before. That would've been the smart move. But Maxine Factor wanted to leave her house in order. That meant finishing grading her students' papers, taking care of a few things at home, and checking on a retired, elderly professor who had been her mentor. Carter was sure, with so much at stake, those things should have been put on the back burner. Delaying the trip for more than twenty-four hours would surely come back to haunt them.

They'd only been on the road for thirty minutes, and trouble was already on their tail. A quarter of a mile behind Carter's rented gray Chrysler was a light blue Chevy sedan. It'd paced them for the entire eighteen miles since they'd left Mount Vernon. On his right, unaware they were being tailed, was the woman he'd volunteered to protect. The professor was intently studying her phone, possibly reading the newsfeed, and at this moment, Carter saw no reason to alert her that she was once again in someone's gun sights.

For twenty minutes, he kept his eyes on the Chevy and his hands on the wheel. After driving through the small town of McLeansboro, he made a left on County Road 1125 before pulling into the gravel parking lot of a small airport. Confirming what he feared, the Chevy mirrored his movements. And as it was Sunday, there was no one at the facility, so it was the perfect place for an ambush. Carter carried no weapons, so the battle would be uneven from the start and surely over in the blink of an eye. Sensing his best odds were getting the car as close to the runway as possible, he made a left and headed for the concrete.

In front of a metal building serving as a hanger for a crop duster, was Carter's refurbished DC-3. The plane had rolled off the assembly line in 1939 and was originally used for passenger service by United Airlines. In the fifties, it was sold to Ozark Airlines and, finally, in the early seventies, was retired. A collector had refurbished the plane and flown it in airshows until Carter, a seasoned pilot, bought it. Since then, he had used the old bird for short flights around the US.

As Carter pulled the car over to the hanger, Factor looked up and inventoried her surroundings. "Is that your plane?" Her tone suggested her surprise.

"Yeah, that's one of them."

"I was expecting a jet."

"This old goose can land and take off in places newer planes can't. It's also as safe as anything that has wings. And we're only going to my cabin in the Ozarks, so speed isn't important. At least not once we get airborne. But getting into the air might be a challenge."

"Why?'

"Don't look behind us, but we've been tailed. There are two men in the car, and by all appearances, I doubt they'll let us get anywhere near my tin goose."

Factor remained amazingly calm. Rather than turn her head, she looked into the side mirror. "So, as my bodyguard and protector, what are you going to do?"

"I'm thinking about just making a big turn, getting back on the highway, and driving."

"And they'll keep following until we run out of gas, or they feel it's time to make a move."

The woman was nothing but logical, and at that moment, Carter didn't appreciate her sound thinking. As he let the Chevy idle, he quipped, "If you can think of something better, let me know."

She didn't hesitate. "Drive into the hanger. The door's open just enough for us to make it through."

"What good'll that do? They're likely armed, we're not. We'll be sitting ducks as soon as we get out of our car."

"Just do it!"

Though the highway seemed like a better option, the woman's assertive tone won him over. Carter made a hard right, hit the gas, and headed straight for the partially open door. He slammed on the brakes as soon as he entered and skidded to a stop ten feet beyond a 1964 Ford ton and a half tanker truck.

"Just like in Kansas," Factor solemnly announced.

"What?"

"It was a long time ago in another life," she explained. "What do you think is in that truck's tank?"

"I'd guess the stuff a crop duster sprays." he pointed to a bright blue biplane sitting on the far side of the hanger obviously used for that purpose.

"Perfect, in concentrated form, the fumes should be overpowering. Can we use the truck to ram their car?"

Carter glanced from the vehicle to the door. If Factor slid the door open enough for the truck to get out, then he might be able to use the old piece of Detroit iron as a weapon. That is, if it actually ran. Right now, the verdict was out on that rather important detail.

"See if you can get it started," Factor ordered as she jumped out and headed toward the door. "We ram them, maybe stun them, and then fill their car with insecticide."

Seeing no reason to argue with what was likely a memory from another time and another place, he rushed over to the truck and opened the driver's door. There were no keys in the ignition, in the ashtray, or over the sun visor, but there was one under the floor mat.

After pumping the gas pedal two times, he turned the switch. The old six cylinder coughed once and then fired up. Glancing through the windshield, he saw Factor, now poised by the door, give him a wave. A second later, she pulled the sliding door open, then ran to the back of the truck, hopped up on the bed, and grabbed the hose used to put the insecticide in the plane. She was ready for action. Yet before Carter could hit the gas, three shots were fired, one striking the crop-duster, the other two the back wall. The time for either death or action was at hand. The billionaire opted for action!

Carter shoved the vehicle into first, hit the gas, and popped the clutch. As the truck's nose emerged from the hanger, he spied the two men. One was still behind the wheel of the Chevy, the other, AR-15 in hand, was twenty feet in front of the car, approaching the hanger on foot. Jerking the steering wheel to the left, he hit the pedestrian before the man could take another shot. The left rear wheel jumped as it ran over the wannabe assassin who'd been pulled under the Ford. The remaining member of the duo, sensing the battle was not evolving in his favor, jerked the Chevy into reverse, but he'd only backed up twenty feet before the truck met the fleeing car nose to nose. The vehicle's airbags deployed but were likely not going to help. The force of the truck's impact knocked the engine off its mounts and through the firewall.

As the Ford rolled to a stop, its busted radiator spewed steam in all directions. While Carter exited the truck and ran back to the shooter he'd run over, Factor jumped off the bed, hose in hand, and began to spray streams of insecticide into the car. After grabbing the gunman's weapon, Carter reversed course and returned to the now incapacitated car. Factor had stopped her assault and dropped the hose onto the ground.

"Is he dead?" she asked as Carter moved toward the Chevy.

"Yeah, they both are." He paused and took a deep breath before grimly noting, "It looks the guy in the car was killed by the force of the steering wheel not what you sprayed. I hate killing."

"In this case, I don't think you had a choice. And just for the record, until the other night, I'd never killed anyone either, unless you count all the deaths I see in my head."

Carter nodded as he considered how many deaths, justified or otherwise, were hiding on the woman's DNA. That thought was numbing. "Let's go through their pockets and see if we can figure out who they are."

A few minutes later, when they'd both accomplished their morbid tasks, they stood beside the wrecked Chevy and compared notes. Factor went first.

"Casey Morris, from St. Louis, thirty-five. That's all I have."

"This one is Bill Zitech, and he's from Milwaukee. The only thing that might offer something of interest is his cell phone and a number he had jotted down on a Post-it note placed inside his billfold. I wish we could hack into his cell. If we could do that, we might stumble into a wealth of information. But everything's encrypted now."

Factor didn't bother answering. Retrieving the iPhone from the front seat of the car, she held it up in front of the dead man's face. The device immediately came on.

"Here you go," she announced.

Carter sheepishly shrugged. Why hadn't he thought of that?

"That obviously didn't come from one of your ancestor's experiences."

"No. Now what can we learn?"

Carter began by going to the messages. There were several previous texts all concerned with tracking Factor. That likely meant the man behind the hit was the person whose number he'd found in the billfold. The most recent message read, "We have them cornered. Do we just take out the woman, or do we kill the man too?"

The answering text was surprisingly restrained. "Do you know who the man is?"

"No."

"Then kill him too."

Factor took the phone and viewed the texts. As she read through them, Carter observed, "The bad news is they were after you and anyone who was with you. The good news is they don't know who I am. Now, let me see if I can manufacture another break. Give me the phone."

"What do you have in mind?"

"Just read along with me," he suggested. Then he typed … "Mission successful."

A few seconds later a reply appeared on the screen. "Are you sure she's dead?"

Carter texted back, "Do you want a picture?"

"Yes."

Carter smiled, studied his companion, and made a suggestion. "Max, lay on the ground and look dead?"

"What?"

"Just do it. I think this might just buy us some time."

As Factor sank to the concrete and arranged her body in a way mirroring someone who'd been cut down while running, Carter pulled a handkerchief from his pocket and sopped up as much of the dead driver's blood as he could. He then turned to Factor, who was now lying on her back with her legs splayed to the side, and dripped Zitech's blood all over her face.

"Hey," she protested.

"If you want to live, you have to look dead."

Once satisfied with his grotesque artwork, he barked, "Keep your eyes open with a blank stare." Using the dead man's phone, he took a couple of photos, studied them to see which one best framed what he was trying to sell, and then attached the picture to the text. As he did, a now bloody Factor pushed off the concrete runway.

"Was that necessary?" she asked.

"We'll soon know." A few seconds later, the iPhone's screen lit up. The text read, "You have to make sure no one ever finds the body."

Carter tapped in an assuring reply. "I have a place where she'll never be found. She'll spend eternity in a gravel pit." He paused for a moment before asking, "Will there be anything else?"

That answer fortunately opened another door. "Your payment will be waiting for you at the assigned place."

Carter immediately shot off a reply. "Too dangerous, must change locations."

"Where?"

Carter thought for a few seconds before answering. "I think I need to cool off in Arkansas. Is there anywhere you could get me the money there? I need it in cash"

"How about Little Rock?"

"When and where?"

"Wednesday, I can have someone meet you at the old Capitol building at three in the afternoon."

"Fine, but I'm going to send another man for the job."

"Why?"

"I need to stay out of sight. Casey met with an accident, and just in case someone saw him with me, I'd rather not be in public view for a while."

"Is Casey dead?"

"Yeah, got caught in the line of fire. I'll be putting him in the pit as well."

There was a pause before the next reply came. "Too bad. Who are you sending for the meeting?"

"His name is Bart. He's about six-two, lean—I'll have him wear a red shirt."

"Okay."

"I'm ditching the phone. I'll text you my new number when I get another cell."

Carter dropped the iPhone into his pocket.

"What was that all about?" Factor asked.

"The meeting in three days might give us a chance to find out who's behind this. If we know that, I'll be better able to protect you. In time, they'll surely learn you're not really dead." He glanced back toward the truck, smiled, then asked, "By the way, how did you know about the truck trick we used?"

"A grandmother, a couple of generations back, used it."

"At an airport?"

"Yep, but that was in 1933, and it took pouring the poison all over the bad guys to silence them. It was a lot easier this time."

"How did your great-great-grandmother get in a mess like that?"

"It was a case of mistaken identity. Two goons, and that's her word for them not mine, were trying to kidnap her because they thought her father had money. He didn't. She just looked like the woman they were after."

"Tell her thanks, that is if she pops back up in your head again. Now, let's grab the stuff out of our car and get moving."

"What about the bodies?" Factor asked.

Carter glanced at the mess on the runway. "We've stripped them of their identification. Let's move them into the hanger, find a chain, use the truck to pull the wrecked Chevy into the hanger, lock them in the trunk, and close the hanger door."

"And what does that accomplish?"

"If they're who I think they are," Carter explained, "which is professional hit men, it'll just look like a payback from one organized crime group to another. No one is going to tie us to it. And as little as this strip is used, it'll likely be days before the bodies are found."

"Still ..." she whispered.

"Let's get to work so we can go someplace where this won't happen again. I think we'll be safe at my cabin."

"What about your rental car? That'll tie you to this mess."

Carter, his mind in high gear, was not rattled. "National delivered it here for me to pick up. I was supposed to leave it in a parking spot in front of the office when I returned with the key locked inside the car. I'll call them before we take off and tell them it's ready. So, it'll be long gone before anyone discovers the bodies. And, even if someone does figure out it was here when I was, there's nothing to tie me to what happened. Why would anyone want to kill the world's most fun-loving playboy? And, as I gave a large donation to your school, I have a reason for being here that has nothing to do with whoever those guys are. We have work to do. Remember to wipe everywhere our hands have touched."

"Who do you think the they are?" a suddenly shaken Factor asked.

"My best guess is they were likely hired by the same folks who tried to get you who few days back. And if we hadn't gotten out of town, you'd likely be dead."

"So, it's not over?"

"It's not even started," he admitted.

Chapter 14

If our missteps and selfish impulses are carried over to future generations, can we ever fully escape our ancestors' sins? History must not only be faced—it must be studied, so we don't continue to make the same mistakes generation after generation.

———◆———

A s the DC3 roared away from Southern Illinois headed to the Ozarks, Max Factor eased back into the seat usually reserved for the copilot and took in the view. Since surviving the crash that proved responsible for ushering her into the world of imprinting, flying was far from her favorite mode of travel. Just looking at a plane usually caused chills. But on this occasion, some eight thousand feet above the earth, she had reason to relax. For the first time in several days, she didn't have to look over her shoulder or jump every time she heard a sound. High in the sky she was safe.

Beneath her were forests filled with trees fighting off Mother Nature's demands for change. For the moment most were green, their leaves clinging to branches, but in weeks those leaves were all doomed to fall. Winding around those trees were ribbons of concrete and people out for lazy Sunday drives. From time-to-time, cattle and sheep could be spotted grazing in fields, and corn, almost ready for harvest, reached toward the sky.

"Do folks still put together jigsaw puzzles," Factor wondered.

"I guess so, I still see them for sale in stores. Why do you ask?"

"There's the potential for one below us right now." She paused before noting, "John Spisbury created the first jigsaw puzzle in 1760. Many of his early puzzles were maps used to teach children the location of the various kingdoms in Europe."

"Do you remember him doing his first puzzle?"

"No, that's the history teacher in me. If any of my ancestors met him, they haven't shared that info with me."

Carter paused, looking almost like a schoolboy trying to find the words to ask out the high school homecoming queen. "Are you having any second thoughts about leaving with me?"

"I was," Factor admitted, her well-known blunt honesty delivered like a club, "until the airport."

"You wouldn't have been at the airport if you hadn't come with me."

"Yeah, but they'd have gotten me in my home or at school."

"Listen," as he spoke, Carter's expression was one of awe, "you saved us back there. It was your plan—you were the cool one, you had nerves of steel, and you faced death without blinking an eye. The poise you showed was unbelievable. I've been all over the world, I've been around people who have won medals for bravery, and you were something."

"Yeah, I was cool on volleyball courts, I didn't get rattled, but this was different. When I was in action back there, it wasn't my plan. In fact, the only original idea I had was opening the cell phone. Max would've been scared to death in a situation like that, so was I really Max?"

"You're okay now," Carter noted as he flipped on the autopilot and took his hand from the wheel. He then looked her way and asked, "Why are you staring at me?"

"I would have thought a man who'd spent his life in the public eye would be comfortable being the center of attention."

She grinned and intensified her gaze. Under her constant study, he was squirming. With all she'd been through in the past week, this was a welcome break. Perhaps in an attempt to break her concentration, his eyes moved to the instrument panel. Yet, she sensed he was still rattled. As her gaze remained locked on his face, as she fully inventoried his features, she asked herself again, who did he remind her of?

A voice came out of nowhere, and suddenly, she was in a different place and time. In an instant, the plane evaporated into thin air.

"Elizabeth."

The man who'd called her from across the pub, dressed in the most recent styles seen on the streets of London and Paris, was obviously from the highest reaches of society. His black boots were polished, and his shoulder length hair appeared to have been recently washed.

"Yes, Mr. Amos."

"What did you call me?" What is my name?"

"Sir Felix."

"Wench, you would do well to remember that. Now refill my ale."

"Yes, my lord."

When she returned to the pub's bar, Johnathon Jenkins' face was twisted in disgust. The forty-five-year-old redhead was no fan of Amos. Turning to where his patron could not see his lips, Jenkins whispered, "He needs to be horsewhipped."

The diminutive Elizabeth nodded. "But they'd put you in the stocks for that. Or maybe something worse."

"How the king could knight a man like that is beyond me. He's not a person to be trusted. I'll take his ale over. You go back in the kitchen and check on Mary."

"You don't have to do that.".

"Let me handle him. You stay in the kitchen until he's gone."

As Jenkins drew the glass of ale, Elizabeth moved back to the kitchen. While she liked Jenkins—he was a lion of a man, gentle, compassionate, and protective—working at his inn was no life for a sixteen-year-old girl. But with her parents dead, what choice did she have? Elizabeth walked through the kitchen and out the back door. In the cool mist that had consumed the fall afternoon, she moved to a stone fence, closed her eyes, and considered her life. She was bright, attractive, and eager to learn. Surely, there was a place for a woman like her.

A hand on her shoulder caused her blood to freeze. Turning, she found herself staring into the grinning face of Sir Felix. Before she could react, he covered her mouth with his left hand, and then, using his right, dragged her to the barn. Closing the door, he dropped his hand from her mouth, and, with lust in his eyes, studied her body. He moved in like a wolf after its prey. A second later, his fingers were at her neck, where he grabbed her dress and ripped it down to her waist. He was reaching for her bare shoulder when a voice pulled her away from a moment in a past that wasn't hers but had somehow become hers.

"You look as though you're a thousand miles away."

Though hundreds of years had passed, Factor still was peering into the face of Sir Felix Amos. Balling up her hands, she hissed, "Don't touch me."

"Max, what are you talking about?"

"I …" And then, she realized the person by her side was not a past tormentor. Even as she came to grips with where she was, the uncanny resemblance between Amos and Carter proved unnerving.

"Did you have a visitor from the past?" he asked.

"Yeah, and in that time a man who looked like you was bent on taking advantage of me." Gaining a bit of poise, she stiffened her lips and posed a biting question. "Anyone in your family tree named Felix Amos?"

Carter nodded. "Yeah, an English knight about four hundred years ago. According to family lore, he was a rogue. He was accused of attacking one of the ladies-in-waiting. The child that came from that rape would be my grandfather eleven generations removed. He was sixteen when he came to America in an attempt to escape the shame of his status as a bastard son of a man executed by the crown." He paused, licked his lips, and shook his head before asking, "Did you just meet Felix?"

"When your voice pulled me back to the present, he was attempting to rape me, or a woman named Elizabeth, whose eyes I was seeing through. I didn't find out what happened. I don't know if he was successful. But he looked just like you."

"It wasn't me, and the woman was not you."

She rubbed her brow. Why did this memory have to come back now? With this image in her head, how could she trust the man who had just saved her life?

"Can you always tell which life you are in?" Carter asked.

"Are you asking if there are moments when I lose myself and this world? Do you want to know if I cease to exist when one of them takes over my brain? Like I zoned out a while ago when I met your ancestor … and his intentions were far from honorable?"

"Yeah, I guess that's it?"

"At first, when the memories came to me, I had no problems. I could experience another life but still have a foot in my own world. But as time has gone on, I've often lost who and where I was. I'll be in another place and another time, and when I come out, I'll have lost two hours of my own life."

"That's got to be weird."

"Not as weird as when I experience life jumping."

"What's that?"

"It's like opening a door and stepping into something an ancestor did in 1850's New England, and then, without warning, I'm pulled into England in 1711, then back to America in 1930. It's like a relay race, and the baton keeps being passed. I come out of those moments with my mind fried. It's like having a hundred different people all talking at the same moment."

"Does that happen very often?"

"Those crazy moments usually happen at night when I'm trying to sleep."

"So, you have no control?"

"What I've discovered in the past few days is that during times when my life is on the line, the ancestors who come calling are there to help me stay alive. Maybe the rush of adrenalin gives me the ability to seek out who I need. But if that's the case, I don't realize I'm doing that, nor could I force myself into that mode."

Carter smiled. "You're miles ahead of Betty Rydell. She could never really find the ancestor she needed at the moment she needed them."

She glanced at Carter. He sounded as if he had empathy, which was a quality she'd never expected to find in the playboy. Yet, that was just the beginning. The attack at the airport had proven Carter was cool under fire. He didn't hesitate when circumstances dictated he save Factor's life and then showed his ability to think under pressure by finding a way to connect with the person behind the last hit. Had she seen the real man today or was what she'd read about him in the tabloids a more accurate picture of the billionaire? In time, if she had enough of that, she might figure that out. But if today was an indication, her life expectancy was going to measured in days not years.

Chapter 15

11:45 p.m.
Sunday, September 19
Carter's Cabin, Outside of Saddle, Arkansas

Safety is not a location, it's a state of mind.

———◆———

Elton Carter's cabin might have been in the middle of the Ozark foothills overlooking the South Fork of the Spring River, but it was anything but rustic. Yes, it was made from logs and native stone, but it featured three bedrooms, three full baths, a massive living area, a fully equipped gourmet kitchen, and a game room complete with pinball machines, pool table, and juke box. On top of that, the DC3 had landed on a paved runway outfitted with remote landing lights on a ridge just behind the house. "Good to see a billionaire who enjoys roughing it," Maxine Factor cracked after completing her walk through.

Carter shrugged, "It's what it is. Much smaller than my other five homes, but I like it. In the daytime, the river view is amazing, but the biggest bonus is we get all kinds of wildlife. It's like having the nature channel in every window.

"And they're showing up to ask, 'What in the world was this guy thinking?'" Factor raised an eyebrow. "You do realize this is luxury to me. The furniture in the place is worth more than my house. I mean, how big is the TV?"

"One-hundred twenty inches. I had it custom built. Oh, and I guess my perspective sometimes is a bit skewed."

"You think?" Factor's sarcasm dripped liked rain rolling off a roof in a heavy thunderstorm. "Your living room has more square footage than my whole house. You could park a Mini-Cooper in your fireplace. I'll bet every bedroom has a Sleep Number mattress."

"How did you know?" Carter asked with a shy grin. "By the way, take your pick of the bedrooms."

"Mine will be the one with the best lock on the door."

"You still don't trust me?"

"My head's full of men whose actions prove they can't be trusted."

"I get that, but I'll try to up your opinion of me. Meanwhile, we can relax here until we pick up the money in Little Rock. That little trip might just give us a lead on who's trying to kill you."

"Yeah," Factor snapped, "that's just the reminder I needed. Surrounded by all this, I'd almost forgotten that I've become a target."

"You can't let yourself forget," Carter warned. "We both have to be on our toes at all times. Just because we're in the middle of the country, don't assume you can't be found. Before we go to bed, I'll have the alarm system fully activated on both the house and property. If a rabbit wanders into the yard, I'll receive an alert."

"Good to know, but still not something I want to hear." She glanced out a window toward the plane. "I'll take the blue bedroom."

"It's yours. I'll go get the bags from the plane in a few minutes. Before I make that trek, do you want something to drink or eat? The man who takes care of this place for me stocked the shelves. We have anything from ice cream to salads to steak."

"I'll hold off. My appetite's not come back since what happened at the airport." She grinned. "By the way, when I make a trip with a billionaire, I expect to go first class. Where was the meal on the plane? Did I miss that?"

He shook his head. "Your students must love sparring with you."

"They lose much more often than they win." Her blue eyes displayed both humor and fire.

"I'm sure they do. And I'm sure I will too."

"So," she announced, her tone more subdued, "you believe they can't find us here."

"I don't see how. The only one who knows who you're with is the president of the school, and he's promised to keep quiet. If he does, it's worth another twelve million to the college. But we still have to plan for the unexpected. If whoever is trying to kill you discovers you're with me, then they'll no doubt start going through the list of the properties I own. But I think we've bought some time."

"Nice to know the odds are on our side," she said. "Unless someone's after you and not me. Surely, with the life you've lived and the money you have, there've been some unsavory types who want to kill or kidnap you."

"I've been in a few scrapes; I've actually made decisions that led to a few deaths. Not murders, and I had no intention of folks dying because of my plans—it happened because I gave the approval for projects—things like construction accidents and deaths on some of the archaeological digs I've financed. While I've got the means to easily payoff lawsuits, the deaths still eat at me."

"What about the deaths of those two men at the airport? Will they haunt you?"

"Yeah, being directly responsible for killing someone isn't something I'll forget. But in this case, I'm glad it was them and not you."

He strolled into the kitchen and retrieved a bottle of water. As Factor watched, the confident man seemed to morph into an insecure child. His expression displayed pain that men normally didn't show.

"Let's be honest," Carter admitted, "being born wealthy is one of the most incredible pieces of luck a man can have. Whatever I wanted, I could have. But it has also made me a target. I was kidnapped when I was twelve and held for ransom. Even after the money was paid, they talked about killing me."

Factor studied her host, trying to peer inside his mind—the view revealed nothing. With that door closed, she opted to do a bit of digging. "Obviously they didn't."

"No, but it wasn't because they suddenly developed hearts." He looked toward the arched ceiling. "There were two of them, just average guys, no one you'd look at twice on the street. One of them worked for my dad as an accountant. When I overheard them arguing about who was going to kill the boy, I decided I wouldn't wait for them to make up their minds. The windows in the room where they held me were locked, so I couldn't get out, but there was an old kerosene lamp filled with oil. I poured it out onto a towel, and when the guy came in to do the job, I lit the towel with a match and threw it at him. It was so heavy with oil, it wrapped around his head like a glove. He screamed and dropped his gun as he fought to get the towel off his face. I grabbed the revolver, and as the second man, my father's accountant, walked in, I fired three times, then ran out of the house and kept running until I found help." He paused before grimly announcing, "Imagine being twelve and killing two men. That was quite a jump-start into adulthood."

"You had no choice. Kind of like me when I knocked Kattan into the flames."

"Yeah, I know. But the only reason it happened to either of us was because we had something that made us targets. If we'd been normal, in my case just another kid from a regular family, and in your case not having the gift, then no one would care about us."

"I'd love to be just another flower on the wall. Just a history professor who only knew what she'd read in books."

"Yeah, I get that. But as for me, I like being a billionaire too much to give it up. Money is a drug that creates an addiction that's impossible to quit." Carter opened the refrigerator and retrieved a Coke this time. After twisting the cap off and taking a swig, he looked back at his guest. "Max, I've been wondering about something."

"What's that?"

"Your name? Why would your parents name you after the king of the cosmetic world?"

Factor shook her head. "They didn't. My former husband's name was Factor, my maiden name was Marks. As I'd already gotten my degrees using the name Factor, I stuck with it after the divorce."

"Maxine's not a name you hear much. Were you named after a relative?"

"I never asked where Mom got it. Knowing didn't seem important. After all, being a girl named Max had a certain cool factor that the Crystals or Heathers couldn't touch. But a few months ago, I figured it out."

He pulled out a stool at the bar and sat down. As he did, she shut her eyes.

"Are you here or someplace else?" he asked.

She opened her eyes and smiled, "I'm here."

"How did you find out about your name?"

"I fell into a great-grandmother's thoughts," Factor explained as she crossed the room and eased onto the stool opposite her host. "As a teen, her favorite group was the Andrews Sisters. Her name was Delores, but she dressed and acted like Maxine Andrews, the lead singer for the act." Factor closed her eyes—her face now displayed a hint of pain. "I've been inside her skin. In other words, I've been there when she looked into a mirror and sang "Boogie Woogie Bugle Boy" holding a brush like it was a microphone. I've put nickels in juke boxes to play Andrews Sisters records. I can tell you all the lyrics to all their hits. And yet, I'd never even heard of them until those memories were awakened." She frowned. "That's what's weird, Maxine Factor has no knowledge of the Andrews Sisters, but Delores Risner does. Note I used present tense, not past. When I see her, she's not in the past, she's very much alive. It's not me going back to the past, it's the past coming to me. My memories and knowledge are hers. And they're vivid, and they're real. It seems like it happened to me, but it didn't. Can you understand that?"

"Actually, because I've known another like you, I think I can."

She pushed away from the bar and walked into the living area. Standing in the middle of the forty-by-forty-foot room, staring into a massive fireplace that tonight contained only a stack of unlit wood, she balled her hands. "How much trouble do you have remembering your life? Is it in sharp focus or are your memories kind of vague?"

"Most are kind of fuzzy. Even things I did last week aren't all that clear."

"And that's the way it is with most of my own memories. But ..." She licked her lips before turning to face her host. "... the memories of my ancestors are all in high definition. The sights, the sounds, the smells, they're all vivid." She considered her words before posing a question. "You said they call people like me imprints?"

"Yeah."

"That's accurate. The memories of others fighting for space in my head are as clear as a mountain pool. And while living with my great-grandmother's fascination with the Andrews Sisters is fun and warm, there are other things I recall in detail I wish I hadn't lived. You see, that's what happens, I don't remember things, I live them." Factor paused and turned her eyes back to the fireplace. "And then they're in my memories forever. And, at times, I get confused. I have to ask myself, 'Was that me or someone else?' That's how real they are."

"I think I understand."

Her eyes still focused straight ahead, Factor shook her head. "Delores was brutally abused by a neighbor when she was fifteen. He burned her several times with a cigarette. He beat her with his huge fists. She never told anyone, but I not only know it, I lived it. Do you understand what that means? It wasn't her, in my mind, it was me! I was assaulted by a monster of a man who was about forty. He smelled of cigars and cheap whiskey. He was dirty, he had a four-day-old beard. There was grease under his fingernails. He beat me up, not just my grandmother—listen to me—he beat us up, not just her, but us, and then threw us away. Consider what it means to have lived that in vivid detail."

"I don't think I can."

"And that ugly feeling is just one of the raw, foul moments I've experienced from many other past generations. I can't just look at them as if they happened to someone else. I feel them as they happen to me. I can't make that separation." Her blue eyes were alive, her face drawn. "All of us try to bury the pain in our own lives. We do everything we can to erase it. But I carry the pain of generations. And it's the bad times more than the good that fight their way into my head. I don't think it's the volume of memories that causes imprints to go crazy or take their own lives. I think it's all the pain and suffering. A person can only handle so much."

Factor walked back toward Carter, took a seat at the bar again, and then folded into herself. She remained mute for a few minutes. When she finally spoke, her words were haunting.

"Back in my office, you called imprinting a gift. It's not, it's a curse. Some of us are not even comfortable with many of the intimate moments of our own lives, but I have to live the very intimate moments of others' lives. I know things that I should never know, and it's horrific.

"My great-grandmother had my grandmother when she was twenty-three. Perhaps after that time, Delores found a way to come to grips with the beating she took. Maybe she somehow found peace. But I'm not privileged to those memories. They aren't on my DNA. So, there's no resolution in my mind. I'm still dealing with the hurt. The wound is still open. And that's not the only one. I kind of alluded to this during our flight, but with each new ancestor who enters my head comes more heartache and heartbreak. Right now, I'm carrying the wounded souls of twenty or more people. I barely have the strength to live with those, much less the others that might soon be knocking on my mind's door. Imagine trying to focus, imagine trying to sleep!"

"Your story, it's not new to me, but if it's any consolation, you're handling it better than the other imprint I knew."

"Well, I guess that's something."

"What about your parents?" Carter asked. "What can you tell me about them?"

"You mean my memories of them or their memories?"

"Either."

"In truth, my mother's memories are vague. One of the few I've ever lived from her life is her senior prom. It's not a story worth telling. Just a boring date with a loser. But she was a wonderful, caring lady, who was a bit of an airhead at times. Still, she was all the mom I could have asked for. When she died, it left a big hole in my world."

"And your father?"

"It's strange, I don't possess a single one of his life experiences. Maybe it was because he was a bit distant. He was an officer at a bank, was in a lot of civic and social clubs, but he never seemed to connect with me, my brother, or even my mother. Rather than ever being in love, I got the idea my parents just settled for each other. He was not a bad man, he gave me what I needed, but it was if we were strangers in areas where it mattered."

"How did they die?" Carter asked.

"Cancer got Mom. Dad committed suicide."

They grew silent—the only sound was the ticking of a wall clock. There was surely much to be said, but neither of them knew where to begin.

"I'll get the bags out of the plane," Carter offered.

"Yeah, I need some sleep. If they'll let me sleep. That's been my biggest problem. They all want to party at night."

"I'll bring your bags to the blue room."

"Thanks for listening. I've never shared what it's like with anyone. It's good to at least put some of it out in the open."

"I wish I had some answers."

"When are we going to see that doctor?"

"I'll set things set up tomorrow. It'll probably be a few days down the road."

"Good," Factor whispered, "The sooner the better. I'm honestly not sure I can handle this for much longer."

Chapter 16

The most difficult questions always seem to center on faith. In a very real sense, when faced with a moral dilemma, those with no faith have a much easier time deciding what to do. They go with their gut and ignore their heart.

———◆———

"Who has the bigger problem, us or the Vatican?"

The question, posed by Ben Greenberg, a small, forty-year-old Brit who had lived in London his entire life, was not rhetorical. He was looking for an answer. His black hair, pasty complexion, and green eyes reflected the fact his family had called the United Kingdom home for five generations, but he was not just another middle-aged English citizen. In his heart and mind, Greenberg was very much a Jew. He had memorized the Torah, could read the book in the ancient languages of the original scribes, and was devout in his devotion to a faith many claimed but few in the island nation actually practiced. He'd even been a rabbi for a few years before being pulled back into his family's business. Today, he had traveled by train to Newcastle, to meet with three like-minded members of his faith on a farm just outside of town. Each had concerns of what the imprint in America might remember about one dynamic event that had shaped almost every corner of the globe and touched, in one way or another, every person on the planet. And it wasn't the event that so worried him, it was how the story ended.

As the group sat around the table in the small cottage's kitchen, the one female in the quartet, Indira Morel, an exotic, dark-eyed Israeli, stared out the window at cattle grazing in the field. Morel was educated at New York University before a move to London, and, unlike Greenberg, who was involved in his family's software concerns and almost a slave to the modern world, she was devoted to the past. In the world of ancient explorers, she was a legend. Archeology had taken her to all the world's major ruins and, most recently, ten months studying an unknown civilization in Brazil. Yet, while her papers had been published in a dozen different languages, and she'd even appeared on a cable television series examining ancient civilizations, she was most famous because of an affair with a benefactor. For almost two years, she had partied across Europe with Elton Carter. Those late-night adventures, the fodder for tabloid newspapers and web pages, had made her one of the most recognized women on the planet. While magical at the time, after being very publicly pushed aside by Carter, that relationship was now one she'd wished she'd avoided.

To Morel's right was Laz Solash. Dressed in tweed, his gray hair and brown eyes gave him the look of a professor, but in truth, the man had made his money in the import business. Born in Italy, but raised in the States, he'd moved to England a decade before. A millionaire many times over, he was a man of deep convictions and completely loyal to Israel. Though he'd never married, he'd nevertheless paid for the college educations of forty Israeli children and, after they obtained their degrees, found them jobs. His character was unquestionable, and his quest to protect Israel at all costs was at the forefront of everything he did.

Between Greenberg and Solash sat twenty-eight-year-old Micah Smith. A stocky man with large cheeks, swarthy skin, and brown, wavy hair, Smith was a rabbi in Newcastle. He'd been educated in the Holy Land, his father had been a local politician, and his grandfather one of the first generals in the Israeli army. A former amateur boxer, Smith was competitive and driven, but was anything but impulsive. The rabbi never acted without intense study and preparation.

The four were part of a secret group of three hundred and seventy-five who worked behind the scenes to make sure Great Britain kept the needs of Israel ahead of those of other Middle Eastern countries. As the chosen leaders of the Star, they met on a regular basis to discuss issues dealing with both politics and economics. No one, not even members of their family, knew of their involvement with the underground organization that had at its disposal hundreds of millions of dollars to influence government policy.

"None of you is very talkative today," Greenberg snapped. "So, I'll answer my own question. In my view, we have nothing to be concerned about. At this time, I feel we need to focus our energies and resources on uncovering radical Islamic cells in Britain and funneling that information to Scotland Yard. Of course, the key is making sure that the Yard, along with anyone else, never discovers our organization and its purpose."

Morel, her eyes reflecting her passion, shook her head. She appeared disgusted, and her tone reflected her feelings. "Ah, a purpose that just keeps changing. When the Star was formed forty years ago, it was to feed information to government officials that would help the Israeli state. Then it morphed into a behind the scenes lobby group that literally bribed politicians for votes. And now, we pretend to fight terrorism." She paused, frowned, and lightly tapped the table with her fingertips. "Gentlemen, what we have really become is a group who has decided that every Muslim in the world is our enemy. Kind of ironic when you consider that each of us had close childhood friends that were Muslims."

"Times have changed," Greenberg argued.

"And," Morel replied, "you called us here today to develop a strategy to keep a part of history in the dark. Now, you tell us that you've already decided what should happen. If that's the case, why did we leave what we were doing?" She cocked an eyebrow before demanding, "Is this just so you can claim we made a decision that was solely yours?"

"That's not what I meant," Greenberg suggested. "I was just giving my opinion. I assumed that you each felt the same."

"Don't assume anything," Morel snapped, "we each come here with a different point of view."

"So, tell me what you think," an impatient Greenberg shot back.

Morel nodded. "Here's the first point. In the matter that brought us to this place today, we don't yearn for the truth, but rather we want to make sure history continues to hide any truth we might not want revealed. Isn't that the only reason this woman in America holds any interest for us? We're afraid of her because we fear the message of the Christian church."

"The Christian church is nothing more than a misguided Jewish cult," Solash argued. "I doubt Jesus ever existed and no one rises from the dead. So, there are billions worshiping a fairytale."

"Then," Morel asked, "what's the fear of exposing that? Wouldn't it be natural for most of those who are Christians to become Jews if they were given the facts you believe? And if that were the case, wouldn't Israel immediately become the most powerful nation on the planet?"

"Jesus existed," Smith argued. He paused, as if measuring his words before dipping deeper into the discourse. "It would be easier if it was not true, but I've found too many references in history written by both Jews and Romans of that period to argue that fact. Now the resurrection, that's another story altogether. That's the fable."

Morel smiled, "I agree with you. So, with that in mind, why are you worried about the imprint? We've been in this same place at other times—"

Greenberg cut in, "And each one of those imprints died long before they remembered back even five hundred years. That's why, now that I've had time to think about this matter, I believe we should just ignore it."

"A man of moral character," Solash explained, "does not gamble. What if this new woman ... what's her name?"

"Factor," Greenberg replied.

"What if Factor is different? What if she can handle the memories? What if she remembers back far enough to have a relative who saw Jesus rise from the dead? Then it proves that we turned our backs on the real messiah."

Smith laughed.

"What's so funny?" Solash demanded.

"A few minutes ago," Smith reminded the older man, "you claimed Jesus didn't even exist. That he was a fable. Now you're worried about the reality of the resurrection." The rabbi pointed a finger at the millionaire. "You can't have it both ways. If what you believe about Jesus is the truth, then this woman, even if her memories go back two thousand years, will never recall the resurrection. In fact, she might be able to verify what we believe rather than what the Vatican states as fact. I think she's more important to us alive than dead. I actually hope she is able to handle this gift and will tell us what happened all those centuries ago."

"I agree," Morel announced leaping back into the debate. "I see this as a way to strengthen our faith. So, I'm with Micah, I also want her to remember back to the first century."

Greenberg pushed his chair back, stood, and walked over to the window. As he gazed out at the rolling fields, he made an observation that he hoped would satisfy all of those present.

"I'm not risking anything." He turned back toward the table. "My sources tell me that, even though the Pope is against it, a small group inside the Vatican is ready to move if Factor's ability to see the past goes back too far. It seems they have even less faith than Solash."

The blood rushed to the millionaire's face. Solash was a man of integrity coupled with emotion, and he wasn't one to take that kind of jab, even if it was delivered with a grin. Yet, before he could speak, Smith jumped in with the one question that needed to be answered.

"So, we do nothing?"

"I think that's the wise plan at this time," Greenberg assessed.

Solash frowned. Without speaking, he got up from the table, put his hat on, walked through the living room, and out the front door.

"He's a man of strong convictions," Smith noted, "but few words." Turning back to look at his host, he added, "Ben, I'm with you on this one, but do keep me in the loop if you hear anything more from our sources in Rome."

"I will."

"Goodbye, my friends," Smith announced as he followed in Solash's steps and made his exit.

Once the front door closed, Greenberg strolled back to the table. For at least a minute, he studied the woman, as if trying to read her mind, before asking, "Would you like some tea?"

"No. What I really want is to meet this woman. Imprints have long fascinated me."

Greenberg eased into a chair and leaned forward. "It sounds like you know quite a bit about them. Where did you get your information?"

"It was one of the few good things that came from my association with Elton Carter. He spent time with one. During our discussions, he convinced me of the importance of imprints' potential to verify historical records. For a woman who has to gain knowledge by looking at bits and pieces of the past found in rubble and ruins, and then comparing those pieces to written history, having the opportunity to question someone who was there would prove invaluable."

"Even if her answers might invalidate something you believe?"

She shrugged. "I've actually thought about that a lot."

"And where did those thoughts lead you?"

"To insecurity. None of us wants to be proven wrong. But if Jesus was the actual messiah, and I were to hear that from the lips of someone who was there and witnessed it ..." She paused and pushed her fingers through her raven hair before finishing her thought. "Well, consider this, as a Jew I have a lot less to lose than a Christian who discovers Jesus simply died on the cross. I could embrace a risen Jesus, but what would those two billion Christians embrace if Christ didn't rise? As the foundation of Western civilization is built on the spread of the Christian faith, that's something to think about. And, and thanks for presiding over the shortest meeting in the history of the Star. Let's make this a habit rather than an exception."

Morel rose, nodded toward her host, and exited the small home. Yet even after she was gone, her words lingered in the air.

Greenberg had never considered Morel's point of view. Pinning down that one fact in history, having proof that it was or wasn't true, would change everything for everyone he knew. It could also bring along with it great insecurity and, maybe, chaos. With that in mind, he wondered if he was wrong. Maybe Factor did need to be eliminated.

Chapter 17

It's not as much what you know as who you know that determines whether you fail or succeed or if you live or die. Just knowing the right person to go to for answers lowers the risk in any situation.

———◆———

"Mr. James?"

Robert Hall was a slightly built, balding man about seventy. He'd begun his academic career as a professor of mathematics before migrating into administration. Open, friendly, curious, and dedicated, he'd been the president of Washington-Lincoln College for twelve years.

In response to the friendly and hopeful greeting, William Dixon smiled and nodded. Today, his cover was Stephen James, a wealthy New Yorker, who had charmed his way into the president's office with the promise of a large donation to the college, but giving money away was the last thing on his mind. What he wanted was information and he was going to get it no matter the cost.

"Please have a seat," Hall suggested, "We can talk more comfortably if we take the chairs by the window. It's also the perfect place to enjoy a beautiful view of campus."

"Thank you, Dr. Hall." Dixon moved quickly to the leather, high-backed chair, but waited until his host arrived before sitting. Then, after spending a bit of time staring out the window, in a gesture to gain trust, he commented, "You're right, the view is just breathtaking. Your campus is the type of place where I'd want my grandkids to come. It drips of tradition and character, and both those things add so much to the educational experience.

"Thank you. I've felt that way since the first time I came to WLC. While I didn't go to school here, when they hired me forty-two years ago to teach math, I knew when I walked in I was home. We've grown since then, but what you see out that window is very much like it was in 1980. Let's just say I feel as though I was born a Statesmen. That's our mascot."

"Very appropriate. And, if I hadn't already fallen in love with this school, your personal testimony would've paved the way for me to embrace it with all my heart and soul. Just wonderful!"

Dixon's words were working magic. Hall was completely buying the visitor's lies.

"I believe," Hall quizzed, "you said you were interested in giving a gift to our history department?"

"That's my intention. I've heard some very good things about one of your professors. And that motivated my coming to Washington-Lincoln. Of course, I'd also heard of your outstanding leadership and wanted to seek you out as well."

"Thank you. And who is the professor?"

"Dr. Factor."

"Ah, Maxine. Yes, she is extraordinary. I keep thinking one of the large universities or Ivy League schools will steal her from us. Yet, she assures me she loves it here in Mt. Vernon. I hope she continues to feel that way for the rest of her career."

"I'm sure." Dixon answered as he took a moment to study the office. The room matched its outgoing host perfectly. The rich, wood-paneled walls were decorated with framed photographs of campus life. The carpet was deep blue, matching the school's color. The furniture was obviously old, but recently restored. It reeked of history and heritage, something the college president himself embraced. Turning to once more face his host, Dixon tossed out a compliment. "Dr. Hall, everything about this place has a very historical feel to it."

"We've tried to make that a theme. It's been our goal to balance progress with a reverence for our past. It's not an easy line to walk. But we must remember our history to understand our future course."

"That's true. Today, more than ever, history guides my life's mission. Which reminds me of why I'm here. Dr. Factor's viewpoints on history interest me. Her articles in *The Smithsonian* and *American Life* make me believe she has traveled to the places and lived in the times she writes about."

"She has a rare gift, and I think it's born of passion. I've found that the great professors feel called to teach."

"I have no doubt. I went by her office before coming over here, but she wasn't there. I was looking forward to meeting her and talking about uses for my donation."

Those words must have been the opening the president was looking for. "If you don't mind me asking, how much are we talking about?"

"Initially, a quarter of a million dollars designated for scholarships for students who otherwise would not be able to financially attend the school. If that works out, then next year, there would be the chance for much more funding."

Hall raised his eyebrows and smiled. "That's very generous. There are many who want to come here but simply can't afford the tuition."

"Now," Dixon cut in and asked, "when can I visit with Dr. Factor?"

"Sadly, that'll be a problem. Maxine left for sabbatical yesterday. A donor offered her an opportunity to do some research that was simply too good to turn down. In order to borrow her for the semester, he gave WLC several million dollars."

Dixon leaned back in his chair and frowned. Suddenly, his job had grown much more difficult. He'd developed a plan that would allow him a clean kill and an easy exit, but that revolved around Factor's presence in Mount Vernon. If she was someplace else, he'd have to do more research.

"Dr. Hall," Dixon politely inquired, "The person who gave the gift, could you share his name? As I travel in the circles of history buffs, I'd bet I know him."

"I wish I could—he was both engaging and fascinating. With your mutual interest in history and Dr. Factor, I know you would have loved visiting with him. But I promised the donor's identity would remain anonymous. I can share this—he seemed a very modest young fellow, much less ego than I'd expected after watching him on television. When I announce the gift, I'll not mention his name. He insisted that if word leaked out it could cost the school the twelve-million-dollar gift he promised for next year. I hope you understand."

"Of course, but could you at least tell me where Dr. Factor went? I'd love to know what project she's working on. Perhaps I could even visit her there."

"I actually don't know. Everything was on the hush-hush. I tried calling her this morning, but her cell goes straight to voice mail. I'm assuming she's going to be off the grid for a few months. A lot of our people work that way when they're on sabbatical."

"And there's no way for me to reach the donor?"

"As I told you, I can't share his name. I wish I could, but I can't go back on a promise, especially one with that kind of value attached to it."

Dixon nodded and smiled. Reaching into his suit coat pocket, he retrieved a small bottle of pills. "Could I have some water? It's time for my medication." There was nothing wrong with Dixon, the ruse was simply a prop to move the conversation into a new direction.

Hall rose, moved quickly to a back wall, and opened a small refrigerator. A few seconds later, he returned and handed a water bottle to his guest.

"What's your medical issue?" Hall asked. "That's if you don't mind me asking."

"At my age, I deal with a myriad of things, most are stress related—I'm sure you know what I mean."

"I certainly do. Though I'm healthy and feel great now, I've actually survived two heart attacks."

Dixon's homework had made him well aware of that fact. After downing the breath mint with a sip of water, he reached for his briefcase. "I believe I promised you a gift."

This was the moment every small college president relished. As Hall smiled, his eyes followed his guest's every move.

Dixon pulled out a checkbook. A few seconds later, after some hurried scribbling, he handed the gift to the president. "This $250,000 must be used for scholarships."

"I'll see that it is."

The president was too focused on the gift to closely watch his guest's actions. He never saw Dixon pull a syringe from a side pocket in his briefcase, quickly move his arm forward, and jam a needle into Hall's thigh. The shocked president looked up, moved his lips as if to speak, and then fell forward out of his chair and onto the floor. As he observed the president take his final breath, Dixon sighed. This had been Plan B. If Hall had just given him the name he needed, it would have never been necessary.

Dixon waited a few seconds, checked Hall's pulse, retrieved the check, then moved across the room and quietly locked the door. Wasting no time, he sifted through the papers on the president's desk. There was nothing there revealing the college's newest patron. The file cabinet also proved a wasted search. Dixon was ready to concede he'd killed a man for nothing, when he noted a file resting on a top of a copying machine. It was simply labeled "Carter." Opening it revealed that a gift of twelve million dollars had been recorded and deposited. Behind those notes was a copy of a thank you letter Hall had written to the donor. Dixon's eyes locked onto the benefactor's name—Elton Carter.

Returning the file to its place, Dixon retrieved his briefcase, and after quietly unlocking the door, stepped into the outer office. The president's administrative assistant was nowhere in sight. With no need to explain his departure or call attention to the dead man, Doctor Death exited the office suite, descended the stairs, and casually made his way to his rented car. Five minutes later. he was outside of town and headed to St. Louis. As he drove, he plotted his next move.

If Carter wanted the woman, it had to be for one of the billionaire's pet projects. The fact the man was a jet-setter meant the tabloid press might just have a lock on his current archaeological pursuit. The area would likely be even more remote than the college campus, making his job that much easier. But there was a troubling question. Why would Elton Carter pay twelve million dollars to obtain the services of an obscure college professor? A small college teacher, no matter how good she was, was not worth that. Could the billionaire have discovered Factor was an imprint? If that were the case, his job had just gotten a lot more difficult. Carter wouldn't just want to tap into her knowledge, he'd want to possess her mind, body, and soul. To effectively do that, he'd keep her out of sight.

Chapter 18

2:45 p.m.
Tuesday, September 20
1301 Holly Avenue, Mount Vernon, Illinois

Sometimes having the devil in sight is the best way to keep from falling into his grasp.

———◆———

Rocky Smith sat in his rented Ford Edge in front of Ulysses Goldsmith's home. Before leaving DC, Smith had gone through everything the agency had on Maxine Factor, and it was her connection to the old AP reporter than rang a warning bell. Goldsmith was a man who constantly found stories others missed. If anyone knew she was an imprint, it would've been the old master scribe. The fact he had left his estate to her seemed to prove they were tight. When Smith discovered Factor had left town to points unknown, the agent opted to take a look through Goldsmith's home. The careful search revealed nothing except that someone had beaten him to the prize.

A vibration pulled a disappointed Smith's attention from the house to his cell. A news notification revealed the local university president had apparently died of a heart attack. On most days, this would mean nothing. But coupled with Factor's disappearance, it didn't feel quite right. After checking a map app, he started the car and motored over to campus. He arrived just as the local police chief finished giving an interview to about a half dozen members of the media. As he studied the small gaggle of men and women, a face stood out. He'd seen one of the reporters' photos in the CIA's Goldsmith file.

"Mason Hardin," Smith quietly announced as he approached a rather haggard-looking writer. As their eyes met, it was apparent the reporter was on edge. Why would a man who'd taken on organized crime and political corruption be nervous while covering the natural death of a small college's administrator? It made no sense.

"Have we met?" Hardin asked, his eyes darting from side to side as if looking for a quick exit.

"The name's Smith, I'm CIA."

"A bit out of your territory," Hardin suggested, "I was under the impression you weren't supposed to operate on American soil."

"I'm not here in any official capacity. I just happened to be in town and heard about the death. My curiosity drove me to check it out."

"That sounds both morbid and inauthentic."

Essentially, Hardin just called Smith a liar, but somehow the fancy words made it sound more palatable. As the reporter continued to crane his neck as if looking for someone he was trying to avoid, the agent tried to keep the line of communication open.

"So, Hall died of a heart attack?"

Hardin glanced over both shoulders before leaning closer and whispering, "You probably know as much as I do. He'd had a couple of attacks in the past, so it all adds up. As there's no story here, I guess I need to get moving."

Smith's instincts screamed the reporter wasn't here because of Hall. If Goldsmith knew about Factor, then he likely shared that information with his friend. Smith stepped closer. "Listen, Hardin, you're a big-time player—they wouldn't have sent you down to Mt. Vernon just to cover the death of an obscure college president. Besides, you couldn't have gotten from Chicago to Mount Vernon that quickly. My gut tells me you were already here for some other reason."

"You're barking up the wrong tree," Hardin shot back. "I need to get going. But if I ever do an investigative piece on the CIA, I'll look you up."

Smith wasn't going to allow Hardin off the hook that easily. Perhaps it was time to be extremely blunt.

"Our file says you're ice cold under fire, but that's not the case right now. You're scared to death. It's written all over your face. So, let's talk about why."

Hardin again nervously glanced around the campus, checking out every face he saw, before leaning closer. "And, if you've read a file on me, you're not here on a holiday."

"Okay, I'll admit that, but it just affirms that we need to talk."

"I doubt it," Hardin muttered as he pushed past Smith and began walking toward the closest parking lot.

Smith quickly considered his options. Locating Factor was the only way to get Clegg and the committee off his tail. So while he couldn't hold the reporter, he still had to find a way to pick his brain.

"Goldsmith and the imprint!" Smith called out.

The ploy worked. Hardin stopped in his tracks.

After the reporter turned, the agent asked, "Now do we talk?"

"I've got nothing to lose. That's unless you're here to kill me."

"What makes you say that?"

"Because someone, my belief is the CIA, took out Goldsmith. And now that someone is trying very hard to extinguish my light."

This was news the agent hadn't expected. He'd been told Goldsmith had died of natural causes. As for Hardin, why would the agency want him out of the picture? Then it hit him. Clegg! He closed the gap between himself and the reporter, leaned close, and made an offer.

"If that's really the case, let's talk somewhere safe."

"Pretty much anyplace is safe for you," Hardin sniped, "for me, not so much. And, if the CIA did take out Goldsmith because of what he knew, why would I want to be alone with one of their agents?"

"My car's at the end of this walk. It's a white Ford Edge."

"Good for you."

"Hardin, if what you say is true, you have every right not to trust me, but we need to talk. Follow me to the car, and I'll prove to you that I'm not the person you need to fear."

Hardin shrugged and briskly walked the hundred yards to the parking area. He stopped and turned when he was in front of the Edge.

After making sure no one was watching, Smith reached under his suit coat and pulled out his service weapon. Without hesitation, he handed it to Hardin.

"I'll drive," Smith announced, "and you hold onto the gun. If I threaten you in any way, pull the trigger."

The agent unlocked the doors and jumped into the Ford. The reporter, who'd spent his professional life taking risks, took a deep breath and joined Smith. Once they were away from the campus, Hardin opened up the dialogue.

"Goldsmith? Is that why you're here?"

"Do I have your guarantee that this is off the record?"

"If you're asking if I'll use your name in a story, I won't. But I'm making no guarantees about what I write."

Smith grimly smiled. "Listen, there's a price on my head too. If what I'm working on goes south, then my life's not worth a plug nickel. So, I'm asking you to protect more than my job."

The reporter considered the confession for several seconds before nodding. "Okay, I'll listen."

"And I get to approve anything you use in stories?"

Hardin grudgingly agreed.

"I'm not here for Goldsmith, though he's linked to my reason for coming to town."

"Then it must be the imprint," Hardin suggested.

"How do you know about that?"

"Goldsmith did, that's the reason he was killed. He shared that news with someone, probably in DC, and it cost him his life."

"So, he was murdered?"

"You don't seem shocked," Hardin noted.

"I don't shock easily. And it makes sense." After turning right onto a rural, tree-lined highway, he looked over at his passenger. "I'm guessing that you know who the imprint is."

Hardin seemed momentarily confused. When he spoke his tone was cautious, much like a high school student who wasn't sure about the question the teacher had called on him to explain. "I might."

The reporter was shrewd. He wasn't going to be tricked into spilling anything valuable. Smith respected that.

"Hardin, I already know who she is—Dr. Maxine Factor. And I guess you know that Factor has left town."

"I found that out this morning."

"Any idea where she went?"

"No. And that's the truth, not a reporter trying to conceal a source."

"Then you and I have two things in common. Neither of us knows where she's gone, and we both need to find her. Now how did you happen into this mess?"

The fact Smith knew Factor's name loosened up the reporter's tongue a little. "Goldsmith contacted me about a story. He was dead by the time I got here, but he left me enough information to figure out who he'd exposed. Yet, before I even left to come down here, someone knew I'd been alerted and tried to kill me."

Smith glanced down the long stretch of highway. Who was behind the hit on Hardin? Was it the agency? Or was it the group that hired the man who had stalked the professor last week? It was obvious Hardin didn't have a clue. That's why he was so jumpy.

"They tried to gun you down?" Smith asked.

"Actually, it was a bomb. Three, if you count the apartments."

"No idea who it was?"

"The same folks who got Goldsmith is my guess."

"What are you doing to protect yourself?" Smith asked.

"Not going back to Chicago. I only came out in the open today because I thought Hall's death might have been tied to Goldsmith and Factor."

"We both know Factor is gone, do you have any idea where?"

"On a sudden sabbatical is what I was told."

"That gives us something. What's your take on Hall's death?"

"I'd say it was a heart attack except ..."

"Except what?"

"How can I trust you?"

Smith shrugged. "You likely shouldn't, but let me remind you, my life is on the line too. If I don't find Factor, then the next bomb might be for me. And those setting it off are the folks I work for. If my neck wasn't on the line, I wouldn't be talking to you. Your best chance at keeping your heart beating might just be to have a pro like me protecting you. Now, you don't think it was a heart attack?"

Hardin paused to consider what he'd heard before opening up. "There was a visitor in the president's office just before Hall died. No one saw him leave. Supposedly, the man was there to give the college a large donation, but there was no check in the office, nor did Hall leave any notes about the meeting. How does that smell to someone in your line of work?"

"Like we need a very thorough autopsy."

"But why kill Hall?" Hardin asked.

"Because Hall likely knew where Factor went."

"And why is Factor that important to you or the CIA?"

"For more reasons than you can begin to imagine."

Smith's vibrating phone caused the agent to pull over to the side of the road. Once parked, he checked the number and answered.

"What do you need?"

"Did you find the woman?" Clegg demanded.

"No, she's left town?"

"Where did she go?"

"That's a mystery. Now it's time you tell me something."

"What's that?"

Smith paused, glanced toward Hardin, before playing a hunch.

"Why did we take out Goldsmith?"

"What makes you think we did?"

"Goldsmith told you about the imprint."

"And if he knew about her," Clegg admitted, "then you know what that could've meant to us and other groups around the globe. If she shared that information with him, he'd have put the story out there and, once he did, all hell would break loose."

"Yeah, you and your old team would have been taken out. So, you protected your own hide."

"I'm not going to debate that, but there was a great deal more at stake. He had to be silenced. Besides, he was just an old man and didn't have that much time left anyway."

"What about the college president who died today?"

"I don't know about that."

"So, you had nothing to do with Dr. Hall's death?"

"No, I had no reason to be concerned about him. What could he know? Now, what about the woman? Do you have a line on her?"

"Not yet, but I'll dig until I get one."

"Keep me informed."

Smith ended the call without a reply. He was still considering his options when Hardin broke the silence.

"So, the CIA took out my mentor and friend."

"Yeah, and I knew nothing about it until right now."

"How's that make you feel? I mean to have an old man assassinated just to cover up the story of a woman with a gift?"

"It sickens me." Smith was not conning the reporter—it really did turn his stomach.

"What about Hall? Did the agency take him out too?"

"Supposedly that wasn't us. Maybe it was just a heart attack." After pulling back onto the road, the agent glanced toward his passenger. Hardin was angry and had every reason to be.

"Listen," Smith explained, "I had nothing to do with this. The call was made well above my head. But I'll tell you something you need to hear."

"What?"

"If the agency took out Goldsmith because of what he was working on, and he told you about it, then you're a target for the same reason he was. You noticed I didn't tell my supervisor I was with you."

"So, my odds of breathing long enough to unravel this story aren't good?"

"If you stick with me, I can protect you."

Hardin's jaw dropped. "Let me get this straight, the only way I can keep breathing is by staying with a man who works for the organization that might have put a price on my head and has already killed my mentor?"

"Exactly. I know our people. I can spot them. And now that I've gotten a good look at what one secretive branch of the CIA is doing, I'm ready to turn on them. But to do that I have to expose them for who they are and you, a reporter with a nationally known name, are my best option."

Hardin considered the agent's bizarre logic. It was obviously he was torn about joining forces. Who could blame him?

"Smith, if I go along with you, what comes next?"

"We have to find Maxine Factor. I think the best place to start is by identifying the man who visited Hall earlier today. Are you with me?"

The look on his face clearly proved Hardin didn't want to play it this way. Who could blame him? He'd just found out that the agency had killed his hero. Still, perhaps a desire to tell the story would keep him in the fold. And as Smith really needed to keep an eye on Hardin, he hoped the ploy would work

"There's another reporter who's working with me on this," Hardin explained. "She's in a room at a motel about five miles up the road. Unknowingly, I exposed her to this mess. You'll need to protect her as well. Plus, I'd feel a lot better if we had you outnumbered."

"Okay, I can go with that." Smith was pleased Hardin had caved. It made everything easier.

"And I want to have a gun with me that's always pointed at you," Hardin added.

"You can keep mine until I need it. Now, let's go get your colleague."

"Just keep driving, I'll tell you where to turn. And for the time being, the gun remains locked on you."

"Considering all my organization has done, that seems fair."

Chapter 19

Lingering guilt is a cancer that eats a person from the inside out, destroying even their desire to go on breathing.

———————◆◆———————

Rocky Smith needed Mason Hardin's contacts on this assignment. The reporter had ways of getting information that even eluded the CIA. Keeping the reporter safe was his most important job until they found Factor. Perhaps, his female partner would prove just as valuable. As he had a way of quickly getting a read on people, it shouldn't take long to find out.

Smith piloted his Edge into the gravel parking lot that fronted a dozen separate cabins making up what was likely a motor court dating back to the 1930s. Each of the buildings were constructed of white stone, with windows on the sides, and a single entry in the front. While they'd been well maintained, fresh paint couldn't disguise their age. In spite of a wealth of vintage charm, this was not a tourist destination. There was one car parked beside the Ramble Inn's small office.

"Not exactly the Hilton," Smith noted as they pulled in.

"We were looking for somewhere to hide," Hardin pointed out. "The fact that no one was staying here made this place perfect. Drive up to #4."

With no concerns, the two men got out, and while Smith waited by the car, Hardin strolled to the entry. As the reporter knocked, the agent sized up the location. The lines of sight were good. He could see a half mile in all directions, which made a surprise ambush unlikely. But he'd still feel much better once they'd picked up the other reporter, retrieved whatever information they could find on Factor's whereabouts, and were well away from Mount Vernon.

"Marsha," Hardin called through the closed door, "it's me."

Smith's gut suddenly twisted into knots. Perhaps there was something to be concerned about after all.

"Marsha?" the reporter called again.

Still no response. Smith quickly made his way the twenty feet to the door. Leaning close he whispered, "Could she have gone somewhere?"

"No, I took her car to town. She was trapped out here."

"Have you got a key?"

"Yeah."

"Then unlock it."

As he heard the sound of a vehicle coming up the highway. Smith glanced over his shoulder and reached for his gun. It wasn't there, Hardin still had it. The agent relaxed when he saw an UPS truck continue down the road. He turned his attention by to the entry just as the reporter fished the key from his pocket, slipped it into the lock, and twisted. The door opened and Hardin walked in, followed by Smith.

The room was a mess. Everything had been turned upside down. As a shocked Hardin took in the scene, Smith moved to the closed bathroom door. He listened for sounds of life before twisting the knob. As the door swung open, his eyes went straight to the tub. An African American woman was there, fully clothed, lying on her back, her eyes open, face battered and bruised, one of her arms obviously broken, and her open mouth revealed missing teeth. There was no reason to check her pulse. Smith quickly backed out and closed the door.

"You find anything?" a shaken Hardin asked.

"Is your partner a young, good-looking black woman about thirty?"

Hardin nodded.

"Then I found her. My guess is she was beaten to death."

"What?" Hardin whispered as he moved toward the bath.

"Don't go in there," Smith warned. "You don't want to remember her that way."

Hardin's hands locked onto to his head, and he fell to his knees. Though he looked as though he wanted to scream, his agony spilled out in little more than a whisper. "My Lord, I killed her."

Smith had no time to mourn someone he'd never met. His job was to protect a source who might help him complete his mission. Rather than offer any words of comfort, he coldly observed, "Actually, you didn't. And knowing reporters, I'm betting she eagerly signed up for this job."

"But ..."

"Get a hold of yourself," Smith barked. "Look around this room. Tell me if anything's missing."

Hardin stood and wiped his face with his hand before sweeping the small cabin. His gaze stopped at the one table in the room. "They took her computer, but I think they left everything else."

"What about her phone?"

Hardin moved to the side of the bed and picked up Chambers's purse. Rather than look through the large maroon bag, he dumped the contents onto the bed. The phone fell out with everything else.

"Do you have a computer?" Hardin asked.

"Yeah, it's in the car back at the college, and so is Goldsmith's thumb drive."

"Does the thumb drive have information on this matter?"

"It does."

"Give me my gun."

"Why?"

"I need to go to the office and check in with the owner. I want to know if he saw anything."

"What do I do?"

"Pack up everything that belongs to you and Miss Chambers. We need to take it with us."

"What about her?" The reporter's voice was dripping pain.

"Quit thinking of her as your friend and look at this mess as a story. You have work to do. Just leave her where she is. I'll handle her when I get back. Now give me my gun."

Once he had his weapon, Smith exited the cabin and quickly covered the fifty yards to the office. As he entered he took a quick inventory of the room. On the wall behind the counter keys hung on hooks. The only one missing was to room #4. The good news was no other guests had checked in.

There was a door at the back that he assumed led to living quarters. Pulling his gun from his holster, Smith walked to the end of the room and stepped around the counter. Sprawled awkwardly on the floor was a short, gray-headed man who appeared to be in his seventies. There was a single bullet wound in his forehead. He probably never knew what hit him.

Moving quickly to the door, Smith stepped into a small, one-bedroom apartment. A walk through revealed no one else was there. The open closet door and the contents of a chest of drawers also assured him the proprietor lived alone. Satisfied that whoever was responsible was gone, the agent exited through the office and jogged back to the cabin. When he opened the door, Hardin was sitting on the corner of the bed, his head in his hands. The bathroom door was open.

"We need to get moving," Smith ordered.

"They beat her to death," Hardin moaned. "Can you imagine what she felt? Can you imagine what she went through during the final moments of her life?"

"Yeah, I can. But we can't do anything about that now."

"I shouldn't have gone back into town to find out about Hall's death."

"Yeah, and if you hadn't, there'd be two bodies in this room, and whoever did this would have access to the information on your computer and Goldsmith's thumb drive."

"I guess we need to call the cops."

"No. We have to do something far more important. We have to clean up this mess. We have to make it look like no one was ever in this room. Other than the manager did anyone else see you here?"

"No."

"Did you pay with cash or credit card?"

"Cash. I didn't want anyone tracing us."

"Good. The only wild card is if anyone saw your partner … what was her name?"

"Marsha Chambers."

"If no one else saw her or talked to her, then no one will think to check this room. They'll just look in, see it ready for a guest, and move to the next one." As Smith evaluated what needed to be done, he grabbed a suitcase from the side of the bed and shoved it toward Hardin. "I told you to pack up. Don't buck my orders again. Get going and don't miss anything."

"But … what about Marsha?"

"I'll take care of her and the manager."

"The manager?"

"Yeah, they got him too. There's a dense woods about four miles back toward town. I saw a dirt road that ran alongside it. We can dump the bodies there."

"But Marsha has a family. Her mother and brother will be looking for her."

"And someday they can be told what happened, but not right now. If anyone finds out about this, it'll implicate you, and that pulls you off this, and we can't afford that."

"What are you talking about?"

"Maxine Factor's life is on the line. There are already several different groups who either know about her or will soon. All of them will be gunning for her."

"And the CIA is going to save her?"

"No, my boss wants her dead too, but I don't. As I see it, the only real chance she has is me. And you're maybe the only way I can find her. So, we clean this mess up, make it look like you were never here, then we go back to your car, get your stuff, and find out anything we can about who visited Dr. Hall."

"I don't understand any of this," Hardin announced.

"I hope when I bring you up to speed, you can make something out of what Goldsmith left you that'll lead us to Factor. Now, we need to get to work."

"Before I buy in," Hardin snapped, "you have to be honest. Did the CIA do this?"

"No."

"How can you be sure?"

"Because they would have cleaned it up, just like we're going to do. Make it look like nothing happened here."

"Then who did this?"

"No clue, not yet anyway, but they aren't pros. Stick with me and we'll find out. And if you want to get even, then I'm glad to help you."

Chapter 20

8:44 p.m.
Tuesday, September 20
Security Offices, Washington-Lincoln College,
Mt. Vernon, Illinois

A picture is often worth more than a thousand words because it tells the story from an unbiased point of view. But viewing the right photo taken at the right time rarely happens.

———————◆———————

G race Destry was about fifty, a stout redhead, and so "no-nonsense," she'd have intimidated a Marine drill sergeant. She'd been the head of campus security at WLC for six years. Up until this past week, her most challenging experience was when a group of male students had snuck into a girls' dorm. As a still shaken Hardin watched, Destry and Smith sipped coffee, traded stories, and casually glanced at the bank of two dozen school security monitors in a room just off the student center's food court. The woman, in the middle of a twelve-hour shift, was obviously enjoying having company, and things seemed to be going well. Yet, when Smith asked a favor, Destry's mood changed.

"I don't care who you are, no one can demand that I show them security footage without a warrant. That's the law, son. If I don't abide by that, I might as well not be here."

"Let me explain," Smith suggested with a smile, "I'm not asking for the world. All I want to see is the footage of who went into Old Main before the president had his final appointment. That's not a big deal, but it may help me answer an important question."

"Why would anyone care about that?" Destry argued. "Dr. Hall died of a heart attack; that's what the doctor said. Who went in and who went out is of no consequence. None! Zip! Nada!" She glanced toward Hardin, and pointed to a table, "Could you bring me one of those donuts—one of the chocolate ones, not the glazed."

The reporter crossed the room, put a donut on a plate, and handed it to Destry. "Thank you, hon," she sweetly cooed before returning her fierce gaze to Smith and barking, "What you're asking for is meaningless, and it's an insult to campus security."

"You and your people are obviously doing a great job. I know you must see this is as a waste of time, and perhaps for your investigation maybe it is, but not for ours. We have reason to suspect the last person Hall talked to was an enemy agent and was tied to that attempt on Dr. Maxine Factor's life."

Destry folded her arms over her ample chest. "Why would an agent be on our campus? What reason would he have to meet with our president? What have you been smoking?" She reached down, picked up the donut, and defiantly took a bite.

As a frustrated Smith jammed his hands into his suit coat pockets, Hardin eased down in a chair and tried to put into perspective what he'd experienced over the past few hours. For a man who'd lived his life on the edge and had never shown fear, who'd been threatened more times than he could remember, he now felt afraid, lost, and helpless. Chambers' brutal murder had torn him up. For the first time, he'd caused a person's death. And it was someone he cared deeply about. The fact he'd helped cover it up made the pain doubly bad.

"Your buddy looks like he's eaten some bad pork." Destry pointed Hardin's way.

Smith nodded. "You'd feel that way too if the man who visited your president killed the woman you loved."

"What?" Destry sputtered. Her tone suddenly displayed a bit of empathy.

Hardin looked up just in time to observe Smith spin a web of effortless lies. And somehow, the deeper he got into the agent's story, the more believable it sounded.

"What's this all about?" she demanded. "Is it drugs or murder? Do you really think the man who visited the president might have killed his …" She pointed to Hardin. "… girlfriend and was tied to the crackpot who tried to kill Dr. Factor?"

"Worse," Smith snapped. "You've got a campus filled with beautiful women.

"So?"

"I think this whole mess is tied to trafficking."

In Hardin's view, Smith had just crossed into the *Twilight Zone*. But judging from Destry's reaction, it may have worked.

The campus security chief tossed the remainder of the donut into the trash, looked back toward the bank of screens, took a deep breath, and then sat down in front of her computer. After a few clicks, she pulled up video from the main door of the administration building. She reversed the footage until the time of Hall's death. She froze the video at the point where a man was leaving the building.

"Is that your guy?"

Smith moved forward and took a closer look. "Can you move in closer on the face?"

A few seconds later Destry completed the task. "That's as good as it's going to get."

Smith pulled out his phone, took a screen grab, slipped the cell back into his pocket, and looked back at Hardin. As their eyes met, the agent grimly nodded. Smith then turned back to Destry. "Thanks, we appreciate your time."

"So that's the guy?" she asked.

"When I get to my computer, I'll run it through a facial recognition program and find out." Smith smiled before warning, "Don't tell anyone about this. If this is our man, and word got out that we're on his trail, he'd disappear. We need to keep him in the dark."

After Destry agreed, Smith moved toward the door. Taking the cue, Hardin followed. Neither man spoke until they were back in Smith's rented Ford. Once the doors were closed, the reporter broke the silence.

"So, do you know who that guy is?"

Smith nodded. "Years ago, a CIA agent dropped off the grid. When he disappeared, he took information with him that could seriously undermine the nation's security. His name was Dixon." Smith pulled out his phone and opened the photo app. "This is the screen shot." He then flipped back a few images. "Here's Dixon from twenty years ago. What do you think?"

The reporter studied the two photos before nodding. "They look like the same man, just with a few years of wear and tear."

"I have software that'll confirm that when I get back to my laptop, but I have very few doubts that it was Dixon who killed Hall."

"Do you think he murdered Marsha?"

"No, he'd have had no reason to. She couldn't have led him to Factor."

Hardin was confused. Why had so much violence suddenly invaded peaceful Mount Vernon? Surely no imprint was worth all this. "Why do you think Dixon was here?"

"He's a hit man," Smith explained. "I studied his file before I left Washington. He was the CIA's top gun for a couple of decades. Then he began to freelance. They call him Doctor Death. He's cold, calculating, and ruthless."

"That doesn't answer my question."

"Dixon has a direct connection to Dr. Maxine Factor."

"What's that?"

"Factor's his daughter, though I'm not sure he knows that."

"What do you mean if he knows that? How can he not know who his daughter is?"

"We don't think Dixon ever realized he had a daughter. We believe he had a brief affair with Factor's mother and left the country months before the child was born. Our research suggests that Factor doesn't know the man who raised her ... Carven Marks ... was not her biological father."

Hardin allowed the facts to tumble around in his head for a few moments before looking back at the agent. One point was really playing with his logic. "Why is he here if he doesn't know that Factor is his daughter?"

"He's been hired to kill her. The fact that Hall's dead leads me to that conclusion. If he was looking for his kid, he'd have no reason to murder the president of the college. So unwittingly he's got his sights on eliminating his own flesh and blood." Smith paused, licked his lips, and then posed a question of his own. "The car you're driving while you're in town, the one you brought down from Chicago. Is it yours?"

"No, it's Masha's."

"Okay, before we leave, we have to remove everything, and then sink it into a pond or lake. We can't have anyone finding it."

Hardin was now so numb to this bizarre thinking, he just accepted what Smith said without question. But, though in shock, his reporter's instincts were still sharp enough to seize on something Smith hadn't said. "How can we find Dixon if we don't know where he went? No one on campus knows where Factor is, at least according to Destry."

"True, but I'd bet Dixon has a good idea where she is and who she's with."

"Why do you say that?"

"Because it's the only reason he'd kill Hall."

"Where do we go from here?"

"After we get rid of the car, I'll call my supervisor. If we can't follow Dixon, then perhaps we can figure out who killed Chambers and follow them. My gut tells me all of us are on the same road, and it's headed to Maxine Factor."

Hardin should've been excited—it seemed they were close to a lead, but he simply couldn't push away the imagines of a bloody and beaten Chambers for more than a few seconds at a time. When he did manage to lose those horrific scenes, they were replaced with the memory of the moment he and Smith dropped her weighted body into a pond. Life was just too fragile and too cheap. Would he ever get over what had happened?

Chapter 21

Life is less about where you are and more about where you're going. If you don't know your destination, you might never get there.

———◆———

William Dixon had been staring at his cell phone for two hours and no matter how hard he looked, it didn't ring. He didn't lack patience, waiting was a part of his life, but to make plans, he needed to know where he was going. There was no use heading to his hideaway in Colorado if Factor and Carter were going east.

Frustrated by his ignorance, he got up and was just about to pull out a pair of sleep pants when the phone finally rang. Moving back to the room's small desk, he plopped down and answered.

"D.D. here."

"I've got the information you requested, but I'm not sure how much it will help."

Dixon picked up a pen. "Give it to me."

"In the fall, Carter spends a great deal of time on his New England estate. That's about sixty miles west of Boston. It's private and very well guarded. I have no idea if he's there now."

"So, you think Boston is that the most likely spot to find him?"

"Listen, I've been working at the *Inquisitor* for two decades, half of that time spent keeping an eye on Carter. Most fall days, if he's not on a dig somewhere, he's at the estate. Who wouldn't love spending fall in New England? But ..."

"But what?"

"No one has seen him there since early August, so I'm guessing he's not returned for his traditional autumn rest. Let me read you my notes. Earlier this year he was in London. For several months, in last year and early in this year, he was seen escorting Indira Morel to all the hot spots. They even dined with the queen. Cameras followed them everywhere they went. But Morel has not been seen with Carter since February. That's when he left to explore ruins in China, and she headed for either South or Central America. Based on that, I'm guessing that relationship is history. Still, she lasted longer than most women do with Carter."

"So where was the last place he was spotted?"

"Two weeks ago, a member of the paparazzi grabbed a snap, photo in your world, in Rome. I can tell you he got on a charter plane there and went to the US. That aircraft landed in Dallas. No one has spotted him since. If I had to guess, I'd say he's either at his mountain home outside of Vail or his cabin in the Ozarks."

"If you had to bet, which one of those places would he take an attractive woman?"

The caller paused for a few seconds before making her guess, "Colorado."

"Why?"

"Still too hot in Arkansas for romance."

"Where's the mountain home?"

"Twenty miles north of Vail. Ask anyone up there, they can tell you where to go."

Dixon nodded while considering his next move. He was about to end the call when a thought snuck in his mind's back door.

"Mia, where's his place in Arkansas?"

"Outside of Saddle on the south fork of Spring River. It's quiet, far away from the crowds, and is a nod to Carter's conservative side. By that I mean, it's not a palace. It looks like a vacation home for the upper middle class. About the only thing setting it apart from a dozen others in that area is the airstrip. That gives him a place to land his DC3. He loves that old plane almost as much as he loves digging for antique treasure."

Dixon smiled. Arkansas made more sense than Colorado. It'd be a spot Carter could take Factor and all but evaporate. And, as this getaway likely wasn't about romance, that'd be the location Dixon would choose if he were in Carter's shoes.

"Thanks, Mia. I'll send you a present very soon."

Dixon ended the call and hit his map app. A quick search showed he was only about five hours from Carter's cabin. The best option would be to drive. Before a kill, especially one that might involve two people, it was always good to get a good night's rest, so he would leave in the morning. Because the location was rural, he could fire from a distance and take out both targets, if necessary, while staying out of Carter's line of fire. The easiest method would be a rifle with a scope. But he didn't have one with him, and with the local gun laws, he couldn't buy one, however, he had a contact in the St. Louis Police Department who could be bribed. A weapon from an evidence locker would be the perfect method of execution. He'd take out his targets then return the gun to his contact where it would be placed back in police storage. This hit had the promise of being very clean.

With his ducks in a row, he climbed into bed, but then what he didn't know kept prevented him from sleeping. Why was Elton Carter interested in Maxine Factor? Had he written a check for twelve million to a small college because he knew she was an imprint? And if so, what did Carter believe she could remember that made her so valuable? Dixon tried to shrug off the mystery. What did it matter? His job was to end her life, not explore the billionaire's motivation. If Carter got in the way, he'd become the wealthiest chunk of collateral damage in history. But not knowing still kept him awake.

Chapter 22

10:15 a.m.
Wednesday, September 21
Old State House, Little Rock, Arkansas

Always plan for the unexpected.

———◆———

The Old State House was one of the first large structures constructed in Arkansas. Commissioned in 1837 by Governor John Pope, the Greek Revival-styled building was completed in 1842. With its white block walls, brick walks, four massive columns, and dynamic entrance, it was impressive when dedicated and just as impressive almost two centuries later.

Wearing a floppy hat and huge sunglasses, Maxine Factor was sitting on a wooden bench about a hundred feet from the drop spot. Elton Carter, outfitted in jeans, an Arkansas Razorback shirt, a baseball cap, and aviator sunglasses, watched and waited by a small hedge surrounding the front fountain.

According to the plan, the payoff for killing Factor was supposed to be delivered at 10:00 a.m. Carter glanced at his watch again. It appeared he'd been stood up. Disappointment etched his face. He'd just wandered over and leaned against an ancient oak tree, when a small man wearing a blue suit and carrying a brown leather briefcase exited the front door, stopped, and seemed to purposely study the handful of people strolling the sidewalks. He then turned right and approached Carter. The billionaire was wearing a hidden mic, and Factor, with a receiver in her ear, had no problem hearing everything that was said.

"I take it you're Bart."

Carter nodded. "You're late!"

"Flight was delayed."

"Do you have the payoff?"

"In the briefcase."

"Let's walk over to the empty bench and sit."

The two men made their way to the suggested spot and eased onto the wrought iron slats. As they did, the contact pushed the briefcase toward Carter.

"You don't have to open it now. Too many folks might see something we don't want them to see. But I guarantee it's all there. When your boss pops the latches, he'll be pleased."

"Open it," Carter suggested.

"Why? I know what's in it."

"Just do it."

The contact shook his head. "I don't think so. This is for your boss."

"I have a gun in my pocket, my hand's on it right now, and it's equipped with a silencer. I also have an associate who's armed and has an eye on you. So, you open the briefcase or tell me why you won't."

"We don't need others seeing the cash. It's not good business."

"Open it," Carter demanded.

The man froze, his eyes darting from side to side. Seemingly unnerved, he reached up, loosened his tie, and frowned.

As she waited, Factor studied the grounds. Down about ten yards, a gardener was pruning a rose bush. A few feet to the left, a mother dressed in yoga pants and a tight shirt, pushing a baby stroller, was getting in her morning steps. An elderly couple were visiting while sitting on the bench opposite Carter. Other than those five, no one else was enjoying the beautiful fall day.

"Let's see," Carter's voice drew Factor's gaze back to the men, "Since you're afraid of opening the case while close to me, the mechanism must contain something directional. And because this is a public place, it's also something quiet. I'm guessing a dart filled with fast-acting poison. Am I right?"

The man nodded.

"Where's the money?" Carter demanded.

"The payoff was always death," the man whispered.

"We're going to walk to my car, see? You'll lead the way. It's located in the lot to our left. It's a blue Lincoln SUV. You'll get into the rear seat and slide across, see? I'll follow. If you make a move to run, I'll shoot you. If I miss, my associate won't. Do you understand?"

"Yes."

Even though the situation was tense, Factor had to grin. Where had Carter picked up his tough-guy lingo? Was it from old gangster movies? The *see* at the end of the sentences was outdated but effective.

"If you want to live to go to bed tonight, you lead the way back to my car."

The little man nodded, stood, and quickly began to walk toward the Lincoln. Just before he got to the vehicle, Carter popped the locks. A second later, the door opened, the hostage slid in with Carter following. Once they were inside with the door closed, Factor strolled up, opened the driver's door and got behind the wheel. After fastening her seat belt, she pushed the start button on the SUV, eased out of the parking spot, and exited the lot. Nothing was said for the next ten minutes as the Lincoln drove northeast on the interstate. As she looked into the rearview mirror, she saw the money-man turned hostage appeared scared to death. His eyes darted from side to side, his fingers drummed the top of the case, and he kept licking his lips. If a person really could come unglued and fall to pieces, he might be the one to prove it.

"Where are we going?" the hostage demanded as they passed the Mayflower exit.

"To someplace quiet. It'll take about an hour, so just sit back and enjoy the view. After all, if you don't come up with the right answers to my questions, this might just be the last part of the world you ever see. Now, where are you from?"

"New York." The quick reply proved he was ready to talk.

"Ever been to Arkansas?" Carter quizzed.

"No."

"It's a good place to live and maybe even a better place to die." The billionaire chuckled before adding, "There's a lake just up ahead. Do you like to fish?"

"I did some as a kid."

"This small reservoir has the biggest bream in the world. Good lake for small-mouth bass too. Shame you can't spend any time there. One of the legends about Conway concerns a body that was dumped up by the dam in 1962. No one ever figured out who it was. As I recall from reading about the case, the guy was about your size. Cause of death was a gunshot wound to the back of the skull."

In the rearview mirror, Factor observed the little man's shoulders sag. He was getting closer and closer to a breakdown. Carter must've sensed that too, because for the next twenty minutes he gave him a rundown on all the cemeteries in the area. He didn't stop his morbid lecture until he told Factor to pull onto a rural highway. It was several more miles, and the time was a quarter to noon when Carter signaled to turn off the lonely Arkansas state highway and onto an even lonelier gravel road. After a mile more, just as the Lincoln pulled up to an old home place, Carter waved at Factor.

"Just pull into that drive. We're going to get out and go inside the house."

After parking the SUV, Factor took a closer look at their destination. The small frame home must have been a hundred years old when the last resident moved out. Nixon was likely president when that happened. The paint was faded, half the windows were broken, and the grass hadn't been cut in years.

"The front door's unlocked," Carter assured his hostage. "We're going to enter that way and then make a right turn into the kitchen. There's an old table and few chairs there. You'll take the one on the far-right side in front of the window. I'll sit on the corner to your left. Our driver will observe from the living room."

"What are you going to do with me?"

"That depends on how you answer my questions," Carter suggested. "After all, I did a job and expected to be paid for it. You've already told me the payoff was supposed to be death. So, if I get the information I need to make sure I get my money, maybe you'll walk away. Now get moving."

The money-man was compliant. He entered the house and quickly found his spot. Two minutes later, from her position under the archway separating the living room from the kitchen, Factor studied Carter. He seemed more than prepared to play the tough guy. What surprised her was how good he was at it.

The table where the silent interrogation was taking place was covered in dust. It appeared, from tracks on the tabletop, that raccoons now called this old farmhouse home. If either man noticed, they said nothing. For several minutes, the billionaire stared into the other man's eyes. The action had its intended effect. The hostage's head sank into his shoulders, as if his neck were disappearing.

"What's your name?" Carter finally demanded.

"Mosby."

"Who instructed you to hand me that lethal briefcase?"

"I don't know his name." Mosby's expression revealed he'd have gladly given the information if he had it.

Carter pushed the briefcase directly in front of Mosby. He then reached his arms around and snapped open the latches. As the nervous hostage looked on, the billionaire put his right hand on top of the case's lid, his eyes locked on his captive. "Here's the deal. My associate has a gun on you."

Mosby's eyes darted toward Factor. As he studied her, she brought the gun up and aimed it as his face.

"Now," Carter continued. "Sometime in the next ten seconds, I'm going to open this briefcase. As it's facing you, you'll receive the gift intended for me. If you move during that time, she shoots you. So, you die either way. Now to avoid that fate, you can start telling me everything you know about the man who ordered the hit and then set me up. Time starts now."

As the seconds ticked by, Mosby glanced from Carter to Factor and then back. At the six-second mark, he made his decision.

"I really don't know the name. Those who know him call him the Ghost."

"Why?" Carter demanded

"Because we always meet him in cemeteries at night. He calls and tells us where and when."

"How long have you been working for him?"

"A couple of years."

"What's the objective?"

"It used to be about making pickups and deliveries. That was all. Then, a few weeks ago it changed. Suddenly, his focus was on an Illinois history professor. He wanted her dead."

"Why?"

"He said it was to get revenge."

Carter glanced toward Factor. She shrugged. She had no idea how anyone could seek revenge by using her as bait.

"Revenge for what?" Carter asked.

"I don't know. I got the idea the Ghost was trying to hurt someone by getting rid of the woman."

"So, this wasn't about her being an imprint?"

"What's that?"

"Don't move," Carter ordered as he got up from the table and strolled to Factor's side. "Any idea who'd be deeply hurt by your death?"

"No."

"Mosby," Carter announced as he swung back to look at the man sitting at the table, "Why was I supposed to be killed? After all, I took out Factor."

"You weren't supposed to be the guy who took her out. You were supposed to deliver the case to him. We figured he'd be the only one who would open it."

"I get that part, but still, when the case ended up in my hands and if I did open it, what was the purpose in killing me?"

"He told me there could be no witnesses."

"And you're sure killing Factor was only meant to hurt someone else?"

"Actually, he said it was so he could get even."

Just as Factor began to consider the haunting words, five quick shots rang out, shattering the window behind where Mosby sat. One second his face was frozen in shock and the next his head was resting on the briefcase, blood spilling out over the table.

"We were followed," Carter hissed.

"I didn't see anyone in my mirror," a suddenly frantic Factor announced.

"I'm guessing there's a tracking device on Mosby or in the briefcase. We're trapped. Any ideas?"

Factor's brain was blank, frozen by both shock and fear. When another round of gunfire tore through the living room window, instinct drove her to the ground. As she hugged the dirty floor, Carter made his way to the front wall and glanced out the window.

"There's one car, looks like an older Impala. That means there can't be more than four of them."

Those words were all Factor needed to hear. Everything around her abruptly disappeared. The year was 1910, and the place was Kentucky. Four robed Klansman had surrounded a farmhouse. And she was inside holding onto her father's old Colt revolver. To her right, two friends, both African Americans, were dead. They'd caught bullets fired through the kitchen window. To her left, Jenny Gardner, the friend who'd come to bring her to the young men, was choking on her own blood. If she had any chance of living, there was only one thing she could do—play dead. Dipping her hand into her friend's blood, she dabbed it onto her back and fell to the floor. She then waited, the Colt tucked under her body, for the white-robed invaders to enter the house.

"We have to play dead," Factor announced as her mind reentered the present.

"What?" Carter demanded.

"Get some of Mosby's blood, we'll put on our necks, then we fall to the floor with our guns under us."

"We played that card at the airport."

"They don't know that. Besides, it's all I've got. When they think we're dead, they'll relax. You take the two nearest you, I'll shoot the other pair.

"A message from the past?" he asked.

"Just do it," she ordered.

Crawling on his knees, he dipped his cap in the blood. After rubbing his back and neck with the blood, he gave his cap to Factor who did the same. This was the second time in three days she'd played dead, and she was tired of it. But if playing possum kept them alive, she'd happily join the animal kingdom for a few minutes.

"Elton," she whispered, "move to the far side of the room. We don't need to be so close. When you get in position, have your weapon hidden but ready."

For the next five minutes, neither of them moved, and Factor had to imagine what was going on outside. Over than a century ago, it had taken more than twenty minutes for the Klansmen to finally enter the house. Would it take that long now?

Five more minutes elapsed before there were footsteps on the porch. A few seconds later, the door slowly swung open. The hinges sounded like the beginning of a classic radio show, but for the life of her, she couldn't remember the name.

"They're dead," a deep voice called out.

"Are you sure," another man asked.

"Looks like it."

"Turn them over," a third visitor barked.

Factor heard a single set of steps walk over to her body. She noted sounds of another man moving toward Carter. When the footsteps quieted, she felt a hand on her shoulder. She waited for him to find his grip and turn her over before aiming the gun. She fired two shots at almost pointblank range. From the other side of the room, she heard two more bursts of gunfire. As the pair of invaders dropped, Factor pushed up onto her knees. She was about to fire again but was a split-second too late. Carter had already squeezed his trigger twice and taken out the last of the gang. All three men were now meeting their maker.

"Your plan worked," a relieved and obviously impressed Carter called out as they both got to their feet.

Factor grimly nodded as she moved toward the kitchen window. Looking outside, she saw no other visitors. It appeared they were only dealing with a trio.

"Grab the briefcase," Carter suggested.

"Why?"

"Because there might be something inside that'll give us more information."

After shoving her weapon back into her belt, Factor yanked the bloody case from under Mosby. His head landed with a thud on the table.

"Don't forget it's unlatched," Carter warned, "might be best to lock it back up."

Factor was reaching for the latches when she heard an unexpected order delivered by an unknown voice. "Both of you need to drop your guns."

There'd been a fourth man, and he'd come in through the back door. That's not the way it had played out in 1910, so she hadn't expected him. The final member of the mob was large, perhaps six-six. The weapon he held in his left hand was big and lethal. Seeing no other alternative, Factor held the briefcase, bloody side up, in her left hand, and pulled the gun from her belt with her right. After quickly considering the odds, she dropped the weapon to the floor. At about the same moment, Carter followed her lead.

"Those were my friends," the guest announced, his tone angry.

"You need to try other social circles," Factor snapped as she walked toward where the guy was standing.

"Where do you think you're going?" the hood demanded.

"If you're going to kill us," Factor explained, "I'm going to stand right in front of you. I want you looking me right in my eyes when you pull the trigger. I want my blood to splatter all over you. I'm not going to let you get away clean. You'll either have to buy new duds or make a trip to the laundry. And blood is so hard to get out."

As the big man considered her taunts, Factor covered the final five steps. When she was standing just three feet in front of the giant, she smiled, grabbed the top of the briefcase, and opened the lid. The lethal dart launched by her unexpected action hit the man in his left cheek. His expression was initially one of shock, followed by pain, and then, within just five seconds, there was a look of death. He wavered for a moment, his knees buckled, and he slumped to the floor.

"Did one of your ancestors give you that idea?" Carter asked.

"No, that was all mine."

Spinning the briefcase around, she looked inside. Except for the hidden weapon, there was nothing. Factor glanced toward Carter. "I recommend we go."

"In case they traced us using the case, let's leave it."

"Fine," Factor replied, dropping the briefcase to the floor."

"I'll drive."

"Is this the way it'll be from now on?"

"It will—until we exorcise the ghost," Carter replied as he walked out the door toward the SUV.

She considered his words as she followed. If Mosby hadn't known the identity of the Ghost, how were they going to find out?

Chapter 23

Make no mistake about this, what you don't know can kill you!

———◆———

After the past few days, Elton Carter concluded his stint as Indiana Jones was no fun, and as much as he didn't want to admit it, he was in way over his head. Except for the escape from the kidnappers when he was a child, he'd never shot at a person, much less killed someone. Now there were seven bodies in need of graves, and he'd had a part in stopping each of their hearts.

As he drove, he checked his review mirror. Each time he saw a car appear, his heart skipped a beat. When those same vehicles pulled off the highway, he sighed with relief. Nothing in his four decades of life had prepared him for this.

To his right, Maxine Factor seemed not as much frightened as lost in thought. Whose thoughts were now taking up space in the woman's head?

As he pushed the SUV around another long curve, Carter wondered when the next surprise would rock their world. Logic dictated they were running out of luck. After all, neither of them was equipped to play this game. They didn't have the skills or experience. Maybe no one did.

"It doesn't make sense," Factor announced, breaking the silence that had lasted since they'd left the abandoned farmhouse.

"You'll get no argument from me," Carter mumbled.

Factor curled in her seat and leaned against the door. She looked at Carter. "Why would they want to kill you? When you were pretending to be Zitech, you told them you were sending another man to pick up the payment. The other man wasn't at the airport, he had no part in this, so why set up his murder? To me, what Mosby said made no sense. Anyone who picked up that case would have surely opened it to make sure the money was there. That would've been a part of their job. Mosby went to his grave with a lie on his lips."

Factor made a solid point. The Ghost, whoever he was, had no reason to kill a pickup and delivery man. In fact, if he'd wanted to kill Zitech, he would've just put a tracker in with the money and thus found the hit man's location. That had to mean he was after the courier. Why? As he eased around a curve that almost met itself coming, he tried to make sense of something that would never make sense.

Meanwhile, Factor continued to think out loud. "Mosby told us the Ghost wanted me dead to even a score. The way he made it sound, this was a personal matter. Until the last few days, I've never done anything to anyone. My parents were even more harmless than me. As many people as your family has screwed, I could understand someone wanting to settle a score with the Carters by taking you out, but—"

"Yeah, and on top of that, Mosby acted as though he didn't even know what an imprint was. That means the last few days don't make any sense at all. Max, are you sure there's no one you've ticked off? Someone with a lot of resources and contacts?"

"Yes, I'm sure. I've done nothing to sign my death warrant. Killing me would have no lasting effect on anyone's life. My brain might be crowded with a lot of people I'm just getting to know, but I can still sort through my life experiences. I've had a dull existence. So, why is the Ghost targeting me to even things up?"

"Tomorrow, B.R. Lenards, the psychologist who has studied imprints, arrives. Perhaps something you'll tell her will unlock why this haunting figure is after you. In the meantime, I don't think anyone knows you're with me. We should be safe at the cabin for a while."

"A while! How long is that? There are at least two different groups after me, and we don't know who either one is. They'll keep digging until they figure out where I am. That's what happened back in 1778, and it was a lot easier to hide then."

"1778?"

"Another visitor. I had a grandmother generations back who worked as a barmaid in an inn outside of Boston. The British found out she was a spy for the colonists. She got away just before they came to arrest her. Rose was on the run for months, staying in the homes of those who supported the revolution. They didn't just offer her safe shelter—they gave her money. She had a number of close calls but managed to maintain her freedom for seven months. In the winter of 1779, a British officer, who'd once talked to Rose during her days working at the inn—in other words, he gave a lot of good information after a few pints—spotted her boarding a coach. She was arrested, brutally beaten, and placed in prison. Her execution was scheduled several times, but the ones holding her didn't have the stomach to kill a beautiful woman. Thus, against all odds, she survived."

"When did that memory pop into your head?"

"Several months ago. At the time, I found it interesting, but now it seems foreboding, and unlike the Brits in 1780, I doubt anyone will show me mercy." She glanced at Carter and delivered a stern warning. "You need to get out of this. You know as well as I do there's only one exit for me, and that's death. There's no reason for you to give up your life in the futile effort to buy me a few more weeks or months. Even if the people who are trying to kill me don't succeed, you and I both realize my mind will explode at some point. And when that happens, when there are too many memories in my head, I'll kill myself. So, pull over, let me out, and drive away while you can. What you're providing is not a rescue effort, it's hospice care."

"Not going to do it," Carter resolutely argued. "I'm not going to give up. Lenards might have some answers and, even if she doesn't, you'd be surprised to find out how much safety an unlimited amount of money can buy."

"It hasn't purchased much security so far."

"But that's on me. I've been cocky. I haven't planned carefully. I'm now awakened to some realities. It's time to put my resources to use figuring out who the Ghost is, and who was behind the attempts on your life in Mount Vernon. You trust Lenards to work on your mental well-being, and let me deal with physical security. Oh, and in your spare time, make me a list of all your ancestors who've helped us escape death in the past few days. I need to thank them."

Factor shrugged, "I guess I do too. But if Lenards can't help, if she doesn't have some way to slow down the family reunions, I'm walking away from you whether you like it or not. I don't want to be responsible for your death." She paused and grinned before jabbing, "The women of the world would never forgive me, and neither would the tabloids."

As he piloted the Lincoln up a steep grade, he smiled. The fact that she could still summon enough of her own personality to dig him with sarcasm gave him hope.

Chapter 24

4:30 p.m.
Wednesday, September 2
St. Giles Hotel, London, England

Ignoring the advice of those who know you best is never a wise course. More often than not, the road you will then take leads to the last place you need to be.

———◆———

F rancesco Russo checked in with Tim Clegg four times, and on each of those occasions, the agent had assured the Vatican's librarian that they were taking care of the imprint. Yet, as much as he wanted to have faith in his CIA source, he couldn't find it in his soul to make that leap. Thus, he created a pretense to go to London on Vatican business in order to meet with a man who might be willing to work with him to stop an imprint. Doing everything he could to shed his clerical identity, Russo entered the St. Giles in civilian clothes. He checked in under an assumed name, Miles Milano, and chose the cheapest room in the stately establishment. After entering, he understood why he'd paid so little. Yet, it seemed the perfect location. No one would look for him here.

Russo put his bag beside the dresser and sat down on the corner of the bed. He felt a need for prayer, but fearing the spiritual act might cause him to reverse course, he focused on the matter at hand. Logic assured him this was not a time for either patience or mercy. The potential wrath this imprint might create was far too great. Still, even as he rationalized future actions, a glaring flaw in his plans prevented him from feeling sure about its success. There was nothing in his background that prepared him for killing anyone. He had never even shot a gun. How in the world could he possibly complete this mission? And, if and when he did, could he live with himself afterward?

A knock on the door brought some hope. The only person who knew he was in London was a man he might convince to join him in his unseemly task. Russo jumped off the bed and rushed to open the door.

Ben Greenberg's green eyes seemed on fire when he walked into the cramped room. The two men forced smiles and shook hands, but exchanged no words, instead they spent several moments sizing each other up before Russo pointed to the room's only chair. After the visitor took the seat, Russo moved back to his spot on the bed. Tense, he opted for small talk.

"How have you been?"

"Does it matter?" Greenberg asked.

"Well, maybe not. It's just that we see each other so rarely ..."

"You're asking me about my life is completely insincere. You don't care. You just want to use me. But to answer your question, with the economy reviving after COVID, business is finally coming back, so my family's software sales are picking up. On a personal note, my mother's upset because I still haven't married nor am I dating anyone. I cut the cable and stream what I watch and have given up meat. Anything else you need to know?"

Russo smiled and nodded. Greenberg was a good person with a birth defect ... he was born with a chip on his shoulder. Because he believed someone was always trying to take advantage of him, he never had time for small talk.

"I'm not dating anyone either," Russo quipped, "but in my case my mother's likely relieved. She always wanted one of her children to choose the priesthood. I was the answer to her prayers"

"I was once a rabbi—guess I still am. My mother doesn't care either way."

"I've never asked you about your faith, is it important to you?"

Greenberg shrugged. "I'm still religious, but the God I believe in seems much further away than when I was young. My heritage is important, but this week it's more about history than faith. What about you? I'd imagine a man who works at the Vatican is immersed in faith."

Russo frowned, looked toward the window, and scratched his head. How should he answer that question? He could trot out the accepted line about service and callings, but why waste those stories on a man like Greenberg? It probably wouldn't impress him.

Tired of the small talk, Greenberg cut to the chase. "Why did you ask me to come see you in this miserable place?"

"The place was necessary to make sure no one saw us together. It's about the imprint."

Those words had barely cleared his lips when an obviously hopeful Greenberg cut him off. "Is she dead? God forgive me for wishing that."

"My source at the CIA doesn't think so."

"Think? I want facts."

"I understand how you feel, and that's why I asked for this meeting. I believe there are a number of reasons our concerns about Dr. Maxine Factor are valid even beyond our mutual interest in maintaining the foundation of our faiths."

"Once again, you could've shared those insights on the phone."

"Ben, has your organization ever dealt with those who eliminate problems?"

"Every group calls in consultants."

"No, I mean human problems."

Greenberg folded his hands together, looked toward the room's lone window, and grew silent. Was he confused or unwilling to offer an answer? To keep the ball rolling, the priest explained, "We've all dipped our hands in muddy water from time to time. And when we did, we turned to those who specialize in cleaning up such matters."

"The Star does not work that way," Greenberg argued.

Russo displayed a knowing smile, "Perhaps it doesn't now, but I know at one time it did."

"Maybe four decades ago. Back then we looked upon the elimination of certain people as an answer, but that was before I was born."

"Have you seen the records from those time? After all, you're the keeper of the archives." When there was no immediate response, it provided Russo with both an open door and an exposed skeleton.

"Ben, in my job I keep track of books—our library is unrivaled in many ways. I deal with rare volumes."

"You aren't telling me anything I don't know. I've been to the Vatican. I'm well aware of its resources."

"But, there are things kept in books that are off the books, if you know what I mean. There are people, places, and events in those books that not even the Pope knows about. And some of them deal with people who became problems. While I wasn't involved in those things, I know of them. Are you aware of similar things?"

"What are you driving at?"

"Did you ever employ a man named William Dixon? Some call him the Grim Reaper or Doctor Death."

"I've read the name. I'm not saying we ever paid him for consulting work, but I'm also not saying we didn't."

"And when the Star used him, was it more than forty years ago?"

"If we did, it would've been."

"Then my friend we share a problem."

Greenberg wasn't connecting the dots. He folded his arms over his chest. "What does this have to do with the imprint?"

Russo stood, walked to the window, and studied the alley. "Let me explain. I was curious why the CIA wanted to take her out. That's not the kind of thing they do now. I discovered that initially they were simply going to observe her, but that strategy abruptly ended."

"Why?"

"Because they found out who her father is."

Greenberg nodded. "So, who is it? A senator? Or maybe a supreme court justice?"

"No, her father is Doctor Death. And that means if she remembers what Dixon did before she was born, then our worlds could turn upside down."

Greenberg frowned as if he'd just taken a sip of straight lemon juice. He allowed that sour taste to linger for a moment before sadly shaking his head. "So, if the CIA is going to take her out, then what's the issue?"

"They can't find her. She's disappeared. The man they've assigned to do the job is walking in the dark. I think we need to go to the States and do our own investigating."

"The two of us?"

"Yeah. I've got the money for the trip."

Greenberg remained unconvinced. "Where do we begin? If the CIA can't find her, how can we?"

"She has to be getting help. We'll start by using our sources to find out who's keeping her out of sight. When we know that name, we can alert the man assigned to do the job for the CIA."

"Once again, why do we need to get involved? They're trained for this, we're not. On top of that, if we can't find the man, then do you expect us to kill Factor?"

"We get involved because we have vital reasons to protect our interests. Maybe more vital that the CIA's reasons." Russo studied his guest before adding, "You're a smart man. You have contacts in American business. I mirror your strengths, but my contacts are in other areas. And best of all, we're behind-the-scenes players. No one's going to look at us twice. We're not going to be associated with anything suspicious. We can ask questions and travel without arousing the curiosity of government officials or law enforcement agencies."

"But what about killing her?" Greenberg demanded.

"Odds are good, that if we locate her, we can find a way to contact the people who're assigned for the job and let them do it. Let's look at it as us just being a part of the final solution.

"You do know," Greenberg frowned, "that's what the Nazis called what happened to Jews in the death camps."

"Sorry," Russo apologized as he moved back to the corner of the bed, "my choice of words was insensitive. I was trying to avoid admitting, though the chances are slim, we might have to kill another human being."

"How do we do that? Kill her."

"We'll improvise. There are two of us and one woman."

"I just don't know."

"Ben, the Bible is filled with stories where God used people to kill. If we're placed in that position, if we have no choice, we'll be given a way to accomplish what needs to be done."

It was obvious Greenberg was not yet buying in. Still, he also wasn't getting up and leaving. It was time to push a bit harder.

"I want to ask you one more time, Ben, did the Star ever use Dixon?"

"Yes, I know we did. The records are clear on that point. We borrowed him from the CIA. I can even tell you the men he killed."

"And if Factor remembers, then those stories will come out, and the Star will be exposed and die."

"We're doing the very thing we hate … finding ways to rationalize immoral behavior."

"Perhaps you're right, but what if she remembers?"

Greenberg through up his hands and signed. "When do we leave?" He wasn't eager to join, but at least he was on board.

"Tomorrow."

"What's the cover for our travel?"

"There's a world-wide gathering of religious leaders in Denver, meeting to discuss better ways of coordinating hunger relief efforts across the globe. It begins next week."

"You've thought this out."

"And, we don't have to sign in to officially be counted as there. I've taken care of making sure our credentials are issued and picked up by a friend. If anyone checks, we're covered. Once we get to America, we can travel under the radar."

"And where do we start? It's a big country, and the woman is hidden so well the CIA hasn't tracked her down. She could be anywhere."

"I have a solid contact in the US. When I spoke with him about a week and a half ago, I told him we'd found another imprint. At first, he didn't care, but his interest shot up when I shared her identity."

"What's his name?"

"Rev. Dallas Arnold."

"Never heard of him."

"His sources are good, so trust me on this. Now go get packed. We have a mission to accomplish for the good of both our faiths."

"The faiths we claim but evidently no longer fully embrace."

As Greenberg walked out the door, Russo sat back on the bed. Faith only got you so far. At times, you had to take matters into your own hands. It was one of those times.

Chapter 25

Music soothes the soul and brings perspective. There are times when a song can literally make the sun shine on a stormy day.

———◆———

S ince the shootout at the farmhouse, all of Max Factor's senses were on edge. While she felt a need to cling to her host, she also still wished he'd walked away, afraid and convinced that his protection would soon lead to his death. And that death would be for nothing. Even if assassins didn't take her out, in time, her mind would fry. Last night, she'd barely slept. Every time she pushed one visiting ancestor away, two more walked in. It was if they all talked at once and shouted louder and louder in order to be heard. A dozen times, she'd crawled out of bed and paced back and forth in an attempt to gain control of her thoughts. But, when she again lay down, they'd come back. Why was it suddenly getting worse? What had changed? The answer was easy—people were now trying to kill her. That epiphany opened a window. More than anything else, anxiety woke her ancestors and caused them to come calling.

Giving up on rest, she got up early, dressed, and moved outside to the porch where she settled in the swing. She watched the sun rise and, for a few moments, embraced the optimism the crisp air ushered in. As she watched the river flow by at the bottom of the rolling hill, she was alone with her thoughts. For an imprint, there was nothing better than having a solitary moment.

"How'd you sleep?" Elton Carter asked as he strolled through the front entry to the porch.

Her host appeared fresh and alive. There were no circles under his gray eyes or obvious fatigue in his posture. Dressed in jeans, boots, and a long-sleeved rugby shirt, he looked like a model for an aftershave company. She was so envious that he'd obviously enjoyed a good night's sleep, she failed to acknowledge his question.

"Cat got your tongue?" he asked.

"No. I was just lost in thought." She paused before confessing, "In truth, I was actually jealous because it looks like you slept well."

"I always do when I'm here. Maybe it's the sound of the rushing river or the songs of the birds, but when my head hits the pillow, whatever's own my mind evaporates."

"Good for you. I'm thinking I may never sleep again." Factor looked into Carter's eyes. "Do you ever have nights when you can't turn your brain off? Are there times when no matter how hard you try your mind just keeps whirling?"

"Of course."

"That happened to me a lot when I was working on my doctorate, but it's different now. Then I was singing a solo. Now I'm giving away space to a choir of voices all singing different songs at the same time. I can't begin to describe what it's like. I fully understand why some of the other imprints committed suicide."

As her troubling thoughts created a cloud of sadness that threatened to smother the entire valley, a car turned off the main road and entered the lane. As it drew closer, Factor's blood pressure raced skyward. She stopped the porch swing and studied the vehicle as if she were looking into the eyes of the messenger of death.

"Don't worry," Elton Carter assured her, placing his hand gently on her shoulder, "that's Dr. Lenards. She called a few minutes ago to get the code to the front gate."

Though her heart slowed, Factor's eyes stayed fixed on the blue Buick SUV, following the vehicle's winding path up from the valley. As she watched she posed a question. "What can you tell me about her?"

Carter's face appeared calm and his body relaxed. The words he spoke came easily. "She's in her early fifties and has degrees from four major universities. She's brilliant and, more importantly, has studied imprints for more than twenty years. I met her when I was dealing with Molly Rydell, the woman in England. I liked her from the moment she first spoke. She has something many lack—real empathy. She's like you in a few ways. About your size, has the same hair color, and is unmarried. She tends to be a loner. Beyond Rydell, she also worked with a Russian professor who was gunned down in 2011. He was a wreck when they met, but I understand he stabilized after their meetings."

"What's her trick?"

"I have no clue."

As the doctor stepped out of the SUV and into the sunlight, Factor realized the accuracy of Carter's description. Lenards did resemble her enough that someone might mistake them for sisters. The psychologist was wearing jeans, a gray sweater, and white tennis shoes. Like Factor, she'd chosen a baseball cap to top off her outfit. Beyond her clothes, Lenards had applied only a touch of lipstick and eyeshadow, but that was all she needed to radiate both beauty and warmth.

"Dr. Factor?" Lenards asked as she approached. Her voice was sweet, like that of a neighbor who always found time for talk and lemonade, and her smile would've lit up a concert hall. On top of that, she oozed both grace and charisma.

"Call me Max."

"Then you can address me as B.R." As the women shook hand, Lenards asked, "How are you doing, Elton?" As she never looked in his direction, her question seemed more routine than sincere.

"For a man who keeps getting shot at, I'm feeling pretty good. So far, I've dodged all the bullets."

"You always were lucky," Lenards suggested as she released Factor's hand. She tilted her head before asking, "Max, let's get straight to the point. Are you able to deal with the invaders in your head?"

The visitor's tone begged for honesty, and Factor complied. "Up until a few days ago, I could handle them pretty well. But they're coming fast and furious now, and I'm overloading."

"What have you been doing to shut them out?"

"I don't have a clue. It's like guests who don't know how to knock or when to leave. It's kind of like being a hotel with loud parties going on in the room next to you."

"Then," Lenards announced, "we need to find a way to lock that door. We don't have time to waste. Where would you like to talk?"

"Why don't we sit out here?"

"The porch is great."

As the women moved to a pair of rocking chairs situated at the far end, Carter followed. "Would you like anything to eat or drink?" Both women shook their heads. "Well, if you do, you can raid the kitchen. Since I'm not needed, I'll make some calls and run an errand."

Lenards waited for their host to exit before turning her attention back to Factor. "You look tired."

"I'm exhausted. Sleep's harder and harder to find. I dread closing my eyes because of what I see in the dark."

"Stress triggers memories," Lenards noted, "and based on what Elton told me, you've been under more of it in the past week than you likely have been in your entire life." She paused and looked toward the ridge on the far side of the river before making an observation. "I feel positive you have the mental ability to control what's happening to you."

"I once thought that, but in the last few days …"

"Did you have a favorite toy as a child?"

"What?"

"I'll explain why I'm asking in a bit. I just want to know if you had a favorite toy."

Factor closed her eyes. As she did, a homemade rag doll popped into her mind. She remembered carrying it everywhere. It had button eyes, yarn for hair, and wore a homemade flower sack dress. It'd been a gift from a favorite aunt.

"Are you recalling something?" Lenards asked, breaking into Factor's thoughts.

Chapter Twenty-Five

"Yes."

"A toy?"

"A doll."

"Why was it special to you?"

"It wasn't. It was my grandmother's. She carried it everywhere. She was eight when it was lost in a flood."

Lenards gently smiled before prompting, "I need *your* favorite toy, not the toy of someone from your past."

"I never really had one. I didn't play with toys much. From the time I was in school, I was always reading."

Lenards nodded and made an admission. "I didn't have a favorite toy either. So, let's try something else. When you were a kid, did you have a favorite song?"

"Yeah, there was one that stood out. When I was really small, I sang it all the time."

"What was it?"

"My grandfather taught me an old country standard, 'You Are My Sunshine'."

"Please sing it for me."

Factor shook her head. "I don't sing in public."

"You will today," the doctor commanded. "Now don't worry about your voice, just begin singing. I want to hear you just like your grandfather did. I'll bet you made him grin when you sang it."

"He smiled like he was proud. He even had me sing it at reunions."

Feeling both silly and awkward, Factor quietly began to push her voice around the familiar words. After a verse, she glanced over at a smiling Lenards who, by waving her right hand, urged her to continue. With newfound confidence, Factor sang a bit louder, and by the time she'd finished, she was almost belting out the lyrics."

"What do you feel right now?" Lenards asked.

"I don't really know."

"Tell me what you're thinking about?"

"I'm not. I'm just kind of floating."

"What about your ancestors, those that live in your head, where are they?"

Factor smiled. "They aren't there. My mind's clear." She grinned before adding, "It's just me."

The doctor nodded. "Coping skill number one. When you're surrounded by too many voices, tune them out. You just did that by focusing on your favorite childhood song. Suddenly the problems, or invaders in this case, disappeared, and you were enveloped by the carefree nature of a time when you were secure and happy. And, because you probably often sang this song while you were alone, you found the solitude you have lost as an imprint."

"It's that simple?" a hopeful Factor marveled.

"No, but it's a start. You see, in a way, imprints have an addiction to the memories of others. Because of your condition, you can't turn them either on or off. They just push the door open and march in even if you didn't invite them. But by drowning them out with one of your own memories, you can keep them at bay."

"Just by singing a specific song?"

"As I said, it's a beginning. Now we have to expand on it. Sometimes that song won't work, so you'll have to have other things to focus on to drown out the other memories. Let's search for other happy moments of solitude from your life and add them to 'You Are My Sunshine'."

"And you know this works?"

"I used this technique on Boris Stravinsky, and he coped with the myriad memories that invaded his head. I think he could've handled them forever if he hadn't been murdered."

"I'd rather die by an assassin's bullet than go crazy and take my own life."

"Let's hope you don't have to make a choice like that. Let's work on some more good memories. What was your favorite place to go as a child? Your safe spot?"

"There was a window seat in my room overlooking an apple tree."

"Picture yourself there now."

Chapter 26

Elton Carter loved the cabin for many reasons, but it wasn't the building that brought him the greatest sense of peace, it was the land. The view of the river from the ridge was hypnotizing. The huge stands of timber reminded him of the grandeur of nature. The rolling meadows, with their colorful wildflowers, were masterpieces of artistic beauty. And then there were the animals. Turkey, deer, raccoons, opossums, bear, and even mountain lions made each hike an adventure. As he watched a bobcat climb a tree as he hiked up to the crest of Eagle's Ridge, his cell rang. The ID he spied surprised him. What in the world did Indira Morel want? When he'd ended their romance, she'd made it abundantly clear she never wanted to see him again.

Apprehensive, Carter answered, "Indy?"

"Yeah, I'm probably the last person you expected to call."

"No doubt. The last words I heard from your lips were encouraging me to head to a much warmer environment. I wasn't aware that folks of your faith actually believed in hell."

Recalling that memory might have been a mistake. It seemed to set her off.

"I'd don't regret any of what I said. You're a jerk and an egotistical heel. You live for yourself alone. You spend more time looking in a mirror than any fashion model I know, and I've met several. You have few manners and no sense of style. I hate your aftershave as well as the way you smack your lips when you chew gum. And your diet's horrible.It's a wonder your arteries have any room left for blood. I'd be worried about your heart if you had one."

"What's wrong with my aftershave?"

"You're hopeless."

He smiled. No woman could dish it out like Morel. "Yeah, maybe I'm hopeless, but we had some good times."

Perhaps Morel didn't agree with that assessment. She immediately moved the conversation away from old memories. "You know my brother is a part of Israeli intelligence."

"If you're asking if I realized he got the brains in the family—"

"Don't go there," she warned.

"Yeah, I know what Jacob does. What does that have to do with us? Did he dig up some dirt that you're going to use to ruin what little reputation I have left?"

"No, he doesn't care enough about you to waste time researching anything in your life."

That stung. Frowning, Carter strolled over to a tall oak, leaned against the trunk and considered what Jacob must've discovered that'd prompted Morel's call. Had to be big! Before he could make a guess, Morel popped back on the line.

"You had an altercation in the past couple of days."

"More than one small skirmish," he corrected her. "How did you know?"

"Because you ended the life of a man my brother had been using as an informant."

"When? Where? There were two scrapes where my life hung in the balance. Yesterday was one of them."

"That's the one I'm talking about," she paused before sarcastically asking, "There was another life-or-death battle? Was it with an irate husband?"

"Later on, the first one," Carter growled. "You said I killed someone Jacob used and that my pulling the trigger has him riled? Excuse me, the men were trying to shoot me, which didn't make me very happy either."

"By killing that man, justified or not, you might've upset an operation that Mossad felt was very important. And I said might, not that you had."

"Was he an informant or hired gun?" a suddenly incensed Carter demanded. "By the way, I had no idea I was such a burden to the Jewish state. Who do I send my card of apology to?"

"Informant. And don't you ever get tired of cracking wise? The world's not all about you, no matter what you might think."

"So," Carter demanded, "does this mean that Israel wants me dead? And, no matter what you think of me, I need an honest answer. If Mossad is on my tail, then I'll need to go to confession for the first time."

"You're not Catholic," she jabbed. "What's the term for those who are no longer active in their faith?"

"Backslider."

"Yeah, that's it, you're a backslid Methodist."

"Which is why I've never been to confession." He allowed that observation to sink in before demanding, "So, am I a target?"

"Don't flatter yourself, Mossad doesn't have any interest in you. There's a reason your cable show didn't air in Israel—no one in my homeland cares about you."

Morel was on a roll. Was this a sign of how much she hated him or a cover to hide feelings she still had for him?

"Elton, I'm going to be honest with you, but you need to be just as honest with me. I obviously have information you need. So, I expect you to answer my questions without hesitation. If you do that, I'll give you the scoop on the man who tried to kill you."

It was an interesting offer. To help Factor keep breathing, he needed to know who had targeted her. But what if Morel was conning him? What if she just wanted information that she could pass along to Jacob so that Mossad could take out Factor? As he considered that possibility, he questioned if the ambush at the airport, and even at the house, were hits ordered by Mossad. It wouldn't take much to believe that Israel wanted Factor dead.

"Elton, I'm still waiting."

"Okay, Indy, we'll play it this way. You give me something that I can be sure is the truth, and I'll pitch something back your way. But you have to start."

She didn't hesitate. "Have you ever heard of a man they call the Ghost?"

That was the name Mosby had mentioned yesterday. But the Ghost he was talking about couldn't be the one Morel had in mind.

"Elton, I asked you a question."

"There's a legend of a man who's supposedly dead who still works for certain intelligence organizations, but I believe he's a myth created by the CIA or MI6 to worry the Russians. I think it's a series of different people who've done jobs under that guise. If the fable of the Ghost is what you're selling, I'm not buying."

"He's real," Morel assured him, "Jacob has worked with him. Be honest, do you know who he is or do you just want to stay in the dark?"

Maybe she wasn't playing him after all. Perhaps she did want him to keep breathing. But it'd take a huge leap of faith to believe the Ghost was real. It'd be a longer stretch to believe this Ghost could also be Mosby's Ghost. Carter paused, watched a squirrel bound from the top of a sweet gum tree to the oak he was under, before spitting out just one word. "No!"

"No what? No, you don't want to know, or no, you don't want to stay in the dark?"

Why did she always have to make things so complicated? Why did she refuse to just lay things out in a nice, neat fashion? "I'd like a little light please," he barked.

"I can give you a lot if you level with me on something."

"What's that?"

"My brother's contacts were watching the gang that tried to take you out."

"Why's that?"

"Because Mossad learned the informant you killed was now playing with Putin's boys. He had information they didn't want Russia to have. As he wasn't working for them yesterday, they wanted him alive so they could find out whose payroll he was on now. You cost them that chance."

Carter considered what Morel had just admitted. The longer he chewed on the scenario, the more enraged he became. If Mossad knew what had gone down, they must have been in both Little Rock and at the farm, and they hadn't stepped in.

"You mean they were watching?" he screamed, his words echoing off the rock wall on the other side of the river.

"Get ahold of yourself," she snapped. "They were there. They planned to step in if it appeared the other team was winning."

"That's a crock, they couldn't have stepped in and saved us. We barely saved ourselves. If they'd stepped in, it would've only been to check our pulses."

"I wasn't there."

"I was, and my life meant nothing to them. I know that for a fact!"

"Why should it? They were there to get information from their former confidant, not to save your hide."

"Tell them they owe me!"

"Actually, you owe them. They cleaned up your mess and got rid of the bodies. You can't leave a bunch of dead people around and not have the law question what happened."

"I didn't have time to worry about that. I had far more important things on my mind."

"Which leads to my question. Who's the woman?"

"Why? Are you jealous?"

"Do you want to know about the Ghost or not?"

"Why should I want to know about him?"

"Because he hired those men."

Carter moved to where he could see the river, but his mind stayed locked on what he'd just heard. If the Ghost was more than a fabricated spy story, then the stakes had gotten higher. Mosby had said the man behind the airport hit wanted Factor dead to hurt someone else. Maybe, in this case, hurt meant more than just mental anguish. Perhaps there was a group that wanted her alive to mine her mind for information to sway the balance of world power. Killing her would thwart that plan. But was the Ghost Morel was talking about the same one who employed Mosby?

"I asked who the woman was?" Morel reminded him.

Carter frowned. He'd play the game, but only one card at a time. Tit for tat.

"She's a university professor. We share interests."

"And she's beautiful?"

"Yes. Now what about Ghost?"

"Forty years ago, he was a top agent at MI6. He got wind of a CIA plot to take out a member of the House of Commons. Four Americans assigned a CIA hit man to the job. When the plot failed, the CIA planted materials in the man's home that made it appear he was a double agent working with the KGB. He had no choice but to fake his own death and disappear. A decade ago, Mossad discovered he was still alive. They tracked him down and convinced him to work a very special mission for which he was paid ten million dollars."

"What was the mission?"

"I couldn't tell you if I knew, and I don't. But after he was paid, he disappeared again. A few weeks ago, while shadowing the man you killed at the farmhouse, my brother saw the Ghost talking to the informant. Ironically, the meeting was in a cemetery."

From what he learned, that made sense. Mosby had told them his boss held meetings in graveyards. The two ghosts were now morphing into one. So, Carter did need the information.

"What else can you tell me about him?"

"His real name is Basil Holmes. He's a brilliant lone wolf operative. He must live in America now, though Mossad doesn't know where. He's in his mid-sixties. When he was with MI6, he was trained in explosives and was at the top of his class in marksmanship."

"So, you think he's after me?"

"I doubt it. He has no connection to you."

"Then …"

"He's after the woman. Now why does he want her dead?"

"If I told you I didn't know …"

"I wouldn't believe you."

"I don't feel comfortable giving the information to Mossad."

"They don't care. The man they wanted is dead. What happens to the Ghost means nothing to them. Though they'd love to know where he is in case they need his services down the road. Elton, I'm being honest when I assure you Jacob only called me because he thought I'd want to know your life was and is in danger."

This *was* really all about Carter's welfare. She did care! It was time to play!

"You won't tell your brother or anyone at Mossad?"

"You have my word. And, while we didn't end on a good note, you know me well enough to realize my word, unlike yours, is solid."

She was right, she always played it level. So, he was almost completely sure he could trust her. Besides, at this point, he needed a friend.

"Her name is Dr. Maxine Factor."

"Factor?" The line went dead for a long moment before she whispered, "Elton, you've got huge problems."

"What makes you say that?"

"Factor's an imprint, and I know you know what that means."

"I know, but how do you know?"

"I'm very high up in an organization called the Star. It's made up of a number of supporters of Israel. We've sworn to do everything in our power to protect the state."

"I thought you said Mossad had no interest in this?"

"It doesn't, at least not that my brother knows of, but there are members of the Star who have argued for Factor's death."

"How did they find out about her?"

"Sources in the Vatican, which means they're probably after her as well. My guess is you're being hunted by several sundry teams who all have much different reasons for wanting Factor dead."

That was not what he wanted to hear. If there were several groups with unlimited resources on their tails, the world wasn't big enough.

"Elton, you must have her at the cabin."

He and Morel had spent many days and nights along the river. And if the groups after Factor knew he was with her, then it wouldn't take long for them to find out about the cabin either. It was time to move.

"Elton, what's she like?"

"You mean Factor?"

"Yes, I've always wanted to talk to an imprint."

"It's not a gift, let me assure you. She's stable so far, but I'm not sure how long she'll stay that way. The voices are beginning to affect her sleep. She might be running on borrowed time."

"But her memories of the past must be intriguing?"

"They come in bursts, but so far there's been nothing that'll change the way we look at history. The problem is there're just too many crowding her mind. She's running out of room."

"That's too bad. If she could control those memories, what a wealth of information she could give to those of us dedicated to human history."

"She's not a resource," Carter snapped, "she's a human being. And a pretty special one at that."

"I didn't mean to sound callus."

"Well, you did. Now, if what you say is true, and people know I'm with her, then I need to find someplace else to hide. I'm trying to give her a chance for a few more months or a year. So, can you do me a favor?"

"You mean you're suddenly putting someone else first?" Morel mused, "She must really be something!"

"This isn't love. Oh, she's attractive, smart, and has spunk, and I was fascinated at first. But now, I pity her. Her mind's about to explode. So, do you have a suggestion of someplace safe?"

"I can make a call. I might know of something there in the States."

"Also, Indy, do you think Mossad could do some digging and discover why the Ghost is after her? I need to know if it's about evening a score."

"Mossad wouldn't, but my brother might. But the odds are long. Remember, he doesn't even know where the Ghost is."

"Could he dig a bit deeper?"

"I'll see." She paused, as if taking time to make a note, but added, "This should give you some peace for the moment, the Star's not going after her. I think I can keep them off your trail. If that changes, I'll let you know."

"I appreciate it."

"Elton, there's one more thing," Morel's tone was suddenly different, a bit softer, and there were hints of apprehension. It was like she was trying to say something and didn't know how. That wasn't like her at all. "Elton," she began again, "I could never get a handle on how you felt about me, but I guess you must've known, even if I never said it, that I loved you."

It's strange how the words he wanted to hear for so long now rang so hollow he wished she hadn't said them. Maybe it was time to level with her too. After all, he might not have much time left and some things didn't need to be left unsaid. It was time to tell her something that was still bugging him.

"I was told you were only using me to get money for digs."

"Who told you that?"

"It doesn't matter."

"Was it Jacob? After all, my family never approved of our relationship."

"They probably had good reason," Carter admitted.

"With all you have going on right now," Morel whispered, "I guess I shouldn't have admitted how I felt about you. I should've waited until a better time."

"No. I just wish you'd said it a long time ago." He paused, trying to put the past and present into some kind of perspective, before grudgingly pulling words from deep in his own heart. "Indy, I loved you too. I loved you so much I hated myself for it. I told you a hundred times I never wanted to be tied down. I promised myself when I was young, I never would be. I didn't run away because I thought you were using me for my money—I didn't care about that—I was just scared of commitment. Deep down, when it comes to emotions, I'm a coward."

"When it comes to snakes you're a coward too," she added, as if trying to make him more at ease. She waited a few heartbeats before adding, "We screwed up."

"I can't bail on Max, but if I could, I'd run back to you right now."

"I wouldn't want you to bail, but …"

"Yeah, I know. As Elvis would say, 'We're caught in a trap and can't get out.' Do you still listen to Elvis when you work?"

"Yeah. You liked him too. Do you still listen?"

"No, I quit when you and I went our separate ways. Too many memories."

"I'll keep you informed," Morel promised. "I'll check on that place to stay. We'll talk in day or so. Good luck."

"Thanks, I'll need it. And—"

"Let's not talk about that." She cut the call.

Pushing off the tree, Carter headed back to the cabin. There was no time to mourn love lost. He had to get things ready for a move and find someplace where no one would expect him to go.

Chapter 27

Noon
Thursday, September 22
Courtyard by Hilton, St. Louis, Missouri

To be good at anything, you need a target; otherwise you end up shooting at everything that moves and hitting nothing.

———◆———

For the past eighteen hours, Mason Hardin had done little more than watch Rocky Smith make a series of protracted telephone calls that were intended to help them find out what had happened to Maxine Factor. The value of all those conversations could be measured in zeros. Going online was no better. No matter where Smith drove down the information highway, there were nothing but dead ends.

As Smith doggedly worked, Hardin mourned. There could be no doubt he'd cost Marsha Chambers her life. Once they found the bomb, he shouldn't have allowed her to accompany him to Mount Vernon. He should have insisted she stay home. He never should've challenged her with the old line about dying for a story. And yet he had. He'd tossed off that remark as easily as a football coach would trot out a "give your all for your team" speech before a big game.

Just the day before, Chambers had shared she'd been working on a story for months, that, when published, would make him proud. "It's your kind of reporting," she'd said, "tough and gritty, fearless and meaningful." Now her story, whatever it was, would never see print. It had died with her.

Eaten up with pain, the morose reporter walked over to a mirror and stared at his reflection. His image presented the definition of exhaustion, but there was more—there was also hopelessness outlined on his face. He'd finally discovered just how cheap and fragile life could be.

Lois Lane! That's what she'd called herself. She was Lois to his Clark Kent. Sadly, he had no alter ego. He wasn't anything close to super, and he proved that when he failed to save her. Worse yet, he'd been drawn into helping Stone clean up the mess and make Hardin's body disappear. So, he was a major player in ending her life and in erasing her death. Thanks to him, her mother and brother might never know what happened to her. Thanks to him, there wouldn't be a memorial service or a grave. Thanks to him, they'd forever look at their front door on holidays hoping she'd come back, but she never would. Her death and her disappearance were all thanks to him.

Smith was glaring at him from across the room. His look of disgust was reserved for times when people failed to live up to the standards needed by a team. "You can't let it eat you."

There was a hint of anger in the Smith's tone, and it lit Hardin's short fuse. His rage exploded, "Easy for you to say—death is in your job description. In your line of work, folks are sacrificed every day. Reporters might be cussed, ridiculed, and even libeled, but torture and death are not part of our world. Neither is erasing us when we die. It's like she never existed. She was a good person ... no, she was a great person. She cared about others, and she lived for the truth. She didn't hide from a challenge. She ..."

Smith's face twisted into something grotesque and almost evil as he screamed. "Don't play that card on me! You report on death all the time. You can't wait to hear of another mass shooting so you can fight to interview people whose children have died at a school. You seek out those who are left alive after terrorist attacks. You write pages about how people have been brutalized. You're drawn to death like a vulture. You thrive on misery and pain. And you think you have a right

to attack me? What we did was because we wanted to save lives—
what you do exploits lives. I might be a rat, but you're a snake!"

Hardin wanted to argue but couldn't. Stone was right. He'd hovered
over tragedies and, in the name of getting the story, had dipped into
others' pain and suffering. Once again, it was time to wallow in guilt.

"She shouldn't be dead. I killed her."

"No, she shouldn't be dead, but that wasn't your fault. She chose
to come even after someone put a bomb in your car. She knew the
risks just like you did. And like you, she wanted to live on the edge.
That's a part of your world and mine. We live on that edge because
we're blessed with a sense of curiosity that boarders on insanity, and it's
matched with a body that pumps out far too much adrenalin. That's
why few of us get to collect social security."

"Okay," Hardin announced with a wave of his hand. Fighting and
screaming where just a waste of time. What they needed was answers.
It was time to focus. "Okay, Smith, you've made your point. Help me
switch the channel. Are we any closer to knowing who killed her?"

"You're like the kid who's constantly asking, 'How much longer,
Daddy?' No, we are no closer, and we won't be until we discover
where Factor is. The key to finding Factor is Dixon."

"And he didn't kill Marsha? Are you sure?"

"Let me explain this again. Dixon couldn't have killed her and
the president of the university. Those events overlapped. Also, Factor
couldn't have disappeared on her own. She had to have help. Knowing
who helped her is the missing piece of the puzzle. That's what we
need, and I'd like your help."

"Do you think Dixon knows who has her?"

"My guess is that he'd still be in town if he didn't."

Hardin's vibrating cell brought a welcome end to a conversation
that was going nowhere. He glanced at the screen and frowned.

"Who is it?"

"A reporter for one of the tabloids."

"Are you going to answer it?"

"Why? He's probably looking for some kind of gossip."

"Answer it," Smith ordered.

"Why?"

"To get your mind on something else for a few minutes."

Hardin shrugged and hit accept. "Yeah?"

"Mason, Deke Ryan here."

"What's up Deke?"

"I'm chasing a wild lead and thought you might have the answer. After all, Illinois is your turf."

"I doubt it, but shoot."

"A student at a college in southern Illinois grabbed a picture of Elton Carter on the Washington-Lincoln College campus a couple of days ago. The guy posted it on social media, and I happened to spot it. I could spin a great yarn if I could tie the billionaire to the death of the school's president. Have you heard anything?"

This was nothing more than the typical gossip Ryan always traded in. Sad when a man educated at a top school spent his days dealing in sordid gossip.

"Deke, I'm sorry, but I don't know anything."

"But tell me, Mason, why would he be in a place like Mount Vernon? My sources assure me he gave a gift of twelve million dollars to the college. Was that cash a cover for killing the president? And, on top of that, one of the professors at the school has disappeared. She's a babe. On looks alone, she fits the profile of the type of woman Carter goes after. And, he's not been linked to anyone since he parted with Indira Morel. Do you think I'm on the right track?"

Hardin considered what he'd just learned. Part of it actually seemed to hint at the missing puzzle piece he and Smith were trying to find. Intrigued, he leaned into his phone.

"Ryan, Carter's a nut for history, isn't that right?"

"That's why he hosted that cable series. He went to ruins all over the globe to uncover secrets. He's also funded scores of archaeological excavations. That's where he hooked up with Morel. They have the same passion for the past. So, am I onto something?"

The last thing he and Stone needed was tabloid headlines about Maxine Factor. He had to steer Ryan in a different direction. It was time to spin a yarn of his own. "Deke, I may as well admit that I know more than I've said. You're onto something, but the history professor has nothing to do with it."

"Really?"

"Yeah. I went to Mount Vernon, did a little digging myself. Factor left for personal reasons. She's a complete bore. There's no story there.

Carter was in town to convince Dr. Hall to allow Indira Morel to lecture for a semester. The gift was just to persuade the president to hire Carter's old girlfriend. It sadly worked out that Hall had a history of heart trouble and died just hours after he and Carter made the deal. It was little more than the billionaire trying to win back the love of his life—Indira Morel."

"That is fantastic! What an angle! So much better than a hook up with a local woman. This might earn me a big bonus. Thanks, Mason."

"You run with that. I have other fish to fry." Abruptly ending the call, Hardin looked over at Stone. "How's your file on Elton Carter?"

"Long and detailed."

"He was spotted on campus in the past few days. He made a huge gift to the college."

"Carter lives and dies history," Smith reasoned, "if he found out that Factor was an imprint, he'd obviously want to protect her as well as tap into her knowledge."

"And, if Deke was right, a twelve-million-dollar gift might just buy him the chance to spirit her away with the college's blessing."

Stone snapped his fingers. "He's got to be the one protecting her, but all his money won't help him against those on Factor's trail. Cash doesn't buy the skill set he needs."

"So, what's next?" Hardin asked.

"Time for me to make a few calls and have Carter's complete file sent to my laptop. Then, we begin to dig into places he might try to hide Factor."

"But what about the people who killed Marsha?"

"Once they put this together, they'll be going the same place we are. We just need to get there first."

This news didn't lighten the grief, but it did restore Hardin's focus. Perhaps it even offered a trail leading to both justice and revenge. It also might just lead to an early death, but that'd surely be better than living with all this guilt.

Chapter 28

5:15 p.m.
Thursday, September 22
Carter's Cabin outside of Saddle, Arkansas

Being in the wrong place at the right time can be fatal. But you rarely know the wrong place from the right place until it's too late.

———◆———

Late in the afternoon, Elton Carter grilled hamburgers and served them to B.R. Lenards and Maxine Factor on the back deck. As the afternoon sun sank behind the ridge, shooting orange slivers through purple skies, Carter used the fading rays of daylight to study his guests. Unlike this morning, both women were relaxed ... almost giddy. It was a welcome sight. If the doctor had managed to provide the professor with a bit of relief, it would surely make their next move, which needed to happen tomorrow and no later, easier. But there was no use worrying about that tonight. For the moment, he wanted to observe Factor, a woman he'd spent four days with but in reality felt like he had never met.

Carter had never seen Factor's face light up with a genuine smile. He'd seen smirks and grins, but nothing reflecting security or joy. Now, she was laughing. Her body language was different as well. She was no longer folded up inside herself. She was loose, open, and unrestrained. Whatever treatment Lenards had employed resulted in what looked like a miracle. But the odds against it lasting were short, not because the cure might wear off, but because there were too many people bent on delivering Factor's final breath. Even now, someone was likely pinning down their location, and if that were true, it was because word had leaked that the imprint was with him.

Carter's vision floated from the quickly fading sunset to the ridge. The animals who pursued prey were often nocturnal, hidden by a canvas of timber and hills. They were watching now, looking into the valley for unsuspecting targets. Under the cover of darkness, the battle for life and death was about to begin. That thought had never bothered him before, but tonight was different. Much different!

"It's starting to cool off," a suddenly unnerved Carter announced as he picked up the plates from a glass-topped table. "Let's move things inside."

As she stood, Lenards stretched, smiled, and announced, "Actually, I need to take off. I'm going to Springfield, and that's a good drive. I'd like to get there before ten. I've got a speaking engagement tomorrow at Missouri State University."

"Not a word of what you did here," Carter warned.

"Of course not. Max's story can't be shared as long as she's alive. And perhaps what we were able to do today will give her the opportunity for a very long life."

"So, you were successful?"

"I'll let Max tell you all about it. Now, I need to grab my purse and hit the road."

As Carter put the dishes into the sink, the two women walked through the house to the front door. They were hugging as he approached.

"Thank you, B.R." It was obvious by her tone and smile that Factor's gratitude was sincere.

"If this works," Lenards answered, "it'll be because of your strength of will. All I did was give you a formula for employing what was already there."

"I think I can cope," Factor assured her. "And if I get overwhelmed, I'll call."

"Thanks for this opportunity, Elton." Lenards opened the front door and stepped out onto the porch. "And when you're not using this place as a hideout, invite me back up for some trout fishing. I have some new, custom-made flies and a rod I want to try out."

"It's a date," he assured her.

As Factor stood in the doorway, Carter escorted Lenards to her car. Once they were off the porch, he whispered, "Looks like it went well."

"This is like a chronic disease—there's no cure, but most of the time she should be able to cope. By the way, she's both brilliant and funny. I've encouraged her to use that sense of humor when dealing with moments of insecurity or danger. Now, what's the best way for me to get to Highway 63?"

Carter was just about to give her directions when a cracking noise came from atop the ridge. The unexpected sound caused him to jerk his head to the right. When he failed to spot the source, his gaze returned to Lenards. Her face was framed in shock. Reaching for the SUV's roof, she steadied herself, then, with no warning, fell to the ground, blood seeping through her blouse and puddling in the grass. Bending, he checked her pulse—there was none. The marksman had found her heart.

Knowing it was too late to help Lenards, Carter, his pulse racing, ran across the yard and leaped up the porch. Pushing Factor inside, he slammed and locked the door, then raced to the back of the home where he repeated the action. Feeling a small sense of security, he rushed to Factor. He found her looking between curtains at the spot where the shot must have originated. Surprisingly, she was incredibly calm.

"I saw a flash," she explained.

"You mean the shot?"

"No, more a reflection created by the final rays of the setting sun. Whoever did this is still up there. They're waiting for us to make a move. They're not going to leave until the job's done."

"How can you be sure?"

"Because two of my ancestors have been in this same position. I can see it just as clearly as I saw that flash." Her voice still flat and almost emotionless, she looked into Carter's face. "By your reaction, I guess B.R. is dead."

"She is."

"There's no time to mourn, at least not right now. Based on experience, we have to get moving."

Factor had been steady during the other two times they'd dealt with death, but now she'd moved it up a step. She displayed no emotions or panic. She was also not looking to him for guidance or help. Even more so than at the airport, she was fully in charge. She was no longer the protectee, but the protector.

"If we could get to the plane ..." Carter suggested.

"We can't," Factor declared. "He'd nail both of us before we got off the deck. But where he was when I spotted that flash means he can't see the far side of the house. We can drop out a bedroom window, get to the brush, and then work our way to the river. Didn't I see a canoe tied up down there?"

"Yeah, but you don't want me piloting a canoe. I'd drown us."

"I can handle one," she assured him.

"Did you go to camp as a kid?"

"Yeah, but I only learned to weave baskets there. Now get moving!"

"Maybe we should stay here."

"Based on what's in my head, he'll burn us out. Besides, staying inside is what he thinks we'll do." She moved away from the curtain, grabbed her purse and briefcase, and walked down the hall toward the far bedroom. After retrieving his phone, billfold, and a bag, Carter followed. When he caught up, she already had the window open and the screen off.

"Let's go."

She didn't wait for him to offer any resistance. After pushing through the opening, she dropped to the ground, stayed low, and jogged to the heavily wooded area just twenty feet across the grass. Glancing through the open door and down the hall, Carter took a deep breath and exited the room through the open window. Once he was safely hidden in the woods, he asked a question. "I've been with you for several days now, and Max, this isn't you. You aren't reacting to death. You're as cool as the other side of the pillow. You're completely relaxed even with an active shooter trying to kill us. I mean, you were good before, but now ..."

"When you're in trouble," she whispered, "it's always best to rely upon experience. I'm not leading you away from the assassin, three different people from the past are. The way the memories are coming, it's like they're all working together and each giving me a different point of view to help solve this problem. I wish you could see what's in my head. If you could, then you'd feel as calm as I do. Just trust me, or better yet, trust who's in my head."

He had to trust her. After all, she was the one with centuries of experience. But how had she changed so quickly from that woman who was fighting off suicide to a warrior ready for action? Was this the result of Lenards's work? Then the nightmare of Lenards's death landed on his shoulders and burrowed into his heart. He could see her face as she died, her dead body as it fell, and the blood oozing from her chest. And just like that, he was paralyzed. Who knows how long he'd have been frozen in place if Factor hadn't grabbed his attention?

"Follow me down the hill. Stay low and keep the trees between you and the ridge. This is important. Avoid stepping on brush of any kind. Watch carefully where your foot lands so you can make each move sure and silent. Become one with nature. When you do that, you can move as quietly as a deer and completely blend into the woods. That way he won't see you or hear you. And keep your focus. We'll mourn later. You get that?" Factor took three silent steps into the shadows before turning and adding, "And, keep this one other rule in mind. Do you remember social distancing from back in the COVID days?"

"Sure."

"Then make sure you stay at least six feet behind me. If we run into each other, we'll make noise. Now, let's go."

She moved down the hill as silently as a shadow. Doing his best to watch each footfall, Carter eased toward the water behind her. When they arrived at the bank, she crept to the canoe, turned it over, and slid it into the water. Pulling the paddles from where they'd been propped against a tree, she slipped them into the canoe. After glancing back toward the ridge, she signaled for Carter to get in the front of the small craft. A second later, she joined him, used her paddle to push off the bank, and began to move downstream.

"Stay low," she whispered, "and don't talk. Even though the moving stream makes some noise, your voice will carry over the water more than it does on land."

"Max, can you really handle a canoe?"

"My guide can," she assured him.

Carter, his eyes on the ridge, stayed low. Once they were around the bend, his heart slowed. The bank now moved by more quickly each time Factor quietly dipped a paddle into the water, and he began to feel more secure. Somehow, they'd dodged death once more.

"We owe B.R." Factor announced, no longer feeling the need to whisper.

He eased back into a sitting position. "Why?"

"I couldn't have done what I just did without what she taught me today."

"How's that?"

"When the memories become overwhelming, I just have to turn down the volume."

"I don't understand."

"I now have several different things I can concentrate on from my own life experiences that will drown out the noise made by my often-unwanted visitors. But she also taught me that when I need the wisdom from the past, when I need guides to show me the way, it's time to let my ancestors freely walk in my mind. In the past, I've fought to keep them out of my consciousness, but I now know there are moments when we need to live and work together. It was B.R. who put things into perspective."

"Instinct," he said.

"What do you mean?"

"When everything else fails. We always talk about relying on instincts. Are those instincts imprinted on each of us? Are they a small window of what you have?"

"Maybe." Factor paddled a bit faster, her smooth strokes barely making a sound. "I'd never thought of that." She made four more strokes before pulling the paddle out of the water and letting the current do the work. As she rested, she allowed a bit of the real Factor to surface. With a tear running down her cheek, she said, "She died in my place."

"Who?"

"B.R. From a distance she looks like me. The shooter won't figure out I'm not dead until he sees her body. If she hadn't looked like me, she'd be alive. I don't want anyone else dying for me. And that includes you. The past four days have made clear that death stalks me." She took a deep breath before adding, "And I wouldn't have run, I'd have let the guy finish the job, if it hadn't been for you. I wasn't going to let you die for me."

As he watched the banks, now bathed in darkness, slide by, Carter could understand her feelings. After all, when he'd brought Lenards into the picture, he'd also set her up to be killed. So, really this was on him. Once again overcome with remorse, he muttered, "Should have left as soon as I heard from Indy."

"What's that?" Factor asked.

"Nothing," he lied.

Guilt was something he'd avoided most of his life. He'd never thought about it when he'd broken hearts or ended friendships. He rationalized those moments by sending expensive gifts as tokens to ease anger or pain. But life couldn't be bought back. This was going to haunt him for a long time. Maybe forever.

"I may have someone from my past who taught me the skills needed to handle a canoe," Factor announced as she broke him out of a pity party, "but I don't know where I'm going. Do you have a plan?"

"Down the river, two more miles, is the home of the man who takes care of the cabin for me. I've got a car stored in his barn, and I've always got a lot of cash in a safe there too. We can then make our next move."

"Where are we going?"

"We'll figure that out," he assured her, though at this moment he had no location in mind.

As she resumed paddling, his thoughts went back to his discussion with Indira Morel. Had the man they called the Ghost been on the ridge? She said he was a sharpshooter, so he'd have had the skills to take out a target with one shot. Whoever it was, the next move had to take them to a place no one would associate with Carter. Where could that be?

Chapter 29

7:55 p.m.
Thursday, September 22
Carter's Cabin outside of Saddle, Arkansas

Age is an unwanted visitor and a cruel master. The lessons it teaches must be swallowed like a bitter pill.

F or over an hour, William Dixon watched the house, his weapon ready. Finally assured there were no signs of life in or around the cabin's perimeter, he judiciously worked his way off the ridge. When he reached the yard, under the cover of darkness and deep shadows, he circled the cabin from a safe distance. Except for the chirping of wildlife, he heard nothing. There was also no movement inside. But for the limp body beside the SUV, it seemed no one was home. But that couldn't be true. He'd seen Carter walking Factor to the car. Where was he?

As he moved to the far side of the cabin, he noted a screenless open window. Carter must have made his escape using that exit. As Dixon had no need to kill the billionaire, that was fine. That'd make this a very clean kill. Creeping closer, he carefully peered inside through the open window. His limited line of sight presented a home void of activity. Leaning the rifle against the house's log wall, he grabbed the window ledge and lifted himself into what was a bedroom. After pulling a Luger from his belt and releasing the safety, he quietly moved through the room and down the hall, checking every room along the way. A hundred steps assured him there was no one left in the cabin.

Satisfied he was alone, Dixon strolled into the kitchen, flipped on a light, and opened the refrigerator. Retrieving a bottle of water, he sat at a table and casually quenched his thrust. As he did, he admired the house. Carter had created the ultimate getaway. The rustic appeal of the logs and native stone combined with the latest in electronics and luxury offered the sense of both charm and style. Still, he liked his remote lair even better. His had history, classic decor, a priceless collection of art, and a view the Ozarks couldn't touch.

Finishing the water, Dixon tossed the bottle in a bin marked recycle, made his way through the living room and out onto the porch. Pulling a small, LED flashlight from his pocket, he nonchalantly ambled down the five steps to get a closer view of his handiwork. He smiled as he noted where his bullet had entered her body—heart, dead center. She'd died within seconds, probably without even knowing what had happened. A good clean kill was a sign of solid work and planning. He prided himself on both.

Leaning closer, he moved the beam of light from the chest to the face. Dixon was not at all surprised by the open eyes or frozen expression of shock, he'd seen that dozens of times, but he was nevertheless stunned. The dead woman was not his target.

Jerking the purse from her shoulder, Dixon retrieved the victim's identification. Her driver's license revealed she was Bethany Ruth Lenards. Frowning, he angrily tossed the bag onto the ground, rose, stepped back, and let his flashlight illuminate the whole scene. The shape of her body, her hair color, her height, and weight all synced with Factor, but this woman was not the professor. For the first time in more than forty years, he'd made the blunder of a lifetime, and for only the second time in his life, he'd killed the wrong person.

He moved back to the steps, sat down, and considered his mistake. No matter how he looked at it, it came down to numbers. His math had been wrong. Dixon hadn't expected there to be anyone at the cabin but Carter and Factor. It never dawned on him there might be a third party. When he'd arrived and spotted the car, he'd just assumed it belonged to the billionaire. So, that meant his target had also escaped through the open bedroom window. Suddenly, his life was a great deal more complicated. Where would they go? That question was going to take some time and research to answer. Pushing off the steps, he walked over and picked up Lenards and slung her over his shoulder like a bag of seed. Pivoting, he carried her inside the house where he dumped her body onto the couch. That task completed, he thought through his options.

The easiest course was simply to walk away. He'd never taken off his gloves, so no one would ever know he'd been here. Yet doing so was like admitting defeat. He glanced back at the body. Perhaps she needed to go out with a bit more style. It was time to show contempt for the man who'd upset his plans and to do it in a spectacular way.

With retribution driving him, Dixon quickly exited the home, walked across the yard, and entered a shed. In the corner, he saw a five-gallon gas can. Discovering it was almost full, he returned to the cabin and began to spill the propellant. After dripping some into every room, he poured the last gallon onto Lenards. Retrieving a match from the kitchen, he struck and tossed it onto the couch. Within seconds, the body erupted in flames. Turning, he exited out the back door and headed toward the ridge. As he walked, he pulled out his cell and made a call.

"Hello." The voice on the other end was obviously unnerved by hearing from Doctor Death.

"It's me," Dixon announced without emotion.

"Is the job done?" Dallas Arnold asked.

"No, I killed the wrong woman."

"What?"

"It's none of your concern. She looked like Factor, she was in the same location, and both of those things worked to her disadvantage."

"But you killed an innocent woman."

"Factor's just as innocent, and you want me to kill her, so get over it."

"What happened to Factor?" Arnold's voice was displaying signs of panic.

"She got away with the billionaire who's protecting her. It might take some time, but I'll track them down."

"The billionaire?"

"Yeah, a guy name Elton Carter. You've probably heard of him. That makes this operation a lot harder. But all you need to concern yourself with is the price. There's no charge for the bonus death."

Dixon turned back to look at the cabin. Flames were now visible through the living room windows. With the closest neighbors a mile away, it'd take a while before anyone was alerted to the fire. There was no rush.

"What's next?" Arnold asked.

"You're going to do some work for me. You constantly brag about your contacts, so I want you to find out everything you can on Carter. I want to know about all the properties he owns and where he hangs out when he's not in his New England mansion. I also need a list of his friends … those he really trusts. He's going to have to have some help in hiding Factor. Whenever you find out anything, no matter how insignificant, text or call this number. You got that?"

"But …"

"No buts if you want me to do my job."

"Okay."

"Get to work right now—don't wait until tomorrow. And don't worry about anyone getting suspicious, you have a long history of cozying up to fat cats, so the fact you're digging up information on a billionaire won't surprise anyone. They'll just think you're looking for another mark."

Dixon abruptly ended the call, slipped the phone back into his pocket, and moved in the direction where he'd left the rented truck. As he didn't know what direction Carter might take, the best thing to do was stay in the central part of the country near a major airport. Thus, he set his sights on a return to St. Louis. About halfway to his vehicle, he noticed a pain in his knee.

"Age" he mumbled. Then, as if he'd grabbed a live wire, a shock rocked him. Would he have made that mistake ten years ago? Even in the twilight, wouldn't he have noticed the target was not Factor? Maybe he'd screwed up because he was getting older. Perhaps his senses were not as sharp. He'd never considered that he might age out of his profession. Was what happened tonight the first sign?

Chapter 30

12:04 p.m.
Friday, September 23
U.S. Highway 63 twenty miles east of Springfield,
Missouri

Sometimes the bridges we burn can be rebuilt. It might time some time, effort, and eating a bit of crow, but with the right attitude, mistakes in the past can be righted.

———◆———

After canoeing to Jarrod Jackson's home and picking up the 2018 Ford Escape as well as a duffle bag filled with cash, the billionaire and Maxine Factor headed north. Their first stop was a Walmart in Thayer, Missouri, for clothes and supplies. Carter paid in cash to avoid his credit cards being traced. With everything they needed, the pair pulled back onto US Highway 63 and began their trek north. Where they were going remained undecided.

Besides his main residence in New England, Carter had homes in Colorado, Montana, Chicago, Reno, Nashville, and San Diego. At least one of the hit men now knew who he was, hence, he'd check each of Carter's American properties beginning with the one nearest the cabin. In time, he'd hunt them down. Survival meant going off grid. But where? Because of his stint on cable TV, Carter's face and name were well known. Rarely could he walk into a store or restaurant anywhere in the world without someone recognizing him. That ruled out a stay at a resort or hotel. Whether Factor realized it or not, her protector was likely a liability. Ironic. They each made the other a target.

Driving a straight stretch, with no cars behind or ahead of them, he glanced to his right. As she had earlier in the evening, Factor seemed calm and assured. She was watching the road and quietly singing a song he hadn't heard in years—"You Are My Sunshine." As he listened to the simple verses time and time again, the final line began to sting. In his haste to protect her, had he taken her sunshine away?

"Too late," he muttered.

"What's that?" Factor asked.

"Nothing, just thinking out loud."

He hadn't lied, he was doing just that. He now understood he should've hired someone to protect her and kept himself out of the picture. But no, his ego wouldn't allow that, he had to be directly involved. He had to be with the imprint. He had to be the one who probed her mind. If he hadn't put himself first, then B.R. Lenards would still be alive. But he couldn't manage this from afar. He hated to admit it, but Morel had been spot on, it always had to be about him.

With no ability to change the past, he returned his focus to the present. He couldn't just drive forever. He had to find a place to hide. If only one of those people sharing Factor's head would speak up and make a suggestion. Yet, even if they did, they were all in the past— what good would that do them now?

As he reran the last twenty-four hours in his mind, a familiar face jumped out. Punching the call button on the Ford's steering wheel, he voiced a command, "Call Indy." A minute later, the woman who he'd realized far too late might have been the love of his life picked up. How good it was to hear that slightly British accent again.

"Hello, anything wrong?"

"A lot of things," Carter explained. "We were attacked. The assassin killed the doctor who was working with Max, and we only escaped because of the guidance of a couple of her ancestors. The bottom line is they know I have her."

"By they, do you mean the Ghost?"

"I don't know. The Ghost is the obvious pick, but maybe there're others."

To his right, Factor had quit humming her song and was closely following the conversation. Carter figured it was in everyone's interest to bring her into it.

"Max, the woman on the phone is Indira Morel."

"Ah, your former girlfriend," Factor jabbed. "No couple in modern history made more gossip pages than you two."

"Most of it was nothing but rumors and lies," Carter retorted.

"Well," Morel added over the speaker, "the parts about his ego were true."

"Earlier you said—" Carter began before Morel cut him off.

"That was yesterday. But enough about a sordid past filled with wrong turns. Dr. Factor, I hope to someday visit with you in person. There are things you could share that might help in my understanding of history. As you likely know, I live to learn more about the past."

Factor smiled. "Your reputation in research is almost as well-known as your relationship with Elton. There are things you've seen in both of those areas I'd love to hear about. Was he controlling when you knew him?"

As it was apparent the women were about to gang up on him, Carter moved the conversation in a different direction. "Indy, because they know who I am, we can't go to any of my properties. Did you come up with anything? And it has to be in the States. Obviously, I can't get on a plane or go through customs without alerting folks where we are."

"Yes, Elton," Morel chimed in, "I was going to call you tomorrow about a safe house. It's in Colorado outside Glenwood Springs. My uncle owns it. It's not fancy but has power and water. He uses it as a fishing cabin. As he is a businessman, it does have internet and cell service. I went there a couple of months ago to work on a research article. In those ten days, no one came up the road."

Carter nodded. "Where's your uncle?"

"New York City. He won't be back in Colorado until next spring. I know the man who takes care of the place. I can tell him I'm coming up with a boyfriend, and we don't want to be disturbed. He'll clean the place, stock the frig, and then stay well away. He'll also keep his mouth shut about my call."

"Perfect," Carter announced, relief evident in his tone. "You just lifted a boulder off my back."

"I'll text directions," Morel continued. "When you get there, you'll see a chainsaw sculpture of a life-sized bear to the right of the cabin. Reach into the bear's mouth, and you'll discover a small shelf at the back of his tongue. That's where we hide the key. By the way, I'm going to connect with the folks I told you about tomorrow. I'll let you know if you need to be worried about anyone at the Vatican."

"Thanks."

"Take care of Dr. Factor and try to keep breathing yourself."

"Bye."

As the call ended, Factor observed, "I know she's beautiful, I've seen pictures, but she also sounds down to earth … even fun."

"You're right on all counts. She not only has an incredible mind, but that mind is open. She listens."

"Then why did you break up?"

"That'd be my doing. I'm not the kind of guy who makes commitments."

Factor grinned. "So, you can face gunfire and overwhelming odds, but when it came to a woman you loved, you got scared."

The last thing he wanted was to be read that clearly, but she was right. In that case, he had been a coward. Why? He didn't know if he was cut out to be faithful to any woman. So, rather than break a vow, it was easier not to make one.

"I'd have broken her heart," Carter explained. The excuse sounded lame, but it was surely true.

"Didn't you do that when you pulled away?"

"It would've been worse later. And I cared too much for her to hurt her that badly. So, I ended the relationship like a smart person removes a band aid—quickly."

"You still love her, don't you?"

Carter shrugged. "You're assuming a lot."

"What do you mean?"

"You're suggesting I can't love anyone more than I love myself." He paused, trying to shake Morel's image from his head, before announcing, "we need to find a route to Colorado. You want the role of navigator?"

If he put Factor to work, maybe she'd quit asking questions. And if she quit asking questions, maybe he'd quit beating himself up.

Chapter 31

11:55 p.m.
Friday, September 23
Holiday Inn Express, Charleston, Missouri

Mistakes that can't be changed or corrected become nagging wounds that will steal focus. They eat at your confidence and keep you awake. They make you question every facet of your being.

For reasons even he didn't fully understand, killing Lenards bothered William Dixon so much it kept him from sleeping. He wasn't suffering from a bout of conscience—it was just the fact that he'd made a mistake. During his long career, he'd only killed one other person by accident, and that was early on. Yes, innocent people had died. He'd once caused an airliner to crash to take out one man, but he marked that up to collateral damage. This was different. He hadn't killed someone to get to his mark, he'd just picked the wrong target. There had to be a reason for each death. When there wasn't, it was like ending a song before the last note.

Dixon spent part of the sleepless night researching Lenards's life. She was an outstanding woman, a professional who, according to numerous testimonials, had helped many using her rich bank of experience and skills. As he scanned through papers she'd written and photos posted on social media, he came across a point where Lenards's life intersected with his own. She'd met the imprint in Russia. Stravinsky had the reputation of being the most stable of all the imprints. Had she been the reason? Had she been at the cabin to work with Factor? That had to be it.

Dixon's phone rang, a look at the screen offering a promise of information he needed. Closing his laptop, he answered, "Well, Dallas, do you have something for me?"

"I've been calling in favors all night," Arnold admitted. "I hope you appreciate it."

"I don't care about how much work you've done—I just want a direction to go. Answer my question and do it without delivering a sermon."

"Well, I made a dozen calls ..."

"Don't waste time bothering me with what you did. Give me what you've got in as few words as possible. If I need more, I'll ask."

"Fine, Elton Carter's not a man who maintains any close friendships. He works with people for a short period of time, usually on a historical project or a business deal, and then he moves on. He doesn't send them Christmas cards, thank you notes, or make follow-up calls when the jobs are done. He just walks away."

"Surely there's someone he plays golf or tennis with or invites to his home."

"No. He's a loner."

"What about women?"

"They're like his business dealings. He's with them for a while and then moves on to the next one. And the time he's with a woman is usually measured in weeks or days. There's been only one exception."

"Who's that?"

"Surely, you can guess."

"No, I can't. If I could, I wouldn't have asked you."

"Don't you follow entertainment news?"

"No. Deliver now!"

"It's an archaeologist named Indira Morel. She has dual citizenship in the UK and Israel. She's not only one of the world's most intelligent women, she's also incredibly exotic. When she walks into a room, everyone else disappears. Anyway, Carter's affair with Morel went on for almost two years."

"Do they stay in touch?"

"I don't know, but they're no longer together and haven't been for months."

Dixon rubbed his chin. People always follow patterns. Once those patterns are established, they rarely break from them. Carter broke the pattern with Morel. Why?

"Dallas, have you met this woman?"

"A couple of times at seminars on Biblical artifacts. She's the most striking creature I've ever seen."

"Is she still single?"

"Yes. The information I've gotten assures me there's been no one in her life since Carter."

"Has he moved on?"

"If he has, the tabloids haven't discovered it. And they hound him."

"Where's Morel now—did you find that out?"

"London was the last place she was spotted. That was yesterday."

"Thanks. If you uncover any more on anyone connected to Carter, text or call."

Dixon ended the call only to immediately make another to his media source in New York.

"I didn't expect to hear from you again this soon," Mia Scott announced. Her tone displayed her lack of enthusiasm. "I take it you need something."

"What's it going to cost me?"

"Tell me what you want?"

"I want the complete story of Elton Carter's love life."

"A grand."

"I'll transfer it to your account today."

"Fine, call me back then."

Dixon frowned. "Let me put you on hold, and I'll send it now." He grabbed his iPad and went to work. A minute and half later, he picked up the phone. "You should have it."

"It came in, Now, how much detail do you want on Carter's conquests?"

"I don't care about names. I just want basic background on how he operates."

"He loves them and leaves them, but he's so generous while he's with them, none of them seem to complain when he moves on."

"How many over the years?"

"It's like a calendar. Usually, one a month. Between money and good looks, he has no problem picking up new ones."

"That means there have been ..."

"Hundreds," she agreed.

"What about Indira Morel?"

"Ah, the Jewish Princess! In the world of jet-setters, she's true royalty. She likely lasted as long as she did because she could challenge Carter both mentally and physically. Added to that, they share a great many mutual interests. It appears he broke it off, but the strangest thing is he hasn't moved on. It's been months, and no other woman has caught his fancy."

"Do they stay in touch?"

"You mean Morel and Carter?"

"Yes!"

"My guess is they at least speak about archaeological matters. Why the interest in Carter?"

"He has money," Dixon lied, "and you know how I love to get in with those with deep pockets."

"You're not his kind of people. So, you're wasting your time."

"Is your organization still covering Morel?"

"Yes, but not as closely as we did when she was with Carter."

"If I dropped another ten grand in your account, could you beef up your focus a bit?"

"Make it fifteen."

"You got it. I just want to know if she leaves London for the US. If she does, I need her followed."

"I can let you know that for the fifteen, but the tailing once she gets here will cost more."

"If she arrives in the States, I'll pay to keep eyes focused on her, and I'll give you a bonus too."

"Can I ask why?"

"No."

The line when silent for a few seconds before she came back on. "I'll have things in motion within the hour. And I'll phone you if there's any movement. How long do we follow her?"

"Until I call you off."

"You've been paying me for information for ten years, but I've never known what you do with the info."

"And we'll keep it like that."

"It's hardly fair."

"Bye."

Dixon's next move depended upon a hunch. When people were in trouble, they always turned to a friend they could trust. In Carter's case, it appeared that list began and ended with one name. If this turned out to be a blind alley, perhaps Dallas Arnold would turn up something else. Until then, he feared his days and nights would be consumed by ending the life of the wrong woman.

Chapter 32

It's far easier to fall off the thin line called deception than keep your balance and get back to a place called truth.

———◆———

It had not been a good three days for Rocky Smith or Mason Hardin. Though both had dug for any lead on where Maxine Factor might have gone, even after using every source at their disposal, they'd come up with nothing. In their lines of work, they were used to blind alleys and the patience it took to track down information, yet, because so much was at stake, both were showing signs of cracking. The man closest to the edge was the reporter.

Chambers's death was still eating at Hardin. The overriding guilt consuming him was something he couldn't shake. In truth, he now was only living for one thing that wasn't writing—it was revenge.

"If only," he whispered.

"If only what?"

Hardin shook his head, "Nothing. Just tired of treading water."

"Those who quit treading, drown," Smith pointed out. "By the way, your phone's shaking."

Hardin glanced toward the nightstand beside his bed. His iPhone was doing a dance. He crossed the room and checked the ID. It was Barry Watson, his boss. He almost let it go to voice mail. After all, he was hiding news the chief should know, but out of a sense of loyalty, Hardin answered.

"What do you need?" His greeting was anything but upbeat.

"Where are you?"

"Chasing a lead."

"Is Marsha with you?"

While he couldn't tell the truth, Mason also couldn't lie. "She's not with me at this moment."

"I've been trying to call her, but the calls go straight to voice mail."

"She must have forgotten to charge her cell."

"Well, I've got some information she wanted, and though it's against my better judgment, I promised I'd share it with her when it came in. In truth, I'm still not sure I need to. Did she tell you what she was doing?"

"I knew she was interested in the attempt on the Washington-Lincoln College professor's life. That's why she joined me in Mount Vernon."

"That was just to kill time. For the last four months, she's been trying to one up you."

"I'm not following."

"Do you remember when she covered the death of Milton Ranch?"

"Yeah, the Chicago homicide detective."

"His death had all the markings of a hit. Though she didn't write about it at the time, she dug enough to find out that Ranch was on the take. He was raking in a lot of dough working with organized crime."

Hardin was suddenly intrigued. That would've been a huge story, one that could put a young reporter on the national stage.

"Why didn't she write about it?"

"Because she discovered a thread that led up the chain of command. The story she's trying to pin down will identify the syndicate head. When she does that, the FBI will no doubt be very busy capturing all the rats as they flee the ship."

"And I'm guessing you want to withhold information from her?"

"Yeah, I want to protect her."

"That doesn't sound like you, Barry."

"Here's the problem. She hasn't covered her tracks like you always do. She's gotten threats that if she doesn't back off, she'll suffer the same fate as Ranch."

Hardin considered what Chambers had kept hidden. Lord, she had been playing with TNT. Hardin was tempted to tell the chief about Chambers's fate, but he held back.

"What are you afraid to tell her?" Hardin asked.

"I just received confirmation on the identity of someone she called the Wizard. She was sure she knew who it was, but she wanted to verify it. She admired you and tried to stay true to what you did. And when you preached over and over again, 'Don't run with the story until you have three separate verifications,' she took it to heart. She needs that third one. So, she had me do some digging too. I went drinking with a friend who has underworld ties. The more we drank, the more he bragged. Still, even after seven shots of high-quality bourbon, he refused to give me the Wizard's name. Then, I let Marsha's information slip. His shocked expression confirmed what she suspected. It's not enough to go print, we still have to verify it, but we are so close."

Hardin was lost when it came to names and nicknames. But Smith might be in the loop.

"Hang on, chief," Hardin hit the mute. "Rocky, does the name the Wizard mean anything to you?"

"In what context?"

"Organized crime?"

"He's the boss, but not even the FBI knows who he is. They have theories, but it could be any of a dozen guys. No one has ever ratted him out."

Hardin released the mute. "Let me get this straight, Barry. You don't want to verify the identity because you're worried about the mob going after Marsha?"

"Yeah, but that's just a part of it. Whether I tell her to or not, she's not going to back off. She's like a dog with a bone—she sees this as the chance to win a Pulitzer. But I thought she might listen to you.

Do you think you could convince her to take a step back until things cool down?"

"I doubt it, she was … is … fearless."

The chief didn't pick up on the reporter's slip of the tongue. "Mason, it might be too late anyway. The reason I didn't mind her going south with you was because I'd gotten wind that there were a couple of guys here in Chi-Town assigned to take her out. Then a few minutes ago, my drinking partner told me the Wizard had ordered her death." The chief paused before adding, "And I was told the Wizard had demanded her death be slow and painful. If I'd known this before today, I'd have told you and had you to keep her with you at all times."

"What's the Wizard's name?" Hardin demanded.

"You really want to know? That might just put your life on the line as well."

"I need to know, and there's already a long list of folks who want me dead."

"Richard Pulino. To his close friends and family, he's either Ricardo or Rick. His cover is an investment banker. He's a friend of numerous congressmen and senators. He's known for his charitable causes. But behind the curtain is the man who runs the mob in the US. Even though Marsha has already found out who he is, she was having problems coming up with anything that would verify that information. And then last week, she told me she had just been given the key element to the story. She was waiting for one more call to break it wide open. In fact, she's already written the entire expose except for that last bit of evidence. So, my question for you—do I assure her she's right on Pulino and let her go for her chance at the big time by digging even deeper or do I shut the story down?"

"Give me a second," Hardin muted the phone again. "Rocky, I need to level with my boss about Marsha's death. He needs to know how she died, and I've got to tell him where the body is. I won't involve you."

"That's not wise," Smith argued. "In fact, it's stupid."

"Actually, there's something you don't know that'll put the whole thing in a different light. Marsha didn't die because of anything I did. She wasn't beaten to death because of Factor. She was about to break another story revealing the identity of the Wizard. He ordered a vicious hit in order to stop her and put my newspaper on notice."

"So, this isn't about the imprint?"

"No. She identified some guy name Richard Pulino as the Wizard. She was waiting on one more lead to break the story."

"The banker? My lord, he was hiding in plain sight."

Hardin didn't wait for Stone's final approval before jumping back on the phone. Except for a couple of minor points, it was time to be straight with the chief.

"Chief, I hate to drop this news this way, but I can't tell Marsha what you found out. Last Tuesday, Marsha was beaten to death at the Ramble Inn Motor Court ten miles outside of Mount Vernon. The Wizard made good on his promise."

"What? Why didn't you let me know?"

Hardin pushed on. "I couldn't at the time, because while I knew how she died, I didn't know why. The motel owner was killed as well. The scene was cleaned up, and the bodies were dumped in a small pond. I've found out where that is and can give you the location. It shouldn't take divers too long to fish them out."

"My lord."

"Barry, can we break the story without the last bit of evidence she was waiting for?"

"No."

"Okay, you start going through everything on her desk and in her files at work. I'm following a lead here. I don't know where it'll take me, but I'll communicate when I can. I taught Marsha to back up everything. So, search for flash drives, hard drives, and even DVD files. Look in the office and at her apartment. They'll be encrypted, but that won't be a problem. I know her encryption code and will text it to you. We have to find that contact, get that information, and finish this story. We owe it to Marsha. And when we do, her name goes on the feature."

"Okay, I'll start to work."

"And Barry, tell no one else about this. This has to be between you and me."

"I don't want to lose two reporters—stay safe."

"I will. As soon as I hang up, I'll send you the code and the location of the pond."

Hardin forwarded the information then looked across the room at Smith.

"I have a target now."

Smith nodded. "Pulino?"

"Yep."

"So, you're moving on?"

"Hardly, I can't work on that story or avenge Marsha's murder until the chief uncovers one final piece in the puzzle. For the moment, I'm still chasing the story Goldsmith asked me to complete."

Smith smiled. "It must be a relief to know you weren't responsible for her death."

"I'll admit what I've learned helps." He paused and shook his head. "But it doesn't ease the pain."

"Nothing ever will." Smith looked back at his computer screen. "We've exhausted everything we have on Elton Carter. His Arkansas property burned, but his and Factor's bodies were not in the rubble. He's not at any of his other homes. Everyone knows his face. So, someone's helping him. Who?"

"Maybe it's time to dig into my connections."

"Yeah, I'll chase the financial leads. Why don't you uncover his friends."

"Let's get to work."

Chapter 33

You can't scout an opponent you don't know. You just have to adapt and react in the moment. And the outcome can be fatal.

———◆———

This trip was not for the faint of heart. The rocky dirt road corkscrewed up the valley, the Escape sliding from time to time. Carter downshifted when needed, but the small SUV still drew far too close to drop-offs of more than a hundred feet.

"No need to ever pay for a ride at a theme park again," Factor cracked. "Perhaps this is Indira's way of getting even for the way you treated her."

"I treated her fine," he argued as he rammed the Ford into second and hit the gas, spraying rocks along the road until the tires grabbed. "I gave her everything she wanted, and we had some good times."

"Maybe she didn't care about the stuff but wanted a piece of your heart."

That stung, but it was also probably true. Morel was a half a world away, and Carter still felt like he was playing two against one.

"That must be the cabin," he announced as they rounded a hairpin curve and spotted a structure. It was small, rustic, and log. A covered porch ran across the front. "Doesn't look too bad."

After Factor retrieved the key, they entered Morel's uncle's cabin. It was like stepping back in time. The furniture looked as though it had been salvaged from thrift shops. While there were few amenities, the kitchen cabinets and refrigerator were stocked, and there were logs stacked and ready to light in the stone fireplace.

"Look," Factor pointed out. "There are graham crackers, marshmallows, and Hershey bars. We can have s'mores and tell ghost stories."

"I'll bet you've got access to some good ones."

"Maybe I'll share, but you'll have to be a good boy."

When people weren't taking up space in her head, she was fun. In a different setting ... he opted to cut that thought off before it went any further.

"Take your pick of the rooms," Carter suggested, "I'll get our stuff out of the car."

Factor tapped on her phone before grinning like a possum. "The Wi-Fi works."

"Good to know."

Carter stepped out onto the small front porch and glanced down the mountain. There were trees, but not nearly as thick as those surrounding his cabin in Arkansas. Thus, there were fewer places to hide, but that might not really matter. Who in the world could trace them to this forlorn spot? The best he could tell, there was no one within miles.

Grabbing bags filled with what they'd purchased, he made three trips in and out of the cabin. When he'd finally retrieved everything, Carter locked and barred the door.

"Do you want a fire?" he asked.

"There're oodles of blankets in the bedrooms—let's wait until tomorrow. If you waste wood, then we'll have to cut more, and that's hard work."

"You sound like you've had some experience."

"Not personally, but I have almost continuously running episodes playing in the theater of my mind that assure me I know what I'm talking about."

He almost let it pass, but after easing into an ancient armchair his curiosity got the best of him. "Who told you about the hard work?"

Factor shrugged, "A pioneer woman. The year was 1822—Missouri. Her husband was off hunting, and she was chopping wood to build a fire to cook over. Their cabin was even smaller than this one."

"Your grandmother?" he asked, suddenly enthralled with a story of survival.

"A few generations back. I can't get a handle on which side of the family. I can see that scene clearly, but the rest of her memories are vague at best. It's like viewing bits and pieces of a movie but having no idea how it turned out. In my head, she has no children, but obviously at some point she did."

"What does she look like?"

Factor shook her head. "I don't know, she hasn't looked into a mirror. Don't forget, I'm only seeing what she saw. So, I can describe her husband and their home, even the view from the front door, but because I'm looking through her eyes, I can't see her face."

That simple explanation opened up the world of imprints in a way that Carter had never considered. Factor wasn't watching a life—she was living one. Her point of view was first person only.

"Max, it just dawned on me, you always have the leading role in the movies that play in your head."

"And they're never completed. I just drop into the lead's mind and body, and then I'm pulled out. Imagine watching a scene from a thousand plays but never seeing all of any of them." She paused, a pained expression etched on her face. "If my count's right, in less than two weeks of my being outed as an imprint, eight people have died. There was Kattan, the two guys at the airport, four at the farmhouse, and then Dr. Lenards."

"Actually, five at the farmhouse. The man we brought with us, Mosby, died as well."

"So, nine," she sadly whispered. "Eight people died trying to kill me, and one died because she had contact with me. I'm worse than the plague. There's no vaccine for me. How many more will stop breathing because of what lives in my mind?"

In an effort to move away from the morbid and onto something that on the surface appeared more positive, Carter made an observation. "You seem more relaxed."

"B.R. gave me a coping strategy, but that gift came with a pretty steep price."

"Yeah, but …"

"But what? Are you going to try to persuade me she died doing what she loved? Are you going to say her death was a noble sacrifice?" Factor pushed off the couch and walked over to the fireplace. She crossed her arms, her expression still pained. "If Kattan had killed me, then B.R. would be alive. I'm the reason both the good player and bad players are dead. I'm both the target and the weapon. And I don't want another good person to die because of me." She turned her gaze toward Carter. "That means you."

"People died because you have great value."

"Once I'm dead, my value's gone."

While Factor didn't sound suicidal, what she said worried Carter. He had to find a way to help change her point of view. But at the moment, he had no idea how to do that.

"Why do you think they're after you?"

She shook her head.

"You scare them," he posited. "You have something they fear so greatly they'll murder to suppress it. As a historian, don't you want to know what that is?"

"Sure, almost more than anything in the world, but not if it kills you or anyone else."

"Right now, we're safe. No one knows where we are. And B.R. gave you a way to harness those voices in your head."

"They're not voices, they're people. They come to life there."

"Okay. Please consider this. We're in a safe place. You don't have to worry about me. We have some time, so maybe we can unlock the memories these people fear—the reasons they want to kill you."

"It's not just me," Factor argued. "It's all the imprints, at least those who didn't kill themselves first. It can't just be what's in my head, it has to be what's in all our heads."

"Yeah, and what might each of your ancestors know that'd frighten them so much? There has to be a link somewhere."

"You knew another imprint," Factor point out. "What's my connection to her?"

Carter snapped his fingers and smiled. He'd found something to build on. "What's the most important thing in the world other than love?"

"You tell me. I'm not sure you value love that highly."

She was wicked when she got an opening. Ignoring her jab, he announced, "Faith."

"You mean religion?"

"That's a part of it, but there's more to it. When someone loses the faith of those who follow them, they can no longer lead. When people lost faith in the USSR's ability to provide what they needed, that government fell. What if Betty Rydell had a relative who witnessed something that could've undermined the British people's belief in their government? Even if the odds were long that one of her ancestors was in the wrong place at the right time, would the government let her live? Would powerful forces believe what she might recall was too big a risk? What if you know something that could do the same thing to the United States?"

"It's a stretch."

"Maybe, but it's also a start. We need to use the next few days to come up with all the theories that make an imprint seem so dangerous."

"And if we figure that out?"

"Then maybe it'll reveal who's after you. Recognizing the enemy is the first step toward stopping him."

"Let's go to bed," Factor suggested. "I've got the room on the right, and I get first dibs on the bathroom."

Alone with his thoughts, Carter was grateful the killing was over. Perhaps, after a few weeks here, she'd gain some peace, put things into perspective, and they could figure out the reason she was being hunted. If they could learn that, then they might be able to put an end to the chaos. But even if they did that, how long would Factor have before she couldn't cope? Would it be years or just months? He was hoping for the former but betting on the latter.

Chapter 34

2:56 a.m.
Sunday, September 25
JFK International, Queens, New York

Guilt is not a good traveling companion. It makes you question every decision and haunts your every step.

———◆———

B ecause of his organization's past sins, Ben Greenberg had let Francesco Russo convince him to join this mission. The more he chewed on the reason, the more he kicked himself for his involvement. His gut still told him the entire exercise was deeply flawed. At its core, this seemed more like protecting the present than covering up what may have happened in the past. And then there was the matter of setting someone up to be killed. Still, he'd committed, and he was going to try to follow through.

After clearing customs, Greenberg and Russo picked up their luggage and hailed a cab. Their plan was to stay at the Washington Hotel until they uncovered the beginning of a trail they hoped would lead to Dr. Maxine Factor. Only streetlights and the headlights of a few passing cars and trucks illuminated the night, yet Greenberg could now clearly see that Dr. Maxine Factor was innocent. She did nothing to push two men of faith to break the most sacred of moral laws. And yet, here they were, seemingly bent on doing just that. It was, beyond any doubt, an unholy alliance.

"Sacrifice," Greenberg mumbled.

"What are you saying?" Russo asked.

Speaking in hushed tones, Greenberg harkened back to a time when sacrificing animals was a common practice. "We sacrificed the purest lamb to God."

"What does that have to do with anything?"

"Really? Isn't Factor the sacrifice? Let's be honest, neither of us worships a God who demands human sacrifice."

"Are we headed toward a theological debate? For Christians, Jesus was the ultimate and final sacrifice."

"And it was barbaric," Greenberg suggested, "but at least in that case there was a semblance of a trial. The government was involved. We might have two different perspectives on the validity of the execution, but we can surely agree that it crossed the legal barriers."

Russo shrugged. "What's your point?"

"There's not a court in the world that would convict Factor of anything. Doesn't that bother you?"

"Sure, but it doesn't change my mind. For a wealth of reasons, she has to die." Russo glanced out the window before adding, "What we need to be talking about is where we can find her. Right now, we're looking for a needle in a haystack. Our sources have been no use at all."

"Perhaps," Greenberg suggested, "as you Catholics like to say, this is God's will."

"No more sermons."

"Okay, I've made this trip to protect the Star. So far, I've let you run the show, but that changes now. You don't get information by asking for it, you get it by letting it come to you. That's the difference between us. You embrace the New Testament activism while my faith requires we wait for someone to speak and show us the way."

"And that's why your people wandered in the wilderness for forty years," the priest grumbled.

"We got there. Now, I'm going to make a call. Watch and listen!"

Greenberg tapped his phone's screen and waited for a response.

"Who are you are you trying to reach at this time of night?" Russo demanded.

"It's morning in London."

The phone rang four times before a bright female voice answered, "Ben, you're lucky to catch me."

"Why's that, Indira?"

"I just landed in Atlanta."

"Really, I'm in the States as well. On my way to a conference in Colorado. What are you doing?"

"Just taking some time off. What do you need?"

"I want to talk to you about something."

"I'm going through customs right now. Can I call you back in a few minutes? I'll have some time during my layover."

"Yes, do that."

When Greenberg ended the call, his eyes met Russo's. As the city streetlights flashed into the cab, it was obvious the priest was perplexed.

"That was Indira Morel?"

"Yeah, you know her?"

"I've met her a few times. Why did you call her?"

Greenberg leaned closer to Russo. "She knows about the imprint. And though she hasn't told anyone, I'm betting she's researched where Factor is. You see, Indira would give anything to spend a few hours with someone who has the ability to view history as an imprint does. So, she might offer us a starting point."

"Her name has always intrigued me," Russo said. "Indira is not a usual Jewish name. Is it?"

"Her father admired Indira Gandhi. He wanted his daughter to have a name that reflected strength, courage, and reason. It seems he made the right call."

As if on cue, Greenberg's cell rang, and he answered. "I take it you've made it through customs."

"I did. Now, what do you need? They managed to get me on an earlier flight, so I don't have much time."

Greenberg considered his words before revealing a hint of his motivation. "I'm worried about the imprint."

"There's no reason to worry," Morel assured him.

"Why do you believe that?" As Greenberg listened to her reasoning, he also heard an announcement in the background. "American flight 449 to Denver is boarding now."

"Listen, Ben, they just called my flight, I have to go."

"Your words have made me feel much better. Have a wonderful holiday. You've earned it."

As Greenberg slipped his cell back into his pocket, an anxious Russo whispered, "Was your theory right? Does she know where Factor is?"

Greenberg ignored the questions, leaned forward, and tapped the cabbie on the shoulder. "There's been a change of plans, we need to return to the airport. You'll earn a big tip if you can get us there quickly and safely."

As Greenberg leaned back and settled into the rear seat, he glanced over at Russo. "Indira didn't tell me where Factor is, but I'm sure she knows. And before you get on me for not asking, realize this, Indira wouldn't have given it to me. We may want to kill Factor, but she wants to protect her."

"So, if we're no better off than we were, why are we going to back to the airport?"

"She assured me I have nothing to worry about. I now know Factor's in a secure location with a friend of Indira's who has all the resources needed to protect her. I'm ninety percent sure I know who that friend is."

"Who?"

"Her old flame, Elton Carter."

"So, we just have to find Carter. How hard can that be?"

Greenberg shrugged. "She didn't say so, but I suspect Indira is headed to where Factor is hiding."

"But you didn't ask where she was going."

"I didn't have to," Greenberg explained. "She's on her way to Denver. So, we'll grab the first flight to the mile-high city."

"Still a big place."

"She'll have to rent a car. She's a beautiful woman. The rental agent will remember her. A bit of cash, and we'll discover where she's headed. And because rental cars have tracking beacons, once we get the information on the car, I can hack their system. Then it's just a matter of shadowing her."

"Your skills—the family software business—serve us well."

As Russo contemplated this new information, Greenberg once more questioned his motives. Yes, he loved the challenge of the chase, but this was a game with an ending he didn't know if he could stomach. When this was all over, Russo could confess and be absolved, but that wasn't in the cards for Greenberg. He'd just have to learn to live with the guilt. Was that possible?

Chapter 35

Hitting a wall is the time when hunches take over. That's when the brain combines experience and instinct, and you roll the dice.

———◆———

Except for grabbing a few hours of sleep, Mason Hardin had done little in the past forty hours but work on finding Dr. Maxine Factor. And though this story was huge, another story tugged at his heart. Marsha Chambers died digging for the information to nail mob boss Rick Pulino and expose his organization. Hardin owed it to her to finish her story. The problem? He was working with information that was a month old, and Barry Watson, the newspaper's editor in chief, hadn't found the missing link. Hardin's hands were tied. Until he uncovered that last bit of information, the story was no more than tabloid gossip.

Adding to the frustration, he hadn't turned up anything fresh in the Factor case either. Yes, he knew a woman was murdered at Elton Carter's cabin in Arkansas, but it was not the elusive Factor. Growing tired of rereading old news stories on a crime that had far more questions than answers, Hardin opted to hit the Twitter feeds.

He was scrolling through tweets when a knock on the door raised his blood pressure. Was it a maid or a stranger with a gun? Apprehensive, he unlatched and opened the entry.

Rocky Smith, looking discouraged, pushed past Hardin into the room.

"No luck?" Hardin observed.

"That sums it up. The fire at the cabin wiped out any signs of who had visited Carter. The dead woman, as you no doubt know by now, was Dr. B.R. Lenards. She was a respected psychologist. From what I can gather, one of the world's best."

"I didn't know they'd identified her," Hardin admitted.

"The media hasn't gotten that information yet, but when they do it'll likely provide little more than a chance to put another photo on their websites. Lenards and Carter had been friends for years."

"How did she die? The stories in the media indicate it was in the fire."

"She was shot."

"By Carter?"

"That's doubtful. She was downed by a rifle shot, likely from a distance." Smith pulled out his phone and pulled up a photo. He held it up. "Who does Lenards look like?"

"Factor."

"The FBI doesn't know what you and I know, but to me that indicates Factor was the target and the killer missed."

"And the killer is?"

"I have a theory, but that's all it is. The most important thing we need to dwell on is what happened to Carter and Factor. I think both of them were at the cabin and escaped. But where did they go? And, with Carter's face all over the news, he has to have some help. So, who's hiding him?"

"His family?"

"I've checked—his siblings haven't heard from him. In fact, they'd love to see him either convicted or dead so they could control more of the family wealth for themselves. And, while Carter knows a lot of people, he has no close friends."

Shaking his head, Smith begin pacing. As he did, Hardin turned back to Twitter. After scanning more than fifty tweets, one leaped out. Jumping back to the search browser, he quickly found the *National Inquisitor's* website. The blurb cited in the tweet was not there. Deleted? Why? Had it been disproved or had someone with money and influence killed it?

"What do you know about Indira Morel?" Hardin asked, "I don't mean the tabloid stuff, I know that. I'm looking for off the radar info."

Smith shrugged. "Because her brother is Mossad, we have a file. I've studied it. We know she works with a secret Jewish group call the Star. She's one of the calming influences in that organization, so we haven't pursued her. While well respected in her field, she was off the radar until she …"

The agent stopped, his expression surprised. Before he could put voice to his thoughts, Hardin chimed in.

"For a short time today, there was a blurb on the *National Inquisitor's* website about Morel arriving in Denver. The person who penned the piece suggested she was back in the US to patch things up with Carter."

"Patch things up? Probably not. But she may well be there to help him. We need to get to Denver before her trail goes cold. Start packing. I'll book a flight. Once we're in the air, we can research places she and the billionaire might meet."

Did the lead have any real value? That was anybody's guess. But for the moment, a snipe hunt beat sitting in a motel room wasting time. And moving might be the answer to burying a few memories that were eating Hardin alive.

Chapter 36

4:56 p.m.
Sunday, September 25
Mountain Cabin, seven miles outside of Glenwood
Springs, Colorado

The times when a person does nothing are often when their perspective is best.

———————

Elton Carter and Maxine Factor spent the better part of the day trying to pick her brain. Yet, in eight hours of questions and answers, they'd come up with nothing connecting her to the other imprints. To give her a break, Carter left Factor alone on the front porch and went inside to throw together some supper. When he returned with ham sandwiches and chips, she seemed lost in thought. Setting the tray down on a table between the two rocking chairs, he glanced down the mountainside. It was a postcard come to life. All around him was the majesty that had inspired songs from "America the Beautiful" to "Rocky Mountain High." At the moment, it also inspired apprehension. He knew danger and death could be hiding behind one of the thousands of trees within his view. So, rather than relax and submerge himself in nature, he remained on edge.

As he began his meal, a sobering thought hit him. He was supposed to be protecting Factor, yet he didn't even have a weapon. They'd left the guns at the cabin in Arkansas. If someone did show up, what would he do, throw rocks?

He glanced over at Factor. Her eyes were now open and seemed fixed on a distant mountain peak. She appeared calm, as she had all day. Perhaps it wasn't the moment to make a confession, but he did it anyway.

"I just realized I don't know how to protect you."

"You've done a pretty good job so far," Factor noted.

"Actually, you've guided us through those times. I've just done what you told me to do. I don't even have a weapon with me. In the world of bodyguards, I'm the bargain basement version."

Factor chuckled.

"What's so funny?" he asked.

"When was the last time you ever heard of a bargain basement? Do they even have those anymore?

Carter shrugged. "I don't really know, but, with all those folks inside your head, you've probably experienced a few."

"It's funny, rather than some random shopper looking for a deal, the ancestor who's roaming through my mind now is a priest."

"A Catholic priest?" a shocked Carter asked. "How could he be on your DNA."

"I don't have an answer to that—I've only uncovered bits and pieces of his life."

As they'd sorted through past lives, Factor's experiences of different eras and places seemed routine, yet this new ancestor was unlike any of the others. Though it likely had no bearing on what made her a target, the how and why she was seeing through a priest's eyes was so fascinating Carter wanted to learn more.

"What's his name?"

"The priest?"

"Yeah."

"Father John is what they're calling him."

"Where and when?"

"Based on the accents, Scotland. The year I don't know. But I'd guess around the fifteen or sixteen hundreds. John was traveling from Fife to Glasgow and found himself in a real mess. It seems the Protestants were accusing people across the nation of sorcery.

There were trials, verdicts, and executions. I watched as women were burned at the stake. It seems, with my modern view, many of them were either suffering from mental illness or a mental disability, but the church leaders determined they were demon-possessed."

"You witnessed it?"

"Those executions made me, or rather John, sick to his stomach. He wanted to step in, but the Catholic church leaders ordered him not to get involved. It seemed they couldn't afford to antagonize the Protestants."

"So, religion was politicized even then."

Factor nodded before continuing her experience inside the priest's skin. "I heard women scream, I could feel the heat of the flames, and smell their flesh burning. And they didn't die quickly. One fire went out before the woman was dead, so they built another one and tossed her onto it. I can still hear her begging for her life."

Factor, her face twisted in pain, stared off into the sky. Carter sensed she was seeing things he couldn't and didn't want to imagine.

"I'm like they are," Factor whispered coming out of her trance-like state.

"Like who?"

"Those women. My gift, if you want to call it that, has or will frighten almost everyone who finds out about it. And like those supposed witches, those around me pay the same price. They're hunted and murdered too."

Factor was not pitying herself—her tone clearly showed she wasn't embracing the role of a martyr—rather, she was displaying deep compassion and empathy for those who died four or five hundred years ago in Scotland, as well as the imprints who'd perished more recently. As Carter watched in awestruck fascination, Factor pushed back in her rocking chair and wiped a tear from her cheek. She was really there, and how he wished he could be there with her.

She remained mute for a few minutes, as more tears streamed down her face, before mournfully announcing, "It was guilt that destroyed the priest."

"What?"

"He was consumed by his inability to help. No one would listen to his pleas for charity and forgiveness. And it broke him."

Carter put his plate down and scooted his chair closer to Factor. "Do you know what happened to him? Can you see that too?"

She nodded. "He asked to spend a few minutes praying for a woman who was to be executed the next day. As thanks for allowing his visit with Ann, John gave the jailer a jug of ale. He'd doctored the alcohol—he didn't call it a drug but referred to it as a potion—and the jailer passed out. John then took the guard's keys, unlocked the cell, and spirited Ann away."

"What did they do?"

"If you are talking about the authorities, I don't know. I'm sure they looked for John and Ann, but they didn't find them. John had two horses and a head start. Once he began running, he kept going. At some point, he took the clerical collar off and never put it back on."

"And the woman? Ann?"

"She was a small lass, as John would've said, but strong. She had fair skin, freckles, light brown hair, and deep blue eyes. Her only crime was hiding a woman accused of witchcraft. She was also a woman with enough courage to show compassion when no one else did."

Factor was fully locked in now. She was describing something she'd seen and experienced. It was a part of her fiber.

"They rode for more than a week. They slept in the open, ate food where they could find or steal it, and finally, they discovered a deserted house just outside a small forest. My last memory of John is of him kissing Ann and then taking her to bed."

"Then …"

Factor finished Carter's thoughts. "All I can figure is a child must have been conceived, and that's why I have a priest's memories on my DNA."

"He gave up everything …" Carter pondered. "… his career, his home, and his friends for Ann."

Factor nodded. "He did."

Still lost in another time and place, she picked up a ham sandwich.

"I guess you see everything." He immediately wished he could take back his observation.

"No," she corrected him. "I experience everything. I don't watch it, I live it. I've been sick, hungry, lost, and abused. I don't know how many different languages I speak or how many times and places I've had sex. I've experienced being both men and women. I've known uncountable joy and inexhaustible pain. And what's most frightening is that with each person whose story I live, the others stay there too. They remain clear and detailed. It's like a room that's getting more and more crowded."

As he listened to her words, he marveled at her strength. How could she contain all those thoughts and stay sane? As he studied her almost serene face, as he peered into her deep blue eyes, she began to hum "You Are My Sunshine." As she did, she turned her gaze back to the view of the mountains. A few moments later, she was once again in the present and fully herself.

"Someone's coming," Factor whispered.

Moving his eyes from the woman to the valley, he spotted an SUV slowly winding its way up the mountain road. Within five minutes, it would arrive at their front door.

"Let's get inside," he ordered.

"Wait!"

"Who are you listening to?" he demanded.

"The same woman who guided us away from danger at the cabin. I'm going to try to keep her at the front of the line. In my head, that is."

Standing, Factor glanced toward the rear of the cabin. "There's an ax back by the firewood. You grab it and take cover in the trees just beyond the lane. Wait until they get out of the car. I'll distract them, then you go on the offensive. To deliver a killing blow, use both arms and bring the ax high over your head."

"Wait, you know how to use an ax as a weapon?"

"Oh, yeah."

Sensing she had more experience than he could get in ten lifetimes, Carter rushed back, retrieved the ax, and then, hid in the pines. When the black SUV arrived, the shadows had grown long, and the lack of light coupled with the vehicle's tinted windows made it impossible to know how many were inside. In the semi-darkness, the driver's door opened, and a person dressed in jeans, a long coat, and a large cowboy style hat stepped out. As the stranger studied the cabin, no one else exited the SUV. A few seconds later, the cabin's front door opened, and Factor strolled onto the porch. She was holding a quart jar in her left hand and a burning candle in her right.

"You must be Dr. Factor," the visitor called out.

He knew that voice. A smiling Carter lowered the ax, dropped it beside a tree, and stepped out into the open. Even though he was only ten feet behind her, the visitor was completely unaware of his presence until he called out, "Indy, what in the world are you doing here?"

Indira Morel turned around and smiled. "I thought you might need some help."

Chapter 37

8:19 p.m.
Sunday, September 25
Mountain Cabin, seven miles outside of Glenwood
Springs, Colorado

Disappointment and suffering shape us far more than the good times.
When pain seeps into our hearts, we see the world differently and thus
react in ways that were once foreign to our nature. Great loss can bring
ever greater empathy.

———◆———

Their first few hours were spent with the women getting to
know each other. Initially, it was Elton Carter who led the
conversation. The more he shared his adventures with Morel, the
more obvious it became that Factor was a third wheel. She lacked
the experiences that connected the former lovers. As the night went
on, she grew quieter and felt more and more isolated. When Carter
volunteered to clean up the kitchen, the women, led by Morel,
stepped outside into a star-filled mountain evening.

"We haven't talked about your gift," Morel noted as they found
seats on the porch.

"Maybe we should call it a curse," Factor suggested. "Hiding from
civilization, dodging bullets, watching people get killed, seeing good

people give their lives for you, and constantly looking over your shoulder is hardly the product of a gift."

"Gifts always come with strings," Morel observed. "The lives of those who win the lottery are more demanding after the win. People are constantly at their door. Relatives become like hungry cats outside a restaurant. Let's face it, possessing something very rare almost always leads to danger. Surely, as a history professor you're well aware of that. More often than not, talent or wealth also lead to isolation." Morel paused, as if weighing what would constitute a legitimate question versus an unwelcome intrusion. "May I ask how far back you've gone?

"In years or generations?"

"Years."

"Good, because I'm having problems keeping track of which order the ancestors come in." Factor glanced toward the sky before announcing, "Six hundred years or so. Now, if you're looking for ancient history, which I know is your field of study, I'm not much help. I can't tell you anything about the pyramids or even the crusades, but I can give you a seventeenth-century recipe for apple pie."

"Can you recall things at will?"

"No, Indira ..."

"Please, call me Indy."

"Indy, I can't force an experience. And it seems I can more easily recall tragic times than happy ones. Perhaps that's because the moments of pain and loss are most deeply embedded in our memories. You know, I've discovered that disappointment and suffering shape us far more than the good times."

Morel nodded. "Dr. Factor ..."

"Max."

"Okay, Max, do any historical events jump out? As a student of the past, have you seen things you've read about and actually—"

"Experienced them?"

"Yes."

"I've been in World Wars, but I never saw Ike, Pershing, or FDR. I see things from the perspective of the common people. So, I can't report on assassinations or tragedies. The moments I live are snapshots of simple lives. So, I've not experienced history as a leader, but rather as people who were shaped by the decisions of leaders. You see, those who've entered my mind and drawn me into their lives simply show me what life was like then. Let me give you an example.

"I've seen this country before the Europeans arrived. I know what it was like to live in an America that was almost like the Garden of Eden. I've breathed unpolluted air. I've walked this place when skies were clear, game and fish were plentiful, and disease was rare. Therefore, I'm well aware of what we've done to our world."

Morel seemed mesmerized. "Max, you've experienced the lives of so many in ways that no one could begin to grasp. I can't begin to fathom what that's like. I mean, I thought I could, but then, when you go there, I mean actually go there, I'm taken aback."

"Consider this, my ancestors' memories are mine—I have lived them. The ancestors are both male and female, so I'm both. Some of those in my past, like a priest whose life came alive to me earlier today, are wonderful people. But others, like a vile French explorer, were the worst. I've not just been raped, I've also raped. So, for every scene of wonder and beauty, there are others that are nasty and ugly."

"I'm sorry," Morel whispered.

"When I was a child," Factor stoically explained, "my grandmother always said everything happens for a reason. When you live as many lives as I have, when you have wronged and been wronged in so many varied ways, that statement doesn't hold much water. I've come to realize that life isn't fair and there are things that happen to each of us that serve no purpose. They're not meant as learning experiences. They're just a matter of being in the wrong place at the wrong time."

"In other words, Max, you're saying none of us have much control."

"Perhaps," Factor countered, "I have a bit more control than you do. After all, I have scores of ancestors helping me through my troubles. They've saved me a few times in the last couple of weeks." She got out of the chair and strolled over to the steps. As she looked at sky, she made a strange observation. "Maybe we need to talk about what's really on your mind."

"I'm not following you."

Factor turned and waited for Morel's gaze to lock onto hers. "You're interested in me as an imprint. With what you study and do, that's natural. But the woman in you also wonders about Elton and me. In truth, that's why you're here."

"No …"

"Don't try fool me or yourself. You don't want to feel jealous, but you are. It's human, everyone experiences it. Believe me, I know that far better than anyone else. I've experienced this a few times in my life and hundreds of times through my ancestors' lives."

Morel looked uneasy. She was obviously a person who didn't like others reading her. But when she spoke, she embraced restraint rather than anger.

"Max, you're a beautiful woman with an extraordinary gift. What man wouldn't be fascinated by that combination? And while I might have made the excuse that I'm here to help you two, the other reason I came was to find a way to get between you. I realized that when I purchased the plane tickets. I hope that doesn't make me look as bad as it sounds."

"Always best to be honest," Factor suggested. "And let me assure you of something—nothing has happened. This is not about romance, it's about Elton's fascination with an imprint. The problem? His fascination will no doubt lead to his death. I hope you find a way to get him away from me before he's killed. In fact, if you don't want to die, you need to get away as well."

"Wait," Morel demanded, but Factor didn't give her the chance to finish her objection.

"I might dodge a few more bullets, but in time, one will catch me. And when it does, you and Elton don't need to be the collateral damage."

Morel stood and walked over to Factor. "Don't write us off as ignorant of the dangers. We know the risks. We know the odds. Elton's here because he wants to be, he needs to be. And I want to protect you as well. What you have could change the world. That has to be saved."

"But can it be saved, and if so, for how long?"

Morel grabbed Factor's arm and turned her so they were face to face. "Do you know who's after you?"

"No."

"Then let me tell you something. I've found those who claim they live by faith have little when it comes to their own beliefs. They fear you and what you might remember. There are Christians who want you dead because they're afraid you'll remember back to the time of

Christ and tell the world that Jesus didn't rise from his grave. There are Jews who want you dead because they're afraid you'll remember back that far and witness a risen Christ. There are Muslims who fear you'll reveal that much of Mohammad's life was legend rather than fact."

"You've thought about this," Factor observed.

"Are you a Christian?"

"I grew up in church—until the last couple of weeks I had a basic faith in what I'd heard and learned."

"You know that I'm Jewish?"

"Yes."

"Well, I'm speaking as an outsider looking in, but here it goes. Jesus said, 'The truth will set you free.' Well, a lot of people would rather be bound by a lie than freed by the truth. Those people are afraid you'll remember a truth that'll threaten everything they stand for. They have to silence you."

Factor smiled, "History has always been more about hiding the truth than celebrating it. And death often comes not from old age, but from being in the wrong place at the wrong time. Make sure that's not your destination."

"What are you ladies talking about?" Carter asked as he walked through the door and onto the porch.

"The truth," Morel quickly explained.

Factor smiled. "And the truth is, I'm sleepy. I think I'll get ready for bed and leave you two to catch up on old times." She shot a wink Morel's way before going inside. Yet, even though she was out of sight, Factor could still hear the conversation.

"She's remarkable," Morel offered, "she's strong, intelligent, and has the wisdom of the ages. She's also a woman consumed by guilt."

"What do you mean?"

"She knows that if you continue to stand by her and with her, it'll surely lead to your death."

"Sobering thought," he observed.

"But it's likely true. The forces that want her dead won't give up. They'll continue to trail her until their mission to silence her ancestors is complete."

"If we only knew what one of her relatives saw that makes her a target."

Morel shook her head. "Odds are they saw nothing, but if there's just one small chance she, through the eyes of others, has witnessed something that'll change the perception of a billion people, then she'll be hunted down and taken out."

"So, my mission is impossible."

"Yes, it likely is. But if somehow she does remember the moment that has placed the bloodhounds on her trail, and we get to hear about it through one who was there, wherever and whenever that is, then maybe that moment's worth a hundred lifetimes. Facing death to uncover truth is a noble path to take."

Factor moved to the open window and looked out just as Morel turned, placed her hands on Carter's arms, and studied his face. "Isn't it better to know the truth for a few moments than live a lie for a lifetime?"

"Sounds like a question someone would ask at two in the morning in a college dormitory."

Morel brought her arms around Carter and hugged him. "I'm with you, and I'll love you until death parts us."

"And I always thought you were smart," Carter cracked.

"What do you mean?" she asked, her face buried in his chest.

"A smart woman would leave this mission right now. There's no reason for both of us to die."

"History has proven that we all die, but few get to die while searching for truth. And even fewer get to share that mission with someone they love."

Factor walked away from the window and back to her bedroom. These two were not going to die for her. Within a day or so, when they weren't looking, she'd sneak away and leave them to find a lifetime of love rather than a handful of minutes spent protecting someone they barely knew. When the time came, she would face death alone.

Chapter 38

It really serves no purpose to kill the messenger because the messenger is only delivering what someone else already knows.

———◆———

William Dixon checked into the locally owned Valley View Motel and went directly to his room to wait for a call from Mia Scott. Earlier, she'd told him that Morel was in the states and headed to Denver. She'd assigned a man to pick up the trail when Morel landed, and then Scott was supposed to follow with an update. That call never came.

After reading *Time* from cover to cover, which was much easier now than twenty years ago, he left and drove to a Waffle House for a midnight meal. He sensed someone watching him. In a counter mirror, he noted two men in a booth spending far too much time watching his movements than eating their meals. Later, the same pair followed Dixon back to the motel. They didn't get out of their car. Instead they parked and waited. The next morning, after checking out of the Valley View and pulling onto the highway, Dixon again noted the duo. Who were they and what did they want?

A few miles down the road, Dixon stopped at a Shell station to fill up his rented SUV. He only needed a couple of gallons, but it gave him the opportunity to more closely observe the tails. They were too well dressed for plain clothes cops or FBI. Both were middle aged, one was a small, tanned man who looked as though he'd just stepped off the page of a fashion magazine. The other was large, possibly a former boxer, whose coat showed a bulge made by something much more lethal than flesh. They were prepared for action.

Pulling the SUV back onto the highway, he headed west. The pair followed at a safe distance. And that's when Dixon noticed something else. A banana yellow Ford Fiesta appeared to be following the car that was following him. If anyone else joined them on the highway, they were going to need a parade permit.

Using a lifetime spent evading those intent on killing him, Dixon sped up, rounded five sets of mountain curves, and then dashed off a rural side road. Safely out of view, he made a three-point turn and watched the main road. The Fiesta flew by, but the other car, carrying the two other men, never appeared.

On a hunch, Dixon got back on the main road and began to tail the compact Ford. It didn't appear the new parade leader realized Dixon was following him. When the Fiesta pulled into a convenience store in Glenwood Springs, Dixon parked and waited. As the little man reappeared and began walking toward his car, Doctor Death started his SUV, pulled forward, and cut him off.

"Watch where you're going," the stranger whined. The message wasn't delivered as a threat, but a suggestion.

As he put the passenger window down, Dixon glared at the seemingly meek man. Dressed like a poor college kid putting himself through school, he was of a much different class than the other two tails.

"Get into the car," Dixon barked, "we need to talk." When the man didn't move, Dixon showed a Luger. The stranger needed no more convincing. Once the man was seated in the passenger seat, Dixon pulled out of the parking lot and turned right on the state highway. A mile later, he posed a question.

"What's your name?"

"Van Goodwin. I can show you my ID if you want."

"Why were you following me?" Dixon demanded.

"I wasn't."

"You were on my tail for miles."

An apologetic Goodwin shook his head. "Maybe that's true, but I wasn't following you anywhere. I was just on my way here."

"For what?"

"I'm a reporter—my boss gave me an assignment. I'm just doing my job."

Could this be true? A bit more probing might give Dixon the answer.

"Who do you write for?"

"Nothing you probably read."

"Don't get smart with me, son. If you value your life, you'll spill the information."

"Okay, the *National Inquisitor*. I know it's a rag, but the pay's good."

Dixon smiled. Perhaps he had drawn an ace.

"Is your boss a woman named Scott?"

"You know her?"

"We've done business."

"Positive or negative," Goodwin apprehensively asked. "I mean the *NI* has made more than a few enemies."

"You've never written about me. In fact, from time to time, Miss Scott has helped me do my job."

"Okay, that's good to know." The reporter was suddenly much more relaxed. "What line of work are you in?"

"Pest control."

Dixon pulled off the main road onto what looked like a logging trail. Once he was sure he was out of view of the highway, he stopped and turned off the engine.

"Let's get out and talk," Dixon suggested.

Goodwin was not going to argue with a man holding a gun; he quickly opened the door and jumped out. When Dixon motioned to move forward, the reporter did so without hesitation. When both men were in front of the SUV, Dixon began digging for information.

"My guess is you've been assigned to track down an Israeli woman named Indira Morel. You're hoping she leads you to Elton Carter. Am I on the right track?"

"I'm not supposed to share my assignments. You know, freedom of the press."

"That tells me all I need to know. So, where's Morel?"

"Once more …" Goodwin's words stopped, his eyes grew as large as saucers as Dixon produced his gun again. When the silencer was spun onto the Luger, the reporter's knees began to shake.

"Look around," Dixon coolly suggested, "what do you see?"

"Trees."

"Let me explain something, if I shoot you here, no one will find your body for days. And if you don't give me the information I want, I will kill you. You see, that's my job. People pay me to stop hearts from beating and mouths from talking. So, have you already written your last story?"

"I hope not," a nervous Goodwin assured him.

"Then tell me what I want to know. Did Scott give you the job of tailing Morel?"

"Yeah."

"Where is she?"

"I lost her."

"What?" Dixon barked.

"I'm pretty sure I know where she went," Goodwin assured him. "I was on my way to check that out right now."

"Where is it?"

"Only about ten miles from here, in her uncle's cabin. She's used it before."

"So, you've got the address?"

"Yeah, and I wasn't following you. I was just on my way there."

"Then, you get back into that car and play navigator, we're going to pay Morel a visit."

Goodwin didn't argue. After pulling out of the woods, Dixon drove in the direction the reporter pointed. The next twenty-five minutes were largely spent in silence, with the exception of the reporter's directions. "Up the side of this mountain. Left at the sign."

Even in the powerful SUV, the drive wasn't easy. Negotiating the road took almost every bit of concentration Dixon could muster. Rocks flew with every turn. But he still had the presence to keep an eye on the gun and on his passenger. When they slowed to ease around a hairpin turn, Goodwin reached for a door handle, Dixon issued a stark warning.

Chapter Thirty-Eight

"If you make that move, you'll be writing your own obituary."

The reporter nodded and pulled back. "There's only one cabin on this road. So, you don't need me to tell you where to go anymore."

"I like having company," Dixon assured him.

As he rounded a bend, he caught a glimpse of a log structure about three hundred yards up the steep terrain. He eased the SUV to the side of the road, set the brake, and cut the engine.

"Why are we stopping?" Goodwin asked. "We aren't there yet."

"I'd rather surprise Ms. Morel. Now stay in the car until I get what I need."

As the reporter waited, Dixon moved to the back and opened the hatch. Tossing a blanket to one side, he picked up a rifle with a telescopic scope and two ammo clips. One he dropped into his pocket, the other he inserted into the gun. After rechecking his Luger, he eased it into his coat pocket and closed the hatch.

"Come on, Goodwin, we're taking a hike." The reporter joined him, and before they took off, Dixon asked, "What's the official address of this place?"

The climb through the woods was rough and steep, and it took almost fifteen minutes to make it to the cabin. Along the way, the men frightened two deer and an raccoon, but they ran into no people. About thirty yards from the destination, Dixon stopped in the shade to evaluate the situation. There were two cars parked in front of the rustic retreat. There was no one outside.

"Do you suppose anyone is there?" Goodwin whispered.

"If they weren't inside, the cars wouldn't be there. Stay right beside me and don't say a word. We're going to duck into the woods, hike up to where the yard starts, and get comfortable. If it takes an hour or a day, we'll wait until someone comes out."

Dixon made the short trek through the pines with Goodwin following step for step. When he found a place that had a clear view of the front porch and adequate cover, he went down on one knee and cradled the rifle in his arms. There'd be no mistake this time. He'd wait until he confirmed it was Factor before he pulled the trigger. As long as Morel and Carter didn't get in the line of fire, they could walk away.

"What do I do?" Goodwin whispered.

"Shut up and watch. Sit down by that tree on your right and do absolutely nothing."

Once the reporter had settled down, Dixon fixed his gaze on the cabin. One minute became five and five became ten. During that time, Dixon opened and closed his right hand. The action kept his fingers limber and his focus sharp. He was about to stand and stretch when without warning, the front door opened, and a woman stepped out. Shouldering his weapon, Dixon peered into the scope. After adjusting the focus, he smiled. There was no doubt. He had Dr. Maxine Factor in his sights. The quest that had been twice thwarted, once in Mount Vernon and then in Arkansas, was now about to be fulfilled. Moving slightly, so her forehead was in the center of his scope, Dixon took a deep breath and readied his finger to squeeze the trigger. But before he could use muscle memory to complete the task, he heard something to his right.

Goodwin rose, pushed off the tree and screamed, "Watch out! He's trying to kill you!"

A distracted Dixon pulled the trigger, but a now alerted Factor quickly turned and stepped back into the house. The bullet intended for the woman instead smashed into a log where her head had been a split-second before. Turning to his right, Dixon rose and muttered, "I should've killed you as soon as we got here."

A terrified Goodwin took off and raced toward the cabin. Dixon cut him down before he'd made it five steps. There were no final words. The shot went into the back of his head and exited the reporter's right eye.

Dixon frowned. In Arkansas, he'd questioned if age was catching up with him. Now, as he studied the body of another person who hadn't been on the target list, he once again kicked himself. In the old days, he'd have dumped, killed, or gagged Goodwin when he'd verified this was the right location. Maybe his mind and body were both failing him.

Chapter 39

1:02 pm
Monday, September 26
Mountain Cabin, seven miles outside of Glenwood
Springs, Colorado

When faced with a situation that's new, always trust the experience of those around you. Not doing so might just be fatal.

———◆——◆———

Maxine Factor dove back into the cabin, rolled over, jumped up, and locked the door. The only thing on her mind was that the shot meant to end her life would've found it's mark if not for someone's warning. She peeked out the window. The nightmare was getting worse. Was the man lying dead on the grass in front of the cabin the person who saved her? It certainly looked that way. Then with no warning, reality slipped away and someone else from a different time and place invaded Factor's head.

"The Germans have us cornered," a hysterical private yelled.

Sergeant Sam Marks nodded. They'd gone into the home to see if any civilians needed help, but the house was vacant. Their noble actions intended to save a French family had turned into a trap. If the three-man team charged out the front door, they'd surely be taken down by the Germans, but they couldn't stay in the house forever.

What was their best plan of action? As no officer was with them, it'd be up to Marks to make the call.

Moving to the door, he cracked it open about three inches. Two more shots rang out. Staying low, he rushed to the kitchen, took off his helmet, and held it up to the window's edge. The move prompted another pair of rounds. Marks smiled. Heading to the rear of the house, he lifted his helmet up to the glass once more. There was no response. He repeated the actions at the back door and another window without consequence.

"Men, we're facing a single sniper, stay quiet and move to the rear of the house. Then we're going out the back door. We'll meet in the woods behind the barn."

"Are you sure?" the fresh-faced private asked.

"I'll go out first," Marks assured him.

With a confused Morel and Carter looking on, Factor mentally forced herself back to the present. Crawling to the front door, she pulled it open about three inches—again a shot rang out. Moving quickly back to the small kitchen, she grabbed a cantaloupe, jammed it down on a broom handle, and pulled Carter's Yankee baseball cap off a chair. She moved back to a window and held her creation in front of the edge of the glass. The move elicited another shot. Even before shattered glass had stopped bouncing across the floor, she raced back to her bedroom and repeated the action in a window. Nothing happened. She did the same in Carter's room with no results. Hurrying to the living room, she once more cracked the door and leaned the cantaloupe into the opening. This bullet caught the melon and blew it to pieces.

Glancing over at Carter, Factor barked out an order. "Quietly take the screen off the window in your room, and then the two of you get out and run to the woods. Stay there until I meet you. If something happens to me, go as deep as you can into those trees and hide. Don't try to come out into the open until this guy is gone. Have you got it?"

"If we can get to my car," Morel argued.

"We can't," Factor answered. "So, don't try. There's only one shooter out there, and he can't be two places at once. I'll keep moving the curtains in the living room while you make your dash for freedom. When you're clear, I'll follow."

As Carter and Morel disappeared into the bedroom, Factor upped her game of cat and mouse. Jamming Morel's cowboy hat onto her head, she moved to the now shattered kitchen window and made a quick appearance, then fell to the ground. A single shot flew just over her head. The guy was quick with his response. Moving quickly back to the living room, she repeated her cat and mouse move. This round was faster and more accurate. While it didn't hit her, it did take the hat off.

Glancing toward the open bedroom door, she observed the window open and no one in sight. Carter and Morel had escaped. Determined to follow in their footsteps, she crawled across the floor. Just as she was about to exit, she noted the duffle bag filled with Carter's cash. After retrieving it, she slipped through the window, dropped to the grass outside, and made a dash for the woods. In ten seconds, she was home free, but her friends weren't there. Had they moved deeper into the pines?

Needing a better angle to see the shooter, she dropped the duffle bag on the ground and worked her way through the trees until she had a view of the front of the cabin. The body on the ground had not moved. She was now sure the man who had cried out and saved her was dead. A few feet behind him, she spotted a man crouching behind a large pine. He had to be the shooter. As long as she stayed hidden, he'd be no problem.

Feeling at least temporarily secure, Factor leaned against a tree to catch her breath. Her heart, which had been racing, returned to normal. But only for a second. She caught movement to her left and turned to see Morel, crouching low, emerging from the woods and racing toward her SUV. How stupid could she be? There was no way she would make it to the car.

The sniper picked up on Morel's movements at about the same time Factor had. Surprisingly, he didn't fire. Instead, he rose and made a beeline toward her vehicle. They arrived simultaneously. Using his weapon's butt as a club, he caught Morel in the forehead, and she dropped limply onto the rocky ground. The assassin, his face emotionless, pulled out a handgun and aimed it at the back of Morel's head.

As if one idiotic move weren't enough, Carter made a mad dash toward the gunman. The effort might've been noble, but it was going to get two people killed rather than one. The sniper aimed at Carter, but before he could fire, a shot came from the woods, zipped past the stranger, and into Morel's SUV's front fender. His focus now on the shooter in the woods, the sniper dropped to the ground and rolled behind Carter's Escape. When several more shots were fired, the assassin slipped into the woods. Within seconds, all was silent.

From her vantage point, Factor watched Carter race to Morel's side. As he did, two men, one large, one small, and both dressed far too nicely for the woods, stepped from behind the pines. The big guy yanked Carter by the neck and tossed him against the SUV.

"Where's Factor?"

"I don't know who you're talking about," Carter lied.

"Dixon was here," the smaller man calmly announced. "He was hired to take out Factor. He wouldn't have wasted his fire if she weren't here." As the big man shoved a gun into Carter's gut, the other continued. "You're a fortunate man, you've dodged Doctor Death twice. Walt will end your lucky streak if you don't give up the woman."

Carter said nothing. With that, the smaller man, the one who was obviously in charge, shrugged. "Do your job, Walt."

"I'm here," Factor called while stepping into the open and waving her arms. With her hands over her head, she moved across the rocky ground to the SUV. "Do what you want with me, but don't hurt him."

The smaller man nodded. "Walt, disable these two vehicles, then we'll march these two to our car."

"What about her?" Walt asked.

"Leave her here. She doesn't appear to be breathing anyway."

Walt fired a series of shots into a tire of each vehicle before signaling for Factor and Carter to move down the lane. Behind him, the man in charge made a call.

"We have Factor. What's the next step?" He paused before adding, "Yeah, I can do that. Just text me the directions on how to get there."

"What's up boss?" Walt asked.

"We take them to the Wizard's safe house." The smaller man quickly moved to Factor's side. "Lady, you're fortunate. You've finally run into someone who wants you alive."

Chapter Thirty-Nine

"Hey, Darwin, what about Dixon? He could still be hiding in the woods."

"No, once exposed, he always moves away and waits for another opportunity. He didn't get to be seventy by taking chances."

"Who's Dixon?" Factor asked.

"No one you ever want to see again," came the quick reply. "Now, let's get moving."

A couple of her ancestors had been captured. The fact she was here proved they'd gotten out of those situations. But not knowing if Morel was dead or alive was a nightmare. Sadly, if the woman hadn't run, they'd all be hiking away from this mess to a spot history had proven was the perfect hiding place.

Chapter 40

4:39 p.m.
Monday, September 26
Mountain Cabin, seven miles outside of Glenwood
Springs, Colorado

A mess is far easier to make than it is to clean up.

———◆———

The world of journalism is not that large, and though reporters often compete against each other, they're also known to provide information when other scribes are in desperate need. Mason Hardin's time on the phone had finally given him an address where Indira Morel might have gone in Colorado. Though he considered the tip from a friend at the *Denver Post* about an uncle's cabin a long shot, he and Smith opted to roll the dice and drive from Denver to Glenwood Springs. When they arrived at the cabin, Hardin fully understood Ulysses Goldsmith's oft quoted descriptions of failed reporters. "They always arrived at the right place too late." With doors open, windows broken, a man's body resting a half dozen feet from the cabin's front door, and two disabled cars, he was sure Goldsmith would've pointed to this experience as a failed venture by a well-meaning scribe.

As Smith pulled out his service weapon and began a perimeter search, Mason turned the body over and looked for the dead man's identification. Everything in the wallet said Van Goodwin, and one card identified him as a member of the press, though the quality of the publication that employed him was suspect. Yet, even if he worked for a tabloid, the poor guy was still a member of his fraternity and died pursuing a story. That made him a brother.

Moving his eyes from the body to the house, he used his imagination to understand what had happened. Obviously, there was an attack. If there were more bodies in the cabin or the yard, then perhaps the story was over. If Factor wasn't here, then maybe there were still leads to follow.

"Who's the dead guy?" Smith asked.

"Goodwin's his name. He works for the *Inquisitor.*"

"Worked," the agent corrected then glanced around the scene a final time. He spent a good studying the woods, before cautiously moving forward and entering the cabin. Meanwhile, Hardin turned his attention back to Goodwin. Thirty-one and gone, not much to show for a life, but he did live a couple more years than Marsha Chambers.

"Hardin," Smith yelled from inside the cabin. "Get in here."

What was it now? More bodies? Hardin was tired of seeing, smelling, and even tasting death. The last thing he wanted to do was visit a new nightmare. But he'd respond anyway. Why? Maybe it was just a reporter's curiosity, or perhaps Smith scared him. After jogging to the porch and entering the cabin, Hardin's gaze fixed on a woman curled up on a tattered couch. There was a cut on her forehead, both her eyes were swollen and blackened, but even those injuries couldn't mask her identity.

"Indira Morel. Is she—"

"No," Smith assured him. "Her pulse is steady—my guess is she'll make it. Besides the reporter, she's the only one here. Now, there might be bodies in the woods, but we'll have to do some searching to figure that out. First, let's move Morel to the car. You drive her to the hospital. I'll do the investigative work and try to figure out what happened to Factor and Carter. Then, when you get her taken care of, come back and get me. And don't tell anyone about this!"

"They took them," a barely audible voice whispered.

Neither man was expecting the woman to hear what they'd said, much less speak.

Falling to a knee, Smith leaned close, "Who took them?"

"Two men." Her breathing was ragged. "One … was large, the other well-dressed and average-sized." She paused again, as if trying to find connections from her brain to her mouth. When she began to speak this time, she sounded stronger and more purposeful. "They thought I was out, but I was just playing possum. The big one was called Walt. I think the other one was Darwin."

She lifted her head, but the pain created by that simple task must've been too great, as she immediately dropped back on the couch. Smith gave her a few minutes to recover before probing more.

"Did they do this do you?"

"No."

"Mason, get her some water."

As Hardin went to the kitchen, Smith resumed digging. "Do you feel well enough to tell me more? I'm CIA—my name's Rocky Smith."

Her eyes fixed on Smith, her mouth tightened, and her body tensed. Something about the agent obviously put her on edge. When she spoke again, her words came more quickly, and her tone now displayed what sounded like either apprehension or anger.

"If that's supposed to make me trust you, it failed. Are you here to kill Factor?"

"I want to find her," Smith admitted. "The man who's about to hand you the water is Mason Hardin. He's a reporter. I don't think he'd be with me if I were going to kill her."

Morel took the glass. After a couple of long sips, she nodded and sized up Hardin. "I've read your stuff."

"Then you know I shoot straight. My objective is to save Dr. Factor, not kill her. Now, do I trust the CIA? No! But so far Smith has been true to his word."

After taking another sip of water, she pushed up to a sitting position. "Wow, that hurts," she whispered. She took a deep breath, seeming to steady herself, and then opened up. "There was another man who shot the place up before Walt and Darwin arrived. He clubbed me with a rifle butt. And he killed the guy in the yard. He just missed Max. She had an idea on how to escape, and it worked until I screwed up and tried to get my SUV. I thought I had enough time and cover, but he met me there. He was going to kill me, but

Walt and Darwin showed up. They took Elton and Max hostage. I know it all sounds crazy, but that's the way it happened."

Morel rubbed her forehead for a few seconds. Though she still looked horrible, she appeared to be feeling stronger.

"My fault," she mumbled. "This was my fault. We could've escaped." She stopped, her battered face now displaying a look of understanding. "I've got it, Darwin made a call to someone, and in that call, he said the shooter was named Dixon."

"Dixon," Smith whispered as he turned back to face Hardin. "He was here. He must be the gun for hire. After all, he has killed two other imprints."

"I don't know if this means anything," Morel continued, "but the smaller man told Max they were taking them to the Wizard's safe house."

Hardin's jaw dropped in disbelief. The story Chambers was writing had just collided with his own. When Morel added nothing more, the reporter dragged the agent out onto the porch.

"Smith, did you hear that?"

"Yeah, we need to do some digging and find his property. Logically, it's within driving distance."

"But why does he want Factor?"

As the men considered that question, Morel wobbled out to the porch. She steadied herself against the door frame. "I think I can provide a theory on that."

"Please do," an anxious Hardin begged.

"I heard you say the word imprint, so I'm guessing you know what Max can do."

They nodded in unison.

"Who's the Wizard?" she asked.

"Crime boss," Smith explained. "He has his fingers in everything."

Morel nodded. "That fits. Some folks want Max dead because of what one of her ancestors may have witnessed, but others want to keep her alive for the same reason. If she recalls the right things, they could extort people, businesses, and even governments for millions of dollars. To someone like the Wizard, she might be a ticket to immense power, and a get out of jail free card."

Hardin frowned. Things just kept going further south. The Wizard could even use Factor as a way to keep Marsha's final story from ever seeing print or ever paying for her death.

"Well," Smith coldly observed, "we now know for sure Dixon isn't working for the Wizard."

"Yeah," Hardin replied, "and that makes us no closer to knowing who's behind the hit."

"There so many choices," Morel noted. "I can assure you it's not Mossad or the Israeli government, but there are some radical Jewish groups who, if they knew what she could do, might want her dead. There're also people in the Rome who'd likely see a reason to take her out."

"No matter," Smith cracked. "Our job is to focus on the Wizard. But first, we need to get you to the hospital."

"I'm fine," Morel argued "The world's stopped spinning. I've got a stake in this, so I want to go with you."

Smith glanced over at Goodwin's body, then turned back to Hardin. "Figure out where they've taken Factor."

"What are you going to do?" Hardin asked.

"I'm going to make a crime scene disappear. I'll start by getting rid of a body. If the locals get wind of this," the agent explained, "if they find out who was here, then Factor and Carter are as good as dead. In time, you can tell the world what you know. Just not now. I'll do what I have to do.

Chapter 41

The key that unlocks future possibilities is sometimes found in the distant past.

———◆———

The Haven was a sprawling ranch style home located in the midst of Colorado's wine region. It was constructed of sand-colored bricks with a slightly sloping roof covered by red tiles, and large windows and doors. With its views of the mountains but nestled in the valley's milder climate and straighter roads, it was a wonderful place to get away from life in New York. Rick Pulino had purchased it in the late nineties, and though he continued raising grapes, he'd never shown any interest in the business side of the fruit. While there was a woman who cleaned the house once a week, and a man who took care of the yard, the only people who were here on a daily basis were those who worked in the vineyards, and they were rarely closer than a hundred yards. The secluded nature of the Haven was what had drawn Pulino to it.

Over the last decade, members of Pulino's syndicate had held a dozen meetings at the getaway. Many of those underworld businessmen had skied in the mountains or played golf in the valley, but their boss stuck to playing pool inside. Except for observing it through a window, he had no use for the great outdoors.

Upon arriving at the house, Larkin and Hill locked Carter and Factor in two different rooms that were hidden behind false walls. Factor, who had been informed that murder was not the men's objective, settled in and grabbed a few hours of sleep. It was only after Hill brought her breakfast and relocked her room's door that she considered a move that might lead to freedom. On her own, Max was completely out of her league in figuring out how to exit a locked room and escape. Fortunately, she'd just met Rachel Jeffers who, four generations back, was her grandmother.

As a young woman, Rachel had served as a magician's apprentice. During her four years in that role, Jeffers learned all her employer's skills. Though barely five feet tall, the pixieish Jeffers was athletic, strong, and determined. One night, when the Great Margino was ill, she took over his act and wowed a crowd who couldn't believe a woman could perform magic. For the next ten years, Jeffers was a star in theaters up and down the east coast. One of her most remembered stunts was having local policemen handcuff her, lock her in a room, and give her five minutes to escape. She always succeeded.

Drawing from Jeffers' fount of knowledge, Factor spent the next several minutes searching for wire to serve as picks. She found paperclips in a nightstand drawer. As the lodge's locks were at least five decades old, getting her room's door open was not much of a trick. Once she had access to the world outside her room, she rearranged her pillows and cover to make it appear she was sleeping, then relocked the door. In the small hall, she ran into a strange panel with a knob, twisted it, and it sprang open. After stepping through, she closed the door and the entrance became a part of the wall.

Moving with the stealth abilities of one of her native American ancestors, she explored the house and two outside buildings. From the master bedroom window, she finally spotted her two captors enjoying the morning sun on the veranda, secure, it seemed, in the knowledge she and Carter were safely locked away. Having overheard, during their car ride, that the Wizard wasn't expected until later today, she began a room-to-room search for both Carter and a weapon. Finding neither, she snuck down the main hall to the living room, where she hid near a partially opened window. She listened to her captors as they talked baseball standings and playoffs. Then a cell rang.

Larkin waved. "Why don't you check on our guest."

Time to move!

Factor scurried to the door and glanced down the hall. Hill was heading in the opposite direction. Hoping Larkin was looking the other way, she followed the big man. She expected him to turn right toward the room where she'd been locked in, but instead he went left, stopped, twisted a knob on the wall, and a panel opened. Behind it was a door. Good to know it was there. But what she needed right now was to even the odds. But how? She was hoping an ancestor with a plan, but those crowding her mind offered nothing. Twenty feet ahead, Hill was digging in his pocket for the key to unlock what she figured was the door to Carter's room. Needing a place to stay out sight, Factor ducked into one of the home's main bedrooms. Some old baseball equipment was enclosed in a display case. As she got closer, she read a plaque. "This bat and glove were used by Mickey Mantle in 1958." Well, one of them was about to be reused.

Employing her homemade picks, she easily unlocked the case. With the Louisville Slugger in hand, she quietly headed back toward the hall. Hill was just pulling the key from the now open door. Thankfully, his back was to her. This was almost too easy. Ten quick, quiet steps later she brought the bat down onto the big man's head, and he crumpled to the ground. "Home run," she whispered.

Pushing by the now unconscious Hill, she signaled for Carter to remain quiet. "We need to get out the back. The man who's behind this operation will be here in an hour or less."

"We aren't going to get very far on foot."

"I know. When I made my tour of the house, I noticed there are three vehicles in the garage. If we want to go off road, I suggest we take the Jeep."

"How did you get away?" Carter asked.

"Evidently, I'm a locksmith. It seems my skill set keeps expanding."

As they moved down the hall and toward the back door, Carter stopped at what looked like a library door and stared inside.

"We need to get moving," Factor urged.

"We also need cash," Carter noted. "Can you crack a safe?" He pointed to a wall safe installed behind a large desk.

"Close the door, let's see if I have that ability."

As Carter watched, she hurried over to study the safe. It was an early Mosler model dating back to the 1870s. Those were a piece of cake even to an amateur, and Rachel Jeffers' skills far exceeded that level. Carter put her ear to the steel door and her right hand on the dial. An obviously impressed Carter chuckled as Factor made four spins and yanked the door open.

"Cash and lots of it," she whispered.

"Fill your pockets," Carter suggested.

After she'd stuffed all she could into her jeans, Carter took his turn. When the safe was closed and locked, Factor reclaimed her baseball bat and led the way out to the garage. She first checked the Jeep for keys, but found nothing in the glove box, console or under the mat.

Carter quickly hurried to the classic Mustang and a Chrysler 300. "No keys in either one."

"I'll hot wire the Mustang," Factor announced.

"You can do that?" he asked as he lifted the garage door. The purr of the engine answered his question.

Carter hurried to the passenger side of the red fastback and got in.

As quickly as possible, Factor pulled the car out of the garage, made a left, circled to the back of the property, and slowly drove out between rows and rows of grape vines. She kept on a tractor trail for more than a mile until it led to a gate. On the other side was a paved rural road. There was no traffic in either direction.

"The gate's locked," Carter observed.

"Picking it will be no problem. Can you drive a stick?"

"Of course."

"Then get behind the wheel, I'll have that open in a couple of minutes, and we'll decide which way to go."

Factor was far too conservative. She had the gate swinging and was back in the car in under a minute.

"Which way?" Carter asked.

"The mountains. It'll be easier to hide there than in the valley."

"Hiding is one thing," he suggested as he got out and returned to the passenger seat. Once he was inside and had his lap belt fastened, he finished his thought, "surviving is another."

"Don't worry, the woman who got us away from your place in Arkansas will be with us on this trip as well."

As she eased back into the bucket seat, Factor had every reason to be proud. She'd not only gotten them out of a tough situation, but she'd been in complete control of her ancestors' memories for two days. Not once had she fallen into the paranoia trap that had all but consumed her before meeting Lenards. Still, with the escape realized, and safety in sight, the adrenaline quickly faded and was replaced by a reality she didn't want to face. She was sure Indira Morel was dead, and that fact would eat at her for the rest of her life. Another life had been lost trying to protect the imprint.

Chapter 42

11:55 p.m.
Tuesday, September 27
Route 65, outside of Delta, Colorado

Most times the vulture leads you to the dead, but there are rare moments when they bring good news.

———◆———

Years before, Elton Carter's grandmother had stressed the key to happiness was to ignore the past and live in the moment. For two decades, the playboy of the western world had done just that. But that all changed the day he walked into Maxine Factor's office. Now he had to look ahead to avoid getting left behind. That meant he was going to do everything possible to keep from having the next tabloid headline refer to him as the late billionaire.

For the first part of the drive, the road had been long and straight, but that was about to change as they headed into the majestic mountains.

Factor glanced his way. "We need to talk about something important."

Carter kept his eyes glued to the highway. He didn't want to think about, much less talk about, what was likely on her mind.

"Indy," her tone was soft but firm.

Carter shook his head as the image of Morel sprawled on the ground filled his mind. "She shouldn't have run," he whispered.

"She was trying to help. She just made the wrong decision."

"But she never made bad decisions," Carter argued. "She never panicked. I don't know how many times she kept me from doing something dumb. And I mean really stupid, like charging into a new dig without checking for booby-traps or snakes." His eyes now misty, "She was like a mom in that way."

"And she was like a mom yesterday trying to save the person she most loved. The decision was all wrong, but her heart was in the right place." Carter downshifted as he came up a grade before quoting something nearly everyone had heard. "No greater love ..."

Factor finished it, "Than to lay down his life for a friend. Let's be clear, Elton. I've experienced enough lives now to know that doing what Indy did is not a natural instinct. Saving oneself is the primary motivation of every person. In that way, we're born selfish. It's in life we learn to give rather than just take."

"Who made you so wise?"

"I could give you a bunch of names if you'd like."

He knew that was the truth. As much to put the pain of loss behind him as to get an answer he needed, he asked, "Where do you think we should go?"

"Do you know the old saying about a criminal always returning to the scene of the crime?"

"Sure."

"Ninety percent of the time, it's a crock. Once a crime's committed, those who participated stay as far away as possible from the place they hit."

Carter didn't make the connection. "And what does that have to do with us?"

"We're going back to Indy's uncle's cabin."

"What?" He was aghast. The last thing he wanted to do was return to look at Morel's and the reporter's bodies. He pleaded more than said, "Anywhere but there."

"No," she resolutely argued. "What we need is there. Computers, clothes, a car we can fix and drive without drawing attention to ourselves. On top of that, I hid your money in the woods. And, if we clean things up and bury the dead, we can hide out there. No one's going to come back to that place to look for us."

While her observation made sense, it'd mean revisiting a spot where someone he loved had died. And she was probably still on the ground! He couldn't fathom doing that. Even if Factor literally possessed the wisdom of the ages, that was asking too much.

"Max, I don't think I can go there. There has to be another place?"

"Where?"

For one of the few times in his life, Carter didn't have an answer. They couldn't get on a plane, not with his face all over the tabloids, and they had to stay away from the guy Larkin had mentioned. Plus, the Wizard was the man who'd paid Larkin and Hill, and they didn't have a clue who he was or what he looked like.

"You didn't answer my question," Factor reminded him.

"Yeah, and you know why."

"There's another reason to go there. I know that area. If Indy hadn't made a dash for the SUV, we could have gotten safely away. There's a place about three miles around the mountain."

"How do you …" He opted not to finish his question. The answer was too obvious.

"The experiences of my ancestors have proven it helps to have an escape route and a guide who knows it. When I saw a certain view from the porch, I realized I knew that spot. There wasn't a cabin there then, but I'd seen that same view of the mountains. And then I remembered more too."

"Was it the Native American woman who guided us in Arkansas?"

"Yes. Her people lived in the valley, but she often spent time on the mountain. She discovered the cave when she was being chased by a group of white hunters. If it's like it was then, it's hidden, but I can find it."

"You're a different woman than you were a week ago." In spite of everything that had happened, she was so calm, so cool, so poised.

"You keep saying that as if it were a miracle. B.R. gave me a way to cope. She was honest enough to explain that this method was likely only temporary. In time, I might become overwhelmed again. Let me share something that's not easy for me to admit. There are ancestors in my head who take advantage of people and situations in order to advance themselves. I'm embarrassed by their actions. They lack character. I find it distasteful that I have their blood in my veins. To them, collateral damage, as we call it, is nothing."

"Believe me, I have a few of those types of lousy people in my family tree too."

"Yeah, but you don't have to deal with them as I do. I become them. At times, I give into their weaknesses. In fact, some of them are the reasons we've survived up until now." She glanced his way and posed a question neither wanted to answer. "What's does it say about humans that we most often value ourselves over all others?"

He didn't answer.

Factor's frown vanished as she added, "Then there are other ancestors that I'm so proud of. They're like Indy, they put themselves last. They're people of deep character." And then the conversation died, and the fading exhilaration of their escape was replaced by the horror of the recent past.

Neither of them spoke for more than two hours. It was finally Carter who, when they were winding up the mountain road toward the cabin, broke the silence and summed up his fears.

"I still don't like it."

"The men who were after us left there when we did."

"But," he argued, "the bodies will be there."

She nodded. "This is not just about my gut feeling. I'm following a wise ancestor who knew the perfect place to hide. That same woman is pushing me to properly honor the dead. The man in the yard gave his life to save mine. Indy was a woman you loved and who loved you. She died for your safety. We can't leave those two there for the animals to scatter their bones."

Again, Factor was right. Still the last five minutes up the mountain were the longest of his life. When the cabin came into view, the horror he'd expected was not there to greet them. Things were just as they had been when they'd first arrived a week before.

"The bodies are gone," he whispered.

Factor didn't respond. When they pulled up beside Carter's Ford Escape, she cautiously stepped out. She then waited for Carter to come to her side.

"Indy's SUV is fixed," she whispered, "the tire's not flat. The cabin's windows aren't broken, and there's no blood on the ground where the man fell."

Carter glanced toward the side of the cabin, there were no signs of life. Except for nature, he didn't hear anything or anyone.

"Let's go around back," Factor suggested.

After scoping out the scene in all directions, she led the way back to the woods. "Wait here," she ordered. She made her way into the dark shade before disappearing into the shadows. When she stepped back into the light, she was carrying a duffle bag. "Between what we got from the safe and what you brought from Arkansas, we're fixed for cash for a while."

She tossed Carter the bag before moving toward the cabin. Rounding the side, she stepped up onto the porch and glanced at the now repaired kitchen window. She then tried the door. It was unlocked. She waved for him to join her.

With Factor leading the way, they both stepped into the living area. Nothing was out of place. As he moved toward the kitchen, she strolled into what had been her bedroom.

"My stuff's still here," she called out.

"So's all the food," he answered.

Hurrying to his room, he pulled up the mattress. His computer and phone were just where he'd hidden them. From the door, Factor watched as he pulled his electronics out.

"Why did you hide them?" she asked.

"Just something I do when I travel."

"Well, whoever cleaned this place up didn't take the chargers. They're on the living room table."

"What do you make of it?"

She shrugged. "My guess? The guy who tried to kill us before Larkin and Hill showed up. I think Dixon was the name they called him, wanted to erase all signs of his presence here. So, in this case, the criminal might have returned to the scene of the crime."

"Why fix the flat and leave the SUV that Indy rented? Why leave all this stuff in the cabin?"

"In case someone came by," Factor explained, "it'd appear the owner's niece was still here. They'd just assume she was out walking in the woods. Remember, she told the guy who takes care of this place she was meeting a friend here."

"Do you still think we're safe?"

"Safer than ever. I hope we can find the keys to the SUV—the vintage Pony is a bit conspicuous. Why don't you rustle up something to eat. I'm going to move the Mustang behind the cabin and out of sight."

"Max, what do you think he did with Indy?"

"I have no clue. But if he dragged the bodies out into the woods, we'll know soon enough."

"How?"

"Vultures," she sadly explained.

Chapter 43

8:15 p.m.
Tuesday, September 27
The Haven, North Fork Valley, Colorado

Even a search that comes up empty always tells us something we want to know.

———•———

Her head still ached. With each passing hour, the area under her eyes was becoming a deeper shade of purple, and her body felt as if she'd lost a bullfight, but there was no way Indira Morel was going to skip the chance to catch up with the men who took Factor and Carter. As it turned out, they picked up the trail much sooner than she'd expected. Smith used his sources to find Pulino's mountain retreat. It was titled in the name of a real estate company, but a bit of homework on Hardin's part revealed the company was one of more than eighty the mobster who fronted as a respectable banker actually owned.

Once the trio had a target, they'd hit the road. Sitting in the rental car, Hardin and Morel waited as Smith moved around the house to make sure they weren't walking into a trap. As they killed time, Hardin reverted to his role of reporter and dug for answers about the woman they were trying to free.

"What can you tell me about Factor?" Hardin asked Morel.

"Why are you asking? You want to do a feature story? That'll set her up as a target for others."

"No, it may have started that way. And I certainly want to finish the story my mentor began, but this isn't about that. My motivation is to find out what she's like. You've met her, I haven't, so I just thought you might give me some insight."

"She's a remarkable woman—bright, funny, deep, and caring. Her natural instinct is to put others first. Still, I'd hate to have all those lives crawling in my head. She told me things that gave me a peek into a world of suffering and pain like I'd never fathomed." Morel licked her lips and turned to face the reporter. "Did you ever disturb an ant mound?"

"Sure."

"Did you watch all those ants climbing out of that hole at the same time?"

"Yeah."

"That must be what it's like in Maxine's head."

"If that's true, it's total chaos."

"Yes, and that's her life. The few hours I spent with her were both amazing and horrifying. Her talent, if you want to call it that, while so fascinating to someone like me, isn't to be treasured but pitied. Perhaps life's greatest gift is that we don't have the memories of all those who've come before us."

Her words were still hanging in the air as Smith slid into the driver's seat and wasted no time bringing them up to date. "There's no one home. The back door's unlocked, so we get in that way, but not sure how much we'll find."

After exiting the car, the trio worked their way around to the back of the house and entered through the kitchen. Because they had no reason to fear being spotted, they turned on the lights. One by one, they worked their way through the home. At the end of a hall, Smith pointed to the carpet.

"Blood, not a lot, but it's there and it's fresh."

"Not what I wanted to see," Hardin observed.

"Don't jump to conclusions," the agent suggested. "We don't know who it belonged to. He studied the carpet. "Okay this is weird. This is a hall that leads to nowhere. As the other two looked on, he began tapping on the walls. "There must be a secret panel here. But how is it opened?"

Morel, who had studied many secret passageways during her archaeological digs, glanced back down the hall. "Why put a coat hook in the middle of a wall that has no outside exit?"

While the men looked on, she walked back and twisted the hook. A second later, the panel opened and revealed a door. By the time she'd worked her way back to the entry, the men had the hidden entry open, had found the light, and were already inside the twelve-by-twelve-foot- windowless room.

"Someone did a lousy job making up that bed," Hardin remarked.

"It was rushed," Smith agreed. "And look at this notepad. Someone's been doodling on it."

Morel strolled over to the small desk and studied the paper. Her heart lifted! She now knew Carter and Morel were alive just hours ago.

"Guys, they were here. I have no doubt."

"How can you be sure?" Smith asked.

"Because that's Elton's handwriting. If he's sitting and thinking, he almost always scribbles 2011 over and over again. This page is covered with those numbers."

"Why that year?" Smith asked.

"It's the last time his beloved Boston Bruins won the Stanley Cup." Morel played a hunch and pulled out her phone. She punched in a familiar number and hit the call button. Ten seconds later, an obviously shocked voice answered.

"Hello? Indy?"

"Are you okay?"

"You're alive?" Elton Carter asked, his surprise obvious even over the phone.

"Alive and free," she assured him.

"We are too."

"Where are you?"

"It's best for you if you don't know. I promise I'll get in touch if we need anything. Stay safe."

"But ..."

"Not now, you don't need to know where I am."

She wanted to talk to him so badly, but perhaps he was right. It was enough, at least for this moment, to know he was alive. Her wide smile brought instant pain to her battered and bruised face, but it was a good pain. "I love you," she whispered

"Ditto."

The line went dead.

"What was that all about?" Smith demanded.

"They got away, and they're fine. But Elton wouldn't tell me where they are. He wants to protect me."

Smith was about to ask another question when Morel's phone lit up. This time, the caller was Ben Greenberg.

"What do you need?" she asked.

"Do you know where the imprint is?"

"No, why should I?"

"Because we've been told she's with Elton Carter, and—"

"Who told you that?"

"The man I'm with has sources."

"Well, they're wrong, Regarding Factor, if you're after her, just give it up and go home. She's not a threat."

"We can't do that."

"Who're you working with?"

"A friend from Rome who has the same objective I do. As should you. Taking her out is good for all of us."

"You're wrong," her voice echoed her anger. "And I don't think you really believe that."

"Can you truthfully assure me," Greenberg demanded, "that you don't know where they are?"

"Yes. I have no idea where they are."

The line went dead.

"Do you mind sharing what that was all about?" Smith asked.

Normally she would have clammed up. Her loyalty to the Star was unwavering. But this was far different. There were times when love trumped everything.

"Have you ever heard of a group called the Star?"

Smith nodded. "It's a Jewish national group that exists outside of the Israeli government. The goal is to make sure key legislation is pushed in countries all over the world."

"There's more," she admitted. "There have been times when people are erased. My associate from the Star is here in the States to take out Max. He's not working alone, he's with someone from Rome."

"The Vatican?" Hardin asked.

"I've been told the Pope knows about Factor and wants her to live," she acknowledged, "but there's a group of priests and cardinals who feel differently."

"So," Hardin observed, "We not only have the Wizard and Dixon, but some religious fanatics are also involved. This just keeps getting worse."

The ring of a cell phone interrupted the conversation again. This time, it was Hardin who answered.

"What's up, chief?" As Morel watched, Hardin excitedly nodded. "Okay, I'll get right on it. Text me the information."

"What's going on?" Smith asked. "You look like the cat who ate canary."

"We got the information we need to finish Marsha's story. It was just delivered to our office."

"What does that mean?" Morel asked.

"It means I can reveal the real identity of the Wizard."

"But you already know that," she argued.

"Yeah, but now we have the final piece of evidence, so I can go public."

"Hang onto that thought," Smith demanded, "my phone's ringing now. It's from my source at the FBI. Perhaps this will help us track Carter and Factor."

"It's Rocky," he answered. He paused, and seconds later his face registered surprise. "Has it been confirmed. It has? Okay, got it. And I think you'll find out something in the next day that'll blow this thing wide open. Have a task force ready to move."

"What was that?" Hardin asked.

"A tip led the FBI to a cemetery in New York where they dug up the body of Ricardo Pulino. He'd been knocked off a few hours before. The Wizard is dead!"

"What does that mean to us?" a confused Morel inquired. "Does it mean the Wizard's two men are out of the picture? Will the guys who brought Elton and Max here pack up and go home now?"

"I have no clue," Smith replied. "But for the time being, let's get away from here. Once they discover Pulino owned this spread, the FBI will be crawling all over this place.

Chapter 44

10:49 p.m.
Tuesday, September 27
Rocky Cliff Inn, Denver, Colorado

Compromising principles is usually very difficult the first time, but it gets much easier after that.

———————

F rancesco Russo sat on his bed staring blankly at a TV screen. His mission had met a roadblock. The quest to find Maxine Factor was at a standstill. And though he'd told no one, including his traveling companion Ben Greenberg, his future likely depended upon his finishing what had been started. This was about so much more than just protecting the interests of the church—it was also about insuring his future.

Russo's vibrating cell phone awakened him to the fact that while he might be alone in the small motel room, he was never really by himself. If you worked in the Vatican, there were always people watching. The caller was Jacob Cole. Had he found out what Russo was doing? If so, he might order him back to Rome. But there was too much at stake. Though tempted, he overruled logic and logged onto the call.

"You're up early on your side of the Atlantic," Russo quipped.

"I take it you're in America," Cole replied.

"Yes, I'm at a conference in your homeland. The Rockies are beautiful this time of the year."

"The higher ups here know you're doing something else."

"Why do they think that?"

"Before you left, you shared the information with Moretti, and you know who he told."

Moretti was such a fool. All he had to do was stay quiet, but when he got around the Pope and his assistants, the fat man just couldn't keep his mouth shut. It was a mistake ever trusting him.

"So what? I'm doing the Lord's work."

"You need to come home. Just cut this off before it goes so far it ruins you and your career. We all surrendered to a higher calling, and this isn't it."

Russo didn't like being addressed as if he were a child. Besides, what right did a priest who had an illegitimate child have to lecture about clerical behavior?

"You're called to do what you do," Russo opined, "and I'm called to do what I do. I suggest you worry about your own morality."

"They chose me to make this call. They thought, as your friend, I might be able to talk some sense into your head. We know why you're there, and it's not a conference. Hear this, the Pope wants Factor protected not dead. Maybe that frightens you, I know it does me, but that's the verdict. So, just turn around and come home."

Russo was fuming, his anger clearly etched on his brow. As Cole was the only one within vocal range, he'd be the one who took the hit.

"I've spent my life submitting to authority. First, it was my mother and then the leaders at the church. I submitted even when I knew it was wrong. This time I'm not going to. Mark my words, in time they'll thank me. Tell them you tried and assure them that if anyone else calls me from Rome, I won't answer."

"If I tell them that," Cole admonished, "they'll strip you of everything including your collar."

"There are times, my friend, that losing everything is the only way to hold onto the thing each of us treasures the most."

"What's that?"

"Our reputations!"

An enraged Russo, his face blood red, ended the call and then blocked any future communication from Cole. Still, refusing to answer the phone was only going to buy him a bit of time. The Vatican had the reach to get powers in the United States to send him back home. To work through the red tape to do that would only take a few days at most. He had to find Factor quickly. It was time to cash in his last chip.

For decades, an American evangelist had used his friendship with Russo to gain inside information on things at the Vatican. Now, perhaps that man could return a few favors. It'd be worth waking Dallas Arnold to find out. The preacher answered on the fifth ring.

"Francesco, it's an ungodly hour to make a call, what do you want?"

"A few weeks ago, I gave you information about an imprint in the US."

"Yeah, Maxine Factor. I told you I'd do some digging on her."

"Have you been doing so or was that just a hollow promise?"

"Yes, I've created a file on her. Why is it suddenly so important to you? You said the Pope was curious about her, but nothing more. Has something changed?"

"The Pope still feels the same way, but I'm of the opinion Factor is a huge danger. I want her to disappear."

"Ah, last rights, you Catholics love that ritual."

"This is no time for jokes."

"Why do you want her dead?" Arnold demanded.

"I have reasons."

"Personal reasons?"

Russo was a priest, but he didn't like confessions. Yet, in this case, perhaps it was time for one.

"I need her out of the way because of something in my own life that she might know about."

"How can a priest be worried about an imprint?" Arnold demanded. "She couldn't know anything about you."

"She could remember something a relative witnessed me doing."

Arnold laughed. "The chickens come home to roost."

"What about you, Dallas, are your robes clean? Now shoot straight with me. My vows prevent me from sharing what you confess."

"Fine, I want her gone as well, but it has nothing to do with theology. I hired a man to do the job. He's on her trail. Missed her once in Arkansas, but the last I heard from him he was getting close to her in Colorado."

"Are you sure it's Colorado? And are you sure the man you hired is up to the task?"

"The man's a pro, I have no reason to doubt him. And yes, it was Colorado."

"Dallas, where does your hit man think she is? I had a tail on her through some modern technology, but it failed."

"I don't like the term hit man," Arnold barked.

"Leave the hypocrisy behind you. You hired a hit man to kill a woman. To take that risk, as well as spend that kind of money, proves you're scared."

"Yes, I don't want to lose what I've worked so hard to gain."

"So, confess what you know."

"The hit man, your words not mine, might've already done the job and be heading back south to give me the proof and collect the rest of the money."

"But you don't have an address?"

"I've got one, and I'll text you what my guy sent me when he was closing in. He was ninety percent sure she was where he was headed. All you'll likely find now is a body."

"Then, my friend, I'll perform last rites and go back home."

"You should have the information," Arnold interrupted. "Check your texts."

Russo now had the information he needed. It was time to get Greenberg and move on. If Arnold was right, perhaps all he would have to do was confirm the kill. Once he did that, he was home free. He could waltz back to Rome, assure everyone he'd done nothing, and the past he feared would be buried forever.

Chapter 45

3:30 a.m.
Wednesday, September 28
Comfort Inn, Montrose, Colorado

There is always time to do something until you've run out of time.

⸺ ◆ ⸺

While Smith was busy trying to come up with Factor and Carter's whereabouts, Mason Hardin was writing the closing chapter of Ricardo "Richard" Pulino's life. To pay a debt of friendship, he was penning the expose under his late partner's name. The byline would cement her reputation as an investigative reporter.

After checking his copy for the fourth time, he emailed the story to his boss along with the Pulino obituary he'd written under his name. While it didn't lessen the pain, there was satisfaction in knowing that Marsha Chamber's work would lead to the arrest of scores of members of the Wizard's organization. His smile, created by the satisfaction of completing this job, quickly dissolved into a sense of sorrow. He'd never see his friend and associate again. There'd be no more ribbing, no more philosophical discussions, nor arguments over when and where to use commas. Sadly, the world had lost a star before she could really shine. Her work was finished, and he would so miss her.

Overcome by a dark, foreboding sense of loss, Hardin stepped out of his room onto the second-floor balcony. From the room beside his, he heard a door slide open. He glanced over as Indira Morel walked out into the open air.

"Did you find anything?" Hardin asked.

Unaware of his presence, Morel jumped at the sound of his voice. Then she relaxed and shrugged. "He's not answering my texts or calls, likely to protect me, so I still don't know where they are. Rocky doesn't want to put out a search for the car they borrowed as it might alert the assassin or assassins. As he said, these guys probably have ears and eyes everywhere. Right now, he's being all CIA and trying to track down Dixon. Rocky did a trace on the car Dixon was using. He checked it back into a rental center in Denver. He didn't get a second vehicle there, but he might rent one from a different company to cover his tracks. That's what he's checking now. Did you finish the story?"

"I sent it off a few minutes ago. You know, publishing a story like this would normally bring a death sentence to the reporter who wrote it. In this case, we don't have to worry about that. He paused and frowned. "She had so much to give. I've never known a talent like her. Likely never will again."

"She meant a great deal to you?" Morel asked.

"As a friend and coworker, yes. She was also like a little sister to me. I was nurturing her, grooming her if you will, to become the best in the business. These days, when the media is seen as the enemy by so many, good investigative reporters are a dying breed. Maybe her final bit of work will show folks how important the news media really is."

Hardin stared at mountains highlighted by moonlight, but he didn't see them. All he saw was Chambers's smile. That image didn't fade until Morel's voice brought reality back into focus.

"Are you going to keep working with Rocky?"

"Yeah, as a favor to my old mentor. I doubt Goldsmith will rest in peace until I finish what he started. And that'll be true whether I get to write the story or not."

"You're the guy who comes in the last few innings and saves the game," Morel suggested.

Hardin grinned. "I didn't figure you'd know anything about baseball."

"Elton loves the Yankees, so I had to learn." She looked over her shoulder. "Just a second, someone's knocking at my door."

Hardin watched her leave and then listened carefully as she said, "I'll tell him." When she returned, her expression seemed hopeful. "Dixon got a car from National. It's to be delivered to him tomorrow morning at ten at the Rocky Cliff Inn in West Denver. Rocky wants us to pack up and get moving. He'd like to get there in time to tail him."

"I'll get my stuff packed up."

"Life's rarely what we want it to be," Morel observed. "Even a man with your writing skills can't pen his own story. No matter how many plans we make, more often than not, things we don't control change them. Maybe that's why I'm a student of the past. History can't be rewritten."

"You might be wrong," Hardin suggested.

"How?"

"Maybe we can't change the mistakes made in the past, we can't go back and prevent Lincoln's assassination, or keep slavery from coming to American shores, but we might be able to fix some of the history in our own lives."

"How?"

"By admitting our mistakes and revealing our feelings. Even offering an apology. As long as people who are part of our history are alive, it's still possible to rebuild a shattered bridge."

Morel thoughtfully nodded. "That's pretty deep stuff."

"I didn't actually come up with those thoughts. A long time ago Ulysses Goldsmith shared then with us on the last day of class."

Chapter 46

7:33 a.m.
Wednesday, September 28
Mountain Cabin, seven miles outside of Glenwood
Springs, Colorado

Courage doesn't always require action, sometimes it's the motivator for walking away from a fight.

————◆————

From the woods just twenty yards in front of the cabin, Francesco Russo studied the scene. There were no signs of life. Yet the Mustang parked behind the structure and the SUV in front indicated someone was there.

"Finally got my software working," Ben Greenberg announced. "The SUV is the one Morel rented. The ID ping matches. My question is who's driving the vintage Mustang. That's a 1965."

"I'm surprised you know American cars," Russo said.

"Everyone in the world recognizes Mustangs. Now, how do we know if they're in there? And then, a much more important question, what do you plan to do about it?"

Russo couldn't really answer either of those questions. Once he'd learned the location, he'd rushed into action and was now just making things up as he went along. That proved he was both desperate and an amateur.

"Give me a second," the priest begged. "I'll figure things out."

If Arnold's hit man had known the location two days ago, then was this a waste of time and energy? But he had to know if Factor was dead. If she was dead, then he could pretend he was following orders and returning to Vatican as Cole had asked. If she wasn't, he had to stay on the trail.

"We're the Three Stooges minus a member," Greenberg sadly observed as he sat down beside a pine tree. "We have this grand goal, but we rushed off blindly without thinking about what it might take to accomplish it. Now, here we are, two men of God trying to rationalize killing a woman, and we have no thoughts as to how to do it. The only weapon at our disposal is that ax leaning up against that tree." He paused and shook his head. "Have you ever killed anyone?"

"Have you?" Russo shot back, as he crawled forward and retrieved the ax. He was surprised it showed no signs of rust and that the blade was sharp.

"No, and maybe it's best we don't start now. I should've never agreed to come with you. This is a fool's errand. No, it's worse. This is a case of two flawed men trying to play God."

"We can't go home after coming this far."

Greenberg glanced toward the cabin. "Yes, we can. In both our worlds, this would be a sin. You said your contact had already paid someone to take her out, so let's just admit we're not up to the task. Besides, even if she's alive, she'll never remember back that far. We know that from what happened to the others."

"It doesn't matter that she can't remember back two thousand years, in my case she doesn't have to. If she's not already dead, we have to stop her from breathing. We have no other choice."

In his rush to convince his friend of the mission's value, Russo may have opened a door to a past he didn't want to share. That admission fueled two explosive emotions. The first was panic, the second was rage.

"What do you mean in your case, she doesn't have to go too far back?" Greenberg asked.

"How valuable am I to you?" Russo demanded as he squeezed the ax handle.

"Seriously, you want me to answer that?"

"Yes, and fully consider that question when you do."

Greenberg looked as though he'd taken a shot of bad medicine. His face reflected disgust. But, as the seconds passed, the expression morphed into one of resignation.

"You're more than just a source for the secrets from the Vatican, you're also my contact to the CIA. From an international standpoint, without you, I'm half blind."

"Then, if we don't do this," Russo explained, "that source you so treasure might be gone forever."

"I don't get this at all. I know your friend issued that threat from the Vatican, but we both know it won't happen. They aren't going to turn you loose. After all, for the past decade you've been the person who files the secrets away. You have leverage. You're safe. Especially if we just walk away. But if you're involved in a murder the Pope doesn't want—you'll literally have hell to pay."

Greenberg was backing out. Russo could read that in his eyes and hear it in his words. If Factor was alive, he needed help.

"Walking away would be the worst thing I've ever done," a determined Russo announced. "If there's one memory that comes back to her, a memory from one generation ago, I'm going to prison. This is about far more than the church—this is about me."

"What are you talking about. Have you embezzled money or something? Did you kill someone?"

"If only it was that simple." Russo took a deep breath. What he was about to admit was a nightmare for anyone, but especially for one in a position of trust. "A lifetime ago," he explained, "when I was a very young priest, I was in America, and I did things with a certain young man I shouldn't have done."

"You didn't," Greenberg said in disgust. The look on the man's face spoke volumes.

"It wasn't only that one teenage boy—it happened a few times, but I eventually woke up. My life has been chaste since then. I promise!"

Greenberg was beyond shocked. He was angry. As he considered the confession, he began opening and closing his fists. It appeared he was finally ready to kill, but the target wasn't Factor.

"So, what does that have to do with Factor?" Greenberg demanded. "How does your perversion tie into this chase?"

"It's her father. If she has her father's memories and figures out who I am now, I'll be exposed in more ways than you can imagine. And you'll have lost your most important source."

"I'm here to cover up your putrid sins. Just when I thought I couldn't feel any dirtier."

Neither man spoke for a few minutes as both stared at the cabin and considered their options. It was Greenberg who finally broke the awkward silence with a stark and honest admission.

"I've used my power to ruin people's reputations in order to get what I felt my organization needed. I've played it dirty in more ways than you can imagine. I drove one man to suicide. Yet, in each of those instances, I convinced myself I was fighting a battle for my faith and Israel. I successfully rationalized my actions time and time again. But in truth, in each of those moves I've sacrificed a bit of my soul. I've told people how to live without living that way myself. And you know what really makes it all so clear?"

"What?"

"If Factor is in there, we have the opportunity to kill her thanks to information you got from a preacher. We're all in the wrong—your source, you, and me. We're influenced by fear, not faith. And if we continue, we have no right to ask God for forgiveness. After all, when the lights are turned off, we've served the devil."

Russo's rage was obvious. Though he was keeping his voice down, his face was red, and his hands were now squeezing the ax so tightly his knuckles were white. Up until this moment, he'd hoped that he could find the will to kill—now he knew he could. In fact, he wanted to.

"Ben," Russo whispered, "if you don't help me, I will never feed you anymore information."

"And, perhaps that's the best news I've had in years."

"So, you're out?"

"I just faced God and confessed my sins."

"You're turning your back on who you are and what you believe in," Russo warned.

"No, I'm just becoming what the world thinks I am and what the Lord knows I should be."

The discussion was interrupted when the cabin's front door opened. A woman walked out to the porch. From photographs they'd both seen, they knew who she was. Dallas Arnold's hit man hadn't struck yet.

Dr. Maxine Factor glanced toward the mountains—her beautiful face was bathed by the sun. She looked at peace and seemed to be considering the majesty that surrounded her, before turning and reentering the cabin.

"You really want to go back?" Russo asked. "Now that you've seen the target, do you still think this is a bad idea? That woman could turn the world upside down. Consider once again what you're giving up."

"I'd already given it up," Greenberg assured him. "I did that a couple of minutes ago when I looked into the mirror in my mind. I didn't like what I saw. I've already done enough things that keep me awake at night. If I do this, then I'll likely never sleep again."

"Okay, then," Russo suggested, "let's go back to the car."

"You're serious?"

"Lead the way," Russo announced with a forced smile while lifting the long-handled ax and resting it on his right shoulder.

Greenberg sighed with relief and began the trek down the mountain to where they'd hidden their car. Russo followed a step behind. They were two hundred yards away from the cabin when the priest whispered, "Forgive me," and raised the ax. Just before he could send the sharp blade deep into Greenberg's skull, he stumbled and that affected his aim just enough to miss the head and skim Greenberg's arm, ripping the jacket but not getting to the skin.

"What in God's name?"

Russo steadied the ax and raised it above his head. The look in his eye was one of madness.

"Frank, you don't want to do this."

Russo grinned and brought the blade down again. Greenburg jumped to the left, then spun and raced between trees down the side of the mountain. An enraged Russo, ax in his hand, was directly behind him.

They were just a few yards from where they'd parked their car, when Greenburg tripped, bounced off a pine and went sprawling on the forest floor. Just as he was about to pick himself up, his hand found a jagged rock the size of a softball. He grabbed it and rolled but was a moment too slow. Russo brought the ax down into Greenburg's left shoulder. The priest was getting ready to strike again, when Greenberg, in desperation, jumped up and flung the rock. The projectile caught Russo's temple. He hovered for a moment, then dropped the ax and fell to the ground.

"I'm leaving, Frank. I'm taking the car. By tomorrow, I'll be back in England. I hope you decide to walk down the mountain rather than turn back to the cabin."

Russo couldn't clear his head. He heard the words, but they weren't making any sense. As Greenberg turned and jogged off, the priest rolled over onto his back. In a few seconds, the world went completely black.

Chapter 47

8:15 a.m.
Wednesday, September 28
Rocky Cliff Inn, West Denver, Colorado

Few things are worse than arriving late for a date. But arriving late is better than missing it all together.

———◆———

After scanning the parking lot and not finding the car that National was supposed to deliver to William Dixon, Rocky Smith left both his confederates in the car and stepped into the old motel's small office. Behind the front counter was a young woman, maybe twenty, playing games on her iPad while nursing a cup of coffee.

"Miss?" Smith asked.

"We won't have any rooms until about one," she announced without looking up. "That's when the maid'll finish her rounds."

"I'm not looking for a room. I'm supposed to meet a man here. He's likely still in his room. He's probably registered under the name Wade Atkins."

Smith figured Dixon was using the same name as when he rented the car. Judging from the woman's nod, he'd guessed right.

"Mr. Atkins was here but checked out early this morning," she mumbled as her eyes stayed glued to the phone. She smacked her gum once before adding, "He said the rental car company had gotten him a ride sooner than he'd expected. He must've forgotten about your meeting."

"I guess he did," Smith acknowledged. "Thanks anyway."

She kept playing her game and didn't respond.

The agent had no way of knowing where Dixon was heading. The one chance he had to track the man down was now toast. Burnt toast. He was about halfway back to his companions when his cell vibrated.

"Meyer, why's the FBI calling me this early in the morning?"

"It's not early in DC. Where are you?"

"Colorado."

"I hope it's for a vacation."

"In a way. What do you need?"

"Just a little follow-up. When I alerted you to Pulino's murder, I had no idea there was a reporter working a story on exposing him. You need to get online. Marsha Chambers's feature is the talk of the news. We have agents picking up the people she exposed for us. This is huge and historic."

"Good to know you all have something to keep you busy." After realizing how sarcastic his response sounded, he changed his tone. "Seriously, you've been looking for the Wizard for years, this is really good news for you all. Congratulations."

"Thanks."

Smith was about to hang up when it dawned on him this was someone who might be able to help with his problems. While the FBI wouldn't know where Dixon was headed, that agency could possibly provide a clue for another man involved in this mess.

"Stan," Smith announced. "I could use a bit of help."

"I've used you as a source a few times, I'll be happy to share anything that's not classified. What do you need?"

"Have you heard of a man who works the crime game named Larkin?"

"Larkin works both sides of the street, but he's not a bad guy. In fact, when we get our arrests taken care of in the Pulino matter and these cases come to trial, he'll likely supply me with the names of witnesses we need to convict these rats."

"This is Darwin Larkin?" Smith asked. "Am I right?"

"Yeah, we're talking about the same person. He runs with a big guy named Walter Hill. Larkin is the brains and Hill's the muscle."

"Do they ever use any aliases?

"Not that I know of. They've managed to keep their records clean, so they have no reason to hide."

"Do you have a number on the guy?"

"No, he contacts me when he has something. What do you need him for? By the way, I thought you were on a vacation. Isn't that what you said?"

"I lied. What I want from Larkin is information that deals with something I'm working on. If you find out where he is, call me."

"Will do."

"Congratulations again," Smith added as he hung up the phone.

If Larkin and Hill flew into Colorado, they likely landed in Denver. It was time to do some more tracing of rental cars. After all, they obviously had wheels when they ferried Carter and Factor from the cabin to the mansion.

As he jogged back toward Hardin and Morel, he focused on Plan B even knowing there was a fly in the bowl of soup. Why would Larkin and Hill continue if the Wizard was dead? More than likely, with Pulino out of the picture, they were headed back to the east coast. Still, he had no place else to go.

Chapter 48

Noon
Wednesday, September 28
Mountain Cabin, seven miles outside of Glenwood
Springs, Colorado

When safety and security are challenged, the only things to cling to are
hope and experience.

—————◆—————

If not nervous, Elton Carter was at least apprehensive. Factor's logic made sense. Who would look for them where they'd almost been killed? But even staying in the state of Colorado gave him the willies. What sold him on returning to the cabin was Factor's promise of having an escape plan and the need to make peace with Indira Morel's death. But she was alive, so the act of saying farewell was no longer necessary. With that in mind, he hoped Factor's confidence in having a way to escape was as solid as she believed it to be.

What most troubled and confused him was the mystery of who'd cleaned up the cabin and what their reasons were for doing so. He was tempted to call Morel and ask if she knew anything about it. If she and the people she was with had cleaned things up, that'd extinguish his concerns. Just hearing her voice would surely provide him with a lift. But making that call seemed like too big a risk.

"You keep looking out the windows," Factor observed.

"Just can't relax."

"Celebrate the good news. Indy's alive and safe." As he nodded in agreement, Factor opened a small cupboard and frowned. "Looks like Vienna Sausage or Spam. We still have crackers and bread for sandwiches."

"Either's fine."

Eating was really the last thing on his mind. Over the last few days, everything he'd put into his mouth had tasted the same. Carter stepped out onto the porch. It was surprisingly cool in spite of the bright sunshine. As he sucked in a deep gulp of mountain air, he considered how good it'd feel to take a run on the mountain trails. Of course, that would require the right shoes, which he didn't have. Once again, he hadn't shown wisdom or foresight. Their trip around the store consisted of little more than hurry, grab, and get out, and when Factor made suggestions, he told her they didn't have time. So, the off-brand sneakers he'd bought a few days ago weren't going to be very good on the mountain trail.

Factor joined him on the porch. "Here's your lunch." Since arriving, she'd seemed surprisingly upbeat. "We still had some corn chips. I'll get mine and join you in a few minutes. Don't wait for me."

He took her at her word and was halfway through the Spam sandwich when she returned. He marveled at how relaxed she was. She acted as if nothing had ever happened here.

"Listen to the symphony. Almost everywhere I've been in my life, there has been noise. I could never seem to get far enough away from civilization to fully escape it. Even in remote areas, there was always the sound of a car somewhere. Until I started communing with my ancestors, I didn't really understand what quiet was. But here it doesn't sound much different than it did two hundred years ago when I …rather a distant grandmother … sat near this spot on a brisk fall afternoon."

"Is she the guide you talked about? Is she the reason we're here?"

"Yes. I'm reviewing moments from her life. And even when her life experiences fade away, the memories stay with me as if they are my own. And for a change, today that's kind of marvelous."

The more he learned about imprints, the more Carter was confused. Rydell was far different than Factor. The English woman never gained control, but the person beside him now had a way of using her visitors to put life into perspective. Lenards's final gift seemed to be a lasting one.

"About this woman," Carter asked, "how much do you know about her?"

"She was Cheyenne. Her name was He'evo'nehe, which means *she wolf*. She had broad shoulders, dark eyes, hair that fell below her waist, and strong hands. She was even a leader of men. She wore her name well. In a time when most women in the world had little value, she was seen as equal to any brave."

"A woman ahead of her time."

"You would've liked her, but she'd have likely frustrated you too. No one could really control her. In these mountains, she did as she pleased. She hunted, fished, and often spent days by herself. Like a wolf, she was comfortable alone."

He had to know more. "The way you talk about her seems different than the way you speak of the others."

Factor smiled. "She carried great peace. Those in her village looked to her for counsel. They said she had the wisdom of the ages. She understood that life was about more than years, it was about service and a reverence for life. I wish I knew what became of her. I can tell you this, she'd met white people, and she knew the English language. So, she was not completely isolated as a child."

At the sound of a twig snapping, both Factor and Carter instantly turned toward the woods. They were no longer alone. A middle-aged man, dressed in slacks and a white dress shirt, emerged from the trees. He carried an ax, blood was streaming down his head, and there was a crazed look in his eyes.

Carter stood, stepped in front of Factor, and demanded, "Who are you?"

"Ask her, she probably knows me."

Carter looked at Factor. She shrugged.

Based on the accent, he was likely from Europe, but which part, Carter couldn't gauge. There was one thing so obvious from the enraged tone, the enflamed look, the way he swayed back and forth ... He was completely out of control.

"I knew her father," the stranger screamed. "My name is Francesco Russo. Her dad called me Father Frankie."

"I have no memories of my father's life before my childhood," Factor explained.

"You lie! You know what I did! Confess now for the good of your soul!"

Factor stood and raised her hands to assure the visitor she meant him no harm. Then, in a calm voice she observed, "You don't hit me as a man who understands what you're saying or how to use that ax. Why don't you put it down, and we can talk? Perhaps we can get something to drink and get to know each other."

Her soothing words did nothing to calm him down. In fact, he was now livid.

"I think I know what I'm doing. I need to kill an imprint. One who knows far too much about me."

There'd be no more words. A man on a mission, he raised the ax even higher and rushed toward them. As he awkwardly bounded up the steps to the porch, he swung. Carter ducked to his left, but while he avoided the ax, he stumbled down the stairs. As the billionaire struggled to get up, the stranger lunged toward Factor. Rather than take the intruder on, she grabbed the porch rail and leaped over it to the ground.

Carter needed a weapon. He spotted a fist-sized rock and raced to grab it. By the time Carter retrieved it, the deranged man had climbed off the porch and was walking steadily toward his prey. Factor, strangely enough, was standing still, just watching as the potential killer moved closer. Just as he lifted the ax over his head, he stepped into a hole and fell to his left. Factor still held her ground. What was she thinking?

As he regained his balance, the stranger made a mad dash directly at Factor. She showed no fear, assumed a defensive position with her arms spread out from her side. When the crazed invader took his last two steps, she ducked her shoulder and drove him backwards. He stumbled and fell to the ground. Springing into action, Carter raced over and yanked the ax from the man's hand. With Factor resolutely looking on, he held it, ready to employ it as a weapon if needed. But the man didn't move.

Factor eased forward, bent down, checked the intruder's pulse, and shook her head. "He's dead. By the looks of things, that head injury was pretty severe. Likely a brain bleed or heart attack."

"Do you know what he was talking about?"

"No, he said something about knowing my father, but Dad's life experiences have never entered my head."

Carter retrieved the man's billfold and passport. He studied briefly. "He's a priest, and the address is the Vatican."

Factor frowned. "Someone else fearing an imprint. I need a scorecard just to keep up with all the folks who are after me."

"What do we do?"

"If this guy found us, others can as well. And I hate to tell you this, but we're about to have more company." She turned her gaze back down the mountain. "Someone's headed this way. I hear a car."

"Are you sure?"

"Yeah. Because that's a one-lane road, we can't use any of our vehicles." She paused and tilted her head as if listening to something Carter couldn't hear. "He just parked a few hundred yards down the road— that surely means he's stalking us rather than coming up for a visit." She glanced back at Carter, "We're about to head to that safe place I told you about. Grab what we need, and let's get moving. We have to be in the woods before he gets here."

Nodding, he ran into the house, picked up his phone, the charger, and his computer and stuffed them in a backpack, then he met her out front. Seconds later, they were in the woods. As she pushed through the pines, she didn't look back, she just kept jogging deeper and deeper into the forest. She finally slowed, but continued at a fast walk for fifteen minutes. With the elevation and rough terrain, it was exhausting. Finally, she pulled up and stopped.

As he attempted to catch his breath, Factor stood erect and still. For what was perhaps thirty seconds, she didn't move a muscle.

"We're not being followed, at least not yet, but we've got some ground to cover before we'll be safe."

"About that crazy guy, do you really think he was tied to your father?"

"Well, my dad was raised Catholic—perhaps this man was a young priest, and they crossed paths. Beyond that I couldn't guess. Obviously, my father knew something the guy didn't want me to remember. If I live long enough, maybe that'll be revealed. We're headed toward a cave I haven't seen in …" She smiled. "Let me rephrase that, a cave He'evo'nehe hasn't seen in almost two centuries. Let's hope it's still there."

"Any guesses on the other visitor, the one we're running from?"

"No."

As they trekked deeper into the mountains, Carter wondered if they would ever be safe anywhere again.

Chapter 49

1:13 p.m.
Wednesday, September 28
Mountain Cabin, seven miles outside of Glenwood
Springs, Colorado

There are a few times when forgiving sins is cheap but covering them up always comes with a high price tag.

———◆———

Dixon had only come back to the cabin to search for clues as to where Factor and Carter might have gone, so he was surprised to see the dead man wasn't the reporter he'd shot on his first trip. His Luger drawn and ready, he cautiously inspected the scene. Nothing made sense. There were three cars at the cabin, but no people. As the minutes passed, he found signs—a scribbled note on the table, some clothes, recently purchased food—it seemed his prey had returned to the scene. As the body in the yard was still warm, they'd left very recently. The tamped-down grass leading toward the woods proved they were on foot. As he followed those tracks, he spotted a trail. He figured they probably had a fifteen- to thirty-minute head start.

Returning to the cabin, he pulled a can of Coke from the refrigerator and opened a map app on his phone to study the possible places Factor and Carter might emerge from the woods. Taking a sip of soda, he frowned. There were too many variables. If he picked the wrong spot to watch, then it could be weeks or even a month before he could again find Factor. Sadly, that meant there was only one thing to do— trail them through the forest. As was usually the case, he'd prepared for almost anything. He had hiking gear and supplies in his car. And thanks to his CIA jungle training, he was a solid tracker.

Dixon was about to leave the cabin and ready himself for his job, when something hit him. He'd shot this place up just a few days before, and now it was in perfect condition. Carter and Factor wouldn't have gone to town for new glass, so who did? Was it the two who ambushed him at this same place a few days before? And, if so, why would they do that? For two men to clean up this scene, they'd have had to come back. There was no reason for that.

Thinking he needed a few more answers before setting out on his wilderness trek, Dixon began to look for traces of blood where he'd killed Goodwin. But the only blood he found was leaking from the unknown dead person's head. That meant the person who'd cleaned up was a pro. His thoughts returned to the two men who'd kidnapped Factor and Carter. They obviously weren't hired killers. If they'd wanted Factor dead, they'd have shot her when she came out of the woods, or they'd have just laid back and let him kill her. So, what was their game?

He glanced at the dead man. Who was this guy?

Dixon walked over, pulled a pair of gloves from his pocket, put them on, then kneeled, reached forward, and retrieved the victim's identification from where it had been dropped on the ground. As he sifted through the wallet, he was both shocked and confused. Though not dressed the part, the man was a priest. On top of that, he worked at the Vatican. Dixon dropped the billfold and stood. There was nothing more to found here—the mystery of what happened would have to remain unsolved—it was time to do some tracking.

When he arrived at his rented SUV, he opened the hatch, pulled out a backpack, a coat and hat, yanked his shoes off, added a layer of socks, and then slipped on some trail boots. Seeing no reason to leave the vehicle on the side of the road, he closed the hatch, hopped into the driver's seat and drove back to the cabin, where he parked the Buick beside the classic Mustang. After dragging the priest's body into the woods, he went back to the place Factor and Carter had slipped into the trees. He dropped and studied their footprints. They were wearing sneakers. They wouldn't be able to travel very quickly. Shifting his rifle over his shoulder, he stepped into the woods only to have his trek interrupted by his cell phone. It was Dallas Arnold. He hesitated, then against his better judgment, answered.

"What do you need?"

"Have you gotten her?"

"I'm close."

"What do you mean?" Arnold asked.

"It appears they were scared away by a priest with an ax. I mean, that's the only thing that makes sense." The line went quiet. "You still there?"

"Do you have a name for the priest?"

"Russo."

"I know Russo. He told me he'd come to the States to kill Factor. I suggested he back off because I'd already taken care of the job."

"How did he know where to look?"

"I told him."

"You what?"

"I figured Factor was already dead—it was my way of proving they had nothing to worry about."

"From now on, keep your mouth shut," Dixon barked. He paused to gain control of his rage and then asked, "Do you know a well-dressed man, about fifty, good shape, who travels with a big guy? They interrupted me when I was here the first time."

"I've used someone for odd jobs who fits that description. His name is Darwin Larkin. The other man might be Walter Hill—he's Larkin's right-hand errand boy. I've been told they've done jobs for the mob. But surely they aren't involved in this mess. They told me they weren't interested."

"What?"

"I tried to hire them before I called you."

"Is Larkin tanned and in good shape? And is Hill a pale guy with dark hair, who looks like a gorilla?"

"Yeah. Someone else must have gotten to them and offered more money. Maybe Russo hired them. I remember telling him a few years back about Larkin."

Dixon shook his head. Why had he taken this job? Arnold was an idiot. He was tempted to just walk away. But perhaps there was a way to work this to his advantage and teach the preacher a lesson.

"Transfer another million right now, or I'm off the payroll."

"That's extortion," Arnold whined.

"No, that's the price for acting like a fool. It's your choice. And if you opt out, it saves me a long hike in the mountains."

Arnold's tone immediately changed. He seemed to grasp that he was over his head with no way out.

"You'll have it in twenty minutes. I'll have you know this will bankrupt me."

"Forgiving sins is cheap but covering up sins comes at a high price. I'm not getting back on the trail until I know the money's in my account."

After hanging up, Dixon walked back to the cabin to wait on the payment. He drained another Coke as he waited. Only when notified payment had been made did he head out again, but before he'd even reached the porch, his cell lit once more. This time, it was Mia Scott.

"What do you need? I already paid you."

"My reporter in Denver is missing."

"That's not my problem," Dixon smugly announced.

"But you know where he is?"

"No, I can honestly say I don't. But I can tell you this, he's written his last story."

"You mean—

"Yeah, that's what I mean. Goodwin seemed like a pretty nice guy, but he was past his expiration date. Thankfully, he did serve a purpose."

"You're the devil," she hissed.

"And you're in bed with me." He laughed.

"I didn't give you what I found out so you could kill someone."

"Mia, each time you've given me information someone has died. Think about that as you count your money."

He dropped the phone back into his pocket, walked out of the cabin and into the woods. He had ground to make up if he was going to corner and kill his prey.

Chapter 50

4:07 p.m.
Wednesday, September 28
A cave eleven miles outside of Glenwood Springs,
Colorado

Illumination does not always require light.

———◆———

Maxine Factor, or He'evo'nehe, guided Elton Carter down the side of a mountain, across a valley, and back up another mountain before reaching a small stand of pines. She effortlessly worked her way through the maze of trees to a massive rock wall. After pointing to a slab of stone, perhaps ten feet high, she dropped to her knees and crawled behind it. Having no choice, Carter followed the woman into the damp, dark crevice. Six feet later, Factor turned on a small LED flashlight and revealed a cave that was at least sixty feet deep, twenty feet wide, and fifteen feet high.

She moved with purpose to the back wall and retrieved something, then pointed to rocks that seemed to have been purposely moved into a position to create benches. Once they were both seated, Factor lit a candle.

"He'evo'nehe …"

"She Wolf?" he asked.

"You can call her that. I don't think she would've minded. Anyway, she stored these. This was her place to think—at least when she was a girl and a young woman. She found peace here. Obviously, my memories stop when the next generation was born."

"When she came here," he asked, "was she running from something?"

Factor paused, as if thinking, but it was likely much more than that. When she finally spoke, her words brought far more light than the candle.

"The tribe called her a seer. I remember falling off a horse …"

"She Wolf?" Carter asked.

"Forgive me if I speak in first person, but that's the way I'm experiencing it. He'evo'nehe fell off a horse, and everything went dark. When she woke, she began to remember other people and other times."

"She Wolf was an imprint."

Factor nodded, "Yes, she was."

"Is she still in your head right now?"

"Not at the moment, you'll have to be satisfied talking to me." She smiled, the flicking light catching the life in her blue eyes. "I wonder how long she handled the memories? That's a question I guess I'll never answer."

Carter pushed off the rock, grabbed Factor's flashlight, and began to explore. While there were artifacts, such as pottery and beaded necklaces placed on several rock ledges, not much jumped out until he came to the back wall. What he found was breathtaking.

"Look at this," he called out. "Someone's painted a mural. It's detailed and goes on forever."

Bringing her candle, Factor joined him.

She pointed to the middle of the wall, "Here's the village, and the painting beside it is of the girl falling off the horse, and …" Factor was now having problems containing her excitement. "He'evo'nehe did these paintings. She was recording the story of her life. Look, this is her face and …" Factor stopped to gain control of her emotions. With tears streaming from her eyes, she whispered, "You can see scores of others surrounding her. These drawings must represent the voices in her head. And here she is holding a baby, probably her own. And look, she's leading her tribe into a battle, and here she's speaking to a group of men. It appears they're listening to her words as if she is a priest."

"And here she is old," Carter pointed out. "She didn't go crazy—the voices didn't destroy her. She found a way to control them."

"And," Factor added, "she lived with a people who saw her abilities as a gift to be treasured rather than a threat to wipe out."

"She must brought you to this place to give you hope."

"No, that's not how imprinting works. I just see her experiences—she doesn't talk to me or guide me." Her face still filled with wonder, she smiled. "Still, perhaps the answer's here, and I can find it myself. Turn off the light."

Once that had been done, Factor blew out her candle. The cave was now completely dark.

"Someone, perhaps another imprint," Factor began, "told He'evo'nehe about this place. That's how she found it."

For Carter, the absolute darkness was unnerving, but as he heard a sense of peace and security in Factor's tone, he calmed. She was completely secure here.

"Elton, this is where she came to visit with those in her head. It was the place she could focus. And when her ancestors came alive, it was like having a council meeting. The memories that came to her were teaching tools. They brought her wisdom. She cherished the darkness because in it, she found the light."

For a few seconds, Factor remained mute. Perhaps she was trying to assemble all she was learning into something she could share. But when she spoke again, she shared her own experiences.

"Ever since the accident, I've run from the darkness, I didn't want to even turn out the lights when I went to bed, but now I realize that it's here in the darkness where everything comes into perspective."

"I don't understand."

"Right now, there are scores of my ancestors all around me. The moments I'm experiencing are the most important things in their lives. And they're not the pain and suffering I told you and Indy about, these are moments when they found peace, joy, and purpose. The darkness erased all the chaos and brought the wisdom of generations into perspective. I haven't been able to properly or consistently use my gift because it's been revealed in an imperfect world. Once I tune out the modern world, it's clear I'm standing on the shoulders of all those who came before me, and that means I have the opportunity to reach higher than they did. If you want, turn the flashlight back on."

When the cave was illuminated once more, Factor shook her head. "I'm not sure I made any sense."

"Perhaps," Carter suggested, "I'm not capable of fully understanding it, but what I heard was fascinating."

Even in the dark light, Factor's face glowed. As Carter watched, she moved back to the mural. Her eyes darted from drawing to drawing and when she found one that spoke to her, she gently touched it with her fingers.

"Have you got something else figured out?" he asked.

"Not much, I'm still a child in this. What does it say in the Bible, I think 1 Corinthians? Now I see in a mirror darkly."

"Perhaps, even if She Wolf didn't actually bring you here, her experiences were what you needed. You had to see that she survived."

"She has given me hope." She glanced both to her left and right before observing, "There are a lot of paintings here, perhaps I need to read the rest of her autobiography." After relighting her candle, Factor stood by the wall. She was once more lost in another time and place.

Giving her time to study and understand the art, Carter opted to search the remainder of the cave. Off to one side, he found a tunnel, about six feet high, and followed it for twenty feet. On a ledge-like outcropping rested something shocking—a mummy. He knew he should alert Factor, but perhaps the sacred nature of this spot activated his mute button. For the moment, he'd take in this snapshot in time by himself.

This was not like the mummies he'd seen in Egypt or Mexico. This one had never been wrapped. The skin had, therefore, dried naturally. Thanks to his experiences with his archaeological digs, he was able to quickly ascertain what he was viewing. The woman had been old when she passed, her hair was gray and long. She was dressed in buckskin and wore knee high moccasins. She was about five feet tall. At the foot of the bench was a female wolf, preserved as the woman was. The animal seemed to have been placed to guard her. It was easily apparent whoever had done this had great respect for the person.

"Max," he finally called out, "you've gotta see this."

A few moments later, Factor worked her way back to him. Rather than showing shock, her face registered a sense of awe.

She studied the body for several moments, her eyes slowly moving from head to foot before whispering, "This is He'evo'nehe. Her power over her village is evident here, they honored her in a way they honored no one else. They buried her in her place of refuge."

"I guess you could say," Carter said, "she brought light to the darkest place they knew."

"My mind has tapped into the lives of scores, maybe even hundreds of my ancestors. I've seen them experience their pain and suffering, as well as love and hate. I can see their best and worst moments just as they did. But there's one thing I can't see. One experience will be mine alone."

"What's that?"

"Death. I have no memories of moments of dying because those happened after the imprinting. It'd be impossible for that to be on my DNA. I was with my mother when she died, but her memories of those moments are something that can't be shared. I can only see that from my own point of view. Death alone is mine and theirs."

As he continued to study He'evo'nehe, Factor backed out of the tunnel and disappeared. Five minutes later, when she returned, her mood was much more resolute.

"There's a man working his way up the side of the mountain. He's following our trail. We need to move on. I know this area much better than he does. If we keep covering ground, he won't be able to stay with us." She then glanced toward the body and whispered, "I'll be back, Kaku."

"What does that mean?"

"Grandmother."

"I get the feeling you won't have to come back here to visit her," Carter suggested as he reached toward the mummy's hands.

"What are you doing?"

"I'm retrieving the knife she's holding."

"Leave it," she ordered.

"No. She'd want you to have it. Plus, this is the only weapon we've got." Carter handed it to Factor, who frowned but still slipped it into her belt.

"Let's move," she ordered.

As they crawled out of the cave, Carter had a deeper appreciation of what it meant to be an imprint. And, perhaps for the first time, he felt it was likely more a gift than a curse. Yet, as they moved down the trail, something oppressive fell over him—when Factor spoke of death, it was like she knew it was coming.

Chapter 51

A forest is an amazing place anytime, but at night it really comes to life. The owls, insects, and frogs provide the background music, the natural cadence of survival. Everything alive is searching for something while looking over their shoulders for whatever's tracking them. It's a dramatic game of live or die that exceeds any sport man has ever created in both risks and rewards.

———◆———

Maxine Factor looked back toward the cave. As the last of the sunlight faded, she caught the glint of a small flashlight. The man following them was a very skilled tracker, but he'd soon have to quit. There was no way he'd be able to trail them in the dark. Still, there would be no rest. She and Carter needed to put as many miles as possible between them and the person intent on taking her life. That meant they couldn't give into hunger or fatigue. There'd be time to eat and rest later.

While she'd mentally mapped their escape route even before arriving at the cabin for their second stay, she'd slipped up on one point. When shopping, they should've gotten gear appropriate for hiking.

Sneakers weren't the ticket for this rough ground. As she came upon a small creek, she stopped and waited for Carter to catch up. In the moonlight, she could see he wanted an update. Yet, before he could pose a question, she put her finger over his lips and whispered, "Sound carries at night. If we talk, we must whisper. Remember that. Now, we'll cross the creek and then follow it down the valley. I don't know the towns around here—they were built well after the memories were imprinted on my DNA, but we'll surely hit a road, and that'll lead us someplace where we can find a place to stay and something to eat."

"Is he still back there?" Carter asked in hushed tones.

"Yes, and as he was able to follow us to the cave, he's obviously a skilled tracker, but as long as we don't use a flashlight and stay quiet we'll lose him. How much money did you pick up before we left?"

His jaw dropped. He sadly shook his head.

"So that means we only have what I've got in my pockets."

"I've got credit cards."

"Too easy to trace." Their options were now more limited. Frowning, she whispered, "Let's get moving."

At night, the valley was unforgiving. They slipped on rocks, tripped over logs, and got tangled in vines, yet much like He'evo'nehe would have, they kept moving. After about eight miles, they'd followed a trail up from the creek to the top of a ridge where Factor paused to let Carter catch his breath. As she studied the valley, she didn't detect anyone following. Still, she pushed on. Finally, halfway down the other side of the ridge, she stopped again.

"You can talk now," Factor announced. "That ridge wall will keep our voices from carrying back into the valley."

Carter nodded and wiped his brow. "I'm surprised we haven't seen more animals."

"They've seen us. If you'd looked, you would've spotted about a dozen deer on the far side of the creek an hour ago. We've startled four raccoons and a couple of possums. There's a bobcat who stalked us for a while too. Each one of them likely wondered why we were using their highway."

"I don't get it."

"The trail we're following was here two hundred years ago and probably a thousand years before that. Europeans were road builders.

They loved to find the straightest point from one place to another. They'd blow up a mountain and knock down trees to create their idea of the perfect road. Native Americans simply used the roads created by deer, buffalo, and elk. As those animals were prey for big cats and wolves, the predators followed this trail as well."

"So, She Wolf walked this same trail?"

"Usually, she jogged. It's time to get moving again."

After four hours of trying to blend in with the wild, a time when Factor was completely at home, and Carter was largely lost, they came out on County Road 313. It was little more than two lanes of worn, shoulderless asphalt. There was no traffic.

"Left or right," Carter asked.

"It's guesswork now, but our trail of broken branches and muddy prints will be easy to follow come dawn."

"I'm exhausted."

"Makes no difference, you have to find a second wind."

"Easy for you to say—every muscle in my body is begging me to stop."

"And, if you do, you're dead. You aren't defined by how far you think you can go but by how far you can go. Sing a song, whistle a tune, do whatever it takes to forget what your gut's telling you. Focus on something else."

Knowing Carter was too stubborn to give up, she pushed forward. On a hunch, she turned right. For the next three miles, he hummed a song she didn't recognize that proved he was tone deaf. But at least he was still putting one foot in front of another. She first heard hints of civilization, a car starting, a dog barking, and the faint strains of a radio, before they came upon a city limits sign. After climbing a steep hill, a few streetlights came into view. It was hardly Denver. Beaver Gulch was little more than a wide place on a mountainside and so small it didn't even have a Sonic or Subway. As Factor contemplated the next move, a police car turned off a side street and approached. The local cop eased his driver's window down and posed a question.

"You folks lost?"

"Well," Factor lied, "we were part of a group that took a challenge for a nighttime hike, and we got separated from our friends. You can tell it was a lark because obviously, we aren't dressed for a trek through that valley. We're not going back up the mountain now, so we need a cheap place to stay. Tomorrow, we'll call our friends to come get us."

"There's a fly-fishing competition this week," the lawman explained, "so the rooms in our two little motels are pretty much gone. It's against the rules for me to give you a ride, but I'll ignore that and take you to Yancy's Motel. Maybe they got a room. It's not fancy, but it's clean. And Tom and his wife are good people. If they're full, we'll check out the Mountain Dew Resort. It's got a fancy name, but it's actually kind of a dump. Why don't you get on in?"

After they piled into car, the lawmen pulled back onto the highway. "Where are you people from?"

"Illinois," Factor answered. "Came up here on a vacation."

"Have an uncle who lives in Bloomington. He works for State Farm. Don't see him much. When he goes on vacations, he heads up to Canada."

"Been there a few times," a still-panting Carter chimed in.

"By the way," the deputy asked. "Do you all know anything about Beaver Gulch?"

"No," Factor admitted.

"Well, we've been here for just over one hundred and fifty years. The place used to be bigger during the mining days. The gold ran out in the 1930s. That's when the town started to die. We lost our school first and then the post office. The few businesses left depend upon hunters and fishermen. We've got a branch bank out of Glenwood Springs, a small general store, a restaurant, and the Dairy Dip ... oh, and two bait shops. That's about it. The motel's up there on the right."

Yancy's Motel, an old motor court, looked to have about a dozen native stone bungalows. The cop pulled up near the office. Before he could give them any more local color, Factor chimed in.

"Let me see if they have anything."

"Tell them Clem sent you."

As Factor got out, she overheard the cop tell Carter, "She's a mighty pretty gal. You're a lucky man."

"Lucky in more ways than you know," Carter assured him.

Factor smiled as she caught the exchange. Perhaps, in this case, it wasn't as much luck as it was instinct. Stepping into the small office, she rang a hand bell.

Chapter Fifty-One

A thin, balding man came through a rear door. "Can I help you?"

"We could use a room."

"How long?"

"Likely a couple of days, maybe more if we find something to do."

"This is not an exciting place," he announced, "so we'll say two days."

"How much?"

"For two nights—seventy. If you pay in cash I'll knock five bucks off."

"Cash, it is."

"Just sign in, and I'll get your key. It's #9, on the far end toward the back. I don't have an open unit with a full bed, #9 just has twins, hope that's not a problem."

"No, that'll be fine," Factor assured him as she handed him three twenties and a five."

"Just sign the register."

She picked up the pen and wrote Sheena Wolf. At the moment, it seemed appropriate.

Exiting the office, she waved to the SUV. Carter said goodbye to Clem and joined her. "It's #9, and we're down to forty-five bucks."

"Should have picked up that duffle bag."

"And the money you left on the dresser," she added.

Once at the door, Factor unlocked it, pushed it open, and hit the light. The room was sparse, but clean. As Carter tossed a backpack on the bed, she looked out through the blinds. The no vacancy sign was now lit up.

"Any of those folks in your head giving you a plan for our next move?" Carter asked.

"No, for the moment we're on our own. The guy who's after us will be back on the trail in a few hours, so we need to get some sleep."

"What are the odds he ends up in Beaver Gulch?"

"Fifty-fifty. Just depends on which way he turns."

"And if he gets here?"

"Sheep."

"What?"

"We're the sheep, and he's the wolf. He's prepared to do what he needs to do—we're broke and have no plan. We can't hide forever, and we aren't equipped to fight."

"What about those voices in your head? Don't they tell you something?"

She nodded. "Yeah, but you wouldn't want to know what they're saying. Just like up on that mountain trail, survival is moment to moment, the hunter and the hunted, and the hunter always has the advantage. We have to turn the tables or we'll die."

Chapter 52

10:14 a.m.
Thursday, September 29
Beaver Gulch, Colorado

Information is often much harder to get in small towns than in big cities. It's not that folks don't want to help, they're just naturally suspicious of your motives.

———◆———

With mounted bass and trout lining the walls, the Mountain Dew Resort was obviously geared toward fishermen. This became even more obvious when an exhausted William Dixon entered the bath in his small room. There was bait crawling up the wall. He crushed one bug with an unopened bar of soap, but two more got away by fleeing to the bedroom and disappearing under the bed. After a few minutes trying to decide if the gray plaster walls had once been white, he pulled out his cell and called Arnold.

"Did you get her?"

"I'm literally on her trail," Dixon explained. "I'm in a small town called Beaver Gulch. If they're here, it shouldn't be too hard to find them. Have you heard anything from Larkin?"

"No."

"Let me know if you do. And, if you talk to him, find out where he is."

"It'd help my life a great deal," Arnold suggested, "if you could work your magic on him too. I'll give you a bonus for Larkin and Hill."

"Only if they get in the way again."

Dixon ended the call, exited the room and strolled back to the front desk. He needed some information. A fifty-something redhead was behind the desk. Her hair, about three shades too bright, matched her lipstick

"I've been hiking and left my car on a mountain outside of Glenwood Springs. Is there someone I could hire to take me back there? I need to pick it up."

"Well, sugar," she began with a smile that displayed two chins and a voice spotlighting the effects of years of heavy smoking, "I get off in fifteen minutes, and if the price is right, I could give you a ride."

"What's the price?"

"Two hundred including the extras."

Dixon grinned. It was obvious the woman with the glowing hair and a week's supply of face paint was offering him a lot more than a ride. While he didn't find her the least bit attractive, she didn't need to know that right now. So, he played along. "You get me to the car, and then the fun will begin."

"You don't know the half of it, sugar," she assured him. "Why don't you wait outside on the bench."

Fifteen minutes later, Molly was behind the wheel of her 2002 Crown Victoria, and they were on their way. As they flew down the road, she shared the story of her life in bursts that came at two hundred fifty-words a minute. It was hardly the stuff of a Hallmark movie … three marriages, a dozen different jobs, and a stint as a high school homecoming queen. But it was colorful.

It was just past noon when they arrived at the cabin. As she waited, he got out to make sure everything was all right. When the SUV started right up, he strolled back to Molly and handed her two one hundred-dollar bills.

"I guess I'll see you later," she said with a wink. "I already know your room number."

An amused Dixon nodded and watched the woman turn around. He followed her back to Beaver Gulch, parked in front of the motel, pulled his bags from the car, and returned to his room. While the bed beckoned, he opted to stroll the small town's streets and ask if anyone had seen an attractive couple who might've hiked into town. He drew blanks until he walked into the small, stark, police station.

"Can I help you," a uniformed woman asked.

"I'm trying to find my niece," Dixon lied. "She and her husband are hikers, and I thought they might've come through here last night. She's a pretty blond in her thirties, and he's a well-built man with a great smile. He looks like a younger Mark Harmon, the actor from *NCIS*. They called me to meet them but didn't tell me when they were going to get here or where they were staying."

"I haven't seen anyone, but one of my deputies mentioned he'd picked up a couple last night. He didn't tell me where he'd taken them or if they stayed the night."

"Could I talk to him?"

"He's not in town now, went up on to Eagle Ridge, but he'll be back here when he goes on duty tomorrow."

"Does he have a cell phone?"

"No, Clem doesn't like them. Thinks they're an intrusion."

"I see. I'll check back tomorrow."

After thanking the officer for her time, a disappointed Dixon walked back out into the cool mountain air. If Factor and Carter were in town, they'd stay hidden. As there was nothing he could do to flush them out, he had no option but to wait for Clem. After stopping for a burger at the Dairy Dip, he returned to his room, killed another roach, grabbed a shower, and fell into bed. He'd slept like a log for five hours when awakened by rapping on his door. He looked at his watch. It was just past seven. Rolling to the side, he retrieved his Luger before calling out, "Who is it?"

"It's Molly-time, sweetheart."

Opening the door, he found Molly in a dress three sizes too small and with even brighter lipstick. This shade of orange must have been reserved for evening.

"Hey, killer," she cooed.

"Hello, yourself," he replied, apprehensive about what was ahead. "Listen, Molly, I was thinking we should grab a bite somewhere. I'd like to buy you the best steak in town."

"Really? Most folks don't want to be seen in public with me." At least she was honest.

"I'm not most folks. Let me get my clothes on, and we'll paint the town."

Closing the door, Dixon walked over to his suitcase and pulled out some dress slacks and a white shirt. His plan was to feed her a big meal, get her very drunk, and then drop her back at her place. He'd soon find out that Molly was a woman who had no problem holding her liquor. In fact, she was the one who won the drinking wars and drove him back to his room. When he woke up around four in the morning, Molly was thankfully gone, but two bugs were fighting a turf war on his bare chest.

Chapter 53

10:47 p.m.
Thursday, September 29
Hideaway Cabins, nine miles southwest of Denver

Trust should never be given until it is earned.

———◆———

After hearing a knock, Mason Hardin pushed off the couch, opened the door, and watched as Rocky Smith marched two men into the three-bedroom log cabin. After tossing the car keys onto a table by the door, the CIA agent barked an order.

"Hardin, I'm sure they're both armed. While I hold the gun on them, get their weapons. The little one is Larkin—the big guy is Hill."

The reporter, while fearing he was not the right person for the job, approached the two, and as they offered no resistance, patted them down. They both had a gun in holsters on their belts.

Smith pointed to the desk. Hardin dropped the guns there before walking over to a bench positioned against the side of a far wall. As he eased down onto the wooden plank, his eyes met Morel's. She was leaning against the log wall on the opposite side of the room. If she was nervous, she didn't show it."

"Who beat the lady up?" Hill asked. His tone indicated he didn't approve.

"I'm the woman," Morel defiantly declared, "you left for dead a couple of days ago at the cabin."

"Glad you survived," Larkin said. He sounded sincere. "If we hadn't needed to get out of there, we'd have helped."

And unmoved Morel folded her arms and turned her head away. She was obviously disgusted.

"Where did you find these guys?" Hardin asked.

"They rented their car and room under their own names. A bit of help from the FBI, and I was able to track them down. Surprisingly, they didn't hesitate about coming over for a visit. Of course, I got the jump on them."

Hardin shifted his gaze back to the unexpected guests. For men who were captives, they were amazingly relaxed. Even though Smith, his face twisted in anger, was pacing back and forth as if to intimidate them, they seemed at ease.

"Larkin," the CIA agent began, "I've read your FBI file. You have no moral compass. You have a track record of taking advantage of people and moments. You've lived a life only playing winning hands. When things get challenging you fold. What I'm saying is this ... when it's a wise thing to do, you've been known to switch sides. You don't show loyalty. Is my assessment fair?"

Smith's verbal assault seemed to have little effect.

"I won't argue with that assessment," Larkin replied. "In fact, it has served me well."

"So, who are you working for now?"

"The guy who hired me most recently suffered a bit of lead poisoning. The story's all over the news."

"Pulino?"

"Pulino," Larkin admitted, "the Wizard, whatever you choose to call him. If you check, you'll discover the FBI has been known to pad my bank accounts as well. Let's just call me a consultant. I work both sides of the street. And neither can claim the moral high ground, at least in my view."

"You've never been a killer," Smith observed, "at least that's what your file says. So, it must've taken a lot of money for you to jump at this job."

"The money promised was beyond your dreams, but it wasn't for killing her. Pulino wanted her alive. He was sure he could use her gifts to his advantage. And you're right, Walt and I don't kill anyone unless it's to keep them from killing us. We're not hired guns. In fact, and I hope Walt doesn't mind me saying this, we're pretty much cowards."

"If you were working for Pulino, and now he's in a morgue, why are you still in town? Last I heard, dead men can't write checks."

"I decided I liked breathing mountain air," Larkin cracked. "And Walt's hoping for some early snow so he can do some skiing."

"I need to know where the woman is!"

"I have no doubt of that—you probably haven't had a date in years.

The flippant sarcasm obviously got under Smith's skin. It appeared he was about to engage in something a bit rougher than verbal attacks when the sound of a car driving up to the cabin stopped the agent in his tracks. This new arrival was unexpected. Everyone froze as they heard steps on the porch, then a knock on the door.

Hardin glanced toward Morel. Now, there was apprehension in her eyes. She obviously feared who was on the other side of the entry. So did the reporter.

Smith stepped to a position where he could keep his eyes and gun on both the door and the two guests. He then waved at Morel.

"Get it," Smith ordered.

She quickly and obediently moved to the entry and swung it open. Filling the entry was someone Hardin had never seen. The man in the dark suit didn't appear happy. When he opened his mouth, he growled more than spoke.

"Is Smith here?"

Morel nodded and stepped aside.

"Clegg," Smith acknowledged, his voice not hiding his disgust. "What are you doing here?"

"I'd just like to know," Clegg barked, "what you're doing period."

"Working on the job you gave me. The two on the couch are a part of the Factor matter. Let me introduce you to Darwin Larkin and Walter Hill. Thought you might have come across them at some point. The woman with the black eyes is Indira Morel. She's an archaeologist—even if you don't know her work, you've probably seen her in the tabloids. The guy on the far side of the room is a reporter … Mason Hardin. I'm sure you've read some of his stories." He paused and tried forcing a smile. He failed. As Clegg glared, Smith tossed out some unexpected derision. "Why didn't you tell me you were coming, I'd have baked a cake."

"What's with the attitude?" Clegg demanded.

Smith was in no mood to damp it down or apologize. "You put me on a case I didn't want. It's been nothing but chaos. I've had to cover up deaths and clean up crime scenes. And by doing so, so far, I've kept the CIA out of it. And now, just when I'm getting close, you decide to step in."

"I don't like your insolence," Clegg barked.

"I don't like it much either," Smith agreed. "Let me remind you, since September 11, the day I drew the deuce, I've tried to complete an assignment you didn't have the guts to do. And in that brief time, the body count reads like a third world war."

Clegg's eyes was ablaze. He obviously didn't appreciate his agent's lack of respect. For the moment, he found a way to turn his attention to matters at hand.

"What are you doing with Larkin and his goon?"

"Mr. Hill is not a goon," Larkin noted. "Walt's a cultured gentleman who leans toward classical literature, modern art, and jazz. In his spare time, he dabbles in sculpting."

"Shut up," Clegg shouted.

"On Larkin," Smith observed, "he's been a step ahead of me all the way. He says he was working for Pulino. Surprisingly, he claims the Wizard wanted Factor alive. He can tell you the reasons if you want to hear them."

"I don't much care," Clegg grumbled, "unless he knows where Factor is."

"Do you?" Smith turned and asked Larkin.

"What's in it for me?" Larkin countered.

Clegg, his mood improving, smiled and made an offer. "You give us what we want, and I'll give you and your friend a free pass. Your payoff died with Pulino."

"Maybe," Landers admitted, "and maybe not. As was pointed out before you arrived, I've been known to switch sides and there are other players in this game. More than you know about. So, don't try to bluff me. We haven't committed a crime that would stand up in court, so don't try to bluff us. When push came to shove, we even saved Miss Morel's life. Your promise of a pass is worthless. We don't need it."

"You didn't answer my question," Clegg countered. "Do you know where Factor is?"

"If I was given information that might lead us to her, that information would come with a price, and it's not cheap."

"Who are you working for now?" Clegg demanded as he walked across the room and stood in front of Larkin. If it was meant as an act of intimidation, it failed.

"I forget," Larkin shot back. He took a moment to fold his arms over his chest, in what had to be a show of calm strength.

Clegg turned back to Smith. "How close have you gotten to Factor?"

"Very close, and I'm about to get much closer."

"And why are they here?" Clegg asked as he pointed to Hardin and Morel.

"They've been helping," Smith explained. "You sent me out here by myself. You gave me nothing. You're the one who's always preaching about the importance of teamwork. I came up with a team of my own."

Clegg frowned, glanced at Hardin and Morel, and shook his head in repulsion before lobbing a bombshell. "I offered you millions and a way out of this business. All you had to do was kill Factor."

Hardin's jaw dropped. He and Morel had been played. They'd been helping a man who they believed was going to help save Factor's life—instead Smith was an assassin.

"Didn't you realize," Clegg shouted, "that by bringing them in you'd have kill them too? Are you that stupid?"

A hush fell over the room. Except for Clegg, it appeared everyone was searching for a path to an exit, yet he was blocking it.

"Larkin," Clegg snarled, while staring at Smith, "I'll give you the same money I was going to give Smith, just tell me where the woman is."

"Did you say a million?"

"No, but I can come up with that much."

Larkin looked at Hill and smiled. The pair seemed sure they'd won the lottery.

"We figured where Doctor Death goes, so does Factor. We were on our way there when Smith kidnapped us."

"Where?"

"Beaver Gulch."

"I didn't kidnap you," Smith observed, "you came with me."

"At gunpoint."

"Beaver Gulch?" Clegg asked.

"My source assured me that was where Dixon was."

"Pulino's dead, so who are you working for?"

"Maybe I'm feeding information to the guy who gunned Pulino."

"Who's that?" Clegg demanded.

"That would cost a lot more than a million."

Clegg nodded. "Smith, lock these guys up. If the information proves correct, they'll get both the money and their freedom." He glanced at the other two people in the room. "Then you'll need to kill Hardin and Morel. We'll dump their bodies on the way to Beaver Gulch."

Things had just moved from terrible to catastrophic. As Hardin contemplated being executed by someone he thought was his friend, he looked toward Morel. Her expression was a mixture of shock and rage. Just like him, she never guessed this was a one-way trip. Smith deserved an Academy Award for the way he'd played his con.

Chapter 54

11:24 p.m.
Thursday, September 29
Hideaway Cabins, nine miles southwest of Denver

There are those who look upon a cross as a sacred symbol of salvation, then there are those who live not for the cross, but for the double-cross. Putting faith in the former can lead to peace and contentment; putting faith in the latter often ends in death.

———◆———

"Stand up," Smith ordered Larkin and Hill as he replaced his service weapon in his shoulder holster.

With Clegg covering the pair, Smith retrieved two sets of handcuffs. He was reaching for Larkin's wrist when Hill stretched. The motion, which mirrored a man simply tired from sitting in a stiff position, was actually something else altogether. Shocking everyone, the big man produced a snub-nosed thirty-eight from behind his neck, a place Hardin hadn't checked, and all hell broke loose. After pushing Smith to the side, Hill aimed at Clegg and squeezed off two rounds, one finding the wall and the second grazing the CIA agent in the left forearm. Though injured, Clegg was ready to respond. He fired off a round that caught Hill in the left shoulder. It should've knocked him down, but it seems to only provide a motivation for rage. A second later, Hill tackled Clegg and the two wounded men began rolling on the floor.

By now, Smith had regained his composure, dropped the cuffs, and was reaching for his own weapon. Just as the agent's hand touched his gun's butt, Larkin's fist connected with Smith's chin, knocking him back into the wall. Seeing an advantage, Larkin raced to the desk, picked up a gun, and turned to watch the wrestling match. Unable to squeeze off a round, likely for fear of hitting his partner, he moved quickly to the door, and stationed himself on the porch. It appeared he wasn't going anywhere without Hill. That loyalty was kind of noble.

On the other side of the room, Smith stood, his weapon ready, and observed his boss and Hill. Neither had an advantage. Strangely, even though he had an angle to finish off Hill, Smith did nothing.

Hardin glanced at Morel who bobbed her head toward the door. To get where he needed to go, Hardin was going to have to get by the wrestling Clegg and Hill. Just when he was about to make his move, a muffled shot went off and Hill went limp. Clegg was pushing the big man to the side, when Morel made her hurried exit. Hardin tried to leap over the rising CIA agent but was a split-second too late. Clegg grabbed his pants cuff and pulled him to the ground. Out of instinct rather than training, Hardin kicked toward the agent, his size eleven shoe finding Clegg's chin. While it didn't knock him out, it stunned him just long enough for the reporter to get to his feet and scramble outside. From behind he heard a second shot and then felt a searing pain race through his arm. Praying Clegg wouldn't fire again, Hardin kept running. He was on a path leading straight into the woods when a hand grabbed him and yanked him behind a huge pine tree.

"I picked up the keys to the car," Morel explained as she pulled Hardin close. "Did Clegg get you?"

"Yeah, in the arm. I don't think it's that bad. Where's Smith?"

She pointed to her left. "Just before you raced out, Larkin took off. Smith followed. They went into the woods."

A disheveled Clegg appeared in the entry, a gun in his hand. A few seconds later, Smith jogged out the woods. He was headed toward the cabin when Clegg erupted.

"Look what you've done! You've screwed up this whole mess. I should've killed her myself."

"Oh yeah," Smith shouted back. "You didn't have the stomach to kill her. I saw that when I met with your old team. None of you did. That's why you set me up. Even if I had nothing to do with it, it was my job to cover up your sordid life. You're a coward."

"I was paying you well," Clegg shot back. After taking a look around the cabin, he demanded, "How are we going to explain this? This whole night was witnessed by one of the best and most respected reporters in the country. He heard me order you to kill him and that jet-setting archaeologist. I shot at him."

"They're not armed, and they can't have gone far."

"Did you get Larkin?"

"No, he got away."

"That's just great!"

"Larkin's not going to squeal. He knows what would happen if he does."

Clegg, seemingly calming down, nodded. "Yeah, and he gave us the information we needed. So, this is going to work out just fine. When we find Morel and Carter, I can use Hill's weapon to snuff them out. The story'll read that Carter dug something up on the big man and Hill was forced to eliminate them. Let's quickly regroup and get on their trail."

"And we trusted Smith," Morel whispered.

Hardin nodded but said nothing. His eyes were fixed on a now relaxed Clegg. The agent shrugged, seemingly signaling to Smith that all was forgiven, then walked back into the cabin. Smith took two steps forward before Clegg, now filling in the entry, turned, grinned, and pulled his weapon up in a firing position.

"Rocky, I'm going to do a rewrite. Here's how the news story will read now. A vacationing CIA agent witnessed Hill murdering the famed reporter and archaeologist, then got into a gun battle where he managed to take Hill out even after being shot several times by the underworld hit man. Agent Smith died before authorities arrived."

The color drained from Smith's face. Obviously, he wasn't expecting a double cross.

"How are you going to get Hardin and Morel without my help?"

"They are no match for me. They've got no firepower or expertise. I'll find and kill them within a half an hour." Clegg smiled, "Any last words?"

"If I had any, they would be to tell you just what I think of you."

"I know that, so don't bother. No, don't pull your weapon. You won't have time to get a shot off. Let's make this clean. I'd rather you not suffer."

"Just tell me, why me?"

"I offered you an easy way to a new life with no worries and lots of money, and instead you screwed up and left me needing a fall guy. It was a simple assignment—all you had to do was kill a history professor. Instead, you left a few bodies around that might potentially be tied to the agency you work for. I'll finish your job, and then, I might just assume the identity I'd worked up for you." The words stopped, paving the way for action.

Clegg pulled the trigger, but Smith felt no pain. The gun didn't fire. Before he could try a second time, Smith raised his arm and squeezed off a round of his own. Clegg was knocked backwards but didn't fall. Pushing off the porch, he stumbled toward the woods. As he ran, he reached for his phone, and made a call. With Smith in pursuit, Clegg screamed into the phone. Twenty seconds later, Smith steadied himself and fired again. This time, Clegg fell forward face first. This time, there'd be no getting up. Smith jogged to the body, bent down to check his boss's pulse and then said, "Die, you sorry SOB."

Morel tugged on Hardin's arm. "I'm getting into that SUV. You find a way to the passenger side. Let's move!"

Morel quickly made her move. She started the vehicle just as Hardin hopped in. Smith, now aware of the escape attempt, fixed his eyes on Morel. Though he had plenty of time to squeeze off a dozen shots, he held his fire and watched them drive away.

"You're losing a lot of blood," Morel observed as she pulled onto the highway, "I need to get you to a hospital."

"Not a good idea," Hardin whispered as he squeezed his bicep to slow the bleeding. "How are we going to explain what happened?"

"In this part of the world, that'll be easy. You were here to hunt and got shot cleaning your gun."

"What about Smith?"

"He's needs to stop you before you write this story, so he's going to be on our tail. Now, can you hold on until we get some miles behind us?"

"Yeah." Hardin sadly nodded as blood seeped between his fingers. "I trusted him, even helped him, and the entire time he was assigned to kill the woman we were trying to save."

"That's the bad news, but the good news is we found out before he got her in his sights. After we get you taken care of, we'll find Elton and Max."

Hardin was more than ready to team up with Carter and Factor. At this point, he felt sure there was real safety in numbers. But in the midst of the chaos he'd just witnessed, there was one thing that made no sense. Why, when given the chance, had Smith not killed them as they drove away? He had the opportunity and the time but did nothing.

Chapter 55

Bad decisions often hide in the dark for decades before deciding to come out and haunt us.

━━━◆━━━

B ristol Owen hated computers, cellphones, and iPads. It wasn't that technology confounded him—it was just that his hands were too big to work the small keyboards. Consequently, setting up and running this emergency Zoom meeting was a frustrating chore he hated. He didn't want to be at his kitchen table in the middle of the night, he didn't want to be staring at his computer, and he didn't want to visit with the two others, who'd once worked with Clegg on covert CIA operations. Yet, events from earlier in the evening had forced him to do whatever it took to bring the old team back together again.

First, Owen sent out texts with links demanding Rick Elder and Elmer Vanover join the meeting. While he'd made the message clear that this was something they couldn't afford to miss, he'd given no details. They'd only receive those when Owen could see them face to face. It was necessary to gauge their reaction, understand their mood, and make sure they remembered a pledge they'd made years before.

He stared at his own face on the screen as he waited for the two comrades to jump online. He thought back to those days years before and the excitement of serving his nation. It was the greatest thing he could image doing—he loved the work, the adventure, and even the risks. Then, in what seemed like a promotion, Clegg had brought him into the group. Suddenly, his life was split. While his CIA missions were fulfilling, the off the grid interactions with the quartet were making him more and more uncomfortable. And, in the end, it was Clegg's operation that defined who he was. He found himself serving two masters, and the evil one was sucking him deeper into a web he might never escape. A second window opened on the computer and pulled him out of his regrets. He refocused on the matter at hand.

As always, the still handsome Elder appeared far younger than his years. His caramel skin showed few wrinkles, but Elder was also a man with troubled eyes. He looked as though he was waiting for a hammer to drop and hoping his head was not the nail.

"Are you alone?" Owen demanded.

"No one can hear our conversation. What's so important that it couldn't wait until morning? Did we add another death to our journal? Is there another reason for me to question my morality?"

"Let's wait for Elmer, then I'll give you the update."

The wait was only a matter of seconds. When the unshaven Vanover appeared, he was wearing faded blue pajamas and hadn't bothered washing the sleep from his eyes. His greeting matched his looks.

"This better be good."

"It's anything but good," Owen assured him.

Vanover frowned. "Retirement is supposed to be spent in days filled with fun and nights without worry. My golden years just get worse and worse. Maybe I should call them the brass years because they are so badly tarnished." He groaned before asking, "What's the bad news?"

"I got a call from Clegg yesterday. His man, Rocky Smith, the guy we met at our reunion, hadn't delivered. Smith hasn't even gotten close to Factor yet, but that hasn't kept the body count from rising.

Let me tell you, Clegg was seething. He was so mad that he jumped on a plane to surprise Smith in Colorado."

"And this couldn't wait until morning?" Vanover grumbled. "Clegg should've done the job himself from the get-go."

"No, it couldn't wait," Owen assured him, "when he got to Colorado, things must have gone south in a hurry. There was a confrontation last night, and Clegg was gunned down by Smith. Just before he died, Clegg called me. His last words were about the pact we made thirty years ago. Then I heard Smith say, 'Die, you sorry SOB.'"

The faces on the screen were suddenly awake and sober. While they didn't appear to mourn Clegg, none of the three liked to be reminded of their time spent on the rogue team, and the pledge given on a hot July night in 1991 was a numbing reminder of how far outside the lines they'd played the spy game.

"We'd been drinking too much the night we made that vow," Elder argued.

"We drank too much every night," Owen suggested, "but that didn't keep us from agreeing to what Clegg suggested."

"We were a team then," Vanover pointed out, "we were young and stupid. In fact, we were asinine for being a part of that unholy alliance. The three of us are retired now. It's different."

"What if it was you who died?" Owen demanded. "Wouldn't you expect us to keep the pledge?"

"If it was me," Vanover replied, "then maybe I'd have some peace. Perhaps Clegg's the lucky one. Maybe he just won the lottery. In death, he won't be haunted by what he did in life."

"So," Owen demanded, "the deal means nothing to you?"

"It should," Vanover admitted, "but this was set up in case an enemy struck. Smith's one of us. He's CIA. That just makes it different."

"Smith's job was to do what was needed to protect us," Owen said, "and when he failed, Clegg dressed him down. That led to Smith killing one of us."

The meeting attendees went mute. Neither Elder nor Vanover seemed eager to commit. It was the former who finally broke the silence.

"You realize what you're asking? We'd be the judge, jury, and executioners. If we regret the decisions we've made in the past, think about what we'll feel like after we do this?"

"That," Owen pointed out, "was the agreement we made. And the fulfillment of that charge means we all work together. We need to meet in Denver."

"You're really going through with this?" a disbelieving Elder asked. "We're not young men anymore. We don't have the skills we once did. And perhaps, we don't have the stomach for it either."

"A pledge is a pledge," Owen argued.

"Where's Smith?" Vanover asked.

"I know where he was last night, not sure today. But we can find him."

Owen searched the other two faces. Though they were not pleased with the arrangement, they seemed to still possess loyalty to the team. But was that enough for them to meet him in Denver and help him track down Smith?

"I'll get us a place to stay," Owen pledged. "Don't tell anyone where you're going."

"What about the woman?" Vanover asked. "If Smith isn't doing his job, does that mean we have to kill her too?"

"The world can't find out what we authorized," Owen pointed out, "so that means the things she might remember are a danger to each of us. If we can track her, then we need to finish that job."

"My whole life," Elder sadly announced, "has been about rationalizing doing the wrong things for a country that claims to always take the high road. When people ask me what it was like to work for the agency, it makes me uncomfortable."

"Most of what we did was right," Owen pointed out. "We all know that."

"That's not what haunts me," Elder observed. "I don't relive all the good we did—I just think about times I justified doing things we can't talk about. And it's those things I'll never be able to live with. If we're all honest, we'd admit that Clegg earned his death ten times over."

Owen shrugged, "It doesn't matter, but what we pledged does. I'll see you in Denver. Be watching for a text with details on where we'll set up our operations center."

"You won't see me," Elder announced. "I won't add anything else to my legacy." Before Owen or Vanover could reply, Elder left the meeting.

Chapter Fifty-Five

"What about you?" Owen demanded.

Vanover nodded. "I don't want to do it either, but there's stuff that can't come out. It'd be horrible for those who know me to learn what I authorized. So, I'm with you."

"What do we do about Elder?" Owen asked.

"The two of us can handle the job. Let Rick spend time with his granddaughter. Between the three of us, he's likely the only one who won't die with a bottle of whiskey in his hands. Text me when you know where we're meeting."

Owen ended the online meeting and shut down his computer. Of the three, Elder was the one who surely had the best moral perspective, but Vanover understood what was most important, and that was saving at least a shred of their self-respect. Perhaps, a shred was all they had left.

Chapter 56

7:30 a.m.
Saturday, October 1
Beaver Gulch, Colorado

Family reunions sometimes bring people together for the right reasons but in the wrong way. In many cases, what's said at these gatherings pulls people so far apart they will never come together again.

————◆————

Maxine Factor yawned, stretched her arms and smiled. She'd found a way to not just live another twenty-four hours but had also controlled those who knocked on her mind's door. She glanced over at Elton Carter, who'd just emerged from the bathroom fully dressed. He'd actually shaved this morning.

"Good morning, sunshine," he announced.

She waited for him to put on his socks and shoes before noting, "It's been two days. If the killer was here, it seems like he would've found us. Maybe we lost him. Am I being too optimistic?"

Carter nodded. "Hunches sometimes pay off. Yours likely do more than mine."

He some flaws, like looking into the mirror too much, but deep down he was a good guy ... the kind you'd love to take home to both Mom and Dad. Money, looks, brains, a bit of courage—he had it all.

Yet, falling for her protector was not in the cards. He might be with her now, but he was in love with someone else.

"You know," Carter announced, his eyes fixed on her. "The last few days, I've seen a side of you I hadn't seen before. You're calm, relaxed, assured, you laugh at stupid things, tell funny stories, and make very bad puns."

"You didn't appreciate the one about the duck walking into a store, asking for Chapstick, and then telling the clerk to put it on his bill."

"It wasn't what I expected. I thought you were getting to something deep. Something tied to your past."

"Oh, it was tied to my past, just not the past of those in my head. You didn't know me before the plane crash. I was always the silliest one at the party. That humor helped with my students, too. I looked for ways to make learning fun. If only life could be that simple again. If only my biggest headache was grading research papers."

Her wistful smile quickly faded. Dr. Lenards had initiated Factor's trek back to herself. That was the first step in controlling the visitors from the past. But it was in the cave where she fully grasped the potential of her gift. And yes, now it seemed like a gift, one she didn't want to lose.

"Did you ever have family reunions?" Factor asked. "I mean big ones where cousins and cousins of cousins came?"

"No," Carter admitted. "Wealthy families tend to exclude those who don't meet the imagined standards of high society. You could be related to us, but if you didn't have power and position, you weren't welcome. In other words, my immediate family was full of snobs."

"Were you a snob?"

"No, in fact, I wanted to hang out with those who were not a part of our social circle. I loved to see my sister's face when I brought my *common* friends to the house. Why did you asked about reunions?"

"Because real reunions are chaotic. They might not begin that way, but they almost always end up with people taking sides. Kind hugs turn into wars of insults or worse. And the reason reunions are a bad idea is that you have to invite all your relatives. If you could just invite the ones who were open-minded, kind, generous, and fun, then reunions would be something to embrace rather than avoid. But there's always that one branch of the family who loves to debate, stir up trouble, and lives to start a civil war."

Carter chuckled, "A good food fight always sounds like fun. Beats talking about art or what's happening at the yacht club. But what does a reunion have to do with you or me?"

"In the cave, I learned how to do something. While looking at the painting of He'evo'nehe's life, I came to see that she had the ability to sort the good from the bad. If she opened a door and there were bad experiences hiding there, she immediately closed it. She could control the people who lodged in her head because she liked them. In fact, she was proud they were her ancestors. It was like she was having a family reunion with only the people who could teach her something or who helped put her life into perspective. I'm now beginning to understand how to do the same thing He'evo'nehe did. In the last two days, I've lived some incredible moments and felt very little pain and heartbreak."

"What kind of moments are so incredible?"

"Little ones. A mother giving birth, a father's joy in teaching a son how to ride a bike, baking bread and taking it to a sick neighbor, floating down a river and watching bears catch salmon, or the moment when, after being away at war, you catch a glimpse of your wife for the first time in years. It's like living the best moments of every feel-good movie you've ever seen, only a thousand times better.

"For the last few years," she continued, "it was the horrific memories that dominated my thoughts. They were the loudest, so they demanded the most attention. You and I both know if we have too much drama in our lives, we fall apart. That's as true for imprints as it is for others.

"So, that's why the sunshine song helped you the other day."

"Yeah. He'evo'nehe lived with the gift, rather than die because of it like so many others. But like every gift, it had to be used in the right way. The sunshine song was the first step in getting to this point."

As she glanced across the room to where Carter was sitting on the bed, she saw something in his eyes she had not seen before. There was a connection. It was warm, honest, and seemed deeply spiritual. As she watched, he stood, slowly walked over in front of her, placed his hands on her shoulders, and leaned forward to give her a hug, and then their lips came together. Inside her head, there were suddenly scores of ancestors kissing. Though many of those were filled with great passion, none could measure up to the power of this new meeting of hearts. Factor was aflush, her face glowed, her eyes sparkled, and long after Carter had pulled away, she still felt his arms around her.

As he stepped back, the billionaire seemed a bit embarrassed. All his confidence was gone. After rocking from one foot to the other, he mumbled, "I need to go get us some money. Then I'll stop by the grocery store."

"Don't forget to wear a cap and sunglasses," Factor warned. "Even here, your face is probably pretty well known."

He grabbed both and rushed to the door. He didn't look back.

Alone, Factor turned toward the wall. What had just happened? Were they two people who came together for reasons of fear, or was she falling in love with a man who already loved someone else? Until she could be sure, this couldn't go any further. She moved to a chair, closed her eyes, and accepted an invitation to a family reunion.

Chapter 57

8:45 a.m.
Saturday, October 1
Beaver Gulch, Colorado

In the blink of an eye, a beautiful day can become ugly. It only takes a moment for clouds to hide the sunshine. And you don't want to be out in a storm without an umbrella.

For the first time in years, Elton Carter found himself whistling. The song he'd chosen was "You Are My Sunshine," or did it choose him? With a spring in his step and a kiss lingering in his head, he walked the nine blocks to the bank, slipped a card into the ATM, and withdrew the limit of five hundred dollars. He'd turned and taken three steps toward the town's only grocery store when his phone rang. It was Morel.

She'd called a few times over the past two days, and to protect her, he hadn't answered. But there was a different feeling in the air today. There was, for the first time, a sense of hope. Yet, as soon as he accepted the call and heard her voice, there was something else too—guilt! Why had a simple hug and kiss affected him so? He'd slept in the same room with Factor and nothing had happened. They hadn't even held hands. But then the kiss …

"Hello."

"I'm glad you finally picked up," Morel said.

He spoke quickly, in hushed tones. "We've been hiding, and I didn't want to do anything that might expose either us or you." What he'd said was the truth, but more importantly, it masked his guilt for seeing Factor in a different way than he ever had before. And in this case his guilt was stupid anyway. Not only had nothing really happened, he and Morel hadn't been a couple in a long time. But if that were the case, why did he feel the need to confess? He'd never felt a need to explain his emotions before, nor had they been so convoluted. Was that kiss, simple without deep passion, showing him he couldn't be faithful to anyone, or was this call that followed so soon after that moment revealing how much he needed Indy? He was so lost in introspection, he also missed Morel's shocking confession.

"Elton, last night Mason Hardin and I were marked for death by a CIA agent named Clegg. Mason was shot."

"What?"

"Don't worry about him, it wasn't serious. In fact, he should be out of the hospital tomorrow. But there's something worse than ducking death."

"What's that?"

"We discovered the man we'd trusted and had been traveling with, CIA agent Smith, was assigned to kill Factor. Without meaning to, we've been leading people to you."

"The guy you called Rocky?" Carter asked in disbelief. What had seemed like a great deal was falling apart, and the kiss was forgotten.

"Are you still in Beaver Gulch?"

"How did you know that?"

"A source, a guy named Larkin, told Smith."

"We're still here."

"You need to get out. Now!"

"That's going to be harder than you might think. We've got no car. Escaping on foot would put us in the open."

"I'll come get you. Where are you staying?"

"Yancy's Motel, number nine."

"Are you there now?"

"No," Carter explained, "As we'd spent all our cash, I had to get some money to buy a few things we need. I'm going to the store next. In trouble or not, we have to eat."

"I'll be there before the cyber trail shows up."

"Thanks for bailing us out. But don't put yourself at risk again."

"You risk things for people you love," Morel assured him.

That made him feel even more guilty. Stewing in his mix of emotions he whispered, "Thanks."

"On my way. Love you, El."

"Bye."

Carter's mood had completely changed. The song was no longer on his lips, and he felt as if there were a thousand eyes locked on him. Failing at acting casual, Carter hurried across the street to Ray's General Store, grabbed a cart and filled it with what they needed and returned to the front of the store. There was one check out aisle and the line was nine deep.

A voice inside told him to leave. If he'd been an imprint, he might have listened—instead, he trusted his own instincts. They had two hours before Morel arrived, the stuff he was buying was needed, and if danger were lurking in this town, it'd have surely already found them. And if all that were true, why didn't he feel safe?

Chapter 58

9:15 a.m.
Saturday, October 1
Beaver Gulch, Colorado

Those who wait are usually rewarded. The problem is few have the patience to allow a moment to come to them. Yet the greatest of all predators are also the most patient. Even when hunger is eating away at their insides, they wait for their prey to appear.

———◆———

P atience. That had been his calling card for decades. There were just times you had to wait for the game to come to you. There was still a fifty-fifty shot Carter and Factor were in the area. If he kept his eyes open, he'd spot them. But even for a patient man, waiting did not come easily.

The deputy who had helped Carter and Factor had taken ill. He was not due back to work until tomorrow. Therefore, William Dixon had been forced to play a waiting game in a town that offered nothing he wanted. What made it worse was having to constantly avoid the amorous Molly. While he couldn't remember the conclusion of their previous night together, she evidently did and wanted more of what he'd forgotten.

After grabbing breakfast at Bill's Restaurant and Bait Shop, a place the locals assured him was a good place to grab some grub—it wasn't—Dixon was walking down the street killing time when he spotted Molly waddling out of the laundry mat. To avoid being cornered, he ducked into a store. With his back to the door, he picked up a pack of gum. All at once, all thoughts of avoiding the woman evaporated. Two aisles over was Elton Carter. He and Factor had been here all this time, and they'd managed to escape detection until now. But now, Dixon's patience had been rewarded.

A quick inventory proved Carter was alone, which meant there was only one place Factor could be. Placing the gum back on the shelf, Dixon exited the store, hurried the five blocks to his motel, and got into his car. He had one destination in mind.

He'd been to Yancy's Motel the day before. He'd checked the register. Nothing had jumped out. And in an hour of observing the place, he'd seen neither Factor nor Carter. But with the billionaire in the store, the motel seemed to be the only hiding place available in Beaver Gulch.

Quickly covering the six blocks to Yancy's, Dixon observed a young woman pushing a cleaning cart filled with supplies exiting Cabin #5. Pulling a twenty from his pocket, he strolled over to greet her.

"Excuse me."

"Yes, sir."

"I'm looking for some friends. They're a younger couple, very attractive. They asked me to meet them here, but I've forgotten what room they said they're staying in."

"Is the woman a blonde and her husband a hunk?"

"I'm sure that's them."

"Then they must be the couple in #9."

"Here's something for your trouble." Dixon handed her the twenty walked back to his SUV, got in, and drove up to the front door of #9.

As the maid had just seen him, as he'd visited with the sheriff twice, and was well known by Molly, killing Factor in the motel was not an option. But not that far from here was a special place he could take her, do the job, put her body in a spot where five others were resting, and no one would be any the wiser. He just had to get her into the car and spirit her away before Carter returned.

Knowing the clock was ticking, he got out of his SUV, marched up to the door and knocked.

"Who is it?"

"The manager. I have some clean towels."

As the door opened a crack, Dixon forced his way in, using the wooden entry as a battering ram. When Factor tried to push him back, he brought the barrel of his Luger to her cheek, knocking her over one of the beds and onto the floor. After locking the door, he whispered, "Get up."

Factor wiped a bit of blood from her mouth and stood. She hovered there for a moment on unsteady legs, and then fell into the chair.

"Give me a second," she pleaded. "I need to wait for the room to stop spinning."

"You've got one minute. Then we're getting out of here. If you cry out or cause any trouble, I'll kill you and everyone else in this place. I don't think you want that sweet little maid's blood on your hands."

"Who are you?" Factor asked as she pulled a tissue from a box and wiped her lip.

"From time to time, there are folks who call me Doctor Death."

"Catchy name. Do you use that on social media?"

"You're not funny."

"Are you the one who killed the reporter at the cabin?"

"He was collateral damage."

"What about Dr. Lenards back in Arkansas?"

"She was a mistake. You were the target."

"You're not very good at your job," Factor observed, and she dropped the tissue in the wastebasket.

Her insult carried no sting. "What I do is not always clean."

"Why not just kill me here? If that's your job, just get it over with. Then you won't take anyone with you. Even you must be tired of innocent people dying."

"There are too many people here. If I killed you, I'd have to wait and kill Carter. And there are a couple of other folks who might ID me, so they'd have to die as well. I'm betting you don't want that to happen." He grinned. "By now you must be feeling pretty guilty over all the folks who've already died because of you. Guilt is a cruel master."

"I'm guessing it's never bothered you."

"Only once."

Factor's weakness in caring about others worked to his advantage. As her head seemed to clear, she picked up a pencil and began to move it from finger to finger as if twirling it would help her focus. As the pencil moved, she studied him. Her eyes, so resolutely fixed on his face, quickly became unnerving.

"Where are we going?" Factor asked.

"What does it matter?"

She stopped twirling the pencil. "I was born on August 10, in Mattoon, Illinois. Now I'd just kind of like to know where and when I'll die."

He smiled—she had moxie. "A lonely place where death is always in focus," Dixon explained with a chuckle. "A place where birds circle, waiting and watching for souls to die."

"Sounds fascinating and poetic," she quipped as her eyes fixed on him again. "By the way, haven't we met somewhere before?"

If her eyes had been weapons, he'd have already expired. They seemed to be two balls of blue fire or perhaps focused lasers. It was like she could look into his mind. To shed her gaze, his gaze darted to a far wall. It lingered there until he regained his composure and only then did he move his focus once more to Factor.

"Get up," Dixon barked. "And remember, before you make a break, what I said about having no qualms about killing any witnesses."

Factor, who'd been doodling on a notepad, stood, and without him even waving his gun, moved to the door and waited for further instructions.

After tossing her the keys to the SUV, he said, "You'll drive."

"No problem." She opened the door and stepped out onto the parking lot. Dixon followed two steps behind. He abruptly noticed two things. The first was the sudden and dramatic change in Factor's face. She was shocked. A second later, he knew why.

Basil Holmes was decades older, but still lean and ready for action. Why was he here?

"Dixon, if it's not too much trouble, you and Ms. Factor need to get back into the bungalow."

As the Brit's gun was ready, there was no reason to argue. Dixon stepped back through the door and dragged Factor with him.

"Who are you?" Factor asked once the unexpected guest had closed and locked the door.

"He's Basil Holmes," Dixon explained. "He was once an agent for MI6."

"It's been a long time," Holmes announced.

"I was told you died years ago," a surprised Dixon acknowledged. "I figured you were in a grave moldering by now."

"You set me up," Holmes suggested. "You made it impossible for me to remain in the sunlight. But I found a way to survive in the shadows."

"Based on how nice your suit is, as well as your custom-made Italian shoes, I'm guessing you did pretty well."

"Yeah, I'm rich. But I'd trade all the money for what you took from me."

"Your reputation?"

"No, my daughter and the rest of my family."

Dixon's cold eyes showed no emotion. "Ms. Factor, only once before in my life have I missed a target, and ..."

"And Basil Holmes is it," she noted. "You killed his daughter."

"How did you know that?" Dixon demanded.

"You don't know who she is," Holmes wryly cracked. "Since I got a call from Rome, I've traveled all over the world just to find this woman and kill her. And my only reason was to hurt you like you hurt me. And now I find you don't know who she is."

"She's an imprint," Dixon explained. "She's someone I've been paid to eliminate. And if that's what you're after, then I suggest you just let me handle the job."

"Who are you working for?" Holmes causally asked.

"You think I'll tell you?"

"Why not? We both have guns and only one of us is going to walk out of here alive. Let me be clear, I wanted to kill her to hurt you, but ending your life is really a better option. The irony of you taking a job to kill Factor is simply beyond comprehension. So, who hired you?"

"A preacher named Dallas Arnold."

The Brit grimly nodded. "Do you know why?"

"Yeah."

"Must be a lulu of a reason."

"She could take down his empire," Dixon explained. "Basil, what have you done the last forty years?"

"For years, I searched for a way to get to you," Holmes explained. "I lived for that. I wanted you to feel the pain that I felt. You did more than kill someone I loved, you couldn't just stop there, you disgraced me, and made me into a fugitive. I had to give up my wife and son. I haven't seen them in more than four decades. Even they believe I sold out the UK."

"You were going to cross the US," Dixon pointed out. "You were going to expose me and a group of men I worked with."

"And, if I had, hundreds of people would be alive now," Holmes argued. "Until you came along, I was clean, I was honest, I was straight-forward. When I found out what the CIA had done to Nigel Watson, I was more than ready to put the spotlight on the splinter group that you were a part of. I was hours away from exposing you, and …"

"Watson had to die," Dixon explained. "He knew about the committee."

"Yeah, the five of you who went rogue and assassinated those you thought stood in the way of America's global plans. Nigel was an innocent man, just doing his job—he had a wife and three kids. Who were *you* to push agendas for the United States?"

"We did what we sensed was in our country's best interests. Even with you, it wasn't personal."

"No, you did what you felt was in *your* interests. And that's why nothing you've done can ever be made public. You see, things that are just and honorable thrive in the light. Your acts require darkness."

"Don't lecture me," Dixon warned.

"Wait," Factor said as she moved back to the bed and sat down, "you're CIA?"

"He once was," Holmes explained, "then he went rogue. Doctor Death became his handle, and I was the ghost that never could quite catch up to him. Each time I thought I had him, the trail went dry. But he sure did fill up the cemeteries I visited."

"You mean," Dixon whispered, "you're the Ghost?"

"Can you think of a better title?"

With guns drawn, the two men stared each other down, and Dixon's thoughts returned to the last time the two met face to face. Dixon had waited in Holmes's London home for hours. When Holmes finally returned from his office, Dixon surprised him and had him square in his sights. All he had to do was pull the trigger. And then Holmes's five-year-old daughter ran in to hug her father. The order had been to show no mercy, and he had. Dixon should've fired twice and killed them both, which he would have if the little girl hadn't looked up at him with those big blue eyes and asked, "Who's this, Daddy?" The pause, initiated by the little girl's question, had given Holmes just enough time to scoop her up and race from the room. Before he could make it to the front door, Dixon regained his concentration and fired. But his aim was off, and he hit the child in the head. Without meaning to, he'd killed one of Holmes's two children. Dixon had panicked and raced out the back. Because of that failure, the committee had been forced to ruin Holmes by planting false evidence. In stories like this, there were no happy endings.

"You know," Holmes announced, his gun still pointed and ready for action, "when I found out who she was, I thought I had a way of really hurting you like you had hurt me. But now I know that my having her murdered wouldn't have hurt you at all."

"Why do you keep saying that her dying would hurt me?" Dixon sniped. "I don't know what you're talking about."

"I guess you don't." Holmes's tongue traced his lips before he smiled and added, "I now know she has to live because Factor can send you to the gallows, and what's far more important, she can also clear my name. I could spend my final years not being a ghost. That's about as sweet as revenge can get."

"Basil, you're not making any sense. An imprint doesn't have the ability to know anything I've done. I have no children."

Holmes nodded. "I think we've talked enough."

"You've got the edge," Dixon suggested, "Why don't you take what you want? Shoot and end this thing now."

"No, now I know you have to live, and the real satisfaction will come when the committee you helped form and run is exposed. My vengeance will be seeing you in a courtroom facing the families of your victims. Killing you is nothing. Making you confront the human cost of your life is everything. I should have known that years ago."

Factor's eyes locked onto Dixon's. He was torn. Like Holmes, she was holding her breath, waiting to see what happened next.

Dixon knew if he moved, Holmes would kill him. If he surrendered, his life would no longer be in his control. A key sliding into the cabin's door caused Holmes to glance that direction. His reaction signed his death certificate. Just the slight shift of attention was all Dixon needed to squeeze the trigger and finish a job that had been left undone for forty years. Holmes, a bullet through his heart, fell to the ground. A second later, the door swung open, and Carter, carrying two sacks of groceries, stood in the entry.

"Get in the car," Dixon ordered. Factor froze, her eyes locked on Carter. When she failed to move, he screamed, "Get in the car, or I'll shoot him in the head. I'll finish him off right here if you don't get moving."

"Get out of here," Factor ordered Carter.

When he didn't move, Dixon struck the billionaire across the temple with his Luger. Elton fell to the ground, the bags' contents spilling across the floor.

"Step over him and get out to the car," Dixon ordered.

"Only if you promise not to kill him."

"Get moving, and there'll be no need to."

Factor nodded, opened the door, and moved quickly to the car. As she scooted behind the SUV's wheel, Dixon got into the back seat. When both doors closed, he put the gun to the back of her head. "Go north out of town. Don't do anything to call any attention to us and drive just enough under the speed limit that no one notices. You got that?"

She didn't reply. After taking a final look at the closed cabin door, Factor put the car into drive, pulled the wheel to the left, and exited. In less than a minute, Beaver Gulch was in the rearview mirror.

With so few people on the road, Dixon should've found a turn off, had her drive out of sight, and ended her life. But with Holmes dead and Carter likely still breathing, he couldn't afford to stay in the area. He needed to get to his lair. He'd be safe there, he could easily finish the job and put the body in a place no one would ever find it.

Chapter 59

Sometimes knowing the truth opens the door to unimaginable pain. In that case, the truth doesn't set you free—it enslaves you forever.

———————◆———————

A few hours before, Maxine Factor was beginning to accept her gift. She was beginning to get her arms around how to control and use it. But after what she'd just witnessed, she once more was forced to acknowledge the gift was causing too much senseless death. Because of all those who died in her place, it was getting harder to live with her own memories than it was to live with the memories of her ancestors. Perhaps her death was for the best.

Not surprisingly, Maxine Factor's mind was hardly on the mountain road she was driving. She didn't notice the breathtaking views of mountain peaks or the lush forest that stretched into the valleys— her thoughts centered on those who'd died or suffered because of her. One face followed another—the most recent, Elton Carter, perhaps hurt the worst. With the promise of her imminent death, she'd likely never know if Carter's injury would cost him his life. The image of his being pistol whipped and crumpling to the floor demanded tears, but she couldn't cry. She might never cry again.

"Turn right at the next side road," William Dixon directed from the back seat.

She glanced into the rearview mirror. The gun he'd held to the back of her head was now resting in his lap, but it was close enough to his hand to assure she'd follow his orders, even if that meant she was driving to her own funeral.

"So," she asked after making the cutoff and straightening the wheel, "how far is it?"

"Further today. Because of what happened back there, we'll take the roads less traveled.

"How long?"

"Maybe two hours. Gives you plenty of time to pray."

A hope and a prayer … a great-grandmother had said those words before she'd taken her first flying lesson. She hoped what she was doing would prove a point for all her girlfriends who considered her a coward. At that same time, she was praying her father wouldn't whip her when he found out. She'd somehow survived piloting a Douglas C-1 biplane as well as the two weeks of grounding that followed. Her grandmother's odds of living to see another day had never been as long as her own.

Factor once more glanced into the mirror. Dixon's dark eyes were ice cold. She knew he could sneer, she'd seen that, but she wondered if he could smile. She also wondered if he could feel guilt.

"Did you enjoy killing Holmes?" she asked.

"Yeah," he admitted, "it offered closure. I don't like leaving things undone."

The man spoke about murder as if he was a mechanic telling a customer he needed brake pads. There was no emotion, it was just a part of the job. Perhaps he was incapable of empathy. Yet earlier, he'd mentioned a time when he'd felt regret. Could she stir up that emotion, or was it buried so deep that it was forever lost? If she could tap into something that haunted him, maybe he would lose his focus.

"So, you killed a child," Factor pointed out.

"She got in the way."

"And you feel no regrets?"

"With Holmes, I hate that I made a mistake. Sadly, there have been several on this job. But remember, Basil admitted he was the Ghost. In that role, he was as lethal as I've been."

"And that makes it okay? You don't feel any regret or guilt?"

As she watched in the mirror, he carefully considered her question before explaining. "If you live then you also die. There's no escaping that fact." He paused, running his fingers over his weapon, before adding, "I was taught to murder. In fact, I was praised when I did my job well. And you know who gave me awards for doing my first kills?"

"The CIA?"

"After several years of using my skills to make already wealthy men even richer and leaders in the government and military more powerful, I figured I could earn a lot more by working independently. Think about that. Essentially, I was killing the same kind of people, but was now making millions. In your case, you're a threat to our government and who knows how many influential people and organizations. The system will run much more smoothly without you in the mix. I'm just the guy making sure the machine purrs."

"And you justify what you do with that kind of rationalization?" Factor caught his gaze in the rearview mirror. "Isn't that the same kind of logic that was employed when people convinced the Roman government to execute Jesus?"

"Yeah," Dixon agreed, "but though you don't claim to be a savior, the situation is similar."

"How?"

"Christ was ripping apart the fabric of the religious establishment of his day. The Jewish world of that time would've been turned on its head if that had gone on any longer. He was moving too fast, and the folks in power couldn't allow him to do that. They'd have lost everything. But that's just one example. History is littered with events where stability was maintained through taking out one man. Looking back, don't you think the world would've been far better off if our government had hired someone like me to take out Hitler in 1933?" He shrugged and then added, "Ms. Factor, as an imprint, you might reveal sins or truths that would destabilize accepted beliefs. You have the power to create doubt, fear, and chaos. You have to be silenced."

"You know the odds are small that I'd remember anything that would spin the world out of its orbit. Everything I've recalled so far is about the stuff of normal life. I've observed nothing earth-changing."

"The power belongs to those who control the odds in such a way the house always wins. You're the wild card that might bankrupt the house."

When his phone vibrated, he picked up his weapon and once more aimed it at Factor's head. When he was sure she'd witnessed his move, he answered.

"What do you need?" He waited for a few seconds before adding, "I have her. I'm taking her to a place where it will be safe to finish the job."

As Dixon listened to the caller, Factor turned her attention back to the road. At this point, she'd have gladly given her life to take out the man in the back seat. Yet, while they were traveling up and down steep grades, guardrails and trees prevented her from steering the SUV off a cliff. As she continued to search for a way to stage a homicide using a car as the weapon, Dixon jumped back on the call.

"It's stupid to do it that way. I can take her out much more easily without spectators. Besides, I'm not sure you'd sleep well after witnessing it." Dixon paused, nodded, and frowned. "You're the man who's paying for this—we'll play it your way. I'll text you directions. But you're going to owe me a bonus."

After ending the call, Dixon fiddled with his phone and sent a text. He then looked back toward the front seat. "You might find this interesting. The man paying me to take you out wants to witness your death. It'll likely take him about eight hours to get here. So, you have a bit more time to put your life in order."

"You told Holmes it was Dallas Arnold. Why is he scared of me?"

"You don't know?"

"I've never met him."

"For two reasons. First, he raped your mother."

Suddenly, Factor was forty years in the past, living life through her mother's eyes. The date had gone well, but now the young man was demanding much more than she wanted to give. Her protests didn't matter because he wouldn't take no for an answer. When she pushed him away, he tried to force himself on her and ripped her blouse open. When she slapped him, he came unglued, and though she fought, he was bigger and stronger.

"I never recognized him," she whispered.

"So," Dixon said, "you can see it."

"I don't see it," she angrily hissed. "I live it. And now, after the way he hurt my mother, he wants to watch me die?"

"For Arnold, what you remember is a game changer. It could destroy his empire. And that's small potatoes compared to what you might be able to do to others. Turn left at the next intersection."

As Factor tried to wipe her mother's pain and humiliation from her mind, she steered the car around the corner. Of all the ancestors to walk into her head at this moment, it wasn't someone giving her a plan to escape and live, it was one plunging her so deep into pain she wondered if she wouldn't be better off dead.

Chapter 60

11:19 a.m.
Saturday, October 1
Beaver Gulch, Colorado

The most important thing at a crime scene is a breathing witness.

———◆———

A frantic Indira Morel, unable to rouse Elton Carter on her cell, raced to Cabin #9, slammed on her brakes, jumped out of the car, and knocked on the door. There was no answer. She tried the knob. The door opened. On the floor, lying face down, was Carter. Five feet away was another man. Blood was staining his shirt and suit. After slamming the entry, she checked Carter. He was breathing.

Her instincts demanded she call 911, but with everything that had happened, she put calling off until she had the chance to evaluate the scene. The man she didn't know was dead, a gunshot through the heart. Carter hadn't been shot, but he did a nasty bruise on his forehead. She checked his pulse—it was steady and strong.

She was about to pull open an eyelid and examine his pupils, when a moan brought her focus back to Carter's pale face. After grabbing his cheeks in her hands, she leaned down and whispered, "Are you all right?"

"I got clubbed with a pistol," he mumbled.

"Was it Smith?"

"No, it was the guy who got you in the face with the rifle butt."

"Dixon."

"Who's that?" he asked as he rubbed his head.

"A hit man who's after Max. Who's the other guy?"

"I don't know, but that Dixon guy must have shot him. I remember hearing gunfire, but my mind's still foggy."

"Can you sit up?"

"I think so."

She first helped him to his feet and then to a chair. As he tried to focus, she looked around the small room. Except for the spilled groceries and the dead body, nothing seemed out of place. As Carter tried to scare away the butterflies hovering in his head, she took a closer look at the body. He was carrying six passports, and all had different names.

"Well, this guy's shady," she whispered. He was likely in his sixties or early seventies. He was well-dressed and distinguished. Grabbing her phone, she took a picture and texted it to her brother. She'd just finished going through all the dead man's pockets when her cell vibrated. The message said, "That's the Ghost!" She glanced back at Carter, who was looking much better, before replying.

"He's dead. He was taken out by a former CIA agent named Dixon."

"Doctor Death," was the answer. Before she could reply, another text arrived. "Text me the address, and we'll send a team to clean things up. You don't need to be involved in this."

"Okay. Do I wait for the team?"

"No, get out as soon as you can and lock the door. Put a "Do Not Disturb" sign up as well."

After texting, Morel put her phone away and looked at Carter. "How are you feeling? Can you get to my car?"

"Give me a minute," he replied.

As she waited for Carter to feel well enough to move, she began an exhaustive search of the room. Using her skills as an archaeologist, she carefully shifted her gaze a few inches at a time looking for anything that might offer a clue. There was nothing until she spied a notepad.

"Have you used that pad to write anything down?" Morel asked.

"No," he answered, his gaze landing on a small table.

Morel moved over and picked up the pad. Someone had written two words followed by what seemed to be a cursive capital J. She pushed the paper in front of Carter. "Is this Max's writing?"

"She's always scribbling on a pad she keeps in a drawer beside the bed—take a look."

Morel moved to the far side of the room and pulled out a second pad. This one was filled with dates and names. "What does all this mean?"

"She was trying to identify and organize the people in her head. One of her grandmothers, a member of the Cheyenne, did the same thing by painting her ancestors on a wall in a cave."

Though she wanted to know more about that story, Morel kept her focus on the matter at hand. The writing matched.

"Look at this," she demanded passing the first notepad she'd found back to Carter.

"Buzzard Roost," he read, "and is that a J?"

"This could be a long shot," Morel observed. "She might have written down where he was taking her. Where's your computer?"

"Who knows?"

Rather than look for the laptop, Morel opened the browser on her phone. A search for Buzzard Roost revealed a few poems and memes, but no locations in Colorado or the surrounding states.

"Never mind." Carter stood. "The fog's lifting. He moved to the bed and pulled his computer from under the mattress, "What are we looking for?"

"Buzzard Roost, and there doesn't appear to be such a place anywhere this side of New Hampshire."

"A few restaurants," Carter noted as he refined his search.

"I don't think he was taking Max out for dinner."

"Wait." Carter pushed off the edge of the bed and slowly crossed the room. "Look at this old postcard that's for sale on eBay."

"It once was a fishing resort," Morel noted. "This must be from the 1950s. But there's no address. Keep looking, we don't have much time."

For five minutes, they turned Google upside down and came up empty. With each passing minute, their anxiety was grew. Time was not on their side.

"I'm guessing the place has either closed or changed names since then," Morel surmised. "Let's dig into tax histories. Perhaps Colorado has old property records scanned and online."

As Morel continued to go through a myriad of searches leading to dead ends, Carter kept tapping in requests of his own. After ten minutes, he had what he needed.

"Here's a small story from the outdoor life section of the *Denver Post* archives. Buzzard Roost sold in 1980, to a man named Dixon Williams. The place had been out of business since 1962. The taxes were reduced because Williams was going to use it as a private residence rather than a business."

"What about an address?"

"None listed, and I can't get into the tax files. I'm not much of a hacker."

"Elton, we need that address."

"And," he observed, "if we get it, we'll need some firepower. I have some old friends in government in Denver. Let's head that direction, and I'll make calls from the car."

She pulled him off the bed and pushed him toward the exit. They had to move and move quickly. Finding the "Do Not Disturb" sign, she hung it over the outside of the room's door.

"Get everything you all brought and anything you wrote on," she ordered.

Five minutes later, they'd loaded up and were heading back toward Denver. She knew time was running out. If they didn't locate where Dixon was going, there was no hope. And though she didn't want to admit it, her gut told her they were already too late.

Chapter 61

There are only so many lies that can be hidden before some of them start falling out into the open.

———◆———

Rocky Smith sat at the kitchen table in the isolated cabin considering his next move. It had taken a full day to clean up the crime scene and dispose of the bodies. He had spent the rest of the time trying to track down Darwin Larkin. He'd failed. He'd then made a trip to Beaver Gulch but had come up empty. On top of that, Morel and Hardin had seemingly evaporated. As he contemplated where he might go for the next lead, he frowned. Clegg hadn't just set him up—he'd then turned on him. He was his own.

Smith was so deeply stewing in his own juices that he didn't hear the back door open. He had no clue he wasn't alone until he felt the barrel of a gun at his neck. He slowly lifted his eyes to see Bristol Owen. He guessed that meant either Rick Elder or Elmer Vanover was holding the gun to his head.

"Clegg called me." Owen's tone was even. "I take it he died, and you killed him."

Stone had regained his focus and remained cool. "It was him or me. I figured life owed me a few more years."

"You have no regrets?" Owen suggested.

"Why doesn't your friend talk?" Smith coldly replied. "Are you the one running this show, or does he have a say?"

"Neither of us wants to be here," Vanover announced.

"Then leave," Smith suggested.

"Move over to the couch and sit down," Owen ordered.

Smith didn't argue. When he felt the man behind him back up, he pushed away from the table and walked to the living room. Knowing he was outnumbered and outgunned, he sank into the sofa and waited for the next move.

"Where's the woman?" Owen demanded.

"I don't know. I'm working on that."

"That's not the right answer."

"I didn't figure it was, but it's the truth. I'd just found out where she was and was getting ready to nail her when Clegg burst in and blew things up. So, blame your best buddy for my having to start all over again."

"You failed Smith," Owen barked.

Smith shrugged. "She has so many people chasing her, I don't think she's a danger to anyone. Dixon's on her trail as well. He's been paid to shut her up. But let me be straight with you. Things aren't the way they seem. In fact, you're walking in the dark."

"Then you better illuminate things before it's too late," Owen said.

"One of you needs to take notes," Smith suggested. When no one bit at his offer, he continued, "Clegg didn't come here just to get Factor—he was also in Colorado to kill me."

The two men glanced at one another before Owen asked the obvious question.

"Why?"

"The agency doesn't know anything about your operations from so long ago and likely wouldn't investigate if they did. No one at the top cares to dig up dirt from the past. I was assigned to work with Clegg because the folks in power thought he was dirty. They believed he was selling information. His ability to offer me a huge chunk of cash to kill Factor seemed to justify their theory. But his promising the money was not enough, I had to earn the chance to prove what the higher ups thought was going on. Clegg discovered that and painted me as the man selling secrets. I did a little checking this morning and found a deposit of several hundred thousand in my bank account. The transfer originated in Russia. So, I was set up as the fall guy for Clegg's recent endeavors. After he killed me, I'm sure he was going to frame me for the murders of Mason Hardin and Indira Morel. I assume he was also going to use the deposit as the proof he needed to get the spotlight off his dirty dealings." Smith rolled his eyes. "You know what's sad?"

"What?" they asked in unison.

"If Clegg had given me a chance, he'd have discovered this was all unnecessary. He literally died for nothing."

"What do you mean?" Owen asked.

"The deeper I got into this gig, the more the money Clegg offered me began to sound good. After the last two weeks of ugliness, I was ready to walk away from this kind of life. I no longer cared if he'd made a bundle by selling a few secrets. So, I wasn't going to rat him out. I was going to let him pay me off."

"And," Vanover asked, "you were going to kill Factor?"

"The only way I could get the cash from Clegg was to take her out. So, I was going to finish the job. Then he showed up. I like money, but I like breathing even more. When he pulled his weapon on me, I opted to respond. His jammed. As I recall, he was not very good about keeping his gun clean."

Owen signaled for Vanover to join him. As Smith watched, the two huddled. He sensed they might be coming over to his way of thinking, but in case he was reading things incorrectly, he pulled his gun from his shoulder holster and slipped it between the cushions of the couch. He made that move just in time. Without warning, the pair broke up their powwow and fanned out. Each now had a gun in hand. Evidently, Owen was the committee member assigned to give the minutes from their meeting.

"We think your story makes sense. We have no doubt Clegg was making some money on the side. He told me before leaving DC he was headed here to shut you up. But you missed one thing."

"What's that?"

"You hadn't figured out that we're still a team. We shared in whatever Clegg took in. So, if you had exposed him, you'd have exposed us too."

The news stunned Smith. He'd never suspected the other three were party to the payoffs. No one at the agency had either.

"So," Owen continued, "we have a choice. We either make you a part of our quartet, or we kill you."

"I can play on the team," Smith assured them. "I'll keep your names out of it. All I want is the money I was promised, so I can disappear once Factor is dead."

"You're cold," Elder observed.

"Yes, I am, and there's a few things you don't know."

"Enlighten us again."

"Once you all conned me into the role of hit man on this mission, I figured I could make a lot of money on the side. I told the Russian mob about Factor and explained that because Dixon was her father, there were things that might come out that could cripple their operations in the US. So, I'm double-dipping. Now, as you guys have the advantage, you don't have to pay the price Clegg offered me. I'll take the money he put in my account to frame me and get the rest from the Russians."

The revelation hung in the air just long enough for Vanover, who still possessed a bit of patriotism, to go for his weapon. But he never had a chance. Smith yanked his gun from its hiding spot and pulled the trigger, catching Elder in the face. Owen fired as Smith rolled off the couch and onto the floor. Smith spun to take out Owen, but the big man had disappeared. Pushing off the floor, Smith raced to the door just in time to see Owen hustle down the tree-covered lane. There was now no way to get a clear shot. A few seconds later, from his position in the open door, Smith heard a car start. Owen had made his escape.

Smith stepped back into the cabin and closed the door. He needed to find Factor, but now he had another crime scene to clean up. He was about to get to work when the cell rang.

"Smith here."

"You asked me to keep an eye on Dallas Arnold."

"Yeah."

"He's on his way to Denver. He'll land at Dunn Field around eight tonight. He might lead you to Dixon."

"Thanks. I'll have things cleaned up by then. Now I've got a bone to pick—why didn't you warn me they were coming?"

"They were my friends for years. I couldn't betray them. I was just going to let the chips fall and see what happened. Obviously, you were up to the task."

"I got Vanover, but Owen's gone."

"Watch him, he's dangerous. He won't stop his hunt until he gets you or you get him."

"Wish it had been the other way around."

The line went dead.

Chapter 62

8:20 p.m.
Saturday, October 1
Dunn Field, six miles north of Denver, Colorado

*When it becomes impossible to tell if someone is lying or telling the truth,
it's always best to believe that every sentence is the beginning of another
lie.*

As Smith already had the necessary cleaning supplies, thanks to
having to tidy up after the Clegg episode, this time sanitizing
the cabin was easier. Yet because of the rain, he was running late
and arrived at Dunn Field just as Dallas Arnold's plane was landing.
Thanks to the storm, the preacher didn't immediately leave the jet, so
Smith still had time to kill.

As he sat in the car Clegg had rented, Smith studied the scene
from the street. He first spotted the car he figured was reserved for
the preacher. Then he noted the SUV parked with its nose just inside
an open hanger. Was it someone waiting for a different private plane
to come in or had Arnold drawn another interested party? He'd
learn the answer soon enough. If the dark SUV followed Arnold's
Mercedes, then things were going to be more complicated.

As he kept his eyes fixed on the private jet, Smith pulled out a phone and made a call. He didn't expect to get an answer, but he'd miscalculated. On occasion, folks who have every reason to hate you are still willing to talk. This was one of those rare moments.

"You still in town?" Mason Hardin snarled. The reporter's tone was anything but bright.

"Are you?" Smith asked.

"I'm not going to answer that. In fact, you've closed the door on my telling you anything. What I'm looking forward is writing your obit."

"Listen, you've got me all wrong. I wouldn't have shot you or Morel, and I didn't lie to you about wanting to save Factor. I was always on your side. I'm actually one of the good guys."

"And I'm supposed to believe that?"

"Hear me out. Clegg offered me a fortune to track and kill Factor. He was afraid she'd remember stuff that'd expose him. What he didn't know was that the agency had already assigned me to get the goods on him for something completely different. He'd been selling secrets to the Russians and Chinese. The reason he burst in the other night was because someone tipped him off I was going to expose his grift."

"That's not the way it sounded," Hardin shot back.

"I know how it sounded. And I had to play along. Understand this, I needed Factor to put the capstone on my case. And I needed her alive. I believed, in time, she'd tap into the memories of her real father. Those memories would be enough to complete my investigation of Clegg and expose those who worked with him back in the day. You have to believe me on this, the CIA I work for wants to clean up their past sins. So, if you'll join with me, I can give you a story that'll rattle governments across the globe. You can even rewrite some of history. This is far better than the story Goldsmith asked you to complete."

"There was a time when I'd have bitten, but no more. Now I've got an arm that will always remind me of who you really are."

"I didn't shoot you," he argued.

"You didn't protect us either."

"Are you okay?"

"It wasn't fatal," the reporter snapped, "but I won't be doing handsprings for a while."

"Listen, Mason, Clegg shot you. My Lord, he was trying to kill me too. Doesn't that prove anything? Today, Clegg's old group tried to take me out. I had to kill one of them. I'm a target. If I were dirty, they wouldn't be after me."

"Too bad they missed," Hardin shot back.

"It'd be much easier to save Factor if we come back together."

"It'd also be much easier," Hardin pointed out, "for you to kill Indira and me if we're in the same room."

"Mason, if you won't work with me, then I'm asking you and Morel to back off. This is far too dangerous for amateurs. I made a mistake asking you to team up with me in the first place. I shouldn't have put your life on the line. So, leave this to the pros."

"I was shot—I have no choice but to back off, at least for a while. But when I get out of here, I'm coming after you. So, start looking over your shoulder."

"Give me a second chance. If she's still alive, and I hope she is, I'll save Factor and give you the biggest story of your life."

There was no reply. Smith frowned. It was a good try, but he hardly blamed Hardin for not jumping back into the game.

Just as the line went dead, Arnold rushed out of the plane and made a dash for the Mercedes. A few moments later, the car started and pulled off the tarmac, through a gate, and onto the road. Smith wondered who was dumber. Was it Arnold, the anxious micro-manager who rushed in to make sure Dixon had done his job, or Dixon for working for a fool? If Arnold was really joining the hit man, both were going to pay for their poor judgment.

As Smith pulled out to follow the preacher, he glanced back through the rain toward the open hanger. The SUV's lights came on, and the car exited the building. They pulled out on the road about hundred feet behind Smith. Then they stayed well back, turning where he turned but never getting any closer.

Who was this, and were they trailing him or the preacher? This extra person in this deadly game of hide and seek had the potential to turn everything upside down in a real hurry. By instinct, Smith reached for his service revolver, pulled it out and laid it on the seat.

Chapter 63

Old information sometimes can become new, it's viewed in the right light.

———◆———

The clock was ticking, the weather getting worse, and Morel and Carter had no idea if Maxine Factor was alive or dead. If only they had a location. Morel's phone pulled her from searching for an address they needed at this moment—no—they needed it five hours ago.

"How are you doing?" she answered while continuing her frantic web search.

"I'm out of the hospital," Mason Hardin assured her, "I'll be wearing a sling for a while. Have you come up with anything?"

"We think we know the name of the place where she might be, but we haven't been able to find a location. Right now, we're searching through newspaper and magazine ads from the forties through the seventies. Sadly, burning up the internet is doing us very little good. It's like the folks who owned this resort wanted to keep people away."

"Well, this might interest you. Guess who called me?"

"Who?"

"Smith. He was trying to get me to join up with him. Claimed he was bent on saving Factor. He weaves an interesting yarn, but there are too many holes."

"Do you think he knows where Max is?" Morel asked.

"No, I think he was seeing if we'd stumbled into it. I'm in a rental car, where are you?"

"Holiday Inn Express, Glenwood Springs, but if I find a location, we'll drop everything and go there. We can't wait for you," Morel explained. She then added, "We're likely too late as it is."

"If you find the place before I get there, text the address."

"I will."

"And take care of yourself."

Just as Morel ended the call, Carter called out, "Bingo."

Jumping out of the chair, she hurried to his side. A small ad, placed in a back section of the May 1946 issue of *Fishing World* finally gave them what they needed.

> *Rooms are large, the food good, the fishing great! Join us at Buzzard Roost for the best fly-fishing this side of England. Rooms begin at $50 a week and are worth every penny. Guides available. Take route 131 to Eagle Crossing, then turn on Mountain Pike. Go two miles and then make a left just after you cross Little Bear Creek. Go three miles and turn left again. The lodge is four miles down the road. For reservations, call Jupiter 3-542.*

"This doesn't make sense," Carter muttered at he studied his map app.

"What doesn't?"

"The road numbers on my phone don't match up with the ad."

"Keep the map on your screen," Morel ordered, "I'll pull up one from that era on my computer."

It took only a few minutes to find a regional map from 1946, but with so much at stake, it seemed much longer. She held her computer up to his phone, enlarged the image on her screen, and began to move it left to right and top to bottom. Tension hung like fog as four eyes followed the movement.

"Nothing," he whispered. "Check the bottom quadrant."

"There!" she announced as she held it up for him to see. "The roads match and here is where rural route 717 crosses Big Bear Creek."

"But," he argued, "there's no cut off that would lead to the lodge. The road just goes on for a while and ends."

"Hit the satellite mode," she suggested. She waited for the image to come up. "Make it bigger right there," she said as she pointed to place near the top left of the screen.

"It's a large structure," he observed.

"That has to be Buzzard Roost."

"I'll bookmark it, then let's get going. But before we leave town, we have to stop by Walmart."

"We can't waste time—she might already be dead. We need to move quickly, and that place is at least an hour away."

"We don't have weapons," Carter explained. "Because of the waiting period, I can't buy a gun, but at least let's get a knife or something."

Morel grabbed a coat and headed for the door. As they raced through rain that was quickly turning to snow, neither of them said anything until they got to what had been Smith's rented SUV. Once inside, Morel looked at Carter.

"Elton, do you think she's still alive?"

He sadly shook his head before saying, "But we have to find out."

"I'll call Mason, maybe he can make it here in time to meet us at Walmart."

She hoped the reporter could get there before they left. They needed every bit of help they could find to take on Dixon. Yet, even at three to one, they were likely outmanned. Carter had a concussion, Hardin's arm was useless, and her eyes were now swollen to the point where her vision was badly impaired. Dixon would likely have no problems killing all of them.

Chapter 64

9:40 p.m.
Saturday, October 1
Buzzard Roost, Colorado

For many, the truth is the most bitter of all pills. It goes down hard and doesn't digest easily. It also sheds light on things that had been dismissed or forgotten.

———◆———

With the snow falling, the lodge and its setting looked like something out of a classic Hollywood Christmas movie. Century-old pines surrounded a cabin constructed of massive logs, and a design featuring steep sloping roofs, large windows, and a towering stone chimney ... it was a Currier and Ives painting come to life. Once inside the front door, the place was even more impressive. The rooms were large, the ceilings high, the furnishings rustic but elegant. On the walls and shelves were pieces of art that would have been prized in museums. In towering bookshelves were first editions of the most revered works in literary history. There was even a display of Native American bows and arrows on a wall surrounded by blankets and wildlife carvings. It would've been a great place to live, but it was a lousy place to die.

Though her life was on the line, and the clock was ticking down to zero, her knowledge of history pushed Factor to carefully study the place where she was scheduled to draw her last breath. The more she looked, the more amazed she was. Her lethal host had to have the world's greatest collection of art outside a museum.

"That's a Raphael," Maxine Factor observed as William Dixon marched her through the great room.

"It's called 'Portrait of a Young Man'," he explained. "It was painted in 1513 and was part of a wonderful exhibit at the Czartoryski Museum in Poland until World War II. Then it disappeared."

"Nazi loot," Factor suggested.

"Looting is such an ugly exercise. Let's just say that a Gestapo officer recognized its value and felt it'd be safer in another place. I bought it about thirty years ago in Argentina from a man named Lutz."

"The Pissarro on the far wall was also stolen by the Nazis," she observed. She strolled closer to a half dozen other pieces before noting, "The world has been searching for a lot of this art for more than seventy years."

"And for the past few decades," Dixon announced with obvious pride, "I've been enjoying it. Let's say it's one of the rewards of my work." He smiled and pointed to a hall. "There's a room with no windows. I use it as a den. You'll be staying there until our guest arrives. And I'm not a hard man, I'll bring you a meal." He pointed straight ahead and added, "By the way, this is my retreat—it's reserved only for me. If I bring someone here, then they have to stay."

Factor fully understood the cryptic message not so subtly hidden in his observation. The only exit from Buzzard Lodge was death. In other words, while Dixon would walk out of here, everyone else was either carried or dragged.

The tour over, Factor was ushered down the hall. As she waited, he reached inside the room, and flipped a light switch. Once she was inside, Dixon closed and locked the door.

Until this moment, she hadn't been in a place where Dixon didn't have gun on her. Now, in a ten-by-twelve-foot room with dark paneling and a wood plank floor, she was finally alone with her thoughts.

Perhaps, just as she had when Larkin and Hill had her confined, she'd come up with a plan that'd literally give her some breathing room. Yet, before she could search for an exit, she saw an antique desk. It seemed familiar. She moved to get a closer look.

It was an oak secretary's desk, not more than three feet wide, and positioned in front of a bookcase. She clearly remembered signing papers on this very desk. And yet the hands holding the fountain pen were not hers—they belonged to a man. She glanced at the walls. If the art was replaced with fishing trophies, the room would be the same as it was then. She once more scrutinized the desk. She was again the man signing the papers. The date on the documents was June 5, 1980. She looked once more at the hand holding the pen, It was not her father's, but it had to be. Imprints couldn't tap into anyone's memories but their direct ancestor's. Carter and Lenards had assured her that was the way it worked. But …

Forcing her mind to stay in 1980, she saw herself shaking hands with a man, about five-five, perhaps seventy years old, who seemed thrilled to accept the check he'd been given. As soon as the deal was completed, the stranger quickly left, and when he did, the person she'd become walked over to a mirror to check his appearance. As he straightened his tie, the reflected face was that of a much younger William Dixon.

That image jolted her back to 2022. Factor dropped into a chair and whispered, "My father wasn't my father." Now she understood why none of Carven Marks's memories had ever surfaced in her mind. She didn't carry his DNA.

As she sat in stunned silence, another scene from another time took over her senses. Her mother was on a date in a fancy restaurant. She was studying a menu and seemed enthralled to be treated so well. She reached across and touched her escort's hand. It was the same hand that had signed the ownership for Buzzard Roost. As her mother's eyes moved from the menu to her date, Factor once again found herself looking into William Dixon's face. As she studied Dixon through her mother's eyes, she locked in on the man. She gasped, she and her executioner shared a jaw, cheekbones, and a nose. There could be no doubt. Dixon was her father.

The truth is often a bitter pill, but no truth could've tasted any worse than this. Factor's father was the man who'd been hired to kill her. Did he know? Shocked and nauseated, she tried to close the door on the events before things could progress any further, but even singing "You Are My Sunshine" couldn't push away this nightmare.

Over the next ten minutes, Factor recalled bits and pieces of a half dozen scenes from William Dixon's life. He reluctantly killed his first victim, a member of the KGB, but the next, a woman who was about to expose a CIA operation—one that had cost a dozen innocent civilians their lives—was much easier. And then there was the jetliner where hundreds of innocent men, women, and children died just to kill one member of the Saudi Royal family. She discovered that in time, Dixon began to relish his work. He reveled in the planning, the operation, and the escapes. It was as if he got a high from each experience. She was sickened by what she was living, and yet, she couldn't escape.

She watched through his eyes as he lined up a shot on a young woman working with the mob. She felt her fingers around the neck of a man who'd turned on the CIA. She saw the blood spraying from where a small girl had been shot and the look on her father's face as he swept her up in his arms. And that father was Basil Holmes. Now she understood why that image had briefly come into her head when they were in the motel room, and Dixon and Holmes were facing off.

The unlocking door awakened her to the present. Dixon, his expression calm, almost benevolent, set a plate on the desk, said nothing, and quickly left. This was no doubt to be her final meal—a turkey sandwich and chips.

Ignoring the food, she quickly leafed through every drawer and cabinet. With each passing minute, it was more evident there was no route of escape. There was nothing she could use as a weapon or even to pick a lock. She was in the perfect trap. She sank into a chair.

A few days before, when she learned He'evo'nehe's story, she'd hoped she might control her gift into her old age. Factor now realized the odds against that were longer than even her cousin the math professor could calculate. Yet, faced with the prospect of death, her thirst to live was suddenly greater than ever. Tragically, when she needed them most, her ancestors had deserted her. She was all alone for the first time in months.

Chapter 65

Revenge is one of the greatest of all motivators. It will drive rational people into in a frenzy from which they can never escape.

———————

Tailing Dallas Arnold had been easy. The preacher's driving was steady and easy, he employed his turn signals well in advance, and slowed at every yellow light. But the person following behind Rocky Smith was another matter. He constantly sped up and eased back, sometimes getting as close as fifty feet. Why was he making no efforts to conceal that he was in this parade?

As the miles mounted, Smith became more concerned. Had the preacher employed someone to make sure he wasn't followed? That was about the only thing that made sense. Normally, Smith would've used his driving skills and lost the tail, but if he did that he wouldn't be able to follow Arnold. So, he was literally stuck in the middle.

As they hit a long straightaway, the SUV made its move. Pulling out as if to pass, the driver flipped on his high beams, accelerated, and began to close. Smith couldn't match speed due to Arnold being ahead. Blinded by the light reflected in the rear-view mirror, he took his right hand off the wheel and reached for his gun just as the SUV pulled alongside. A moment later, it swerved right and collided with Smith. The impact knocked the service weapon from his hands and into the floorboard. With sparks flying from metal on metal, Smith hit the brakes, but he was a second too late. The SUV's driver braked and turned his wheels sharply to the right. Both vehicles now moved as one, and suddenly, there was no road under the wheels. A split second later, they crashed into a rock wall, Smith's crumpled car partially flipped onto its side, passenger doors down, while the SUV skidded to a halt fifty feed further forward.

The exploding airbags momentarily stunned the agent. For about a minute, he struggled to stay conscious. When he finally shook the cobwebs from his mind, he reached down onto the floorboard for his weapon. In the dark, he couldn't find it. Grabbing the handle, he forced the door open, climbed out, and jumped down into the snow. As flurries blew around him, he peered through the darkness. Arnold was out of sight and the SUV's driver was no longer in his vehicle.

"You looking for me?"

Smith spun and found himself staring into the face of Darwin Larkin.

"My friend would be alive if you hadn't screwed things up."

Smith frowned. "Do you know who was in that car?"

"Arnold, and I knew you'd found out that he was landing tonight because I fed the information to your source. The trap you fell into was mine. You're not nearly as smart as you think you are."

"How did you know?"

"I've worked for him a lot, at least in the past. Dug up a lot of dirt he needed. But I don't kill people, so I passed on taking out Factor."

"But Pulino?"

"Rick wanted her alive, and I have no problem with kidnapping. If you hadn't gotten in the way, I might've been able to retire." He shook his head. "Walt and I worked together for twenty-two years. He was the only real friend I had. Suddenly, the money's not very important."

"What is?" Smith cautiously asked.

The snow picked up, the flakes bigger, and the night became whisper quiet. For a few seconds, neither man moved. It was Larkin who finally broke the silence.

"What's important is knowing you failed. I figure that you believed Arnold would lead you to Factor."

"Is that where he was going?"

"The pilot didn't tell me that, he only said they were flying to Colorado and gave me the scheduled arrival time. I just figured the final destination had to Factor."

"So, you must be working for Elder?"

"Let's just say that Elder's not on your side, and he let me know that. He didn't want you to get to Factor. He was afraid you might go against orders and save her."

Smith grimly smiled. He'd been played.

"Were you going to kill her?" Larkin asked.

"No, I was after Dixon. She was the best way to get to him."

"Why?"

"Dixon killed a friend of mine. He took him out for the Russians."

"Guess Dixon's responsible for Walt's death too."

Larkin lowered the gun, turned, and headed back toward his SUV.

"Aren't you going to kill me?" Smith asked.

"I don't kill," Larkin reminded the agent. "I told you that." He turned. "I just wanted to stop you from completing your job. That way Walt didn't die for nothing."

"That's what was this was about?"

"Yeah. Why should I kill you? Besides, Elder and Owen are both after you, and the CIA thinks you've traded sides. You've got targets all over you. I have places I can disappear—you don't."

Larkin turned and headed back to his car. Smith watched as he slid behind the wheel and put the SUV in gear. Though dented, it was roadworthy. Within seconds, it disappeared into the snowstorm. Shoving his hands into his pockets, he considered his options. There were none. The gig was up. Without Arnold, there was no way he could find out where Dixon had taken Factor. As there were people gunning for him, he had to disappear or die.

Chapter 66

10:54 p.m.
Saturday, October 1
Buzzard Roost, Colorado

Sometimes the most lethal traps are of our own making.

As the snow grew heavier, William Dixon bet Dallas Arnold wouldn't make their scheduled meeting. So he set a deadline. If the preacher was not at his door by eleven, Doctor Death would claim another victim without spectators. As he sat in the living room checking his weapon of choice for this mission, a Beretta M9, a bell rang. Someone had driven through the front gate. After loading the clip, Dixon walked to the front door.

The visitor had arrived in a Mercedes SUV. It took the driver a while to get out of the vehicle and march through the foot of accumulated snow. The man's gait and bearing gave away his identity.

"It's about time," Dixon announced as he swung open the door.

"The road up here's horrible. Doesn't it ever get graded?"

"That'd only encourage visitors," Dixon explained as he closed the entry.

Pulling off his overcoat and tossing it onto a chair, Arnold studied the great room and kitchen. "Nice place."

"Thanks, but don't get too comfortable, this is mine alone. Do you have the cash?"

"In the bag I dropped on the porch."

Dixon frowned, reopened the door, and retrieved his payoff. After setting it on the table, he unzipped the top. As requested, the black leather bag was filled with Euros.

"Where's Factor?" Arnold asked while his eyes darted around the home.

"She's locked up." Dixon studied his anxious guest and chuckled. "Do you really want to watch me do this? Death can be messy."

"Yes," Arnold nervously answered. "I've only seen old or sick people die, I've always wanted to know what it was like to have someone who was young and healthy ..."

"In other words," Dixon cut in, "you want to see an execution."

"I've thought about attending them in the past. I had a chance once and backed out. But in this case, I made the trip because I need the assurance that she's really dead. I have to see it with my own eyes. I have to know her heart is stopped. I won't sleep if there's any chance she could tell the world about my slips."

"Slips? You're trying to make murder and rape sound like whoops moments? Like, I spilled this glass of milk, here, let me get a towel and clean it up. What you did is far more than that."

"You kill people," Arnold snapped.

"But you're missing two points."

"What's that?"

"I don't kill for sport or to get some kind of emotional high—you did both. And, secondly, it's my job. Others, including you, are the judges, I'm just there to carry out the final verdict."

Arnold frowned. It seemed he didn't like the way the truth tasted. As he chewed on the hit man's sermon, he paced three steps one way and three steps back. When he stopped, he resolutely declared, "I can't take a chance on her remembering."

"She remembers," Dixon calmly assured the preacher. "When I mentioned your name, the rape came back. She lived it again. I knew from the actual victim's testimony—you were out of control. It sounded as if it was brutal. Know this—in a very real way, you have now assaulted both the mother and the daughter. On the other hand, I don't know if she knows about the African American man you helped lynch. She might not have unlocked that episode in your sorry life."

Arnold was now even more uncomfortable. His face flushed, and he shifted on his feet as if he needed to find the men's room in a hurry. Dixon drew satisfaction in watching his guest puddle up as if he were melting. Best of all, the preacher couldn't guess what was ahead. He was in for the surprise of his life.

"How will you do it?" Arnold whispered.

"A single shot to the heart. There's less to clean up than if I hit her in the head."

"And what happens to her body?"

"I have a place where I put them. She'll join a few others who took their last breath at Buzzard Roost. In case you're wondering, I didn't make up that name, this spot has been called that for more than a century, but it does seem appropriate. Don't you think so?"

Arnold grimaced and moved his right hand as if he were asking a congregation to stand. "It doesn't bother you to have them so close to your home?"

"No, because no one will ever find them. It's the bodies that are easy to find that bother me. And recently there've been several of those."

"Sorry."

"Sorry? You think that covers your sins? Do you know how many died because you couldn't keep your mouth shut? There's a psychologist who was renowned for her work who's dead thanks to you. Her name was B.R. Lenards. She could've helped a lot of people. Then there's a writer for a tabloid who took his last breath thanks to you. His name was Van Goodwin. He might've never won a Pulitzer Prize, but he likely had folks who cared for him and will miss him. You also killed a priest named Russo, who wouldn't have been where he was without your mouth. For all I know, earlier today, I might have killed Elton Carter. I didn't stay around to see if he woke up. If he's dead, think of this—Carter might have been a jet setter, but he still gave hundreds of millions to worthy causes. His family likely won't continue his charity work. If you just had the ability to keep your mouth shut, all of those people would still be alive, and Factor would already be dead."

"I had to …"

"Yes, you had to cover up because of all the people you've screwed. But you know something, you were stupid long before you called me. I can't fathom how you built such a following. Today, I'm going to solve this problem for you, but I want you to consider this—how many years until your past sins or the fact you fleece your flock are exposed?" Dixon paused and smiled. "If there is a God, then I doubt you'll ever meet him. You see, you're worse than I am. I don't pretend to be something I'm not. I don't tell people how to live their lives and then do the opposite. I'm not a hypocrite."

As Arnold continued to shuffle his feet, Dixon placed his gun on the table and retrieved a folded plastic sheet from the kitchen. Once he returned, he moved a coffee table out of the middle of the room and against the wall, then walked over to an open spot about ten feet in front of the massive native stone fireplace and spread out the plastic. It was fifteen-by-fifteen-feet.

"She'll stand in the middle," Dixon explained. "I'll be just off the plastic, just out of range of the blood splatter. One shot—that's all it takes, that all it ever takes, or until I met you, that was all it took. If you want to watch, move over to the couch. You'll have the perfect spot to see her fall and observe her final struggling breaths. If you're really lucky, you might hear a death rattle."

Arnold, his face now drawn, nodded, but before moving to the suggested seat, he pointed to a table by the entry. "What's the second gun for?"

"Just a backup in case this one fails. Guns do jam from time to time. Now, find a spot—if not on the couch, then any place you want that's out of the way."

"Can I stay here by the door?"

"Sure, I'll be right back."

Dixon picked up his gun and a key and casually strolled down the hall. After unlocking and easing the door open, he found Factor sitting on the corner of the desk. "Come with me," he ordered as he stepped away from the entry.

She didn't balk. Showing no signs of fear, she exited the room and turned toward the right. She stopped just short of the couch and stared at the unexpected guest.

"Dallas Arnold," she hissed.

The preacher took a step back but said nothing. As she stared holes into him, he turned his face toward the wall. Dixon smiled. He knew the power of Factor's gaze. He too had experienced it.

"Move over to the middle of the room, to the center of that plastic sheet."

Rather than follow his orders, she turned and uttered a name. "James Q. Bryant. He stood in that same place in 1981. You were paid one hundred thousand by the mob to take him out. One clean shot to the heart. You used a cloth sheet back then rather than plastic. You buried him behind a stand of pines in the back, about a hundred yards from the house. That was back when you dug the graves by hand. It was August 6th. The weather was clear, there was a slight breeze. After you covered him up, you went fly-fishing. You caught three trout and had them for supper."

Dixon was stunned. He rubbed his suddenly dry lips with his fingers but said nothing as Factor continued outlining his greatest hits.

"A few months later, it was Karen Costello. She was a petite blonde, pretty in a way, with a figure that turned heads. She was planted inside the CIA by the Chinese. They were looking for information on American spies in Asia. Before you executed her, she'd passed on information to China that led to the capture of six of the agency's men. While Bryant was scared, Costello was rock solid. She was smiling when you pulled the trigger. You broke a shovel digging that grave."

The normally cool Dixon was now sweating. Factor was retelling events that only he knew. How had she found out about them?

"Did the CIA know you were freelancing even before you left them?" Factor asked. "And you never told Clegg about your extra work. You really hated him. You found his arrogance sickening. He gave you the assignments, but he's the one you wanted to kill. But because no one ever paid you for that job, he continued to live."

"How do you know all this?" Dixon demanded.

Factor smiled. "Do you remember a pretty woman, about my size, who was separated from her husband? You met her at a party in Chicago in 1986. Her name was Kathleen Marks, but she didn't give you her married name—she used her maiden name that night. So, you knew her as Kathy Hammond."

"I've known a lot of women," Dixon observed.

"You slept with this one—just once, but that was all it took. I'm your daughter. Every horrid thing you did before that night is imprinted in me. I know the names of those you killed and the fact you used to have a dog named Romney. In your entire life, he might have been the only one who ever liked you."

"You're my daughter?"

"Until tonight you were sure there were no witnesses to your crimes, but you hadn't thought about what you might've left on someone else's DNA."

Stunned and shaken, Dixon let the hand holding his weapon fall to his side. As he tried to process what he'd just learned, Arnold went into action. He grabbed the gun from the table and pointed it at Factor.

"You're not getting paid for this one," Arnold grumbled as he aimed. Though he had Factor in his sights and went through the mechanics of action, nothing happened.

"The safety's still on," Dixon explained without emotion as he pointed his weapon at the preacher.

"No," Arnold begged as he realized what was about to happen. "You can have the money. I overreacted. It's all yours."

Dixon shrugged. "No one who steps into this house ever leaves. This was a one-way ticket for you as soon as you made that call. The rule has always been … no witnesses. So, your desire to watch signed your death warrant. I was going to kill you after you helped me clean up. It's time for your maker to judge you. That should be an interesting meeting."

There was no time for a prayer before Dixon's shot entered Arnold's chest and stopped his heart. He collapsed onto his back. There was no death rattle.

"Such a stupid man," Dixon grumbled as he studied the body. "This whole thing would've been easy if he hadn't gotten in the way."

Chapter 67

10:27 p.m.
Saturday, October 1, 2022
Buzzard Roost, Colorado

The past can never be completely buried. When summoned, it has the power to crawl out of the grave.

———◆———

Her memories of the father she didn't know until today had bought her a little time. Yet, the shock of watching Arnold try to kill her, and then his own death, had numbed her too much to make a break. Before she'd taken two steps, Dixon would have surely drilled her anyway. Or would knowing she was his child make a difference?

"I never knew about you," Dixon said, his voice displaying no hint of emotion. Ironic, as Arnold's blood was still dripping onto the floor. How could he ignore death easily?

"I'm sure Mom wanted it that way. She and Dad got back together soon after that night. I don't think she ever told him I wasn't his. I didn't know until you brought me here. Though I had a flash earlier in the day that should've spelled out who you were and my relationship with you."

"Did you enjoy seeing Arnold get the justice he deserved?"

Her eyes darted to the body. She studied the pathetic figure who abused his position and had gotten rich preying on the weak. The fact he was dead didn't ease the pain of what he'd done, a pain she'd personally experienced.

"No. I've lived a lot of abuse through the lives of others, and it's taught me there's no real satisfaction in justice. The only peace comes with forgiveness. My mother forgave him a long time ago."

"She told you that?" Dixon asked.

"No, she never mentioned it to me. But the way she lived her life proved she did. That doesn't mean the pain went away—it just means she learned to live with it. Given time, I might actually remember the moment she did forgive him. That is, if it happened before the night she met you."

"You don't have much time," Dixon warned. "What you've already told me has assured me I can't let you live. If you have anything else to say, you better say it."

"Know this, I didn't just remember your deeds, I lived each of them. I saw, heard, and smelled everything. I bet I can recall those moments in greater detail than you can. I even know how you felt the moment you pulled the trigger. I still feel the satisfaction you felt when you checked the pulse and found none."

"Then, rather than carry all those moments in your head, you should want to die. Only people without a heart can do what I do."

"So, you'd kill your daughter?"

"Your father raised you, I was never your dad and you were never my daughter."

"I can live with that." she assured him. "Still, I wish I could be around to see if you'll really be able to live with my death. I'm betting it'll be different this time. I'd like to know how it eats at you. I think you'll never get a good night's sleep in this house again."

Dixon frowned. He obviously didn't like the taste of those words. They didn't go down easily.

"You said you don't have a heart," Factor observed, as she readied another vocal volley, "but do you have a soul?"

"Does anyone?"

"I feel pretty sure we do, based on what I've seen through the eyes of many others."

Dixon stepped around the couch and over Arnold's body, then moved to a wingback chair on the other side of the room where he sat.

"I've killed two other imprints."

"You must be very proud."

"They were jobs, nothing more."

His face suddenly seemed to display a touch of regret. Did it mean the man had some feelings, even if they were buried down deep inside? If true, Factor was going to dig those out if it was the last thing she did. And it very well might be just that.

"About your dog," Factor said, "you never forgave your father for killing him. Even if Romney was killing the neighbor's sheep. You cried when you buried him. Have you cried since?"

"No," Dixon admitted.

As she studied Dixon's stoic expression, she was transported back to another time and place. The home was small, there was a barn visible out the kitchen window. A calendar that read November 1959 was tacked to a wall. There was no one else in the one room, shotgun-style home until the front door flew open. James Dixon was a big man, dressed in faded bib overalls and a blue-checked flannel shirt. His expression was gruff and unyielding. His voice was raw, raspy, and loud.

"Where's your maw?"

"She went to her sister's. Grandma's sick."

"You been hunting squirrels, boy? Is that why you're holding my rifle?"

There was no answer. A blast echoed off the walls, and the man was driven out the front door into the yard. He kept his balance for a moment, then fell. The boy walked out and put another round in the man's head.

Now, knowing where the killing started, Factor forced herself back into the moment. "You murdered your father. You ambushed him when he came in the front door after work."

"He killed my dog, and he beat me and my mother."

"He was your first," Factor observed.

"I still owe him. Without him, I might never have had such a successful career." Dixon smiled. "They'll never find his body, but I guess you know where I buried him."

"I haven't experienced that, at least not yet." As she studied him, Dixon looked to be in a different place and time. Had recalling this experience made a difference?

"I've killed two of your kind," he admitted for the second time, "but I never talked much to either of them. At least not about what they'd experienced. I never thought about that until now. Can I ask a question?"

At this point Factor was looking to kill as many minutes as possible. Though she didn't really expect anyone to rescue her, she at least wanted to use every chance to change Dixon's mind.

"What do you want to know?"

"Could I talk to someone in your past, like my father or your mom?"

"It doesn't work that way. I don't channel people. This isn't a séance. Neither of those people is alive. None of them are in another world waiting for an invitation to come back to this one. I can't ask them questions. I only get to reexperience what they did when they were living. And I don't choose who I see or when their stories are revealed. Why do you want to talk to your dad and my mother?"

"I just wanted to know how they really felt about me."

"If I could see though your father's eyes right now and remember the moment you were born or when you took your first steps, then I might be able to give you something to hold onto. Maybe he was proud of you at times. But his memories aren't in my head. I've not experienced them."

Dixon nodded. What he was dealing with at the moment appeared to be more than just a desire for knowledge of those from his own past.

"I never regretted my jobs," he muttered.

"But you're regretting this one," Factor countered. "Why did you want me to channel your father?"

"I wanted him to know he earned his death. He needed to understand it was justified. I should've laid out his crimes before I pulled the trigger."

Factor nodded. She had another bombshell to drop and how Dixon reacted might determine how long she lived. "You said your father didn't deserve to live. What about you? If you hold yourself to the same standard as your father, do you deserve to live?"

It was quickly apparent she'd failed to touch his soul. That is, if he actually had one.

"The strong live," Dixon explained. "My father was weak. Now, it'd be easier if you moved to the plastic."

"I'm not going anywhere. I won't do anything to make this easier on you."

Dixon nodded. He lifted his weapon, his movement slow, almost lethargic.

Factor watched, waiting for his eye to twitch, an action she now knew happened right before he fired. As soon as she saw the twitch, she'd drop to the ground and roll behind the couch. After that, she'd hope for a miracle.

Chapter 68

11:50 p.m.
Saturday, October 1, 2022
Buzzard Roost, Colorado

Fear is the universal imprint that each generation shares with the last.

———◆———

F actor closed her eyes and thought about the cave. It was the place
that offered her perspective. It was in that darkness she'd seen a
real path to light and hope. For a brief moment, she once again saw
through He'evo'nehe's eyes. She felt peace.

"What are you seeing?" Dixon demanded.

"Not you," she assured him. "I refuse to allow my last moment to
be consumed by your miserable life."

He lowered the gun. Their relationship was eating at him. This
kill would be hard. But now that she'd experienced his life, she knew
he would still go through with it. That's just how he was wired. She
heard a voice, speaking in Cheyenne. "Fight." Her only weapons
were words and memories, and it was time to use them.

"You killed Holmes's daughter, and it still eats at you," she jabbed

"I didn't mean to," he whispered. "She got in the way."

The verbal lob had worked. His thoughts were on another time
and place. There was pain and regret written on his face. Now it was

time to pull from the wisdom she discovered in He'evo'nehe's life. Working together, they might be able to create a miracle.

Dixon's still wasn't looking at her. Free from his gaze, Factor looked around the room. It was three steps from where she stood to the light switch. Taking a deep breath, she eased to her side. Just as Dixon noticed her movement, she leaped forward and flipped the switch. Maybe it was an ancestor guiding her or perhaps it was instinct, but she immediately fell to her knees. Just as she did, a shot rang out and a bullet flew over her head.

Employing a technique taught to her great-grandfather during his basic training in World War II, Factor rolled across the floor to a position behind the couch. Holding her breath, she crawled over to the Native American artifacts. Standing, she reached into the display and, in the darkness, found a bow and two arrows.

Dropping back to the floor, she crawled back behind the couch. To her back was the dining room, somewhere in the dark living room was Dixon.

"There's no way out," he announced.

Knowing her voice would give away her hiding place, she didn't answer. Using the few moments she had, she ran her hands over the bow. While she'd never been involved in archery, the weapon felt right in her hands. She knew how to grip the bow and hold the arrow and string. Best of all, in darkness, she saw the light. Now, she had to locate her prey.

Bow in hand, she crawled toward the unlit fireplace. Once there she stood, pulled the string back, held the arrow, and listened. At first, she heard nothing, but then the sounds seem to come to her. The hum of the refrigerator, the tick of a clock, and the breaths of a man. She closed her eyes. Where was he? A minute became two and then three. Nothing. Then he shifted his weight from one foot to the other, and his shirt or coat rubbed against the wall.

She guessed Dixon to be about six feet tall. Doing a bit of math, she figured she'd have to aim at about the four-and-a-half-foot mark to find the heart. After willing her pulse to slow, Factor pulled the string back as far as she could, recalculated her aim, and let go. As soon as the arrow was launched, she dropped and rolled back behind the couch.

The security of hiding behind the couch beckoned her. Here

Factor felt safe. But she had to know if she hit her mark. Stringing another arrow, she stood and once again listened for breathing. She could hear him. He was still alive. She must have missed. She only had one more chance.

Factor tried to picture the room. He'd obviously moved, but she couldn't figure out where. She had to get him to move.

Sliding over to an end table, she picked up a sculpture. Would it be better to roll it or throw it? She opted for rolling it as that would give her time to have her bow in position. Laying it on its side, she gave a strong shove. It hadn't gone two feet when three shots rang out. The fire had come from behind the chair. There was now no doubt the man had intended to kill her all along. As he moved back to cover, the bow caught under her knee and snapped. Now she had no weapon.

"You're good," Dixon called out. "Are those voices in your head telling you what to do, or maybe you're channeling what you learned from my life."

Crawling back to the display, she reached up and retrieved a knife. It was a larger version of the one that Carter had found with He'evo'nehe's body. With its sixteen-inch, hand-carved blade, it was an instrument of death, but she was going to have to be very close to the target to deliver a fatal blow. And she'd likely only have one chance. She had to draw him out. As long as he was behind the chair, she couldn't get to him. Ducking back behind the couch, she went to Plan B.

One minute became two and two, four, but there was no movement. Then someone or something bumped a chair. A second later, Dixon brushed a curtain. He was headed toward the door and the other light switch.

Rising, she visualized the light switch and Dixon. He was right-handed, so he would have to cross in front of the door and use his left hand to turn on the lights. That meant, for a brief moment, his back would be to her. Four feet, nine inches, she thought. That would put her blade in the area of his heart. As soon as he flipped that switch, she might, if she could work her way to the door without him hearing her, have enough time. At this point, the darkness was her friend, but once he got to that light, there was no cover.

Armed and ready, she slowly moved forward. Was he having second thoughts? Was he really headed toward the light switch? Or maybe that was a ruse, and he was circling from the other direction? Why couldn't she hear him breathe?

Patience and self-control, that's what had governed He'evo'nehe's life. She could sit in the darkness for hours until she gained control of the visitors in her mind. Just slow the heart, take shallow steady breaths, and get to the spot your instincts tell you that you need to be.

Factor moved forward. She was four feet from the door, the knife pulled back, when she heard the switch. The bright lights disoriented her. For a split-second she froze. But Dixon was dealing with the same problem. He was blinking as he attempted to search the room. If she waited to get used to the light, it would be too late. Just like in the dark, she had to trust her instincts. Though the target was still blurry, she shoved her right hand forward with a fury she'd never known. She pushed with such force the knife went clear through the agent's body and pinned Smith to the door. He wasn't dead, just hanging like one of the paintings. His eyes were open, but they weren't focused.

As Dixon moaned in agony, Factor stepped forward and pulled the gun from his hand.

"It's over," Factor announced. "This time, the Indians won."

"Can you live with killing your father? he whispered.

"You were never my father."

Factor grabbed the knife in both her hands, jerked it out of the door, and then pulled it through the man's chest. As it reversed course in his body, Dixon's screams bounced off the walls and cathedral ceiling. Before he crumpled, Factor put her hands under the agent's arms and lowered him to the floor.

"Never underestimate the experience of an imprint," she whispered as she tore open his coat and shirt. The wound was nasty, blood was gushing out both his back and chest. The knife had surely pierced a lung and maybe the heart. As far as they were from civilization, the best she could do was make Dixon comfortable. If he was lucky, he'd pass out and die without feeling much more pain. Yet, tonight Lady Luck wasn't his companion. His eyes were like saucers, and his face displayed both fear and agony. He knew he was dying, but rather than get there in a hurry, he was fighting for life one second at a time. It was a horrible thing to witness.

"If I'd had a different father," he whispered.

"There's no reason for this," Factor gently said. "Just relax. The pain won't last much longer, and the confession's not necessary."

He nodded but didn't quit trying to put voice to his thoughts. "I'm glad it was you."

"I'm not," she whispered. "I never want to kill anyone again."

"I hope you ..."

He never finished the sentence.

Chapter 69

1:22 a.m.
Sunday, October 2
Buzzard Roost, Colorado

Turn out the lights, the party's over.

———◆———

For thirty minutes, Maxine Factor sat on the couch studying the two bodies sprawled on the floor. It was if she were in a trance. She felt nothing. She might have stayed that way for hours if she hadn't heard a car approaching. Well aware there were still people who wanted her dead, she retrieved Dixon's gun, moved against the far wall, and waited to see who would enter. Though she had no stomach for it, if forced she would shoot.

She steadied herself against the wall and raised the weapon as the door swung open. Then she smiled.

Elton Carter, his face bruised, was the first through the door, then came Indira Morel. The last to enter was a man she didn't know.

Armed with baseball bats, the visitors seemed ready for battle. As they studied the room, their confused expressions were replaced by relief.

"Is one of these Dixon?" Carter asked.

"The guy at your feet," Factor answered, dropping the gun to her side. "The other guy's Dallas Arnold."

"The preacher?" Morel quizzed.

"One and the same," Factor confirmed as she dropped into a chair.

"I'm Mason Hardin," the stranger announced with a wave.

"The writer," Factor noted.

Carter looked at the two bodies and then back at Factor. "We came to save you, but …"

"I could've used some help," she assured him.

"The guy next to the door," Morel asked. "Was that your father?"

"No. I just carry his DNA."

"I think I'm glad I don't know my family tree like you do," Morel observed.

"There're always some rotten limbs," Factor admitted, "but I've found the trunk's pretty solid." She pointed to Dixon before adding, "Even with people like that inside my mind, I've decided being an imprint is a gift not a curse." She forced a weary smile, "The key to being able to use it is making sure no one else knows what I am. The Cheyenne might've accepted and revered He'evo'nehe, but my people aren't going to be that tolerant."

"Max," Morel asked. "Elton and I have to know something. It's been bothering us since we found your note in the motel room. How did you know he would bring you to this place?"

"What do you mean?"

"You left the name on the notepad." Morel pointed to Dixon before asking, "Did he tell you?"

"No, but his grandfather used to bring him here when he was a child. At that time, I hadn't guessed Dixon was my father, but the fact I could experience those trips in my head should have clued me in. Maybe because he was going to kill me, I didn't connect what I was seeing in my mind to who he had to be."

"And you knew he would bring you here?" Morel asked.

"The best days of Dixon's childhood were spent right here. Perhaps, if his grandfather hadn't died when he was young, or if his father hadn't been abusive, things would've been different. He hinted at that right before he died."

"What was the J for?" Carter asked

"What J?" Factor asked.

"The one you scribbled under Buzzard Roost on the notepad?"

Factor chuckled before admitting, "That was a fishhook. This used to a fishing lodge. I put that in there as an extra clue."

"Oh," Carter grinned, "I can kind of see that … now that I know what it is. It's good you teach history and not art."

Factor smiled briefly, then looked back at the bodies. "This is a mess."

"And," Morel added. "Smith isn't here to clean it up."

"Who's Smith?" Factor asked.

"Not someone you want to know," Hardin chimed in. "I don't think we even begin to explain this to the cops. So, let me propose this. Dixon's so far off the radar, no one will know he's dead. Arnold's disappearance will make the news, but in time the story will fade except for those 'whatever happened to' shows on cable. We might not be as effective, but I think we can do what Smith did."

Morel nodded, "It's not right, but it's the best thing for Max. We need to keep the imprint story out of the news." She glanced toward Hardin and added, "Sorry if it costs you a big story."

He shrugged. "This is one story I'll only write if I'm the last of this quartet still standing. Let's make sure that's a lot of years down the road."

The four looked at the bodies for a few more minutes before Factor made an observation. "It's all about fear. All this death, all the pain and suffering, all the loathing and doubt, is centered on fear. And it's not just the fear of having sins revealed, it's also the fear of losing power, influence, and status." She paused, once again considering the needless waste of life littering the floor of the lodge as well all the wasted lives she'd viewed through the eyes of scores of ancestors. Sadly, nothing had changed. "The greatest of our fears, that of having what we believe in turned upside down, might be the most deadly of them all. There's nothing worse than fearing what could be the truth and doing everything possible to avoid learning if it is true."

Everyone grew silent. There were no words to complete the closing lines of this haunting ballad.

Factor opened the door and walked out into the clean, fresh snow. She'd been a target and would continue to be a target, because in her memories, she might know a truth the world was not ready to hear.

In the end, fear seems to be the emotion most deeply imprinted on everyone.

Chapter 70

Peace is fragile and so easy to break; therefore, peace has always been temporary.

———◆———

M axine Factor sat alone in the darkness. She was lost not in thought, but in peace. In this place where He'eve'nehe had found herself and discovered how to use her gift, Factor was savoring a few moments to come to an understanding of who she was and what it could mean to her and the world.

As she looked for light in the darkness, she heard footsteps outside the hidden entrance. They were followed by a familiar voice.

"Can I come in?"

"Elton, can you find your way in the dark, or do you need a guide?"

"I brought a light."

Factor observed a small flashlight illuminate Carter's face. It was a bit unsettling—he looked like Jack Nicholson in *The Shining*. His steps unsteady on the uneven stone floor, he slowly made his way to where she sat.

"When I woke up and looked into your room," he explained, "you weren't there. I didn't find a note, but I knew where you must be. I'm sorry if I'm intruding, but we need to talk."

"Have a seat."

Once he was on the ground, she reached over and turned out the light. "In here," she explained, "this is the way it should be. It makes the words ring louder and their meaning resonate more deeply. What do you need to talk about?"

"I bought this place," he explained. "The cabin and more than a thousand acres are now mine. Indy's uncle sold them to me. I'll pay the taxes, but the title's in your name. That way you can come here whenever you need to be in your sanctuary."

"I should say you shouldn't have, but I'd be lying if I did."

"Max, we've shared a lot," he observed. "I don't know how to define our relationship." He paused, likely searching for words to explain his thoughts. When he finally found a way to connect the dots, his tone lacked confidence. "I've been wondering if maybe I love you."

"Elton, that's flattering, and I really mean that, but you can't love me because being with me means you'd have to embrace and accept all those who, from time to time, I might become. I wouldn't ask you or anyone else to commit to that. I mean, consider if you were to lean forward to kiss me. I might be inside some man's experiences. You could be kissing someone named Elmer."

"I think, as long as Elmer had your lips, I could get used to it."

"It's more than that. You love Indy, and she loves you. I'd always know that I'd be running second place to her. And while second's not that bad in the Olympics, it's lousy in the game of love."

Carter sighed. "Maybe you're right, but I'll have to give it some time. I have feelings for both of you. And then there was that kiss."

"Ah, the kiss. How many women have you kissed?"

"I don't know."

"The moment we shared was interesting. We were both wondering if we'd live another day. You can't base love on that."

"Okay, I'll take some time and try to figure things out. But I still need to be at your side. There're still people who are after you. And your battle to live isn't one that you can win all by yourself. You need resources. And you need a friend. And until you're truly safe, then I'm your best bet."

"But …"

"Max, hear me out. I want you to know my mind and heart. I've spent most of my life living for myself. I've been selfish. Perhaps it's time I try to at least come halfway close to noble."

"Don't waste days you could spend with Indy. She's amazing. You two are meant for each other."

"That's bit of advice your ancestors can't give you. And, when it comes to love, Max Factor is not much of an expert."

There was no use talking to him. He'd made up his mind. So, this was a battle for another day.

"Did you know that Rocky Smith disappeared?" Carter asked.

"No."

"The CIA's looking for him, but no luck so far. And Indy's trying to talk the Star into believing you're not a threat, but it's tough sell. Some of them still want you dead. Don't forget about the two guys who worked with Clegg. Besides that, we still don't know who was behind ordering that first attempt on your life. And the guy named Larkin knows who you are and what you can do. He might be selling that information right now. And …"

"And there are other groups too," she finished. "But right here and right now, we don't have to worry about any of them. Here in this place and at this moment, I'm in control. Right now, I can deal with the gift. As I don't know how long that control will last, I have to concentrate on learning from those who walked before me. And the best place to focus and learn is right here. For now, I'm not going out into the world and make myself a target."

"But make me a promise?" Carter demanded.

"What?"

"When you leave here, you'll let me protect you."

"Okay."

He was right. She really didn't need to fight this war by herself. And his resources would help.

"How far back do the memories go now?" Carter asked.

"I really can't answer that. My mind jumps. Let me give you some perspective. Let's say there are four generations in each century. That means when you factor in my parents, grandparents, and great-grandparents, there are fifteen different memories counting my own that go back one hundred years. If you go back another century and a half there are eight thousand one hundred and ninety memories, plus my own. If the door opened, and all my direct relatives from the past four hundred years tossed a reunion, there would be tens of thousands in my head at the same time."

"So how far back have you been?"

He just didn't get the way it worked. And if he couldn't, who could. So, it was best to humor him.

"1437."

"Tell me what you're seeing," Carter begged.

"Listen, Elton, so far, if you don't count William Dixon, there's no one in my family line that has seen anything earth-changing. So, it's not just me, an almost forty, divorced professor who's boring, but my whole family tree is boring."

"But what about 1437?"

"It's just a glimpse of life in a fishing village.

"Where's this fishing village?"

"It's on the Irish coast …"

"Tell me more."

"I'm seeing through the eyes of a woman named Jane. She's a farmer's wife. Her father was a fisherman. When you walked in, she was baking …"

The Beginning of the Next Adventure

10:30 a.m.
Wednesday, October 19
Roosevelt Hotel, New York

You can't have a secure future until you put the past to rest.

———•———

"She hasn't shared any information yet."

"At least none that we know of."

"If someone's going to leak the story, it'd be the reporter. Hardin was with her, she likely shared with him what Dixon did. He surely knows the names, dates, and places."

"I still think we need to focus on Factor. She's the source."

"We don't know where she is. We can find Hardin. We silence him, then we'll go after the imprint."

About the Author

Citing his Arkansas heritage, Christy award winner **Ace Collins** defines himself as a storyteller. In that capacity, Collins has authored over a hundred books that have sold more than 2.5 million copies for twenty-five different publishers. His catalog includes novels, biographies, and children's works as well as books on history, culture, and faith. He has also been the featured speaker at the National Archives Distinguished Lecture Series, hosted a network television special, and has appeared on all the morning TV shows.

Ace's hobbies include sports, restoring classic cars, watching and reading about classic films, tinkering with Wurlitzer jukeboxes, and playing guitar. He is married to Dr. Kathy Collins, Chair of the Department of Education at Ouachita Baptist University. The couple lives in Arkadelphia, Arkansas and has two grown sons and a daughter who is in college.

Ace is represented by Greg Johnson, WordServe Literary Group Ltd

To find out more about Ace, including a list of his books, go to his website, https://acecollins.com.

www.ingramcontent.com/pod-product-compliance
Lightning Source LLC
Chambersburg PA
CBHW070543030726
47505CB00001B/144